PRAISE FOR THE EARTHSONG SERIES AND MARY MACKEY

"Mary Mackey's *The Village of Bones,* gives us the vivid adventures of *The Clan of the Cave Bear,* the magic of *The Mists of Avalon* and *Lord of the Rings*, and the beauty of *Avatar.* Filled with the belief that love drives out fear, it contains stunning twists that will leave you wanting more."

—**Dorothy Hearst, author of the** ***Wolf Chronicles***

"Brilliant, accurate…an unforgettable work of fiction… Mary Mackey combines a researcher's precision with a storyteller's magic."

—**Dr. Marija Gimbutas, author of** ***The Civilization of the Goddess***

"Vivid, dramatic, compelling…Mary Mackey joins the company of Jean Auel and Elizabeth Marshall Thomas."

—**Marge Piercy, author of** ***Woman on the Edge of Time***

"[A] heart-pounding evocation…whose lessons lie in the hearts of the characters."

—**Thomas Moore, author of** ***Care of the Soul***

"Mary Mackey has taken ancient history and created a land where the feminine principle of love and creation rules…"

—**Floyd Salas, author of** ***Buffalo Nickel***

"With all the literary grace and storytelling power we have come to expect of her, Mary Mackey leads us back on an imaginary trek to the prehistoric origins of modern sexual politics."

—**Theodore Roszak, author of** ***The Voice of the Earth***

Also by Mary Mackey

The Year the Horses Came, Book One of the Earthsong Series

The Horses at the Gate, Book Two of the Earthsong Series

The Fires of Spring, Book Three of the Earthsong Series

The Last Warrior Queen

The Notorious Mrs. Winston

The Widow's War

Sweet Revenge

The Stand In

Season of Shadows

Kindness of Strangers

A Grand Passion

McCarthy's List

Immersion

The Village of Bones

Sabalah's Tale

A Novel

Mary Mackey

Prequel to the Earthsong Series

This book is a work of fiction. Names, characters, places, and incidents are the product of the author's imagination or are used fictitiously. Any resemblance to actual events, locations, or persons, living or dead, is coincidental.

Lowenstein Associates, Inc.
115 East 23rd St., Fl. 4
New York, NY 10010
www.lowensteinassociates.com

Cover design by Mark and Mary Roberts www.maryroberts.org

Visit the author's website at www.marymackey.com

LIBRARY OF CONGRESS CATALOGING IN PUBLICATION DATA
Names: Mackey, Mary. | Mackey, Mary. Earthsong series.
Title: The village of bones : Sabalah's tale : a novel / Mary Mackey.
Other Titles: Sabalah's tale
Description: New York, NY : Lowenstein Associates, Inc., [2016]
Identifiers: ISBN 978-1-5308-0457-3 | ISBN 1-5308-0457-4 |
Subjects: LCSH: Mothers and daughters–Europe–Fiction. | Women, Prehistoric–Europe–Fiction. | Magic–Fiction. | Goddess religion–Europe–Fiction. | Battles–Europe–Fiction. LCGFT: Historical fiction.
Classification: LCC PS3563.A3165 V55 2016 | DDC 813/.54–dc23

for Angus and Marija

CONTENTS

PART 2
The Dark Forest

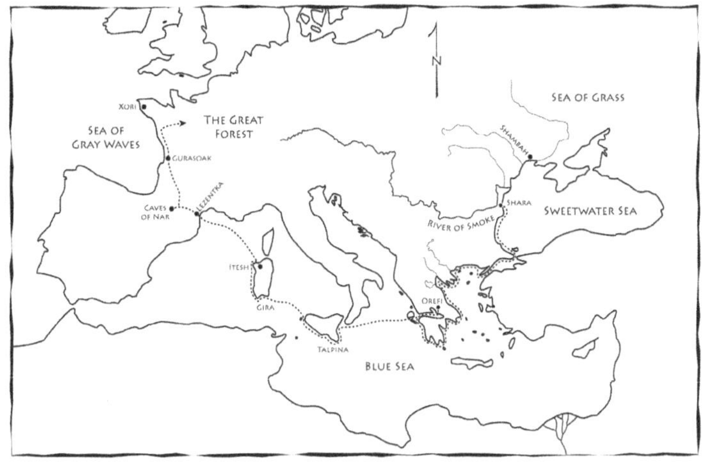

SABALAH'S FOURTEEN-MONTH JOURNEY ACROSS OLD EUROPE

4386 B.C.E. TO 4385 B.C.E.

Historical Note:
Although there is no conclusive evidence that the people of Old Europe had a written language, some archaeologists have theorized that the untranslated hieroglyphic script of ancient Crete known as Linear A was based on a much older script developed by ancestral non-Indo-European speakers. If such a script existed in Sabalah's time, it was probably primarily used for religious and ceremonial purposes.

INTRODUCTION

In the Fifth Millennium B.C.E. the human beings who inhabited Europe had only just begun to clear the great forests that stretched from the Atlantic Ocean to the Black Sea. Lions ranged over much of the continent until well into the early Middle Ages, but horses, which had died out during the drastic changes in climate that followed the last glacial period, were unknown until they were reintroduced from the northern steppes by invading nomads about the time Sabalah's story begins. Possibly the first Europeans to encounter men mounted on horses saw them as the Aztecs saw the first Spanish conquistadores whom they described to Montezuma as "beasts with two heads and six legs"—in other words: "beastmen."

The invading nomads worshipped a Sky God while many of the peoples of Europe worshipped the Earth as a Great Goddess who brought forth life. Mammals and birds that are now extinct still thrived, some in great numbers: wild cattle; giant elk; Caspian tigers; and mountain goats called "ibex," which only disappeared in the early 1890s. What other creatures, now extinct, might have survived into Sabalah's time to roam the forests of Europe? Would they have been dangerous, friendly, deadly?

INTRODUCTION

PART I

BEYOND THE SEAS OF SHARA

Let me bury my face in your hair
for it smells like wheat and roses
Let me bury my body in your flesh
for it smells like wild lilies and spring

Am I singing of the Goddess Earth
or my love who sleeps here beside me?

Of both, I sing of both
of the grace of Her brown hills
and the brown curves of your breasts
of your ankles and wrists
and Her saplings that tremble
when the south winds blow

I am singing of the vast seas
of your journeys
and the infinite ocean of Her love

Song carved on a fragment of a wooden lute
Europe, Fifth Millennium B.C.E.

Beware! There are things that are not human out there!

Warning engraved on the handle of a stone knife
Europe, Fifth Millennium B.C.E

1

Walking on Water

The West Coast of the Black Sea: 4387 B.C.E.

Sabalah dug her paddle into the water and raced toward shore. Her arms were burning, her shift was soaked in sweat, and her breath was coming in gasps. She paddled with all her strength, not daring to look over her shoulder. She had to go faster, or she wasn't going to make it.

Twenty-one seasons old and barren, the midwives had said. What a fool she'd been to try to run away from their words, but how could she have known? She'd gone down to the wharf this morning in a bad temper and a defiant mood, and now she was paying the price. When she set out, the sun had been shining and the Sweetwater Sea had been as calm as a lake. In front of her, sunlight still lay on the water in big golden puddles, and she could see the fishing boats bobbing gently beside the wharf in waves no more than a handspan high.

Beyond the wharf, Shara rose up, white and lovely, its twenty temples and hundred motherhouses perched along the south bank of the river like a flock of doves. As far as she could tell, nobody in the city had noticed the approaching storm yet. Why should they? There was no need to keep watch on the sea. This wasn't storm season, and the city had never been attacked or invaded as long as anyone could remember.

Dear Goddess, she prayed, *please let me get to safety before the wind hits!* At least she was making progress. She was close enough now to see the procession of mothers and children winding their way up the honey-colored cliffs to the Temple of Batal. The ceremony that bound them together today was the reason she had gone off by herself for what should have been a quiet sail on a calm sea. She could not bear to watch them celebrate their love for each other, because she had no children and never would have any. She didn't want a life dedicated to mothering other people's. She wanted a baby of her own, and if the midwives were right and the Goddess had other plans for her, that was just too bad.

Still feeling defiant, she dug her paddle into the water again and felt the boat lurch forward. She was close enough now to see the fishing nets drying on the beach. *I'm going to make it!* she thought.

The instant the words formed in her mind, the sun went out like a lamp, the air turned green, great black clouds boiled over her, and bolts of lightning flashed so close the mast of the boat seemed to jump sideways. Looking over her shoulder, she saw that a giant wall of water higher than the walls of the city had risen out of the sea. Above it, there was nothing but churning darkness.

As the darkness engulfed her, the boat bucked and rose out of the water like a kite. The linen sail shredded and the mast snapped like a dry stick. *Into your hands, oh Goddess,* she prayed as her body arced through the air and slammed into the great wave. And then everything was water, fury, salt, terror, and drowning.

Later, she sometimes wondered if she had died at that moment. How else could she explain the peace that settled over her when she finally stopped struggling and let the wave pull her under, or the feeling that she was no longer in her body, but outside of it looking at it as if it belonged to someone else?

Slowly, she sank toward the bottom until she seemed to float above a garden of stones. Her shift billowed around her like a cloud. Over her head, just below the tossing waves, schools of fish flew like flocks of wingless birds. So this was death. A simple return to the Mother. Nothing to be feared.

Or perhaps this wasn't death. Maybe she was merely crazed from lack of air and hallucinating the way the pearl divers of Shara sometimes did when they came to the surface with pearls in their mouths and couldn't remember their own names or recognize the faces of those who loved them; because the next thing she knew, she was being sucked back up toward the surface through a tube of churning foam.

As her head broke out of the water, the pain and fear came back. She fought to breathe, but the air was such a mix of rain and saltwater that each time she inhaled she felt as if she were still drowning. Kicking her feet, she flailed at the waves, but she wasn't strong enough to resist the force of the storm. She could feel herself getting weaker. She was going to go under again, and this time she wouldn't be able to fight her way back to the surface.

Suddenly, her right hand struck something solid. Grabbing for it, she found herself clutching the broken mast of the boat. The wooden spar bobbed up and down in front of her, hitting her in the forehead and chest. Ignoring the battering, she wrapped her arms around the mast and pulled herself on top of it.

As she lay there, panting and gasping, the storm suddenly stopped—not all of it, just the part that was raging around her. One moment, she was fighting to stay on top of the mast so she wouldn't drown. The next, she was drifting in a tranquil circle of green water. Within a space about the size of the floor of a temple, the wind had died down so completely that she could hear the soft lapping of the waves beneath her, but when she looked outside of that circle of peace, she could see the storm still beating its way toward shore. It was as if a wall of transparent fury enclosed her. Where the waves still roared and the wind still screamed, everything was dark and terrifying. But where she floated, there was a green-gold light that seemed to come from no obvious source.

Trembling with cold and fear, she took a deep breath and allowed herself to relax her grip on the mast. This was too real to be a dream. She could feel the splinters of the mast digging into her chest, taste salt in the water she was coughing up.

As she lay there giving into the sobbing that had been bubbling up in her throat ever since the boat capsized, a woman emerged from the wall of crashing waves and walked across the sea toward her. Sabalah abruptly stopped crying and stared at the woman, stunned. This was impossible! She had to be dreaming! But if it was a dream, it was different from any dream she had ever had.

The woman kept walking, stepping over the waves as if they were furrows in a field of wheat. Her flowing dress was blue as a summer sea; her hair long and green, twined with seaweed and pearls. Her skin was dark and light at the same time, her eyes so bright, they glowed like the last flash of the sun when it falls into the sea in midsummer.

Sabalah closed her eyes and clung to the mast trembling. Was she going mad? Was she dead after all? A sweet scent suddenly filled the air like the perfume of roses blown across water. Don't be afraid, the woman said. *I'll do you no harm. Open your eyes and look at me.*

"I'm afraid if I look into your face, I'll die," Sabalah whispered.

Nonsense, the woman said with a touch of impatience that reminded Sabalah of her mother. Open your eyes right now.

Sabalah opened her eyes and saw that the woman was standing on the water so close to the mast that the hem of her robe was touching it. Repressing an urge to scream in terror, she summoned all her courage. "Who are you? How can you walk on water?"

You don't recognize me?

Sabalah shook her head and felt saltwater drain out of her ears.

The woman's laughter was like the sound of a wind chime. *I am Amonah, Goddess of the Sea, and water is my path. I can walk above it or beneath it as I wish.*

"Could I walk on water too?" It was a crazy question under the circumstances, but Sabalah was in no condition to think before she spoke.

The Goddess laughed again. *No, my child. You would sink like a stone.*

Sitting down beside Sabalah, Amonah let Her feet dangle in the water. They were bare except for toe rings of rose-colored coral. She must have weighed nothing, because the end of the spar didn't tilt the way it would have if a flesh-and-blood human being had sat there.

I have news for you that will bring you great joy. Amonah's tone was casual as if She and Sabalah were two friends sitting on a bench in Shara sharing a piece of honey cake and talking about the weather. *You're going to bear a magical child.*

"But I can't. I'm barren." The word "barren" was bitter in Sabalah's mouth.

For a third time the Goddess laughed. Not anymore. Leaning over She gave Sabalah a kiss on the cheek. At the touch of the Goddess's lips, Sabalah felt her womb leap in joy.

Rising to Her feet, Amonah again stood on the water. She was fading now, becoming transparent. "Wait!" Sabalah cried. "Please don't go. Tell me who the father of my baby will be. Where will I find him?"

Don't worry. The father of your baby will find you. Amonah was fading fast. By now, Sabalah could see through Her body.

"Wait! Dear Goddess, will my baby be a boy or a girl? How will my child be 'magical?' Will she be a great priestess? A Queen of Shara? A seer? A ..."

There are some things you are better off not knowing. Amonah waved Her hand, and a school of dolphins rose up out of the water and surrounded the mast. Their gray and white bodies glowed in the strange green-golden light. *You must go back to Shara now. My dolphin children will see you safely to shore.*

As Amonah disappeared, there was a crash of thunder and the storm closed back over Sabalah. A huge wave smashed into the mast, sending it straight up into the air and tossing her back into the sea. But this time she didn't sink, because the dolphins surrounded her and bore her up all the way to the wharf where the fishnets had been torn to shreds and the boats of Shara floated, wrecked almost beyond repair.

Staggering through the surf onto the beach, Sabalah took a few steps and fell face forward in the sand.

She woke in her own room in her own bed. The first thing she saw when she opened her eyes was the face of Uncle Bindar, her mother's youngest brother. He was her *aita,* the man who had joined her mother in raising her, protecting her, and loving her from the moment she was born. Every child in the Motherlands had an *aita.* Not all were blood relations to the babies they cherished and nurtured, but no man who had not helped raise a child was considered whole.

"Sabalah, my dear child," Uncle Bindar said. "Can you hear me?"

Sabalah tried to speak, but her throat was so burned with saltwater that the word "yes" came out as a croak.

"Don't try to talk. Just be still and rest." Uncle Bindar wiped off her forehead with a cloth dipped in lavender tea and offered her a sip of water through a hollow straw. Sabalah sucked at the water greedily and almost vomited. Her whole body ached. Worse yet, the room was spinning in a way that made her feel as if she were still being tossed around by the waves.

Coming up beside Uncle Bindar, Sabalah's mother Lalah picked up the cloth, dipped it in the bowl of lavender tea, and began to wipe Sabalah's arms gently, as if she were afraid Sabalah might shatter like a doll made of unfired pottery. Anyone looking at the two of them would have known immediately they were mother and daughter. They both had the same brown eyes; long, slender noses; full lips; high cheek bones; and glossy black hair. The only important differences, besides their ages, were that Sabalah's eyes contained small golden flecks and her hair was heavy and straight, while Lalah's eyes were pure brown and her hair sprung away from her head in a halo of short curls.

Lalah, who was in line to be the next Priestess-Queen of Shara, always chopped off her hair because she claimed it got in her way when she leaped up on the roofs of houses to re-roof them or climbed a ladder to repaint the great snake on the walls of the city. She was a born fixer, never so happy as when she had a trowel of wet stucco or a paintbrush in her hand, but when she tended the sick, her touch was as gentle as the flutter of a butterfly's wing.

"We found you on the beach after the storm." Tears filled Lalah's eyes. "Oh, my darling, we thought you were dead."

Sabalah opened her mouth to say that not only wasn't she dead, she had spoken to Amonah, Goddess of the Sea, who had walked toward her over the waves, saved her from the storm, and promised she would bear a magical child, but the words wouldn't come. It was as if she had been struck mute.

Perhaps I am not supposed to tell these things to anyone.

As soon as she thought this and realized it was true, her voice came back. "Mother," she whispered.

At the sound of Sabalah's voice, Lalah began to cry in earnest. All at once all of Sabalah's relatives were standing around her bed laughing, weeping, and welcoming her back to life: her brothers Gradush and Tarah and her sister Alana; Great Aunt Nasula, the present Priestess-Queen of Shara; her cousins and cousins of cousins; her friends, her neighbors—so many people that the small room grew warm with the heat of their bodies.

Sabalah looked from face to face. She had known most of these these people her entire life. In the years since she first became a woman, several of the men had been her lovers. Would she share joy with one of them again and would he father her child? Or would the father of her baby be some man she had not yet taken into her bed? She liked men of all shapes and sizes, handsome and not so handsome, as long as they were kind, interesting to talk to, and thoughtful when it came to giving her pleasure.

Would it be Landar with the curly black hair? Zand whose wispy beard made him look like an eager young goat? Reloc who, despite a twisted leg, danced as gracefully as a crane? Chindar who had always left her gasping with pleasure? Some of the men, like Uncle Bindar's partner Enal, only liked men, but that left more than enough possibilities. The Goddess had promised that the father of her baby would "find her." Well, hadn't all these men just "found her" by coming into her room?

I only need one, Sabalah thought. *Surely whoever he is, he'll be from Shara.*

But she was wrong. In fact, she could not have been more mistaken.

2

Songs in the Night

Sabalah belonged to two of the great societies of Shara: The Society of Those Who Fish and The Society of Those Who Gather Wild Food. In the months following her vision, her stews never burned, her threads never tangled, her nets always came back filled with fish, and when she went out to gather berries, she returned with so much fruit that bands of children waylaid her outside the city walls to beg for handfuls. *The Lucky One,* everyone called her. *Sabalah, Daughter of Lalah, who is blessed by the Goddess.* But Sabalah did not feel lucky, and she did not feel blessed. She felt cursed and betrayed.

Since Amonah had promised her she would bear a magical child, summer had turned to winter, and winter was turning to spring, yet although she had lain with several of her old lovers, her womb was still empty. Everywhere she went, she carried that emptiness with her. For twenty-seven generations, Shara had prospered under the rule of its priestess-queens, each descended in an unbroken line from the First Mother who had built the original temple dedicated to Batal on the cliffs above the river. No queen had ever ruled Shara who had not borne children.

As each month brought new disappointment, Sabalah began to sleep more, eat less, and take no pleasure in the things that had once delighted her. Halfway between the winter solstice and the spring equinox, Great Aunt Nasula summoned her, settled her down on a pile of stuffed cushions, fed her dried figs and freshly baked flatbread spread with goat cheese, and assured her once again that her barrenness didn't matter.

"You're next in line to be Queen of Shara after me and your mother," Aunt Nasula said. She was in her early sixties, lean and long-armed, with shell-white hair, a square chin, and penetrating eyes with exceptionally large, black pupils. As far as Sabalah could tell, Aunt Nasula saw everything that went on in Shara, which meant when she spoke, you listened, even if you would rather be off by yourself brooding on the unfairness of life in general and Amonah in particular.

"You have the twin gifts of seeing and prophecy and the common sense to know that a good queen listens to the Council of Elders," Nasula continued. "The priestesses say you've learned all they can teach you. If your mother and I, may the Goddess spare us, should die tomorrow, I have no doubt that you'd be one of the best priestess-queens Shara has ever had."

"How can a woman who is not a mother be a queen?" Sabalah said. She looked wearily at all the objects in the room that proclaimed her aunt's fertility: walls decorated with red triangles; storage jars whose billowing sides resembled the bellies of pregnant women; windows shaped like full moons; strings of onions; baskets of dried fruit; sheaves of wheat that hovered over her head just beyond reach; not to mention the thirteen small pregnant snake goddesses, each no bigger than her thumb, who sat in a circle on the stone altar by the kitchen door as if discussing who would give birth next.

"How could I be queen?" she repeated. "My barrenness would spread like oil from a spilled lamp. I'd bring bad luck to Shara."

Nasula made a clicking noise with her tongue and stared at Sabalah sternly. "I'd better not die tomorrow, and we better hope your mother remains in good health, because you're speaking like a fool. Listen to me, niece. Forget luck, bad or good. You're not important enough to control whether or not fields bear crops or babies are born. The Goddess Earth is so much greater than we are, that nothing we do can change the destiny She has marked out for us. If She wills Shara and its people to be fertile and happy, they'll be fertile and happy whether or not you're barren."

Nasula picked up a piece of bread and cheese and ate it in two quick bites. Sabalah could tell she'd made her aunt angry, but she still believed what she'd said. It was on the tip of her tongue to confess that things were even worse than they appeared.

I've been abandoned, she wanted to say, *betrayed by the Goddess Herself. Or else I'm not entirely sane, and see visions that are not true visions and imagine women who walk on water when no women are there.* But instead of speaking, she pressed her lips together and held the pain of her barrenness in her heart where it stung like a fresh cut.

It was good she didn't speak out, because her aunt never liked to be interrupted, and she was not finished. Licking the cheese off her fingers, she reached out and gave Sabalah an affectionate pat on the arm.

"My dear child," she said, "you're not to blame for your lack of understanding. You've never been more than a two-day walk from Shara. When I was your age I sailed all the way north to the city of Shambah where they worship butterflies as the messengers of the Goddess."

She grinned broadly, exposing her missing front teeth, and gave Sabalah another friendly pat on the arm. Then she helped herself to a second piece of bread and cheese. This time she nibbled at it slowly.

"In Shambah, their priestess-queen was barren. In fact, they had had three barren priestess-queens. Were the fields of Shambah barren too? No, they were green and lush with barley, and the gardens! Ah, the gardens! I wish you could see the gardens of Shambah. Perhaps someday you will. The Shambans plant flowers that attract butterflies: especially purple and white ones. And they paint flowers on their houses. What a beautiful place Shambah is with the Sweetwater Sea on one side and, on the other, a sea of grass that extends as far as the eye can see."

She paused, picked up the largest fig, stared at it, and then put it back down on the plate without eating it. "My point in telling you about Shambah is to help you understand that the Goddess Earth is worshipped in different ways in different places, but nothing exists that isn't part of Her. So let's not have any more nonsense about how a barren woman can't be a priestess-queen. What you are feeling is self-pity. Put that aside and go on with your life. I never again want to hear you complain about what you don't have when you have been blessed with good health and so many people who love you. You don't have to take care of children of your own to be a mother. There are plenty of children in this city who need love and mothering. Devote yourself to them and be grateful for what you have instead of longing for what you don't have. I give you this as an order, not as your aunt, but as your elder and your queen. Do you understand?"

Sabalah nodded. "Yes, Aunt," she said meekly. But her meekness was insincere, and by the sharp look Aunt Nasula gave her, it was clear she knew Sabalah was not going to follow her advice.

My ears hear your words, Sabalah thought, *but they don't reach my heart. The fact that some butterfly-worshipping city on the edge of nowhere has had barren priestess-queens doesn't make my own barrenness more bearable. How can you ever understand me, Aunt Nasula? You have four grown sons. I won't have any children, ever.*

Again she was tempted to speak of the vision she had had and of the promise Amonah had made to her.

"Meanwhile, be patient," Nasula said. "You're still young. Anything can happen."

But nothing is happening! Sabalah wanted to cry. *Nothing!* As for patience, she had never had much to start with, and these days she had even less.

"Are you Sabalah, Daughter of Lalah?"

Sabalah turned at the sound of the question and found herself facing a man who was holding a strange-looking stringed instrument shaped like a bow. He was about her age, tall with a finely-shaped face, long nose, dark skin, full beard, and eyes so green they looked as if they had been chipped out of jade. His hair, which hung down below his waist like a cape, was black as the jet stones the western traders brought to Shara to be used in offerings to the Dark Goddess. Deerskin clothing, deerskin headband, deerskin boots embroidered with shells, no fur trim on his gloves, but still Sabalah would have been willing to bet her share of tonight's feast that he was a trader from the West Beyond the

West who had come to the city to celebrate the Festival of the Ewes.

Ewes was a men's celebration that marked the start of spring when the snakes came out of hibernation and the first lambs were born and suckled. Each day of the festival the men made beds for the Goddess out of rushes and sheepskins and invited Her to join them in sharing joy. At night they lit torches which they carried around the city walls in long, snake-like processions. For a solid week, everyone danced, feasted, and sang, and since sex was sacred to the Goddess, Ewes was the time when half the babies in Shara were conceived.

The most exotic visitors were the traders from the West Beyond the West. Like all pilgrims, the westerners spoke Old Language, the common tongue of worship and trade, but given the way they looked, it was impossible to mistake them for anyone else since they wore their hair very long: the women braiding it into coils on their heads in imitation of snakes, the men letting it hang down below their waists.

"Are you Sabalah?" the long-haired stranger repeated. "Sabalah, Daughter of Lalah?"

Sabalah realized she had been staring. Putting down the basket of fish she'd been lugging to the cleaning stone, she placed the tips of her fingers together and bowed to him the way the Mother People always bowed to welcome a stranger.

"Yes," she said. "I'm Sabalah."

The stranger smiled pleasantly, exposing a row of slightly crooked teeth so white they could have been bleached shell. There was something about his smile that made her think he wasn't going to have any trouble finding a partner to share joy with tonight. Oddly enough, it didn't occur to her that that partner might be her. So many things didn't occur to her the first time she met him, but she liked him from the very first.

"Good," he said. "Then I'm in luck. Your sister Alana sent me to find you. She says you're the best singer in the city."

"My sister praises me too much. The best singer in this city is Xan."

"Is Xan a man or a woman?"

"A man. In our language 'Xan' means 'beloved son of the Goddess'."

"That's a lot of meaning to put into such a short name." The stranger smiled again, took off the instrument he had been carrying, and balanced it against his leg. The strings cast long shadows on the white gravel path. Sabalah found herself wondering what kind of music they made when he plucked them.

"Xan won't do. I need a woman, a young boy, or a girl to sing with me, someone who can hit the high notes. I prefer a woman, because the young ones tire more easily, and my singing sometimes goes on all night."

"You sing?"

"Ah, I'm being rude. I haven't introduced myself properly." Putting the tips of his fingers together, he returned her bow. "I'm Arash, Son of Wanala, and this," he gestured to his instrument, "is what I accompany myself on when I sing. My people call it a *shuala*."

"What sorts of songs do you sing?"

He smiled more broadly this time. She could see he loved singing so much that just hearing her say the word "songs" made him happy. "I sing love songs, songs of praise to the Goddess, songs for those who fish and those who hunt and those who weave–songs for people who do almost anything really. I also sing long story songs that recount the history of my people and the histories of all the peoples I've encountered during my travels. Tonight I'd like you to do me the honor of singing with me, because I have a story song to sing that requires more than one beautiful voice."

Sabalah laughed. "You aren't very modest, are you?"

"No," he said. "Not about my singing. Will you join me?"

"What kind of story is it?"

"A dialogue between two lovers who have met for the first time. So will you sing with me or won't you? If you won't, I'll have to keep wandering around this city bothering people until I find another woman who can carry a tune."

For many months Sabalah had felt too sad to sing, but there was something about his smile and his simple, good-natured invitation that tempted her to say "yes."

"You see before you," he said, "a supplicant who will happily throw himself at your feet if it will persuade you to join me at on the singers' stage tonight."

"You're a very silly man. If you throw yourself at my feet, you'll regret it. The ground is dirty, and my boots smell like fish."

"And yet when you speak, your voice is as sweet as the song of a nightingale."

"Do you always give such outrageous compliments to complete strangers?"

He grinned. "Yes, because they work. From the look on your face, I can tell I'm persuading you. So tell me, Sabalah, Daughter of Lalah, will you sing with me tonight or won't you?"

Sabalah bent down and picked up her basket. "What choice do I have? Yes, Arash, I'll sing with you. It's not every afternoon that a woman on her way to gut a basket of perch gets compared to a nightingale."

That night Sabalah and Arash sang together for the first time. Afterwards, they went to the sheepskin bed Arash had made for the Goddess and shared joy so passionately that it left both of them breathless. For the rest of her life, Sabalah remembered the soft sweep of Arash's long hair over her nipples and eyelids, the sweet scent that rose off his body like freshly baked bread, the skill of his tongue, the strength of his embrace, the way he laughed and rolled around with her after the first time, and then came back for a second and a third. Each time they made love, she gave him a soft tap on the thigh, that universal sign of the Mother People that the woman was inviting the man to enter her.

"You are sweeter than all the honey in all the hives in all the world," he said to her when at last they lay side by side looking up at the shadows of the lamps playing across the white plastered ceiling. Turning toward her, he brushed her hair off her face and gave her a kiss on the forehead. "My sweet Sabalah, I shall have to write a song about you."

"A love song?" she asked.

"What else?" Arash murmured, drawing her closer.

3

The Temple of Dogs

Seventy-nine nights of passion and tenderness. Three full moons, six quarter moons, two nights when the moonless sky was as black as Arash's hair. *I want us to lie together where I sleep most nights, he told Sabalah. I want to take you out under the stars.*

So except when it rained, they left the city, walked into the darkness, and made love under warm sheepskins, curled around one another, so mixed and tangled and close that they soon forgot where the body of one ended and the body of the other began. Sometimes they pitched their bed on the beach. Afterwards, as Arash played his *shuala* and sang to Sabalah, his voice would move in rhythm to the waves. On other nights, they lay in the meadows or beside the gardens where as they kissed, they could smell the scent of wild roses mingled with the scent of their own bodies.

For seventy-nine nights, Arash taught her the songs of his people, and she taught him the songs of hers. One of his most beautiful songs traced his journey from the West Beyond the West to Shara. As they sat side-by-side singing it, Sabalah began to understand how vast the Motherlands were.

> *When the Queen of the West*
> *calls to her dolphins*
> *the sea trembles*
> *white foam climbs her thighs*

they sang.

Gira, island of soft nights
Gira, island of love

Would she and Arash ever visit the island of Gira, or the Caves of Nar where "the animals danced"? Would they follow his song map west to Lezentka the village of "rockfish and clams," and then travel through the forest for months until they reached the village on the "Sea of Gray Waves" where he had been born? She couldn't imagine ever leaving Shara, but if she did, she wanted to travel with Arash to all the places he sang about.

The nights passed so swiftly that, almost before she knew it, the scent of spring was in the air, and the earth was coming back to life. Sometimes when Arash lay sleeping, she would crawl out from beneath the sheepskins, kneel, place the palms of her hands on the earth, and pray.

Oh Goddess, she would whisper, *oh you who are the sacred force that makes the ewes bring forth lambs and the wild birds nest, move through me. Make me fertile. I have never loved a man as much as I love this one. Let us make a child together.*

The joy of it was, Arash loved her too, not gradually but from the very first. In Sabalah's experience, this didn't often happen, but by the grace of the Goddess it had. That first morning, he gave her a present: a small crystal bead that shattered into rainbows when she held it up to the light. The next morning and each morning after, he gave her another bead until by the time the new wheat was sprouting finger-high in the fields, she had an entire necklace of crystals.

"Sweet Sabalah," he said, "I would give you the stars over our bed if I could, but I can't reach them, so I am giving you these small stars. In the West Beyond the West near the village where I was born, there's a cave where my people go on starry nights to harvest crystals. When we lift up our torches, the whole inside glitters in rose and white and purple."

Besides teaching her the songs of his people, Arash told her stories about them. They worshipped the Goddess as an owl, he said, erecting great circles of stones in Her honor. He himself had helped raise one of those stones when he was only fourteen, pulling on the ropes with all the young men of his village. As for his family, he had a loving *aita* but no brothers or sisters. His mother had died when he was young, and he had few memories of her, only that she was gentle and beautiful *(like you, Sabalah).* At the Feast of the Dead, his people had laid her bones in the crystal cave along with the bones of her ancestors.

Discovering that he had a talent for singing and playing the *shuala,* he had joined a band of traders heading east shortly after his fifteenth birthday. From then on, everywhere he went, he was welcomed by people eager to hear his songs.

One night as he and Sabalah sat together around a small fire, he told her that north of the city of Shambah, there was an endless sea of grass. Somewhere in that waving ocean of green lived tribes of beings who were half-animal, half-human.

"They are said to have six legs and two heads," he told her. "Their front part is like a person, but their back part is like a long-tailed, fur-covered beast. They move so rapidly no one can out-run them. The people of the north call them 'beastmen.'" Suddenly he stopped speaking, and Sabalah saw an expression on his face she'd never seen before.

"What's wrong?" she asked.

Turning away, he poked at the fire with a stick, sending a cloud of sparks into the air. "The beastmen do terrible things."

"What sort of things?"

"I don't know. All I know is that the traders who have ventured into the Sea of Grass fear them more than any beasts in the forest. That's why none of the trade routes go farther north than Shambah."

"Do you believe these beastmen really exist?"

"Yes."

"Have you ever seen one?"

"No."

Sabalah laughed, drew him close, and hugged her to him. "Dear, silly man," she said. "You can't combine a person with an animal. There can't be such things as beastmen. I bet it's just a made-up story like your stories of birds that speak and rabbits that wear boots."

Arash smiled, shrugged, and then laughed with her. "You're probably right. I make up a lot of stories about impossible things when I sing. I wonder if people believe they're true." He poked at the fire again and sent it flaming. For an instant a host of dark shadows fled across his face, and Sabalah felt a chill creep over her. But that meant nothing. The evening was cool and the wind was rising.

Later as they lay together looking at the stars, he promised he would never leave her. "I'll stay in Shara," he said, "and learn to fish or hunt or farm so I can be useful. When you're ready, we'll travel west together, and I'll show you the Motherlands. There are so many things I want you to see: great temples built in the shape of birds, mountains that breathe fire, the River of Smoke, the Snake Dancers of Itesh. We'll sing together, and everywhere we go, people will welcome us."

That night they made love with more passion than ever. The next morning, he handed her the seventy-ninth crystal bead, picked up his *shuala,* and went off to check on a line of snares he had put out to catch rabbits. They said goodbye as usual with a kiss. Nothing seemed wrong, and as Sabalah went off to join The Society of Men and Women Who Fish, she felt happy. As she walked toward the beach, she imagined Arash sitting under a tree practicing the songs they would sing that evening. There was one song she particularly liked, and she hummed it to herself as she put up the sail.

But although the day started out well, the wind was blowing from the wrong direction, and every time she cast her nets into the sea, they came up empty. Convinced her luck would change if she just kept at it, she went on fishing until sunset. When at last she entered her mother's house, everyone had finished dinner except Arash who had not shown up yet.

She waited for him all evening and far into the night, but he never appeared. Finally she fell asleep in her own bed, alone for the first time in weeks. Near dawn, she started awake with the sense that something was in her room. As she watched, frozen in terror, a strange, headless shadow rippled over the walls. Opening her mouth she tried to scream for help, but no sound came out.

That was when she realized she must be dreaming. Falling back, she pulled the covers up around her neck and closed her eyes. In the morning when she woke, Arash had still not returned.

When he did not return the next day either, she began to worry in earnest. Leaving her fishing boat moored to the wharf, she started to search for him. Where was he? Why hadn't he come back to Shara? What had happened? Had he been injured? Attacked by wild beasts? His *shuala* was gone, which made sense since he'd taken it with him; but his pack was gone too. How could that be? She was certain he had left it hanging from the rafters in the storeroom when he went out to check his snares, but when she went to look for it, it wasn't there.

For an entire week, she combed every thicket within a half day's walk of Shara, calling out his name only to be greeted by a silence that seemed to mock her. There was no sign of a struggle, no indication that he had been injured in any way. In the end, all she found were a few muddy footprints at the edge of the farthest field, which might or might not have been his.

Finally, she was forced to accept a harsh truth: he had come back in the middle of the night, picked up his pack, and left without even bothering to say goodbye. Maybe he had realized he didn't love her or maybe he'd decided against living in Shara. In any event, he had gone, leaving her with nothing but memories of seventy-nine nights of love and passion, a crystal necklace, and a longing so intense that in the first weeks after he disappeared, she could not look at the stars without crying.

For days, she grieved, not eating, not sleeping, not able to take joy in any of the things that had formerly made her happy. Once she walked down to the beach, faced the open sea, and cursed Amonah. *How could you have tricked me like this!* she cried. *What kind of Goddess are you! I will never offer you flowers again! I might never have shared joy with Arash if I hadn't thought he was the man you promised I would meet!*

Then something happened that changed everything. It didn't happen all at once, but little by little. When she first noticed, she refused to let herself hope. She'd been wrong so many times, and she didn't need another cruel disappointment so soon after being abandoned by Arash. *I am not,* she told herself. *I can't be. It's impossible.*

But day by day, the indications were harder to ignore. She missed her menses once and told herself it was because she was grieving. Two weeks later on the first day of the new moon, she woke up feeling nauseated, and when she examined her breasts—still hardly daring to hope—she saw they had grown fuller and the pink part around her nipples was turning brown.

Amonah, she thought, *have you not abandoned me after all? Could I be with child?*

She told no one her suspicions, not even her *aita* or her mother. If she was wrong again, she didn't think she could stand to face their pity.

The prudent thing would be to wait until she felt the baby move inside her, but she couldn't bear to wait, so instead, she went to a small building near the healing hot springs known as the Temple of Dogs. The temple, which was constructed entirely of fired blue and white tiles, was one of the prettiest of the twenty temples of Shara. In it lived seven sacred dogs who were tended by three elderly priestesses. The Sharans believed dogs had been created by the Goddess to teach humans how to love one another. Dogs herded Sharan sheep, hunted with Sharan hunters, played with Sharan children, lived in Sharan houses, ate with Sharan families, and sometimes slept in Sharan beds, but the dogs in the Temple of Dogs were like no others.

When Sabalah entered the temple, she was greeted by three dogs who had not gone out for a morning run. The dogs—a little black one, a large white one, and a shaggy brown one with foxlike ears—stood around her looking up at her with what appeared to be curiosity. Maybe, Sabalah thought, they were as eager as she was to know if she was with child.

For a few moments there appeared to be no one in the temple but the dogs. Then one of the priestesses entered through a small door that led to the room where the dogs and priestesses slept and took their meals.

The priestess walked slowly toward Sabalah. She was white-haired and bent with age, so thin that her brown linen robe fluttered loosely with each step she took. Sabalah knew her well. Her name was Valina. A cousin of a cousin many times removed, she was one of the midwives who had assisted at the birth of Sabalah's mother.

"Sabalah, Daughter of Lalah," Valina said, "what can I do for you today? More prayers?" That was a reasonable assumption since Sabalah had visited every temple in Shara more than once to ask the priestesses to pray for her to conceive. Mostly she had gone to the Temple of Batal on the cliffs since the Snake Goddess was the greatest giver of fertility, but she'd also come to the Temple of Dogs a few times.

"It's not prayers I come in search of today." Sabalah paused, reluctant to go on. She knew there would be a look of pity on Valina's face as soon as she told her what she had come for, but that couldn't be helped. She had to know.

"I've come for the dogs," she said.

Valina's eyebrows went up. "The dogs?"

"Yes."

"Then again you think you may have reason to hope?"

"I'm not sure. That's what I want the dogs to tell me."

"How many times have you missed your menses?"

"Once."

Valina cleared her throat and looked down at the three dogs who were still waiting patiently. "It's early," she said. "I don't know if they can do it this early."

"But they can try, yes?"

"They can try, but think about how you're going to feel if they tell you you're not with child. You won't know if they're right or wrong. Have patience, Sabalah. Wait another month. You've already been disappointed too many times."

"But what if the dogs tell me I'm with child?"

"If the dogs tell you that, then I will be the first to kiss you and congratulate you and bless you in the name of the Goddess. The dogs are never wrong when they say 'yes'; only when they say 'no.' But it's early. Why rush?"

Tears filled Sabalah's eyes. "Because, dear cousin, I can't bear to wait another month or even another week. Please let me consult the dogs now. Perhaps they'll put my mind to rest; perhaps they won't. If they tell me 'no,' I'll wait until it's time to try again. But if they say 'yes'—dear Goddess, if they say 'yes,' there will be no happier woman in Shara."

"You're sure you want to do this?"

"Absolutely sure."

"Then how can I refuse you?" Gently wiping the tears off Sabalah's cheeks with the sleeve of her robe, Valina took her by the hand and led her over to a low platform at the far end of the temple. The border of the platform was decorated with tiles that showed the Goddess at play with Her sacred dogs.

"Did you know I was the one who brought the dogs to your mother on the day they told her she carried you in her womb?"

"No."

"Stretch out and close your eyes. I will bring the dogs to you and pray they tell you what they told her."

Sabalah stretched out on the platform and obediently closed her eyes.

"Come," Valina commanded. As the dogs approached, Sabalah heard their claws clicking on the floor tiles.

Valina began to chant softly. The chant was wordless, low-pitched and soothing as the sound of surf or the humming of a hive of bees.

The next thing Sabalah knew, three small, cold dog noses were sniffing her from head to foot. The sniffing tickled, but she forced herself not to move. *Dear Goddess, Mother of us all,* she prayed, *Please let your blessed dogs say 'yes.'*

Suddenly, one of the dogs placed a muzzle on her belly. Then she felt a second muzzle, then a third.

"Sabalah, Daughter of Lalah," Vilna cried, "the sacred dogs have scented a living child in your womb!"

Sabalah opened her eyes, sat up, gathered all three dogs to her, and hugged them. Then she began to cry; but for the first time since Arash abandoned her, her tears were tears of joy.

4

THE BEASTMEN

Sabalah settled into a deep sense of contentment. She still missed Arash every night when she climbed into bed alone, still ached for his touch and the sound of his voice; but she no longer felt the almost unbearable pain she had felt when he first left. Instead she thought of the child growing inside her, how it would live in the same motherhouse that had sheltered her family for generations and play with the same toys she had played with as a child. Next summer when the mothers and their children walked up the cliffs to the Temple of Batal, she would walk with them carrying her baby in her arms, and someday when she was very old, her child might carry her.

Every seven days on the new, full, and quarter moons, she gathered blue and white flowers and walked down to the sea to offer them to Amonah. First she tossed them into the waves. Then she scooped up a handful of water, poured it over her head, and prayed that her child would be born whole and healthy; that it would not die of any of the diseases that took young children; that it would thrive, and that—if Amonah willed it—she might someday give it brothers and sisters.

These were her days and they were good; but her nights were different. Often—much too often—she had disturbing dreams. Once she dreamed Arash was drowning. On another occasion, she dreamed that golden beasts with claws were lurking beside her bed. Twice she woke in the middle of the night with the feeling that she was being smothered by something heavy and invisible.

"It's not uncommon for pregnant women to have nightmares," the midwives assured her. "Drink a cup of peppermint tea before you go to bed and sleep on your side or put pillows under your knees and these dreams will stop."

But no amount of tea or pillows under her knees made any difference. Her days were filled with joy, including the joy of asking her brother Gradush if he would be her baby's *aita;* but at night, the bad dreams continued. The worst were the ones she could not remember, but they left her so exhausted, she felt as if she had not slept.

Why was she having so many nightmares? She was healthy, happy, loved by her friends and family, and carrying the child she had always longed for.

The next time she went down to the beach to offer flowers to Amonah, she prayed a different prayer: "If it is your will, Goddess, let me have no more nightmares."

The waves took the flowers out to sea and then returned to toss them up on the sand. Was that a sign? Was Amonah saying "yes" or "no?" Sabalah gathered up the flowers and tossed them back. They returned a second time, then a third. She stood on the beach waiting for something more to happen, but nothing did.

The next morning, she climbed up the cliff to consult Batal whose long gold-and-green body coiled around the walls of Shara. Batal had protected the city for time out of mind. On rare occasions She sent visions warning of earthquakes, destructive storms, or plagues. She was also the Goddess you went to if you wanted to ask for a dream that would tell you if you would find love or happiness, bear a boy or girl child, survive a bad illness, or live to a ripe old age.

When you asked for a dream from Batal, you went into the Dreaming Cave next to the temple. The entrance was a dark hole that sometimes made pilgrims nervous, but there was nothing to be afraid of. The Cave was actually three caves, two small and one large, reached through a well-lighted tunnel that twisted and turned until the silence was absolute. The walls of the third cave were painted red to symbolize the life-giving blood of the Mother, but other than that it was undecorated except for several clay lamps that were always lit and a stone platform covered with deerskins where the dreamers lay.

When Sabalah entered the third cave, she felt as if a heavy weight had been lifted off her shoulders. There was no more peaceful place in Shara, perhaps no more peaceful place in all the Motherlands. Confident that Batal would send her a dream that would help her get rid of her nightmares, she stretched out on the platform, closed her eyes, and fell asleep.

She was walking on a path made out of light. On either side of her for as far as she could see there was a green meadow filled with wildflowers. As she crossed it, she heard the voice of Batal, high and sweet as the ringing of silver bells.

"I who shed my skin each year, I who am immortal, I who take messages deep into the womb of the Goddess Earth welcome you, Sabalah, Daughter of Lalah. You will bear a girl child whom you will name 'Marrah,' which means 'seagull' in a language you do not yet speak. Marrah will be the savior of her people, but only if she lives long enough to become a woman."

Batal's words struck Sabalah like a blow across the face. What! Her child would become the "savior of her people" but only if she didn't die! She fought to wake up. This dream wasn't going well. Everything was changing. The path of light was fading, the wildflowers withering, the meadow turning brown.

Fear. Confusion. Beastmen. Monsters with six legs and two heads: one human, one the head of a giant animal. Racing faster than wind. Coming toward Shara from the north and destroying everything in their path. Bared teeth, foaming lips. Short, bristling brown hair on one head; the other head covered with a tangle of something that looked like flax. Breathing fire. Eating whole cities. Turning the green womb of the earth to ashes.

"Rise up, Sabalah! Save Marrah or the beastmen will take her!" Batal cried. *"Time is running out! Your enemies are drawing closer. Flee! Go south to my shrine at Orefi where you can give birth to Marrah in safety. Then take her to the West Beyond the West. Leave tonight. Don't tell anyone where you are going. Don't say goodbye to your mother or*

aita; don't bid your sister or brothers farewell. Be brave. Be strong. Be— "

Sabalah woke up screaming to find herself back in the Dreaming Cave lying on a tangled pile of sweat-soaked deerskins. For a moment she was too stunned to move.

Leave Shara tonight? Why so soon? Why should she suddenly run off under the cover of darkness without telling anyone? They'd think she was dead. Why should she leave her mother, Uncle Bindar, and her brother Gradush whom she'd already asked to be her baby's *aita*? Why should she abandon her home, her friends, and everyone who would help her raise her child?

This couldn't have been Batal speaking. This was another nightmare created from her longing for Arash. Arash was the one who had told her about the beastmen and taught her a song to guide her to the West Beyond the West. Or maybe it was that pork she had eaten for dinner last night. She'd thought it tasted a little off. Nothing like bad pork to give you nightmares, even in the Dreaming Cave.

She started to sit up, but before she could move, she felt a forked tongue brush across her eyelids. A sharp current of pain ran down her spine, and a light brighter than the sun exploded in her head. Screaming, she opened her eyes to blackness and for a moment was utterly blind.

When her sight returned, she saw the red wall of the Dreaming Cave. Between her and the wall, a huge snake floated in endless coils. Her eyes were blue as the sea on a sunny day; Her scales, yellow and gold.

"Go now," the Snake ordered.

Sabalah knew the difference between a vision and a dream, and this was no dream. This was Batal speaking, the Great Goddess whose commands could not be denied.

"Spare me," she pleaded. "Let me stay in Shara, Goddess. I've never been anywhere. I'm frightened."

"You are one of my Chosen and my Chosen are never spared," Batal said. *"Go to Orefi, my beloved child. The Motherlands are peaceful. South and west of here there is no war or hunger, and a woman with child is always welcome. Don't tell the sea, confide in the gulls, or whisper to the*

temple dogs where you are headed. Go in secret and go tonight or you will lose your baby to the beastmen! Do you understand?"

Sabalah put her hand on her belly feeling the full terror of what it would be like to lose this precious child who was growing inside her. "Yes," she said in a trembling voice. "I understand. I will obey you."

Seizing Her tail in Her mouth, Batal curled into a single floating coil, spun for an instant, then vanished.

When Sabalah finally stopped shaking, she got up and left the Dreaming Cave as fast as she could. If she was leaving Shara tonight, she had to gather water, food and blankets, and get her leggings mended without rousing suspicion. She'd take a spare shift, a pair of boots and her warm wool cloak for when it got cold. She'd also take the fringed linen skirt, the blue stone necklace, and the ceremonial earrings her mother had given her on the day she became a woman, and the crystal necklace Arash had given her, because even though he had abandoned her, she couldn't imagine leaving it behind.

That night, as she made her way toward the South Gate, the streets of Shara were deserted. High above her, a sliver of moon rode through a sea of stars. No dogs barked at her, and she met no one as she silently said farewell to the familiar places where she had lived since the day she was born.

She passed Aunt Nasula's motherhouse, the healing hot springs, the Temple of Dogs. *I will never see them again,* she thought. *And then she thought: Who am I to predict the future? Perhaps someday Marrah and I will return to Shara.* The baby in her womb was "Marrah" now. She could no longer imagine giving her any other name.

Since the Motherlands had never known war, the south entrance to the city was only closed with a flimsy wooden gate to keep out animals. As Sabalah opened the gate, she thought of all the times she and Arash had left the city at night only to return at dawn half-drunk with love and contentment.

That was a good thought, and she was grateful to have had it, because from the moment she stepped onto the trail that led through the fields to the forest she stopped feeling nostalgic and started feeling terrified. She couldn't have said why, because nothing was different. There were the same sheep she and Arash had seen on the nights they went outside the city walls to make love, muddled white shapes with their winter fleeces sheered, some sleeping with drooping heads while others kept watch. There were the cattle, standing like shadows. There was the wheat, moving gently in waves like a small, tossing sea. Everything was peaceful and familiar, and yet—

She stopped at the edge of the last field and looked back at Shara, which gleamed faintly in the moonlight. She could just make out the Great Snake that wound around the city walls. Again she had the sense that someone was following her, but she could see no one.

That was the moment she realized she had never been alone before. Not that she hadn't been by herself. She had fished for days at a time with no one to help her draw in the nets, taken long walks on the beach, and ventured into the forest on this very trail to gather food. Yet she had never before been without friends and family. All her life, she had lived surrounded by people who knew and loved her. Now she was about to become like the traders who visited Shara: a stranger far from home.

Yet it was more than that. She couldn't shake the feeling that something was watching her. Bending down, she picked up a dead branch to use as a club if she were attacked. But who would attack her? Batal had said the beastmen were coming to take Marrah, but Marrah wasn't even born yet so they wouldn't be arriving for months, perhaps years. Meanwhile, the trails that led south were safe, and no one in living memory had encountered a lion or bear in the forests that bordered the Sweetwater Sea.

Throwing the branch down, she told herself to stop imagining things and walked into the forest. *Be brave,* she told herself. *Be strong.*

As soon as she took a few steps, the moonlight disappeared, leaving her in darkness except for the trail, which was made of hard-packed white clay. The sensible thing would be to spread her blanket under a tree and get some sleep until sunrise, but if she did, members of The Society of Those Who Gather Wild Food might stumble on her and ask questions. Then too, there was that very disturbing thing Batal had said about her enemies drawing closer and the need for haste.

As far as she knew, she had no enemies, yet for the first time the forest felt unfriendly. She walked on, and with every step she took, the feeling that she was being watched grew stronger. Something was stalking her. Something silent and invisible. Could she still be asleep in the Dreaming Cave? Had she not left Shara after all?

She knew every bend in the trail and could have walked it with her eyes closed, so why was she feeling a prickling at the back of her neck? Why were the hairs on her arms standing up?

She grew more and more frightened. Finally, she came to a stop, trembling so hard her teeth chattered. So much for being brave and strong. She'd had enough of this. She was going back to Shara as fast as possible. In the morning when she could see where she was going, she would obey Batal's command. It would be awkward to try to sneak away when people were up and about, but anything had to be better than this feeling of being stalked.

Turning around, she made her way back toward the dim line of moonlight that marked the edge of the trees. She had only taken a few steps when a hand was slapped over her mouth, her arms were pinned to her sides, and she was pulled backwards into the brush.

She tried to fight off whatever held her, but it was much stronger than she was, and all she managed to do was knock it over. There was a creek below the trail. As they rolled down the side of the gully toward it, branches whipped across her face, thorns tore at her clothing, and her eyes and nose filled with dirt. She bit at the hand hard enough to draw blood, but it kept pressing over her mouth, suffocating her.

Plunging through a dense clump of blackberry bushes, she struck a large boulder and came to a stop face down in a pile of dead leaves. Again she tried to fight the thing off, but it lay on her back, making it impossible for her to move.

"Quiet," it hissed in her ear. "You have to be quiet, or they'll find us."

Looking over her shoulder, she saw a pair of yellow eyes that glowed in the dark like the eyes of an owl. Again she tried to scream.

"Stop fighting me, my love," her captor whispered. The voice was familiar. She looked again and saw that his eyes weren't yellow after all, and they didn't glow. Only her fear had made her imagine they did.

Seeing recognition dawn on her face, Arash removed his hand from her mouth and hugged her to him.

"Arash?" she whispered. She felt such a mix of love, anger, relief, shock, and confusion that she couldn't think straight; but it was Arash who now held her in his arms, no doubt about it.

How could this be? She had been sure she'd never see him again. Why had he abandoned her? Why had he come back? Why had he attacked her and knocked her off her feet?

"Sabalah," he murmured, and kissed her. The kiss was long and as sweet as if they had never parted. She fell into it, forgot her anger, and for a moment became part of him again.

When they stopped kissing, he put his lips to her ear and spoke in the same whisper that had seemed so terrifying a few moments ago but which now seemed filled with love and reassurance. "We need to be quiet, or they'll find us."

"Who?"

"The beastmen."

"They're here already!"

"Yes. Lie very still, my love, and don't move or make a sound. They can hear the smallest twig snap, and they have a sense of smell sharper than dogs. Three of them are hunting us right now."

Putting his arms around her, Arash pulled her back under the blackberry bush so they were completely hidden. For a moment Sabalah heard nothing but the beating of her own heart and the hoot of an owl. Suddenly the owl's hoot turned into a scream of warning, and the silence of the forest was broken by a strange clopping sound as if someone were banging seashells against dirt.

As the clopping came nearer, Arash drew Sabalah closer and pointed. Above them on the trail, three beastmen were passing by, headed away from Shara into the forest. She only got a quick glimpse of them because it was dark, and there were trees and bushes in the way. She couldn't see if they had two heads: only arms and shoulders that would have made them look human if they had been walking. But they weren't walking. Instead they moved up and down the way you might move if you were standing in a boat. Or, she thought with growing terror, the way you might move if the bottom half of your body were the body of a beast.

They waited until the clopping faded away. When the silence of the night had closed around them again, Arash pulled her to her feet.

"Run!" he whispered.

Climbing back up to the trail they ran silently toward Shara. When they came to the main fork beside the vegetable gardens, Arash took the trail that led to the wharf. Sabalah started to ask him why they weren't going back to Shara where they'd be safer, but he put his finger over her lips and shook his head, so she kept running.

A stiff breeze sprung up. When they got to the wharf, they found several dozen boats bobbing up and down, tugging at their lines.

"Which boat is most seaworthy?" Arash whispered.

Sabalah pointed to a sturdy *raspa* that had sailed into Shara only that morning with a load of flint and honey. The *raspa* belonged to three sisters who had come to Shara bringing trade goods every summer for as long as Sabalah could remember.

Running over to the spot where the boat was moored, Arash untied the line that anchored it to the wharf. "Get in," he said.

"We can't take the Xuruna sisters' boat!"

"We'll send it back to them. Get in. We have to get out to sea. The beastmen can't travel on water, and we don't have much time before they find us. I'll explain when we're safely away."

Sabalah stared at the boat with grave misgivings. She had never stolen anything before. What would the Xuruna sisters think when they learned that both she and their boat were missing? She thought of Batal's warning, the safety of her unborn child, and the beastmen who were hunting her and Arash and who might well attack Shara if they thought she had taken refuge there.

Deciding she had no choice, she climbed into the boat with a silent apology to the Xuruna sisters. Arash climbed in beside her and pushed it away from the wharf. As soon as she put up the sail, it filled with wind. Soon Shara was only a small, whitish spot on the horizon.

When they were well out to sea, Sabalah lowered the sail, secured the lines, and turned to face Arash. She was angry at him for abandoning her, glad he'd come back, frightened by the vision she'd had in the Dreaming Cave, and so shaken by her brief glimpse of the beastmen that her heart still felt as if it might jump out of her chest. She opened her mouth and then closed it, searching for words. When she looked down at her hands, she saw they were shaking.

"Explain," she demanded. "What's going on? Why did you leave me?"

Arash took her hands in his. For an instant she was tempted to pull them out of his grasp, but instead she let him hold them. There was something comforting about his touch that made her feel less frightened.

For a while he sat staring into her eyes. He looked different. His lips were badly chapped, his long hair tangled, his face thinner as if he'd hardly eaten in the weeks since he disappeared.

"You're not going to like hearing what I'm about to tell you," he said at last. "I wish I could spare you. It's terrifying."

He was right. As they sat in the Xuruna sister's *raspa* under a sky filled with stars, he told her things that made her feel as if everything she had ever believed about the world was wrong.

"When I went out to check my snares, I was taken prisoner by the beastmen who took me north into the Sea of Grass. They spent weeks trying to make me tell them everything I knew about Shara. In particular, they wanted to know about a magical girl child who their shamans predicted would someday destroy them. For some reason they seemed to think the mother of this child was you.

"They knew your name, and no matter how often I told them you had no children, they kept insisting you were the mother of the baby they were looking for. As soon as I realized they intended to sacrifice this child to their God—yes God, not Goddess—I refused to tell them anything else." He shuddered. "I won't describe what they did to me to try to get me to talk, because it's too horrible, and with luck, you and I will never see them again."

He paused as if waiting for her to speak, but the horror of what he was saying had again rendered her speechless.

Lifting her hands to his lips again, he kissed them passionately. "I'd never betray you, my love. Never. When the beastmen realized this and saw that they couldn't get more information out of me, they dragged me back to Shara and tried to make me identify you and point out the motherhouse you lived in. They've been watching the city for days, pointing out woman after woman and watching my face to see if they'd found the right one. They're very cunning beasts, and they were sure I'd give some sign of recognition."

He bent forward and kissed her on the forehead, and she saw there were tears in his eyes.

"Oh my love," he said. "I wanted to warn you, but they kept me tied up at night, and in the daytime they never let me out of their sight. For weeks I tried to escape. Two nights ago, I finally succeeded, but I couldn't go to Shara to warn you that you were in danger, because if I'd gone anywhere near you, they would have known you were the woman they were looking for. So I hid in the forest and watched the city, hoping you'd come out on your own, and tonight you finally did."

"How did these beastmen know that you knew me?"

"I have no idea. They seemed to know a lot of things that there was no way for them to know. Like your so-called child—they said they knew her name."

Sabalah felt an icy fear congeal in her chest. "What did the beastmen say the name of my magical child was?" she asked.

"'Marrah.' The beastmen kept insisting your child's name was 'Marrah.'"

Sabalah gasped. Then, taking Arash's hands in hers, she placed them over her belly. "And so it is," she said.

For a moment he stared at her, confused. Then, suddenly, he understood. Pulling her into his arms, he kissed her. "This is wonderful!" he cried. "You've wanted a child for so long! Praise to the Goddess for giving you this joy!"

He did not ask if he had fathered the child since this was not the way of the people of the Motherlands, but Sabalah told him, and he was pleased to hear it had been him. Bending forward, he covered her belly with quick, light kisses. "Welcome, little Marrah. I who love your mother, love you with all my heart. Be born to us, and we will make sure no beastmen ever get near you!"

Sabalah took his long, black hair in her hands, stroked it, then lifted his face to hers. "So you think we're safe?"

"Almost safe, and with every moment we sail south, we'll be safer. No beast can move as fast as a boat on the open sea. And just to make sure, I have this for you."

Reaching into the pouch that hung around his neck, Arash pulled out a single, blood-red crystal. "I was going to give you this on the day the beastmen kidnapped me. It's from the crystal cave. My mother gave it to me on my fifth birthday. Red crystals are very rare, and my people believe they have magical powers."

"What sort of powers?"

"They're a mystery. All we really know is that as long as you wear a red crystal, nothing bad can happen to you."

Sabalah took the crystal from him and held it up to the starlight. It glowed as if it were on fire. "So beautiful. So very beautiful."

Taking the crystal from her, Arash unstrung her necklace and restrung it so that when she put it back on, the red crystal lay a little to the left, directly over her heart.

5

THE SIX COMMANDMENTS

They had left Shara on the longest day of the year. At this season the weather was dry, the sunsets spangled with long red clouds hazed with yellow dust. The winds were unpredictable, but with luck they would reach Orefi before the fall rains set in.

With every day that passed, Sabalah grew stronger and more confident. The nausea that plagued her in the early weeks of her pregnancy gradually disappeared, and as she filled her lungs with great gulps of fresh air that left the taste of salt on her lips, she imagined she could feel her waist thickening and her belly growing rounder.

Inside her, Marrah was getting bigger. She imagined the tiny baby unfolding like a flower. Would her eyes be green or brown? Would her hair be curly or straight, or would she be born with no hair at all? What would Marrah think the first moment she came into the world? Did babies welcome their birth, or did it frighten them?

She wished she'd paid more attention to the midwives when she'd had the chance, but she'd thought she had months to learn about such things. Even with Arash to keep her company, it was strange to be so far from home with only one person to rely on. In the Motherlands, women often did not live with the men who got them with child; and even when they did, they always slept in a motherhouse surrounded by dozens of people including the child's *aita*.

Sometimes Sabalah would sit in the stern of the boat and stare at the wake spreading out behind them like a ribbon of bubbles. That ribbon pointed back toward Shara. Every moment it grew longer and thinner until somewhere out of sight it ceased to exist.

Mother must be terribly worried about me, she thought. *The Goddess commanded me not to tell her where I was going or even say goodbye. I miss Mother terribly. I want her to be by my side to comfort and encourage me when my time comes. I want her to be the first to hold Marrah's head in her hands.* Then she would cry a little, secretly so Arash would suspect nothing, because she knew he was doing his best to protect her and Marrah from the beastmen.

Although she was frequently homesick, she gradually came to love this unfamiliar world, which was beautiful almost beyond description. As she and Arash sailed slowly along the shore of the Sweetwater Sea, the Motherlands unrolled like a green carpet embroidered with red poppies. There were no cities immediately south of Shara, only small villages; wide grassy meadows; stony cliffs; small, sheltered bays; and vast stands of forest. Most of the motherhouses in the villages were round and faced with white stucco so that when Sabalah and Arash looked at them from the sea, they shone like freshwater pearls.

Each village had a small temple where the Goddess Earth was worshipped. If they saw snakes painted on the side of a temple, they knew it was sacred to Batal, but often it was hard to tell in what form the Goddess was being celebrated. The carved wooden deer they saw on the fifth day probably meant that in that particular temple the Goddess was worshiped as a pregnant doe who ensured fertility, and the two temples shaped like birds were undoubtedly sacred to the Bird Goddess who brought life-giving rain to the crops, but many of the others were too far away to see clearly.

In any case, whatever form the Goddess took, She was always part of the same great whole, for this was the eastern edge of a vast, thinly settled continent of hunters, traders, and small farmers united by a single religion that held that the earth and every living thing on it was sacred. It was not a perfect world, because human beings would always be driven by passions that sometimes led to acts of violence, but it was a world filled with compassion and simple human kindness, so much so that, for thousands of years, the

Motherlands of Old Europe would linger in myth and legend as an earthly Paradise.

Above all, this was a land where strangers were always given a warm welcome, pilgrims were supplied with anything they needed, and a woman who was with child could travel in safety and be honored wherever she stopped to rest, for nothing was more important to the people of the Motherlands than children and their mothers. Thus when Arash finally declared they were safe from the beastmen and they put into shore for the first time, they found a crowd of villagers already gathered on the beach waiting to help them pull their boat out of the water.

"Where are you from?" the village elders asked. They had put on their best clothing, and although it was their holy duty to greet strangers with kindness, they must have not had many visitors, because they were clearly excited to see Arash and Sabalah.

"Why did you stop here? No one ever stops in Chaunna except the traders, and they only come twice a year."

When Arash and Sabalah said they were traveling to Orefi so Sabalah could give birth in Batal's temple, the elders produced two pilgrims' necklaces made of shells. "Hang these around your necks," they commanded, "so anyone who meets you will know you're traveling under the special protection of the Goddess. Why aren't the two of you already wearing pilgrims' necklaces? All pilgrims wear Her sign."

Not wanting to frighten the elders of Chaunna by telling them that she and Arash were being hunted by beastmen, Sabalah said they had left Shara in too much of a hurry. If the elders thought her excuse was unconvincing, they were too polite to show it. They watched as Sabalah and Arash hung the pilgrims' necklaces around their necks, and then took turns admiring Sabalah's crystal necklace.

"We've never seen such a thing," they told her. Several asked permission to touch the red crystal. "So bright. So beautiful. That red bead looks like a beating heart. Yes, dear guest, you should wear both necklaces. A woman with child must be protected in every possible way."

That evening the villagers prepared a huge feast, and danced a lively dance of welcome that involved much laughing and stumbling thanks to the bottomless bowls of wheat beer that were passed around with the roast venison and honey cakes. Since she was with child, Sabalah was not expected to join in the drinking, but by the time the feast was over, Arash could hardly stumble back to bed.

The next morning, they woke up to find a crowd standing outside the guest house. As far as Sabalah could tell, everyone in Chaunna had gotten up early to offer them help. Did they want someone to sail the Xuruna sisters' boat back to Shara? Here were two strong young people who had already volunteered to make the trip. Did they need another boat to continue their journey to Orefi? Then they were welcome to borrow any boat in the village.

"Return it if you can," the leader of The Chaunna Society of Those Who Fish said, "but if you can't, please accept it from us as a gift and ask the priestesses at Orefi to bless our village with a good catch in the coming year."

"We're honored," Sabalah said, putting the tips of her fingers together in the sign of the Goddess and bowing to them. "You are very kind. Thank you."

They stayed in Chaunna for eight days, feasting every night and leaving with their boat provisioned with so much food that it rode low in the water.

"I can never remember being treated with such generosity," Arash said as the little village grew small in the distance. "They must have given us one of their boats because you're with child. They probably thought it would offend the Goddess to make a pregnant woman walk to Orefi."

For a moment Sabalah was too surprised to reply. "I don't think that's the reason," she said. "You yourself told me that when you traveled with the traders, you were fed, housed, and honored as a guest wherever you went."

"Why?"

She stared at him, not understanding. "Why? You're asking me why?"

"Yes, why was I honored?"

"You were honored because you sang to your hosts." She felt her confusion growing. "You were honored because you played your *shuala* and entertained them with stories. But I'm sure you would have received a warm welcome everywhere you went even if you hadn't sung. After all, the first commandment of The Divine Sisters is that we all live together in love and harmony. Guests are sacred. Guests are..."

"The Divine Sisters? Who are The Divine Sisters?"

"Arash, please. Don't talk like this. Everyone knows who the Divine Sisters are. At the beginning of the Great Spring, the Goddess sent Them to us to teach us how to farm and weave and live peacefully with one another."

"Ah, yes," he murmured. "Of course. Now I remember. What were the Sisters' other commandments?"

What? Was he joking? Was it possible he didn't know? A cold sense of dread crept over her. She had been watching him closely ever since they left Shara, but up until now she had seen nothing to indicate that he hadn't healed and put his ordeal at the hands of the beastmen behind him. She'd thought he'd come back to her whole and in one piece, but there was something wrong with him, something deeply wrong.

What had the beastmen done to him that was so dreadful he couldn't bear to talk to her about it? Why had she been so slow to understand how devastating it must have been for him to be their prisoner? Had they done something to him so painful that he had to forget it to go on living, and while he was forgetting the pain, was he forgetting other things too? Was this why he couldn't remember the commandments any child in the Motherlands would have known?

Taking his hand, she rubbed his palm with her fingers in slow circles the way you massaged the hand of a crying child. *Calm down, my darling,* she thought. *Calm down. You're safe now.*

"The Goddess sent The Divine Sisters to us to give us six commandments," she said gently. "You remember, Arash."

"No. I don't." His eyes were filled with distress and confusion.

Sabalah felt a mix of pity and fear that was so strong she could hardly speak. She forced herself to keep her voice encouraging. Maybe if she kept reminding him about the things he had forgotten, he would begin to remember them on his own.

"The Divine Sisters commanded us thus: Live together in love and harmony. Cherish children. Honor women. Respect old people. Remember that the earth and everything on it is part of the living body of your Divine Mother. Enjoy yourselves, because your joy is pleasing to her."

"That's all? No other commandments?" Arash tossed his head nervously, and his hair fell over his face.

"No." Sabalah had no idea what to say next. He looked the same: as handsome, as tall, as long-nosed, green-eyed, and fine-featured as he had on the first day she met him, but there was something different about him, something unfamiliar, as if the Arash she had known had not come back to her after all. That was a foolish thought. This was the same Arash—the Arash she loved who had been wounded in some way that didn't show on the outside.

"They took my *shuala*," he said suddenly. "Broke it over my back."

Sabalah didn't have to ask him who "they" were. My poor, dear love, she thought. How you must have suffered. "We'll get you a new one," she promised. She reached up and stroked his hair, straightening it and pushing it away from his face.

"*Shualas* are only made in the villages that border the Sea of Gray Waves."

Homesick, sad, injured by the beastmen in ways that didn't show on the outside. *He must sing again,* she thought. *Maybe if he sings, he'll get well.*

"Then we'll get you a *lixah* like our singers play. They're smaller than a *shuala*, have more strings, and aren't as beautifully carved, but I'm sure you can play one." She stood on the tips of her toes, and gave him a kiss. "We'll spread a blanket in a field under the stars. You'll play the *lixah* and we'll sing together the way we used to."

He looked at her uneasily. Had he also forgotten the words to his songs? Had the beastmen taken those from him too? If so, she would teach them to him, so he could sing and be himself again.

6

CHAUNNA TO OREFI

As they sailed slowly south along a coastline that grew increasingly rugged and dry, the forests became sparser, and they began to see purple mountains looming to the west, their summits wreathed in clouds that looked like heaps of sun-bleached flax. Often they were delayed when the wind refused to blow in the right direction or didn't blow at all.

Luckily, most of the time the only storm clouds they saw lay far to the east. As one calm, dry day followed another, Sabalah's belly gradually grew rounder. It was plainly visible now, taut as a summer melon. Although she was happy to see that the child inside her was thriving, she continued to worry about Arash. Something was wrong. She didn't know exactly what it was, but she could feel it hovering over him like a dark cloud.

The days grew warmer, and the winds that filled their sails began to take on the scent of salt mixed with dust. Often on hot nights, they didn't head in at sunset. Instead, they reefed the sail, tossed out the anchor, and slept in the boat where it was cooler than it would have been on land. As they lay in each other's arms on a pile of blankets under the stars, Arash pointed out the constellations and told her the names his people gave them.

"There's the Lake of Fire. There are the Four Hunters. Over there to your right is the Great Ireki."

"The Great Ireki?"

"One of our names for the Goddess Earth."

"What about the Owl? Is there an owl up there?"

"An owl?" He looked puzzled.

"You told me your people worshipped the Goddess as an owl."

"Oh, of course. The Owl Goddess is right over there."

"I thought you said that was the constellation of the Great Ireki."

"My people call it by both names." Turning away from the night sky, Arash pulled her to him and began to caress her, and soon she was no longer thinking about the stars.

He had always been a good lover: tender, passionate, the kind of man whose ways in bed Sabalah would have thought it difficult to improve on, but the Arash who had come back to her from the Sea of Grass was all he had been and much more.

His lovemaking was still tender, but it was more erotic, more powerful. Before they had been equally active: whispering to each other what they wanted, saying what they liked, trying out new positions, and sometimes laughing so hard that they couldn't continue when one proved awkward. Now the laughter was gone. Now, more often than not, Sabalah closed her eyes and let Arash take the lead with no sense of loss, because where he was leading her was so intensely pleasurable.

How had he learned to make love this way? Had he been opened to pleasure by pain? She'd heard that happened sometimes. Or had he always been this way? At first she didn't want to ask for fear of stirring up bad memories. Then she no longer cared.

They shared more than joy now. They shared something so powerful, she couldn't put words to it. Each time they made love, Arash took her, consumed her, swept her away, satisfied her, and still left her hungry for more. When he kissed her, when he touched her breasts, entered her, played with her hair and wrapped it around her neck, ran the tips of his fingers down her arms and up her legs, buried himself in her body, she lost all sense of who she was.

Often she felt as if she was being caught up in a great current, pulled under, and carried to a land with no boundaries where she was being given visions of places she had never seen, places no human ever could actually see: A lake of fire that burned blue and gold. A great wall of blackberry thorns. A city built of blood-colored stones. Black sunsets so bright they burned her eyes with darkness. Crystal caves that sparkled in the light of a thousand unseen torches. A stand of trees so tall they seemed to hold up the sky. A range of mountains that looked like human teeth. Temples of salt and amber. Giant birds with leather wings and the heads of snakes.

Why am I seeing such things? she sometimes wondered in those brief moments of clarity when the tides of passion had temporarily receded. Then Arash would put his lips to hers again, inhale her breath, run his hands over her body, and the question would remain unanswered as she trembled in long, exquisite spasms that left her breathless.

Afterwards as she lay beside him catching her breath, she discovered that she could hardly remember anything that had happened. He was doing something to her, doing it over and over. She had no idea what that something was. She only knew she wanted more of it.

During the day, she watched him closely, worried that he continued to suffer from memories of the three months he had spent as a captive of the beastmen. Was he getting well? Was he becoming himself again? Perhaps he was, for as the days passed, he began to speak more confidently and the haze of bewilderment left his eyes.

On a hot afternoon in late summer, they finally sailed out of the Sweetwater Sea and entered the Blue Sea, which lapped the southern shores of the Motherlands. Here the winds were stronger, and the currents less predictable. Yet although the threat of storms always hung over them, their luck held and the weather remained fair.

As the equinox approached, Sabalah grew increasingly eager to stop traveling. It was becoming awkward to move around the boat, and although Arash helped her as much as he could, he knew nothing about sailing except what she had taught him.

One afternoon he did something so amazing that she decided it was time for her to stop worrying about him. They were hugging the shore as usual when a small island came into view, so far to the east and so obscured by mist that it looked like it was veiled in fine linen. Directing Sabalah to anchor near shore, Arash kicked off his sandals. Then, before she could stop him or ask him what he was doing, he dove into the water and began to swim with strong, steady strokes toward the island.

"Arash," she called, "come back!" But instead of coming back to the boat, he turned, blew her a kiss, and continued swimming.

She pulled up the sail, heaved in the anchor, and tried to go after him, but the wind was blowing in the wrong direction. For what seemed like forever, she watched him, terrified that at any moment he would disappear, overpowered by the waves or dragged down by the currents. She had fished all of her adult life and knew how far a strong person could swim through open water. That island was well beyond the range of any swimmer she had ever encountered. Had he gone insane? Was he trying to kill himself?

"Amonah, protect him," she prayed, but if the Goddess was listening, She gave no sign.

On Arash swam, never stopping until he became a small black spot that she sometimes lost sight of in the tossing waves. At last she saw him, or at least thought she saw him, emerge from the sea and crawl up onto the rocks that ringed the island. Yes, there he was! He had stripped off his shirt and was waving to her with it.

She felt almost sick with relief. The fool! What had he been thinking! He'd probably have to spend the night over there with no food and no fire since there was no way she could get to him until the wind changed, but at least he hadn't drowned.

She reefed the sail, threw out the anchor, and sat down feeling as exhausted as if she'd made the swim herself. When she picked him up, she was going to insist he never take such a risk again.

The sun at this season was warm and pleasant without being too hot. At least he'd dry off rapidly and not suffer too much from the cold after sunset. She sat for a long time staring at the island as the small dot that was Arash moved back and forth doing something she couldn't make out.

She was just wondering if she should eat her midday meal when she saw him do something so alarming that she jumped to her feet and screamed out a warning despite the fact that there was no possible way he could hear her: he dived into the sea and began swimming back.

Again she watched in an agony of suspense as this time he grew larger and larger. Not once did he falter or seem to tire. When at last he swam back up to the boat and pulled himself over the side, his black hair slick and wet as the pelt of a seal, he looked no more weary than she would have looked if she'd swum across a pond.

"Did you worry about me?" he asked.

"No," she lied. "Why did you decide to take such a long swim?"

"To bring back these." He displayed a small net bag filled with clams. "I thought that island would be a good place to find them, and look, I was right."

Clams. He'd gone to dig clams! How could she tell him she had thought he was trying to kill himself or let him know she had doubted his ability to make it to the island and back? He had shown a strength and skill she never imagined he possessed. This was a man who clearly had come back into *lixahs* his own power, a man who was well on the way to healing from the terrible things that had happened to him at the hands of the beastmen, and even though he'd frightened her badly, she knew she should be grateful.

Perhaps, she thought, *Amonah answered my prayers.*

Three weeks later, they put in at Ishuna, a village famous for making the best *lixahs* on the shores of the Blue Sea. It was time to keep her promise to Arash, so while he was arranging for new supplies of food and water, Sabalah paid a visit to a local temple named Shrine of the Birds. Painted inside and out with beautiful, brightly colored birds, it was sacred to the Bird Goddess who had first taught mortals to sing.

Inside, she found the workshop where the *lixahs* were made. Many crafts were sacred to the Goddess including bread baking, weaving, and pottery-making, so it was not uncommon to find workshops in temples, but this one was more interesting than most. Six skilled *lixah* makers—three women and three men—sat across from one another carving the frames, while three others prepared and put on the strings, and two more tuned the instruments.

The carvers worked slowly but constantly while the stringers and tuners, who worked infrequently since it took several months to produce a finished *lixah,* spent their days playing the instruments and singing praises to the Bird Goddess.

For a few moments, Sabalah stood in the doorway listening. She could not make out the individual words, but the voices of the singers were high and sweet as a chorus of birds, filled with complex harmonies that vibrated off the walls and domed ceiling, crossing over one another and multiplying to produce a sound so sweet it could have been the voice of the Bird Goddess Herself. *This must be the most beautiful music in all the Motherlands,* she thought.

Could Marrah also hear the *lixah*-makers singing? She hoped so. She put her hand over her belly, which by now was so big it felt like a shelf. The gesture must have caught the eyes of the singers. Suddenly they all stopped singing and turned toward her, but because the temple had been built to amplify sounds, their voices kept on reverberating in tones and overtones that were complex and utterly enchanting.

Putting the tips of her fingers together, Sabalah bowed to them. "Greetings, singers of divine songs," she said. "I am Sabalah, Daughter of Lalah. A pilgrim and a stranger in your village."

The singers looked puzzled, as if they did not understand what she was doing standing in the doorway of their temple. Still, they seemed friendly. Walking over to the carvers, Sabalah stood for a moment and then bowed again. "Respected crafters of the divine instruments," she said with great formality, "I am Sabalah, Daughter of Lalah, and I would like to barter with you for one of your *lixahs.*"

The carvers looked at her uncertainly. That was the moment she realized she had come so far south that people no longer spoke Sharan. Bowing for a third time, she repeated her name and her request in Old Language.

"Many come here asking to barter for our *lixahs,*" a lean, white-haired, square-chinned woman replied in Old Language. "But we do not trade them. We make them as gifts for temples of the Goddess all up and down the western shore of the Blue Sea. You must travel to another village where they trade in *lixahs.*"

This was not only disappointing, it was embarrassing. She should have known the *lixahs* of Ishuna were too sacred to be exchanged like furs or flint, but none of the traders who had come to Shara from the south had brought this information with them. She stared at the *lixahs* longingly. She had to get one for Arash. Perhaps flattery would work.

"But your *lixahs* are the best, are they not?"

The square-chinned woman smiled. "There are no better *lixahs* in all the Motherlands," she said proudly.

"Then let me say with the greatest respect that I do not want to travel to another village to get a *lixah.* I want one of yours. Please, great crafters. I will give you my knife and the sandals off my feet. I will give you anything I own, but I must have one of your *lixahs* to heal my dear friend Arash and make him whole again."

"You have not understood the words of my sister," one of the men said gently. "We do not trade these *lixahs.*"

Sabalah felt sick with disappointment. How was Arash going to finish healing himself if he couldn't play again? She couldn't afford to spend time searching all the villages along the western shore of the Blue Sea to find one that made second-rate *lixahs.* Marrah's safety had to come first.

She bit her lips to hold back tears. She'd had such high hopes when they sailed into Ishuna, and now it appeared she wasn't going to be able to keep her promise to Arash after all. She was about to thank the *lixah*-makers for their time and bid them farewell, when the square-chinned woman spoke again.

"Wait," the woman said, putting her hand on her brother's arm. "Stop." She turned to Sabalah. "Did you say you wish to have one of our *lixahs* because it would heal your friend?"

"Yes. My friend Arash is a singer. His instrument was taken from him, and now there's something in him that's been broken. He can't remember his past or the words to his songs. But I think if he had a new instrument to play, he'd get well."

"Was his instrument stolen? People almost never steal things, but it does happen."

"No, it was not stolen. Not in the ordinary sense of the word. It was taken by bad people."

"Bad people? What bad people? Please explain."

"I can't explain." Sabalah suddenly realized that if she told the villagers about the beastmen and how they had kidnapped Arash and done terrible things to him, her story might spread terror all up and down the coast. Or else, they might assume she was lying. In any case, this visit to the Shrine of the Birds had clearly been useless. She wasn't going to be able to get Arash a *lixah* here or anywhere else for that matter. Even if they had been willing to trade, she had nothing of value to barter except the blue stone necklace her mother had given her on the day she became a woman, which was a sacred gift that could not be given away. There was her crystal necklace, but Arash would be upset if she showed up at the boat without it, not to mention that she was wearing it to protect her unborn child.

"You can't explain?"

"No."

"Sacred vow?"

"No."

"Something you're ashamed of?"

"No. I'm sorry. I should never have asked. Thank you for taking time to talk to me." She turned to the stringers and tuners. "And thank you for your singing. It's very beautiful."

"Wait, don't go yet," said a short, middle-aged stringer. The woman had a round face, a very small nose, long calloused fingers, and eyes that radiated the joy that came from spending day after day singing. "Come here and give me your hands."

Sabalah approached and stretched out her hands. The stringer took them, turned them over, and stared at her palms for a long time without saying a word. Sabalah tried without success to read the stringer's face, but it was as blank as an early morning sky.

Suddenly, Sabalah felt a rush of wings, and her mind filled with birdsong. Dropping her hands, the stringer smiled. "Ah," she whispered.

She turned to the others. "Give this Daughter of Lalah a *lixah*. She speaks the truth; she wants to heal someone she loves, and as we can plainly see, she's with child. In the Shrine of the Birds we cannot refuse a woman with child anything she asks for."

Almost before Sabalah knew what was happening, the carver with the square chin had bundled up a lixah in a fine linen cloth and put it in her arms. "Go," she said.

"Give it to your singer, and may the Bird Goddess give him back his voice."

Sabalah looked down at the bundle. Then, to her surprise, she began to cry. "Thank you," she said through her tears. "May the Goddess bless you for your kindness to a stranger."

That afternoon after they made love, Arash disappeared into the woods with his new *lixah,* saying that he needed to learn how to play it. The whole time he was gone, Sabalah was plagued by the fear that he would never return, but he did, walking into the village not long after sunset, playing the *lixah* with such skill that everyone gathered around him was amazed.

All night he played, singing the same songs he and Sabalah had sung months ago when they went outside the walls of Shara to lie in the fields and make love. Somehow he had remembered every word. He was healed at last, strong and well and even able to recall other things he had previously forgotten.

This is a miracle, Sabalah thought, and she wondered if the sacred *lixahs* made in the Shrine of the Birds were filled with the voice of the Bird Goddess Herself.

The only thing that marred the evening was the loss of her crystal necklace which had apparently fallen off sometime not long after she left the Shrine of the Birds. That night she searched for it everywhere with no success, only to find it the next morning caught on a bush outside the door of the guest house. Since there were no crystals missing, she re-tied the broken string, put it back on, and never mentioned the incident to Arash, who might have been upset if he'd known how close she had come to losing it.

She must not have tied the necklace tightly enough, because a few days later it fell off again. Picking it up, she retied it much more firmly, but before she put it back around her neck, she noticed something strange: the red crystal wasn't quite as red as it had been when Arash first gave it to her. It looked as if some of the color had leaked out. Since that was impossible, Sabalah decided this was an illusion created by the new, stronger light of the far south.

By the next afternoon, the light of the south was no longer strong. Dark clouds began to gather on the horizon. The storm that followed consisted of a few cloudbursts that left no more than an inch of water in the bottom of the boat, but it was a sign that the dry season was finally coming to an end.

They had turned west some time ago, still following the coast, which meant they would reach Orefi in a few weeks, but Sabalah, who was now nearly seven months with child, worried that if the heavy winter rains set in, they would have to stop and take shelter for weeks—perhaps for months–until the Blue Sea was calm enough for them to set sail again. Batal had commanded her to give birth at Orefi. What if she didn't make it?

"I'm worried about the winter rains," she told Arash.

"Water is a wonderful thing," he said. Which was true, of course, but a strange thing to say.

7

ADDER AND THE SACRED SNAKES

They arrived at Orefi in a torrential rainstorm, tossed by seas so wild they had to lash themselves to the mast to keep from being hurled overboard. The bay was deep and well-sheltered. Three times they tried to enter, and three times they were blown back as if the sea itself did not want them to make landfall.

"Pray to Amonah to get us in without capsizing!" Sabalah yelled to Arash over the howling of the wind. If they went over in a storm this fierce, she would drown and the baby in her womb would drown with her. Even Arash, who was the best swimmer she had ever met, wouldn't be able to save them.

"Don't worry!" he yelled. "We'll make it!" She peered at him through the driving rain. Water was dripping off his long black hair, running down the sides of his face, and pouring off his beard. He didn't look afraid. In fact, he looked as if he were enjoying himself.

He smiled at her and threw her a kiss, and Sabalah felt her courage return. "Again!" she cried, wrenching the tiller and turning the boat about.

Perhaps Amonah heard their prayers, because as they headed toward land for the fourth time, the rain stopped, the sun came out, the wind shifted, and they were driven forward into the bay. For a moment they were too shaken to move. Arash spit water out of his mouth. Sabalah flung her wet hair out of her eyes.

Gradually, she realized she was no longer having to fight to control the tiller. She looked up at the sail and saw that it was frayed but still intact. A stiff breeze was blowing and the waves were still topped with whitecaps, but the wind was steady now, and the boat was no longer careening violently.

Turning away from the sight of the dark storm clouds still clustered on the far horizon, she looked toward Orefi. Of all the shrines in the Motherlands sacred to the Great Goddess, it was always said to be the most beautiful, and now she understood why. White limestone cliffs rose from a low valley like sheer walls. Behind them, a range of mountains capped with a light dusting of snow pierced a sky so blue it seemed to be tiled with lapis lazuli. Above all this, a double rainbow arched like a message of welcome.

Orefi, center of the universe, navel of the world, site of the most sacred shrine in all the Motherlands. Orefi, birthplace of The Divine Sisters, who in ancient times had emerged from the Earth's holy womb and gone forth to teach the First People how to grow crops, tend animals, and live in harmony with one another. Orefi, where the Great Python breathed in the breath of the Goddess Earth Herself and the past met the future. Orefi, where life began, and where according to the oldest prophecies of the Mother People, it would someday end.

"Let's untie ourselves," Arash said.

"What?"

"Let's untie ourselves."

Sabalah looked down and realized she was still lashed to the mast. "Cut me loose." Drawing his knife, Arash cut them both free. As the ropes fell to the bottom of the boat, she saw they were standing ankle-deep in water.

"We need to bail out the boat."

"We've lost the bailing bowls."

"Then we'll have to make do with our hands."

Bending down, they cupped their hands and began to throw water out of the boat. Strangely, this felt like a blessing: water falling back into water, their fingers and palms pressed together in something close to the sign of the Goddess. And so they made it to shore, already blessed, only to find more blessings waiting for them.

As they dragged their boat up onto the beach, they saw that some of the people of Orefi had come down from the shrine to greet them. At the water's edge, nine priestesses of Batal were dancing in a serpentine line that undulated back and forth like the coils of a snake. Their hair was braided into snake-like coils, and their faces were painted red, the color of fertility. All were dressed in black, the holy color of the Goddess Earth. Their robes fell to their ankles in long strips, embroidered with green and yellow snakes and decorated with small bells made of shell.

As soon as Sabalah and Arash drew close enough to hear, they began to sing:

Welcome pilgrims
Your long voyage is over
You are safe in the womb of Orefi

The tallest of the priestesses produced two pairs of finger cymbals which she clashed together, and the singing turned into a sibilant sound that was nothing like anything Sabalah had ever heard.

Sssssssssssssss, they hissed,
We are the Nine Sacred Snakes of Orefi
Who serve the Great Python
Sssssssssssss

As the last of the hissing died away, the tallest of the Sacred Snakes approached Sabalah and Arash and placed the tips of her fingers together in the sign of the Goddess. Her arms were unusually long and Sabalah couldn't help thinking that they too were snake-like.

"Welcome," the priestess said. "My name is Adder, spiritual daughter of the First Adder who is said to have brought music into the world." She gestured to the eight priestesses who stood behind her. "These are Red Snake, Blind Snake, Spotted Snake, Rock Snake, Smooth Snake, Viper, Long-Nosed Snake, and Sand Boa."

Sabalah noticed that the priestess named Long-Nosed Snake had a nose not much bigger than a good-sized pebble. Apparently the Snake Priestesses of Orefi were not named for the snakes they resembled.

Putting the tips of her fingers together in the sign of the Goddess, she returned Adder's bow. "I am Sabalah, Daughter of Lalah," she said.

"You are with child?" It wasn't really a question. Anyone with eyes could see Sabalah's swollen belly.

"I am."

"Have you come to give birth in Batal's temple?"

"Yes. The Goddess appeared to me in a vision and ordered me to travel here to have my baby." At her words, a ripple of excitement passed through the crowd. Viper and Sand Boa gasped; and then to Sabalah's astonishment, all the Snakes put the tips of their fingers together and bowed to her three times. What was going on? What was all this bowing about?

"The Goddess really appeared to you in a vision?" Adder asked. "She really commanded you to come here to give birth?"

"Yes. She came to me in the Dreaming Cave of Her Temple in the form of a Great Snake with blue eyes and gold scales and commanded me to come to Orefi to have my child."

"Then you must be the one we've been waiting for."

"What?"

"You must be she who is foretold in the prophecy." Adder looked stunned. "My dear child, we often have women come here to give birth in Batal's temple, but none in living memory have been sent by Batal Herself." She turned to the priestess called Viper. "How long has it been since Batal sent us one of Her own?"

"More generations than anyone can count," Viper said, looking at Sabalah with a mixture of awe and amazement. "Some say that in the time of the Ninth Great Python, Batal sent a woman to Orefi who bore magical twins who were more than human. The boy named the stars. The girl named the animals and plants."

Sabalah stared at Viper and Adder in disbelief. Could this be true? She had assumed Batal often sent pregnant women to Her shrine at Orefi to give birth. Something very strange and powerful was unfolding here, something wonderful and more than a little frightening.

Adder nodded at Viper and then turned back to Sabalah. "Sabalah, Daughter of Lalah, we are honored to have you among us and happier to see you than you can imagine. We have waited for you for so long, and now, thanks to the Blessed Goddess, you have come at last." She turned to Arash. "And you, pilgrim, you are welcome too. Who are you, and what mother bore you?"

"I'm Arash, Son of Wanala."

"Are you going to be her child's *aita*?"

"Of course he is," Sabalah said quickly. "I originally asked my brother Gradush, but he lives so far to the north, I may never see him again, and Arash has protected my child from the first moment he knew she was in my womb." Sabalah turned to Arash. "You will be Marrah's *aita,* won't you?"

Arash smiled and took her hand. "Of course. I've been hoping you'd ask."

"Good." Adder placed the palms of her hands on their foreheads. "Blessings on you both. Now, come. It's time for us to lead you to Orefi. We will dance you up the mountain with joy for the prophecy is fulfilled and our long wait is over."

At these words, the line of priestesses gave a long hiss and began to dance again, moving in the direction of the trail that led up the cliffs toward the shrine which was located some distance away on the slope of a high mountain.

Arash and Sabalah followed the dancers, and the rest of the people who had been standing on the beach followed them. The trail was long and steep. Paved with alternating strips of black and white gravel, it too looked like a snake as it wove back and forth along the cliffs.

I'm glad I'm not afraid of heights, Sabalah thought as she trudged up the slope. Walking up a mountain carrying a nearly-ready-to-be-born baby in your womb was not like strolling through Shara with a basket of perch. Her lower back ached, and her big belly kept throwing her off balance.

The climb to Orefi took the better part of the afternoon. By the time they reached the last part of the trail, Sabalah was footsore and out of breath. Turning, she paused and looked back at the way they had come. Far below, the beach was a tiny strip of sand blued by distance. She could not see their boat, but beyond the beach was a vast expanse of ocean, blue inside the bay, still gray and troubled outside.

A cold wind swept up from the sea, teasing her hair. *I'm not walking back down there until my baby is weaned,* she thought. *This is where we'll spend the winter.* Turning, she struggled up the last part of the trail which was so steep she felt as if she might topple over backwards. Then, at long last, she was in Orefi.

Or was she?

In front of her, she saw a village built in a large, flat space among white boulders. It had no source of water—at least no creek or spring she could see—and soil so rocky and barren that it would be hard to grow anything edible unless you planned to survive on bark and juniper berries. She had expected Orefi to be larger than Shara, but she and Arash had stayed in fishing villages no bigger than this. There were only a dozen motherhouses, perhaps fewer, all made from mud and sticks and thatched with straw. Where were the sacred shrines she had heard so much about? Where was Batal's temple?

True, there were snake images everywhere, most made of wood and a few of clay, all gaily decorated with red, green, black, and yellow scales. And possibly in the spring when real snakes came out of hibernation, there would be no shortage of them curled up on the rocks. But this village did not have the look of a great pilgrimage center. Was Orefi still farther up the slope? Was she going to have to do more climbing before it came into view?

"Is this Orefi?" she asked Adder.

"Yes and no. It is and it isn't."

"I don't understand. Are we in Orefi or must we keep climbing?"

Adder tossed her braid over her shoulder to keep the wind from blowing it into her face. "Here you will hear many riddles."

Sabalah stared at the mud huts and miserable soil. To have come so far for this! She might as well have stayed in Shara. Sitting down on the nearest rock, she stared at her belly. She couldn't go back. She had no choice but to stay here and give birth.

"I've traveled for months. I'm cold, tired, hungry, and dizzy. My back hurts and my feet ache. For the sake of the Blessed Goddess, Adder, please tell me if this is Orefi."

"Do you feel faint?"

"No, I just need to know where I am."

"You don't have to climb any further. You are in Orefi. The motherhouses you see are built from the flesh and bones of the Goddess Earth, that is to say of mud and wood and straw, as they have been built for time out of mind."

"Where's the Temple of Batal?"

"Batal's temple is all around you. It's not a building. It's the entire Earth and all things on Her, in Her, and above Her. You see that stone over there, the large round one that looks a little like half an acorn? Do you know what that is?"

Sabalah shook her head. This conversation with Adder was not making her feel any more confident that she had come to the right place.

"It's the Horn of the Goddess," Adder continued, "which means you are sitting on Her belly right above Her womb."

Sabalah jumped to her feet. "I'm sorry. I didn't know this was sacred ground."

"No need to apologize. You can sit anywhere you like. All ground is sacred."

Sabalah looked at the stone. "'Horn' of the Goddess?" She walked over to it and inspected it more closely. "Horn?"

"It's the Great Mother's clitoris, the center of the universe and greatest fount of fertility in all the Motherlands. You couldn't have come to a better place to give birth. All babies born under the sign of Her Horn live."

"All?"

"Well, a few go back to the Mother right away, but those usually have mothers who are already sick before they come to Orefi. Often when these babies die, their mothers follow them; but you have nothing to worry about. You're healthy and strong, and there are no better midwives in the Motherlands than the Snakes of Orefi."

Sabalah was still not convinced. She stared at the barren patch of stony ground that surrounded the Horn of the Goddess. "If all the Earth is the Temple of Batal, does that mean I'll have to give birth out here in the open? What if it's raining?"

Adder came up beside her and put an arm around her shoulders. It was a gentle, motherly embrace that made Sabalah feel homesick for her own mother. "Don't worry. We'll take good care of you. There are things here that you've haven't seen yet that will calm your fears. Be patient."

Arash, who had been standing some distance away, walked over to them. "Is everything all right?" he asked.

Sabalah gave him a brave smile. "Yes, everything." They were stuck in Orefi for the winter. What would be the use of giving him cause to worry about her before she knew if there was anything to worry about?

A few moments later, two small children appeared carrying a basket of freshly baked bread and a jug of water. A snake of black reeds coiled around the rim of the basket, and the bread—warm, fragrant, and sweet—had been baked into crisp coils.

When they had finished resting and eating, Adder led them on a short climb to a cave that lay a little north of Orefi. The opening was concealed by a thicket of brush and small trees. The rocks around it had been smeared with red, and a smaller version of the Horn of the Goddess stood directly inside the entrance.

"This is the doorway that leads into the Womb of the Great Mother," Adder said.

Sabalah and Arash stepped closer. A faint, sweet smell was wafting out from somewhere deep inside. They could see a long passageway lit by torches. The sides and ceiling were rough, but the floor was smooth, polished by the feet of countless pilgrims. On one wall, a line of ancient handprints and red triangles disappeared into the depths.

Arash pointed to the farthest end of the passageway. "There are crystals in the next cavern!" he cried. "It's another crystal cave like the one near my village!"

Sabalah peered into the darkness, but could make out nothing. As far as she could see, the lighted passageway of the first cavern ended in a black hole.

Adder grabbed the nearest torch. "Go in," she commanded. "This is where the Great Python lives."

Arash started to step into the cave and then stopped abruptly. "How large is this snake?"

"About as tall as Viper but a great deal older with white hair and eyes that can no longer see."

"The Great Python's not a snake?"

"No, it's a human being just like the rest of us, only more blessed with the gift of prophecy. Please go in. We're wasting time out here. The Great Python wanted to see you the moment you arrived. Don't be afraid. There's nothing in these caves more dangerous than a colony of bats, and they sleep during the day."

Reassured, Arash followed Adder into the cave with Sabalah bringing up the rear. At the end of the first passageway, she saw an entrance to a second cavern just filled with white crystals that rose up from the floor and hung down from the ceiling. As the torchlight struck them, the crystals glittered like sunlight on water.

How could Arash have seen these? she wondered. She looked at him, already far ahead of her and Adder, striding confidently through the darkness.

"There are forty chambers in this cave," Adder said. "Call out to your child's *aita* and bid him come back. We don't want him to get lost."

8

BEWARE!

The Great Python's chamber was filled with a sweet scent that seemed to be coming from everywhere at once. On the ceiling and walls, painted snakes twisted around one another, forming a labyrinth.

"Sabalah, Daughter of Lalah, I've been expecting you," the Python said. "Come closer, and let me bless the child you carry."

Sabalah approached the Python who sat on a three-legged stool which symbolized all the sacred things that came in threes: Past, Present, Future; Maiden, Matron, Crone; Earth, Sky, Water; Birth, Life, Death. Sabalah had expected the Python's famous stool to be made of silver or at least marble, but like everything else at Orefi it was simple and unadorned, carved out of unfinished wood and by the look of it, a bit unsteady. You'd think the greatest priestess in the Motherlands could afford to get herself a new stool when the old one wore out, but perhaps this one was so ancient and sacred that it was unthinkable to replace it until it disintegrated entirely.

Actually, calling the Python "her" was a leap of imagination. Although priestesses were almost always female, the person sitting on the stool could have been a man, a woman, both, or neither. Later Sabalah learned that an ability to flow between genders was one of the most important traits the Sacred Snakes looked for when they traveled through the Motherlands searching for a new Python after the death of an old one.

The current Python had long white hair, sunken cheeks, and a face threaded with wrinkles, but its eyes were as clear as the eyes of a baby. *Eyes that can no longer see,* Adder had said, yet when Sabalah looked into them, she saw love, compassion, and something so strange it made her wonder if she was looking into the eyes of a living Goddess.

In their depths, shapes were moving, souls or perhaps spirits from other worlds. The shapes swarmed back and forth like ants, and as they tumbled over one another, she imagined she could hear them whispering to her in a language that sounded like surf hissing across sand.

Suddenly, the whispering voices fell silent, the shapes disappeared, and she found herself staring straight into the Python's sightless eyes. A sense of peace enveloped her. She knew she had been frightened, but she couldn't remember why.

The Python laughed. "Come closer, child. What are you waiting for? I can tell you're still standing out of reach."

Sabalah drew closer. When she was a few steps away, the Python stood up and walked toward her. Stretching out its arms, it ran the tips of its fingers over her face and then laid the palms of its hands on her belly. At its touch, everything seemed to shatter into rainbows. She stared at the colors, trying to see beyond them, but they hung in front of her like a curtain, blinding her with their beauty: reds redder than the reddest reds, yellows that glowed like embers, blues that flickered like cold fire. Inside her womb, the baby stirred. Leaping in joy? Perhaps, but there was something dark at the edges of those colors, something disturbing.

Removing its hands from Sabalah's belly, the Python gave her a kiss on each cheek. Its lips were soft and dry, and its breath smelled like crushed bay leaves. "The child growing inside you is healthy," the Python said. "You've already named her 'Marrah,' yes?"

"Yes, Honored One." Sabalah groped to retain the memory of what had just happened, but again it was gone. There was something she had wanted to ask the Python, but what had it been? "Yes, Honored One," she repeated. "But how did you know her name? Did Batal reveal it to you in a vision?"

The Python laughed and shook its head. "Not necessary."

A cryptic answer and far from satisfying. The utterances of the Great Pythons of Orefi were famously hard to understand, and Sabalah suspected more questions would not be welcome. Again, she tried to remember what had frightened her, and again she failed.

The Python turned to Adder. "Leave us," it commanded.

Adder left, taking her torch with her. The cavern grew darker. Sabalah wondered if the Python could sense this, or if light and dark were both the same to it. In the silence that followed Adder's exit, she heard a soft hissing which seemed to be coming from a crack in the cavern floor directly under the Python's stool.

"The Goddess is about to speak," the Python said. The smell Sabalah had noticed earlier when she stood at the entrance to the cave suddenly became stronger. The Python pointed toward Arash. "I hear breathing. Who is standing over there?"

"Arash, Son of Wanala, the man who will become the *aita* of my child."

"He must leave too, but first I want to read his face. Come here, Arash, Son of Wanala." Arash didn't move. "Come," the Python repeated. "We don't have much time left before the Goddess speaks."

Reluctantly, Arash approached the Python and bent down so it could run its fingers over his face. "Ah," the Python said, "yes, I thought so. It's the breathing, you see. I can always tell by the breathing."

Suddenly, it placed its fingertips on either side of his neck. Arash started and tried to straighten up, but the Python let go of his neck, wrapped its hands in his hair and pulled him closer. "You are different, Arash, very different, but we are all children of the Goddess, are we not?"

"Yes," Arash said in a voice so low Sabalah could hardly hear him.

"Do you love this woman? Will you care for her? Protect her and her child?"

"Yes." He looked frightened, but more likely he was nervous. It wasn't every day that the Great Python of Orefi grabbed you by the hair and pulled you close.

"You realize that the words you have just said are a vow, yes? You understand that you cannot break a sacred promise to the Great Mother. Arash, Son of Wanala, I ask you again: do you love this woman, and will you protect her and her child?"

"Yes."

"Good. Now go. After the Goddess speaks, you can return and sing me 'The Dolphin Calling Song of the Yashas of Gira.' Do you know it?"

"Yes."

The Python let go of his hair. "You'll find Adder waiting for you in the second cavern, the one filled with those crystals you could see when no one else could."

Arash left quickly without looking back. Sabalah could tell he was upset. Probably he hadn't liked the Python forcing him to repeat that he would take care of her and Marrah. Or maybe he just hated having his hair pulled. What had the Python meant when it said he was "different?" Again, she knew there was no use asking.

When Arash was gone, the Python commanded her to go to the other side of the cavern and stay there no matter what she saw or heard. The cavern was large, and by the time she got to the far wall and sat down, the light of her torch barely reached as far as the Python's stool, so what she saw next, she saw mostly in shadows.

A few moments passed. Then the floor trembled a little, and the hissing grew louder. On the other side of the cavern, she could see the Python bending forward as if bowing to an invisible spirit. Again that sweet smell, even stronger now, odd, a little unpleasant with a bitter aftertaste that lingered in Sabalah's nose and on her tongue like ground peach pits.

Gradually, she realized the smell was making her dizzy. She wondered if the Python was feeling dizzy too. Perhaps so, because she could see its silhouette swaying back and forth.

Suddenly it made a horrible sound halfway between a scream and a cry. Words flowed out of its mouth, but not words in any language Sabalah had ever heard before.

"Agapahash, lashahaka, nevvitich, shaool! Da, da, kintah! Aiii! Aiii!" Reaching up, the Python tore at its braid as if trying to pull it out of its head. *"Aiii! Aiii!"*

Sabalah jumped to her feet and started to run to it to stop it from hurting itself, but then she remembered it had ordered her not to move, so she sat down again and waited, torn between fear and fascination.

The Python chanted the word "Aiiii" for a long time. Then, suddenly, it fell silent. Sabalah waited anxiously for whatever was coming next, but all the Python did was straighten up and sit on its stool with its arms at its sides.

It could have been in a holy trance or asleep for all she could tell.

Gradually the smell grew fainter. When it was almost gone, the Python called Sabalah back to her. When it spoke, its words were slurred and hard to understand.

"A crystal snare. A fish that's not a fish." Reaching out, it ran its fingers over Sabalah's belly. *"A baby born on the longest night. Never tell her she was born at Orefi. The Blind Singer wanders forever, not knowing who he is. Beware."*

"Please, I don't understand, Honored One. What do you mean 'beware'? Does some danger threaten my child? Is it the beastmen? Have they followed us?"

But the Great Python of Orefi never explained its prophecies, and when Sabalah looked more closely, she saw it had fallen fast asleep.

"I have no idea what the Python's prophecy means," Adder said. "I'm going to have to think it over." They were standing outside the cave. The sun was so warm that Adder and Arash were sweating, but Sabalah was trembling with a coldness she couldn't shake off.

"If you can't interpret the Python's words, Adder, who can?" Sabalah drew her sheepskin cloak closer, blew on her hands to warm them, and stared anxiously at the tunnel that led into the cave. "The Python's prophecy clearly states that my baby is going to be born on the longest night of the year. That part I understand. I also understand that I'm not supposed to tell her she was born at Orefi. But why can't I tell her?"

"Maybe it would put her in danger," Arash suggested.

Adder sighed. "I wish it were that simple. You've both made reasonable guesses, but reason is rarely the key. For example, Never tell her she was born at Orefi sounds like a prophecy for your baby. In fact, that's the way I would interpret it. But there's always the chance that it's a prophecy for some other child. We can never be sure we've correctly interpreted the prophecies of the Python. Still, don't despair. You're in luck. This is one of the clearest prophecies the Python has uttered in years. For example, before you arrived, it spoke at least a dozen times about a 'Bee Wolf' that is going to jump into a lake of fire to battle monsters."

"What's a Bee Wolf?"

Adder shrugged. "I have no idea, and it seems likely that when the Python is not breathing the breath of the Goddess, it doesn't know either. Some of its prophecies are about things that took place thousands of generations ago; some probably won't happen for thousands of generations. We Snakes are supposed to interpret the prophecies, but no matter how hard we tried to puzzle out the Bee Wolf one, we came up with nothing that made sense. Our best guess is that the Bee Wolf, whatever it is, must live in the future, but we aren't sure. The Python used the words "is going to" but that doesn't necessarily mean the Bee Wolf didn't fight those monsters in the past. Sometimes the more we try to understand the prophecies of the Python, the more confused we get."

"'Crystal snare,' 'fish not a fish,' 'blind singer.'" Sabalah turned her back on the cave and looked out across the cliffs to the Blue Sea. She felt confused and discouraged. Why had the Goddess commanded her to go to Orefi? What was the use of traveling so far to receive a prophecy no one could understand? She thought of all the months she and Arash would still have to travel after Marrah was born to reach the West Beyond the West and all the dangers that still lay ahead of them.

"Please, Adder, help me. What am I supposed to beware of?"

"My dear child, I wish I could tell you. You have my word that the Snakes will do their best to interpret the entire prophecy for you, but meanwhile, all I can do is go on guessing. 'What is a *fish not a fish*?' you ask. My first thought is that it could be a dolphin since dolphins swim in water but breathe air, but it could just as easily be something that lives so far in the future we can't imagine it. What is a *crystal snare*? Once again, it might be the second cavern in the Python's cave. Perhaps, Goddess forbid, someday the roof will fall in and someone will be buried under the crystals. Yet it could just as easily mean that you're going to be caught in a big ice storm, or that the whole world is going to be covered by ice.

"As for the *blind singer wanders forever not knowing who he is,* I can't even venture a guess." She pointed to Arash. "The only singer the Python spoke to was you, and you're not blind."

"But I sing, and I could go blind."

"But you aren't wandering around not knowing who you are, are you?"

"No."

"Well then, I suggest you don't waste your time worrying about losing your sight."

Sabalah stared out at the sea again and shuddered. How could she sail off into all that nothingness knowing that some terrible danger was waiting for her and her child? She was starting to wish she'd never gone into the Python's cave. "I thought a prophecy from the Python would help us travel safely to the West Beyond the West, but it's worse than useless if we can't figure it out."

Adder sighed. "That's not the Python's fault. It has no control over what it says. It merely channels the voice of the Goddess. Try to be patient. Perhaps the meaning of this prophecy will be revealed to us before you leave Orefi."

But patience was hard to come by. Three days later, the real winter rains set in, and the sea turned permanently gray and stormy. No more pilgrims would be coming to Orefi until spring, and although the Snakes would take the Python food and water every morning, by long custom it would not speak again until the first narcissus bloomed.

The days passed slowly as the people of Orefi gathered wood, fed their animals, formed pots from clay, or did other winter tasks. Since Sabalah was a skilled weaver, she joined Adder and Rock Snake at their looms. It was peaceful to sit in Adder's house in front of a warm fire pushing the wooden bobbin between the threads of the weft. She would start out with nothing but a net of stings. Gradually as the colored threads of wool filled her loom, shapes would appear: dolphins, birds, and long sinuous snakes that ran from the top of the cloth to the bottom. Once she even tried to weave an image of the walls of Shara, but the sight of the city made her so homesick, she ripped it all out and wove a flock of doves instead.

During those winter weeks, she grew very close to Adder and Rock Snake. One day when Adder found Sabalah secretly crying from homesickness, she took Sabalah in her arms and held her until she stopped sobbing. "I know how hard it is to be separated from those you love," Adder whispered. "I lost my mother when I was five years old. I've never doubted that the Goddess greeted her with love and sent her on to another life, but I've never really gotten over her death; and sometimes the memory of her sweet face still makes me cry."

Rock Snake was equally kind. She often rubbed the small of Sabalah's back when it ached and cooked her special treats including tiny honey cakes that were as good as any sweets baked in the ovens of Shara.

Gradually the three women came to love one another like sisters, and although Sabalah never stopped missing her mother and *aita,* this friendship with Rock Snake and Adder made her feel less lonely.

Like all weavers of the Motherlands, they sang as they wove. Sometimes they chanted the many names of the Goddess, but often they sang old story songs, love songs, and bawdy ballads. On days when it was too cold to gather wood, Arash, who could not weave, would join them and play his *lixah.* Sabalah loved to hear the sweet notes of the *lixah* and the even sweeter sound of his voice when he could be persuaded to sing.

With every day that passed, she was loving him more. It was a quiet love that grew like the child inside her: slowly and steadily, which was not to say that it lacked passion. The winter nights were long and dark, and the Mother People had always believed that sharing joy did not hurt unborn children.

As the rolls of cloth grew longer, Sabalah grew more uncomfortable and more eager to give birth and be done with it. Finally on the longest night of the year, she went into labor. As soon as her pains began, the midwives took her to the small birthing temple that stood near the Horn of the Goddess. Like all the houses in Orefi, it was a simple place whitewashed with lime inside and well chinked against the winter winds. Throwing fragrant cedar logs on the fire, the midwives dressed Sabalah in a birthing gown embroidered with snakes, and tended to her, sponging her forehead with cool water, walking her around the room to make her labor shorter, and giving her the traditional teas that made birthing easier. Some of the teas were so bitter that she wouldn't have been able to choke them down under ordinary circumstances, but as her pains grew more intense she found herself begging for more.

Her labor was long and hard. There was nothing wrong with the baby, but it was her first, and first babies, the midwives told her, always took longer.

"I want this to be over!" she yelled.

"Cry out to the Goddess," the midwives told her. "She hears you. She is with you. Cry out to Her." But instead of crying out to the Goddess, Sabalah cursed the birthing pains.

"*Rak!*" she yelled, "I'll never share joy with a man again!"

The midwives laughed and embraced her. "All women in labor make that vow, and almost none keep it." Picking her up, they carried her to the birthing stool and sat her on it. One stood behind her to support her, while another massaged her belly. "Push! Push! Soon it will be over."

Sabalah pushed and yelled, and cursed, and called on the Goddess for help, and a little after dawn, Marrah was born healthy, strong, and squalling with a full head of dark, curly hair and eyes as blue as the sea. When she emerged from the womb, her face was veiled by a thin white membrane which the midwives immediately removed.

"She's a lucky child," they told Sabalah as they washed Marrah, rubbed her with salt and oil, swaddled her in a soft blanket, and placed her in Sabalah's arms for the first time. "She was born with a caul over her face. A caul-born child can never drown."

Unwrapping the blanket, Sabalah examined Marrah's tiny toes, perfect fingers, and the magical smoothness of her skin. She had a small cowlick that looked like a rose. Giving a little yawn, Marrah stopped crying, closed her eyes, and fell asleep as if her journey into this world from the world of the Goddess had been a long one, which indeed it had.

Sabalah was almost afraid to move for fear of waking her. She had never seen anything as beautiful as this little creature who had come from her own body. At last, bending over, she kissed Marrah gently on the forehead. A sweet scent wafted off her baby flesh. As Sabalah inhaled it, she was overwhelmed with a love for her daughter so great it brought her to tears.

"Welcome to the world, little one," she whispered.

"You gave birth on the longest night of the year just as the Python predicted," Adder observed as she massaged Sabalah's arms and legs with lavender oil.

Sabalah was too tired to reply. Closing her eyes, she let the soothing touch of Adder's hands lull her into a dreamy state. The necklace Arash had given her still hung around her neck, each bead commemorating a night of love. As he had promised, the red crystal had protected her all through her labor and protected Marrah at the moment of her birth.

She ran her fingers slowly over the beads, thinking again of her mother and all the friends and relatives she had left behind in Shara. Would she ever return? Would she and Marrah ever walk through the South Gate and visit the Temple of Dogs and then go down to the beach and throw flowers into the sea as an offering to Amonah? They had come so far from Shara and still had so far to travel. *Mother,* she thought, *I miss you. I wish you could have been here with me when Marrah was born.*

One bead after another passed under her fingers. When she got to the red crystal, it felt warmer than the others, but perhaps that was her imagination. There had been quite a bit of poppy juice in those teas the midwives had given her.

She woke sometime later to find Rock Snake and Adder standing beside her. Rock Snake was holding a large bundle.

"We have a gift for you," Rock Snake said.

"What is it?"

"Open it and see."

Sabalah sat up, took the bundle from Rock Snake, unwound the cloth wrappings, and found herself looking at a flat wooden board. There were two short wooden poles attached to one side, a number of straps and ties, and a small, curved, basket-like contraption at one end woven from yellow and red reeds. All in all, this was one of the strangest objects Sabalah had ever seen.

"Thank you," she said.

Adder and Rock Snake both laughed. "You don't have any idea what this is, do you?" Adder said.

"No," Sabalah admitted.

"It's a cradleboard." Rock Snake took the object from Sabalah and turned it so the basket part was at the top. "It's for carrying a baby on your back. This part," she pointed to the basket, "is a collapsible sunshade. These," she pointed to the straps, "are for strapping your baby in so she won't tumble out. This," she pointed to a small wooden board that Sabalah had not noticed, "is a foot rest, and this," she pointed to a square of stuffed deerskin, "is a pillow. The poles are for attaching the cradleboard to your back. You've probably never seen a cradleboard before because people who live in this part of the Motherlands don't take their children on long journeys until they're old enough to walk. But north of here, especially in the West Beyond the West, the Forest People use cradleboards all the time because they're always wandering from place to place searching for food."

Her face grew somber. "We don't want you to leave Orefi, but the Great Python has told us you have a long journey ahead of you. This way you can carry Marrah safely."

Tears welled up in Sabalah's eyes. "Thank you," she whispered, thinking how much she was going to miss Adder and Rock Snake when she and Arash finally left Orefi.

Ten days after Marrah was born, on the feast day of the Sea Goddess Amonah, the Sacred Snakes blessed her in a naming ceremony and consecrated Arash as her *aita.* It was a fair day, filled with bright winter sunshine, and as Sabalah stood beside Arash watching Adder rub sacred rosemary oil on Marrah's forehead, she felt a joy beyond words.

Naming ceremonies were usually short, followed by a celebration that lasted well into the night, but as first Sabalah and then Arash held Marrah in their arms and promised to care for her, something unprecedented happened: the Great Python came out of its cave to hold Marrah too.

For years beyond counting, no one but pilgrims and the Sacred Snakes had seen the Python's face, and perhaps no one else ever would, for on Marrah's naming day the Python wore a gray robe and a thick white veil that looked like a caul.

The Python did not speak. Taking Marrah from Arash, it lay her on the Earth, Great Mother of all living creatures. Then it picked Marrah up, handed her back to Arash, and returned to its cave, moving up the trail with quick, sure steps as if it could see every twist and turn.

9

THE MOTHER BOOK

That spring Sabalah appeared before the Great Python for the last time carrying a bouquet of wild iris. Entering the Womb of the Great Mother, she passed through the cavern of crystals and followed the line of red triangles and ancient handprints that pointed the way to the Python's chamber.

After the winter storms had stopped and the narcissus had bloomed, four more women from neighboring villages had come to give birth at Batal's shrine, but the Python had not been willing to see any of them. Its seclusion had been so complete that even Adder had not seen the Python's face when she came to bring it food and water.

"The Python is still wearing the veil it put on when your daughter was born," Adder said. "None of us know why. It's never happened before. Viper thinks maybe it's preparing for its death. Sand Boa and Blind Snake are convinced it's veiled itself from this world so it can see the Dark Forest more clearly."

"What's the Dark Forest?"

"It's the place between life and death where souls wander until they go back to the Mother. The old songs say that in the Dark Forest there are paths that lead into different worlds. No one knows for certain, because when the dead go into the Dark Forest, they never come back. Only the Great Pythons have gone there and returned, and they've taken a vow never to reveal anything about it. Sometimes when a Python feels that it's about to die, it spends most of its time in the Dark Forest."

"The Great Python didn't look sick the last time I saw it."

"Not sick perhaps, but it's very old."

"How old?"

"No one is sure because no one living can remember a time before it began uttering its prophecies. Our best guess is that the present Python has seen more than 100 springs, but it may be much older. It still has one lover alive that it took when its hair was already white. The Python's lover has seen seventy springs. Some say that the Breath of the Goddess lets Pythons live forever, but that's not true. Sooner or later, all Pythons die, and the Snakes must search the Motherlands for a new Python. There have been over a thousand Great Pythons at Orefi. If the Goddess wills it, there will be a thousand more."

Sabalah thought about Adder's words with every step she took. She wondered if the Great Python really was spending its time in the Dark Forest. She imagined it following dream-like paths through thick stands of strangely shaped trees, but she never imagined the ordinary, yet extraordinary, thing she saw when she entered the Python's chamber.

The Python was holding a book. At least Sabalah thought the thing the Python was holding was a book. She had never actually seen one and knew no one who had except an elderly priestess named Liada who had served for many years at the Temple of Dogs. Liada had been initiated into the secrets of the Dark Goddess in Kataka, a city north of Shara, and when Sabalah was nine, Liada had described books to her.

A book, she had explained, *is made out of pieces of deerskin sewn together into a scroll. There are marks on the skins that look like bird tracks. When the priestesses of the Dark Goddess unroll the scrolls and look at those marks, the marks speak. This is called "reading."*

When she saw Sabalah did not understand, Liada knelt and began to scratch in the dust with a stick. *This mark stands for the words "Amonah Goddess of the Sea." This mark stands for the word "Queen," and this little mark that looks like a snake with its tail in its mouth stands for "All time past, present, and future." Put the marks together and you get:*

"Amonah, Goddess of the Sea, is Queen of all time, past present and future."

If you heard these words spoken out loud you wouldn't be able to understand them. This is because the books of Kataka aren't written in Sharan. They're written in Xchimosh, a sacred language that's even older than Old Language. In Kataka the priestesses say Xchimosh is the language of the Goddess Herself. Would you like to learn it?

Crouching over the marks Liada had made in the dust, Sabalah formed the mark for "Amonah" and then the little snake with its tail in its mouth that stood for "All time, past, present, and future." By the time she stood up, she knew she wanted to learn how to read and write in Xchimosh. In the months that followed, the lessons became a secret game the two of them played whenever Sabalah had free time. She was a fast learner, and by the end of the second spring, she could read and write Xchimosh.

Now she hesitated. Should she enter the Python's chamber, or should she turn around and leave as fast and as silently as she could? She had always suspected Liada had taught her something forbidden. Reading was one of the secrets of the Dark Goddess, and she was fairly sure Liada had taken a solemn vow not to reveal it to anyone.

Before she could decide whether to go or stay, the Python turned its sightless eyes toward her. "You are here," it said.

"Yes," Sabalah admitted.

"Come closer."

As Sabalah walked across the chamber, the painted snakes on the walls seemed to follow her. This morning the Python was not veiled, but there was something different about the way it looked. In such dim light, it was hard to make out what that difference was. Suddenly, Sabalah realized the long, white, snake-like thing that lay curled around the bottom of its stool was its braid. It had cut off its hair and shaved its skull clean. There was no deeper sign of mourning in all the Motherlands.

"You can read?" the Python asked.

"Yes," Sabalah admitted, quietly placing the bouquet of iris at the Python's feet. Iris symbolized good news, and it didn't seem right to hand it to the Python when it was in mourning.

"Xchimosh?"

Sabalah was almost too startled to answer. "Yes," she stuttered, "Xchimosh."

The Python held up the book. It wasn't a scroll and it wasn't made of deerskin. Bound in snakeskin, it was square and about as thick as four hands pressed together. On the cover, Sabalah saw an image of a snake swallowing its own tail.

"The prophecies of the Eighty-Sixth Python predicted that one day Batal would send a pregnant woman to Orefi who would bear a magical child. That woman would be able to read Xchimosh because she had been taught by dogs. Were you taught by dogs?"

"Not exactly. I was taught in Shara by a priestess of the Temple of Dogs."

"Still, you can read Xchimosh. That was how the prophecy of the Eighty-Sixth Python said we would recognize you. What a long time we have waited for you, Sabalah, Daughter of Lalah. For forty-five generations, women have come to Orefi to bear children. For forty-five generations each Great Python has asked each mother if she could read Xchimosh. None could. In fact, few could read at all. Come closer."

Sabalah moved so close to the Python that she could see into its eyes, but today no shapes were moving in the depths. This had to be a mistake. They couldn't have been waiting for her for forty-five generations. She was not that important.

"I'm only a woman from Shara who fishes."

"Only a poor little unimportant fisher from Shara who saw the Goddess Amonah walk to her across the waves. You do not know who you are, do you? Well then, I will tell you: you are a good thing and a bad thing. I welcome you, and I wish I had never heard your voice. You are the mother of Marrah who it is said will save our people from the beastmen; and at the same time, you are the first sign of a catastrophe that will bring an end to the Motherlands."

The Python tapped the book with its finger. "I know this because I am holding the Mother Book, Orefi's greatest treasure. The Goddess Herself dictated it to the First Great Python, and as the little snake on the cover indicates, all things past, present, and future are written in it. I've not always been blind. When I was not much older than you, I read the Mother Book, and like all the Pythons before me, I memorized every word. Even now, I can tell by feel where each passage is."

The Python opened the Mother Book, placed it in Sabalah's hands, and pointed to a line in the middle of the page. "Read this to me, so I can have the pleasure of hearing it again."

Sabalah stared at the inside of the book in astonishment. "The pages are so white," she whispered.

"They're made of vellum. As far as I know, there's no other square, sewn book made of vellum in all the Motherlands. But never mind how it looks. What's important is what it says. Read."

Sabalah took a deep breath and began reading. *"How sweet he will be, your tender lover, the one with the crooked finger."*

"And sweet he was, the sweetest man or woman I ever lay with. I was always grateful to the Goddess for telling me to look for a lover with a crooked finger. I might have missed him otherwise."

Taking back the Mother Book, it turned to another section. "Read this."

Sabalah looked at the passage the Python had selected. What she saw surprised her so much she almost dropped the book. "It says: *'Rise up, Sabalah! Save Marrah or the beastmen will take her! Time is running out. Your enemies are drawing closer. Flee! Go south to my shrine at Orefi where you can give birth to Marrah in safety. Then take her to the West Beyond the West.'* Those are the exact words that -"

"—the exact words that Batal said to you as you lay in the Dreaming Cave at Shara, yes?"

Sabalah nodded, too stunned to speak. So this was why Batal had sent her to Orefi!

"So you see, we really have been waiting for you for forty-five generations. Of course, forty-five generations ago, those words appeared to be complete nonsense. No one knew what they meant. Even now, we can only understand a small part of the Mother Book. There are passages in it that speak of birds heavier than stone that cross the Great Western Sea, songs sung by invisible singers, giant mushrooms brighter than the sun. But here is a prophecy which I'm afraid I do understand."

The Python riffled through the Mother Book until it located the section it was searching for, but this time it did not hold the book out to Sabalah. "Adder tells me your partner Arash says he was taken captive by the beastmen. Is this true?"

"Yes. The beastmen did terrible things to him."

"Is it also true that he has said these beastmen worship a sky god, not an earth goddess?"

"Yes, I remember him telling me that on the night we fled from Shara."

The Python stared down at the open book for so long that Sabalah began to wonder if it had forgotten she was there. Finally it spoke.

"There is a prophecy in the Mother Book that says someday Orefi will be destroyed. According to it, the last Python will be killed by a sky god. On that day, the Horn of the Goddess will become a Phallus, and the Mother People will be vanquished. The Sacred Snakes will become a symbol of evil, and the Goddess Earth Herself will begin to die."

The Python closed the Mother Book. "We cannot know exactly when this attack on Orefi will take place, but if these beastmen worship a sky god, it might come in the lifetime of your daughter Marrah, if not sooner. I don't fear the Sky God. I've lived a good life, and if he kills me, I will go back to the Mother in peace. But no matter what happens to me or to Orefi, the Mother Book must be saved. Whoever possesses it, possesses the greatest power to do good or evil ever placed in human hands."

The Python handed the Mother Book to Sabalah. "Take it."

Sabalah's hands trembled so hard as she took the Book, she almost dropped it.

"Carry it to the West Beyond the West where it tells us you will find a people who will know how to keep it from falling into the wrong hands. I can't tell you anything about these people, but you will recognize them when you meet them. They are not like us, really not like us. For all I know, they may not even be human. The Mother Book says they have three eyes, *one blue, one brown, one dug out of the ground.*"

"But how ... ?"

"It's useless to ask questions. There are no answers. Just remember: *'One blue eye, one brown, one dug out of the ground.'* I don't think you're going to mistake any other people for the people the Goddess has chosen to watch over the Mother Book, but until you meet them, you are to tell no one that you have it in your possession. Above all, you are not to read the Mother Book no matter how much you are tempted to do so. These prophecies are dangerous. Only a Great Python or a Lesser Python who has been initiated into the Mysteries of the Dark Goddess is allowed to see them. If you ultimately place the Mother Book in the hands of a Lesser Python who cannot read Xchimosh, you may, at its command, read the book to it. So let me say again: you must tell no one you have the Mother Book, and you are forbidden to read it. Do you understand?"

"Yes, but ..."

"No, not 'yes but.' I'm going to make you take a vow so sacred that if you break it you may die. It's the vow each Python takes the first time she is told about the Mother Book. Stretch out on the floor face down and embrace the Earth."

Sabalah put down the book and stretched out on floor of the cavern. She spread her hands and felt the rough edges of the stones dig into her palms. She had come into the Python's cave carrying a bouquet of iris. She was going to leave with something so powerful it could destroy the world. Taking the Mother Book to safety was a heavy responsibility, one that she might have declined if the Python had given her a choice. How could she protect it? All she had was a knife for skinning fish.

"Repeat after me," the Python said. "I will never tell anyone the Mother Book exists. Not strangers, not friends, not lovers, not even my daughter. I will keep its existence a secret, carry it to safety, and defend it with my life. I will not read the Mother Book. I will not even open it unless a Python commands me to."

After Sabalah finished repeating the Python's words, it told her to get up, take the Mother Book, and hide it under her cloak. Before she left, it spoke for the last time.

"There is one more prophecy you should know about. This prophecy says that someday human beings will want to love the Goddess Earth again and nurse Her back to health. That day may be far in the future, but when it comes, the Mother Book must be there to guide future generations. Now, go with my blessing, and may your journey to the West Beyond the West be safe and your path smooth."

The Python's blessing was meant to be comforting, but there was something in its voice and the way it turned its head away from her that made Sabalah fear it knew far more about her journey than she did. Or perhaps it was its own journey the Python was thinking about that morning, for three days later it died, withering away so suddenly that the nine Holy Men who came to carry it out of the Womb of the Goddess said its body felt as light as the castoff skin of a snake.

10

THE ATTACK ON OREFI

The Python's funeral feast was the greatest celebration held at Orefi for over a hundred years. For three days everyone was too occupied eating, drinking, and dancing the Python back into the arms of the Dark Mother to notice that Sabalah wasn't tending the cooking fires or gorging herself on roasted goat. Arash was too busy singing and playing his *lixah* to keep track of her. The children were too busy gathering flowers. The Snakes, Holy Men, and villagers were too busy drinking fermented honey, matching each other cup for cup.

Sabalah could have been back in the guest house sleeping. She could have been nursing Marrah in some quiet place where the drumming wasn't so loud you had to shout at the top of your lungs to make yourself heard. But she was in none of those places. The Mother Book had to be hidden, and there was only one place to hide it where no one, not even Arash, was likely to stumble on it.

The problem was, that place didn't exist. Sabalah had to create it, and creating a secure hiding place in a small village where people noticed every stick of wood you gathered for your fire would have been impossible if the Python's funeral feast had not been in full swing.

Before she realized where the only possible hiding place was, she spent two days anxiously waterproofing the Book. This was tedious but fairly easy because, having fished most of her life, she knew a lot about keeping things dry. First, she wrapped the Book in a thin piece of doeskin to protect it from stains and spots. Then she made a waterproof jacket for it out of dried goat intestines sealed together with glue. Over this, she put a second jacket of leather coated with pine pitch, and then a third layer of doeskin.

It looks like a pillow, she thought as she stared at the result; and suddenly she knew where she should hide it. There was only one pillow she would be carrying with her to the West Beyond the West, and that was the pillow Marrah lay her head on every time Sabalah strapped her into her cradleboard.

It took her the better part of another day to refashion the Mother Book into Marrah's pillow and lace it firmly to the cradleboard, but she finished in time. On the final night of the Python's funeral feast, she joined in the celebration, carrying Marrah on her back as she danced with the Snakes. Arash sang, Marrah slept, the drummers drummed, and no one asked Sabalah where she had been or noticed that Marrah had a new pillow.

The next morning, Adder led a procession up the mountain to the Womb of the Mother. As everyone stood outside the entrance waving laurel branches and singing praises to Batal, Adder carried the jar that contained the Great Python's ashes into the cave and placed it in the Grotto of the Pythons where it joined the jars that contained the ashes of every Python who had prophesied at Orefi.

As she waited for Adder to emerge, Sabalah wept for the Python. The Python had guided her, blessed her, warned her, and entrusted her with the Mother Book. Who could she turn to for help now that it was dead?

Come back! she thought. *Please come back! I never got to ask you to bless the fishers of Chaunna so they'd have a good catch this year. I never got to tell you I loved you.* But even as she asked the Great Python to return, Sabalah knew this was impossible.

Blinded by her own tears, she began to pray. *May you walk safely through the Dark Forest. May you find that old lover of yours, the one with the twisted little finger, and share joy forever with him.*

A week passed, then another. The Python's death felt like a hole in the fabric of life that could never be repaired. Often when they sat together weaving, Adder, Rock Snake, and Sabalah sang the funeral songs of the Mother People. One song in particular always brought them to tears. It was a very old song, so old no one knew when it had first been sung, and it told of the journey of the dead back to the Great Mother whose love was infinite and whose arms were always open. Sometimes Arash accompanied them on his *lixah,* and as the sweet sound of his playing filled the room, Sabalah imagined the Python had returned to comfort them and tell them not to grieve.

But the Python did not return. It was painful to think of its chamber sitting empty and its stool remaining unoccupied, but slowly the pain grew less intense, and they took up their daily lives. The potters of Orefi made pots, the weavers wove, the bakers baked, the Snakes met to plan their search for a new Great Python, and Sabalah and Arash watched Marrah grow and blossom.

Marrah was no longer a tiny newborn. She was lifting her head now, swatting at things, smiling at Arash when he sang to her, and babbling as if she were trying to speak, and with each day that passed Sabalah loved her more.

As she nursed her, she sometimes wondered if Marrah remembered where she had been before she was born. Perhaps as she babbled, she was trying to describe what it had felt like to be held in the arms of the Goddess Earth, the Great Mother of all babies.

As Marrah changed, the weather was also changing. It was soon clear that the worst of the rainy season was over, which meant it was time for Sabalah and Arash to continue their voyage to the West Beyond the West, but they lingered on, unwilling to set a date for their departure. Orefi was comfortable and safe while somewhere ahead of them lurked the danger the Python had warned them to beware of.

Perhaps they would have stayed through the summer or even through another winter, but three weeks after the Python died, something happened that destroyed everyone's illusion that Orefi was a sanctuary.

The trouble began with the arrival of the first pilgrims. The boat that brought them into the Bay was the largest ever to come to Orefi. Like the *raspa* Arash and Sabalah had sailed in from Chaunna, it had a deep keel and gaff-rigged linen sails reinforced with battens, but it also had six oars mounted in rows so they could all be used at the same time. This was a boat that could keep moving even when the wind failed. Yet as quick and graceful as it was, there was something ominous about it.

The hulls of every boat Sabalah had ever seen had been painted with good luck symbols: dolphins, schools of fish, labyrinths, triangles, moons, snakes, flying fish, and waving blue lines that ran from stem to stern. But the boat that brought this new batch of pilgrims to Batal's shrine was completely white, and in the Motherlands white was the color of mourning. When Sabalah saw all that whiteness descending on Orefi, her breath caught in her throat, and she felt a shudder of foreboding.

As the pilgrims waded to shore, she saw that they were dressed in white linen and their faces were painted with white clay. The women in the party were not with child, so even before they spoke, it was obvious none of them had come to Orefi to give birth. Six people in deep mourning. This could not possibly be good. *Please,* Sabalah thought, *don't let this have anything to do with Marrah.*

She pulled back the sunshade of the cradleboard and rested the palm of her hand on Marrah's head. The warm sweetness of the sleeping baby spread down her arm and filled her heart. She had never loved anyone or anything as much as she loved this child. *Please don't let those women be mothers who have lost their babies.*

As the pilgrims walked up the beach toward the waiting crowd, the Snakes danced and sang for them. "Welcome in the name of the Goddess," Adder said, placing wreaths of sweetly-scented pink flowers around their necks. "Where are you from, and why have you come to Orefi?"

"We have sailed from the eastern shore of the great Western Sea through the Stone Gates that lead into the Blue Sea," the tallest man said. "We live in three villages that neighbor one another. To the west of us, there's nothing but water. We've made this pilgrimage to Orefi to offer combs of honey and baskets of ceremonial axes to the Great Python."

"I'm sorry to tell you that you've come too late. The Great Python died a few weeks ago."

When they heard Adder's words, the pilgrims stared at one another in dismay.

"Dear Goddess," the tall man said in a husky voice. "Tell us this isn't true."

"Alas, it is."

The man took a step back as if he had been struck. Then to everyone's astonishment, he began to wail like someone who had lost the mother who had given him birth. "No!" he cried. "No! This cannot be!"

"Why do you grieve so excessively?" Adder asked, throwing her arms around the tall man and pulling him close. "Hush, my son, hush. The Great Python was very old. It had a good life. We miss it, but no one lives forever. Hush, hush. Don't cry. You can still offer the gifts you've brought to Batal and take the Goddess's blessing home with you when you leave."

"You don't understand," the tall man said in a ragged whisper. "We needed to consult the Great Python and now—" His voice broke. He moved out of Adder's embrace, struggling for control. "You say the Python died only a few weeks ago. This is terrible luck. We've traveled far from our homes and suffered great hardships all in vain. We'd hoped a prophecy from the Python might help us understand what kind of animal has been taking our children."

Everyone stared at the pilgrims in stunned silence. Children? Some animal was taking their children?

Sabalah felt a wave of terror so intense it stopped her breath. For an instant, she swayed as if the ground had suddenly moved under her. *No!* she thought. Regaining her balance, she fought to push the pilgrim's words out of her mind. This stealing of children had nothing to do with Marrah. Nothing. It had taken place far away. Again she touched Marrah to make sure she was safely asleep in her cradleboard blessed by the Mother Book, which lay under her tiny head.

"Are you saying your children are being eaten by lions or attacked by wolves?" Adder asked.

"No." The tall man waved his arms in a gesture of complete helplessness. "They just disappear. The things that take them come out of rivers or out of the sea. They walk on two feet, leaving behind prints like those of no animal we've ever seen before. The prints look almost human, but the spaces between the toes are webbed." He suddenly stopped speaking, put his hands over his face, and wept uncontrollably.

One of the women stepped forward. "Forgive my brother," she said. "He hasn't been himself for months. He was the aita of a little girl named Chala who was taken last fall." She looked at Adder and the rest of the Snakes hopefully.

"Can any of you prophecy? Can any of you tell us what these things might be? We live at the ends of the earth, as far west as people can live. In our land there are beings left over from ancient times: little people who aren't exactly human, people-like things with big heads who live mostly underground, birds with leather wings, long-necked lizards. They're all very shy and mostly keep to themselves. Every generation or so, a hunter spots one of them, but no one in all the history of our people has ever seen a five-toed animal with webbed feet that stands on two legs like people."

"Alas," Adder said, "none of us can help you. Only a Great Python can inhale the Breath of the Goddess and speak in Her voice, and our search for a new Python will take at least a year."

"Then we will have to return to our own land and tell all the mothers who have lost their children that we've failed."

"You don't have to go back immediately. You're welcome to stay here for as long as you like. You must be exhausted after a journey of so many months."

"Thank you, but it took us three weeks to get here, and we need to get back to our villages before any more of our children are taken."

Adder stared at the woman blankly. "I'm sorry. I must not have heard you correctly. How long did you say it took you to get from the Great Western Sea to Orefi?"

"Three weeks."

There was an audible gasp from the crowd.

"But how can that be? It takes the better part of two months just to get to Gira, and if I understand what you said, you came from a land much farther away than Gira."

"We came across open water."

"But ... I still don't understand. No one ever sails out of sight of land, and those who do never return."

The woman gave Adder the ghost of a smile. "We knew that, but we were desperate. That's why we spent all winter building a boat we could row if the winds failed. We had hoped to come here, receive the Python's prophecy, and return to our own land before that beast, whatever it is, came out of hibernation. It sleeps in the winter, or at least we think it does, although some of us fear it lives under the ice watching us as we pass over its head. In any event, by getting here in less than a month, we hoped ..."

The second time the woman uttered the word "hope" the light went out of her eyes. She looked at her brother who still had his face buried in his hands. "But it seems we hoped in vain."

The Snakes came up to the pilgrims, put their arms around them, held them, and tried to comfort them; but it was no use. Their grief was too deep. Before sunset, the white boat sailed out of the Bay of Orefi carrying the mourning pilgrims back to their distant land.

That night for the first time in months, Sabalah had a nightmare. In it, she found herself walking through darkness so thick it felt like a blanket, following a small silver line that was no wider than a strand of flax. To her right and left, she could sense immensely tall things rising straight up like the masts of boats.

I must be in the Dark Forest, she thought, and as the words formed in her mind, she was again overcome with a feeling of terror so great she began to stumble. *I must get out of here! I must get out!*

Something barked that wasn't a dog. Something moaned that wasn't the wind. A stick snapped, and the hairs on the back of her neck stood up. Something was hunting her. Panicked, she broke into a run. Behind her she heard the sound of her pursuer's footsteps coming faster and faster. The footsteps didn't sound human.

A thing with webbed feet that walks on two legs like people, the pilgrims had said. If it caught her, would it kill her? Take her as it had taken their children? Drag her underwater to drown?

Suddenly, she broke out of the forest into light so bright she was temporarily blinded. In front of her stretched a vast sea, frozen solid. She skidded to a stop at the edge of it and looked down. The ice was so clear she could see all the way to the bottom. Half way between the sand and the surface, she saw the Great Python suspended in the ice, its head shaved, its face painted with white clay.

"Beware!" the Python cried. *"Be..."*

Sabalah woke up screaming. Before she had time to understand that she'd been dreaming, Arash had thrown his arms around her and was holding her and comforting her. "Hush," he said. "You're safe, my love. I'm here."

"I saw—" But she couldn't remember what she'd seen or what had frightened her so badly. Her mind was like ... She groped for the words. Like the Dark Forest. That was it. Her mind was like the Dark Forest, but when she tried to tell Arash this, he didn't understand, and she couldn't explain.

The rains stopped, yet still they lingered on in Orefi. Sooner or later they would have to leave since Batal Herself had commanded Sabalah to take Marrah to the West Beyond the West, but why should they embark on such a long, dangerous journey when Marrah was so young and there seemed to be no need to rush?

The answer came all too soon. The pilgrims in the white boat had only been gone for a few weeks when a trading *raspa* sailed into the Bay bearing two pilgrims who were traveling as passengers. The *raspa* had set out many weeks ago from Shambah, which lay on the very edge of the great plain known as the Sea of Grass.

These pilgrims looked like no people anyone had ever seen. They were tall and lean with muscles that made them look as if they had spent their entire lives pulling in fishing nets, but they could never have fished, because the traders who brought them to Orefi said they knew nothing about boats or the sea, plus they had been horribly seasick during most of the journey south. The body of one man was covered with scars that made his chest and back look as if they had been raked by bear claws. The other was missing an eye.

Sabalah never saw the strangers, because as soon as they landed, Adder sent Rock Snake back to the village to say that she and Arash should take Marrah into the Womb of the Mother immediately and stay there until it was safe to come out.

"Adder doesn't trust them," Rock Snake said. "None of us do. We think they're lying to us. Remember the Python's warning that you should tell no one your daughter was born at Orefi? Well, now we think we know why. These so-called 'pilgrims' say they've come from the north seeking a magical child who was born here on the longest night of the year."

Sabalah gasped.

"It gets worse. They claim they worship the Goddess Earth, but when we asked them what made them think a magical child had been born here, they said their holy men looked up at the sky and saw that prophecy in the stars. They've brought gold necklaces shaped like sunbursts which they claim they want to offer to the child they're seeking. As you know, there's a prophecy that Orefi will be destroyed by people who worship a Sky God. We think these men may be the first Sky-God worshippers to come to Orefi. Obviously they can't destroy us. There are only two of them. But we fear their arrival is the first sign of the invasion to come."

Sabalah didn't wait to hear more. Picking up Marrah, she strapped her into her cradleboard, put her on her back, and hurried to the cave so fast Arash could hardly keep up with her. When they were safely inside the second cavern, she sat down and tried to gather her wits.

"Could they be beastmen?" she said, pressing the palms of her hands together to keep them from shaking.

"No. From Rock Snake's description, we know they aren't half beast." He paused. "There's something I need to tell you. I didn't say anything about it before, because I didn't think it mattered." Again he paused.

"In the name of the Goddess, Arash, don't keep me in suspense! What is it?"

"I've heard tales of a northern tribe called the Tcvali who worship a Sky God. The Mother People who live near the Sea of Grass are terrified of them. They say they'll do anything for gold."

"Do you think the beastmen gave the Tcvali gold and told them to find Marrah and kill her?"

"It seems possible. Rock Snake said they brought gold necklaces with them."

"Dear Goddess, how did they manage to find us?"

"I don't know. We came by water. We didn't leave any tracks."

They took each other's hands and sat silently for a few moments.

"I'll fight to protect you and Marrah," Arash said grimly.

"We'll both fight," Sabalah agreed.

"No one is ever going to hurt our baby."

"No one."

Getting up, they moved deeper into the cave. As Sabalah followed the line of red triangles and handprints that led to the Python's chamber, she remembered that brief glimpse she had of the beastmen the night she fled from Shara: the eerie, terrifying way they had moved up and down as if the bottom half of them wasn't human.

You'll never get your hands on my child no matter how many Sky-God worshippers you send after us! she thought. She'd never so much as struck another person in anger, but she knew that what she'd told Arash was true: she'd fight to the death before she let these so-called pilgrims touch a hair on Marrah's head.

Time passed slowly underground. Sabalah unstrapped Marrah from her cradleboard and held her, feeling the warmth and weight of her tiny body as she babbled happily, mercifully unaware that there was anything wrong. *My sweet child,* Sabalah thought. *My darling.* Putting Marrah to her breast, she nursed her back to sleep, gently strapped her back into the cradleboard, and put her in a quiet place where she could sleep undisturbed.

Too upset to sit still, she paced back and forth. Twenty-three steps to one side of the chamber; twenty-three steps back. In the lamplight the painted snakes on the walls and ceiling seemed to coil restlessly.

"Try to relax," Arash suggested. "We're safe here. The entrance to the cave is hidden. They'll never find it."

"I can't relax." She kept on pacing. What was going on outside? Were the strangers still down on the beach or had they climbed the trail to Orefi? If they were in the village, they might stumble on the path that led to the cave.

She looked around the chamber for some kind of weapon to use in case they were attacked, but the only thing that might have served was the Great Python's rickety, wooden stool.

Sometime later, perhaps in the late afternoon or early evening, they were startled out of a fitful sleep by moaning and weeping. Leaping to their feet, they ran to the entrance of the chamber and saw Adder walking down the tunnel toward them holding a baby in one hand and a torch in the other. With her were half a dozen women who also carried infants and another woman who was clutching her arm as if it had been broken. There was blood on the women's faces and clothing, and they were all sobbing and shaking except for the woman with the broken arm who stared straight ahead with a stony expression that was more upsetting than tears.

"The strangers are searching Orefi for a girl child!" Adder gasped. "Take care of the mothers and babies. I have to go back!" Thrusting the infant she was carrying into Sabalah's arms, Adder turned and ran out of the Python's chamber, leaving the sobbing women behind.

Sabalah cradled the baby in her arms and rocked it until it stopped crying. Then she handed it to Arash and put Marrah to her breast to quiet her.

The woman sat down and waited. Several of them also began to nurse their babies. They had all fallen unnaturally silent. Perhaps they were grieving or paralyzed with fear. It was hard to tell.

Taking a deep breath, Sabalah asked them a question she wasn't sure she wanted to know the answer to: "What happened?"

The story they told her was short and terrible. Convinced the strangers were up to no good, the Snakes had informed them that they'd made a mistake: there were no baby girls at Orefi. Despite this, the men had insisted on visiting the village, and since the Goddess had commanded the Snakes never to turn away pilgrims, they had no choice but to lead them up the mountainside.

Once they got to the village, the men had yelled, "Bring out your girls!" When no one did, they began to go from house to house, kicking in doors and terrorizing people. When they found a nursing child, they ripped it out of its mother's arms, pushed the mother aside, and stripped off the baby's swaddling clothes to see if it was a boy or a girl. If it was a boy, they cast it aside, uttering curses in some strange language no one had ever heard before. Then they set the house on fire.

By the grace of the Goddess the men did not find a single girl child before Adder, seeing what was happening, gathered up all the remaining mothers with nursing babies and led them to safety under the cover of the smoke and confusion.

"The strangers kept yelling that they were going to kill any girl child they found," one of the women said, clutching her baby daughter to her breast. "Why would anyone do such a terrible thing?"

"They threw my baby boy onto the floor," another woman said. "Look." She lifted the edge of the makeshift bandage, and Sabalah saw a nasty cut on the little boy's forehead. The child whimpered in pain. Bending over, his mother gently replaced the bandage, kissed her son on the cheek, and put him to her breast.

"Why didn't you fight when they tried to take him from you?"

"Fight? I couldn't. Orefi is sacred ground. Everyone here has taken a vow to keep the Peace of the Goddess."

"Even at the cost of your own lives? Even at the cost of the lives of your children?"

The woman went pale. "I don't know. Maybe we could have fought for our children without breaking our vow, but the strangers took us by surprise. We didn't know what to do. No one has shed blood here for thousands of generations. No one has ever harmed a child on purpose. Such things never seemed possible."

As she watched the woman nurse her injured baby, a deadly calm settled over Sabalah. There was no time left for fear. Carrying Marrah over to the cradleboard, she laced her in and strapped the board to her back. Adder had said there were forty chambers in this cave. If the strangers showed up, she wanted to be prepared to run.

When Adder finally returned, she was alone. "The strangers have gone. No one was killed, and none of the boy babies has been seriously injured." Sitting down beside Sabalah she put her head between her knees, and sat there shaking.

Reaching out, Sabalah placed her hand on Adder's shoulder, thinking to comfort her. At Sabalah's touch, Adder started as if she'd been struck.

"It was terrible. Indescribable. What should we have done? We couldn't fight back. Did you know we're all sworn to peace?"

Sabalah nodded. *Yes,* she thought, *I do. No one in the Motherlands knows how to fight like those strangers because no one has ever had to, even me. I've told myself I'd fight to the death to protect Marrah, but Arash and I don't know any more about fighting than that woman who let them throw her baby boy on the floor.*

"Besides," Adder continued, "we had no weapons. They took us completely by surprise. Thanks be to the Goddess none of our beloved children was murdered. It could have been much worse. They could have killed us all."

Rising to her feet, she walked over to the Great Python's stool and ran her fingers over the wooden seat, which was covered with fine white dust. "I wish the Great Python were alive to guide us, but since it has gone back to the Mother, I'm the person responsible for everyone at Orefi. What should I do? What does this all mean?"

She turned to Sabalah. "Did you know the strangers would do this? Did the Great Python warn you?"

"The Python told me the prophecy about the Sky God which you already know, but other than that it only told me to 'beware' without telling me what to beware of."

"Yes," Adder said. "Now I remember. You begged me to interpret the Python's warning, but I couldn't tell you what danger lay ahead." Seizing hold of one of the torches, Adder jerked it out of its holder.

"All of you, stay here. I'm going back outside to see what's going on. When I left, the strangers had broken every snake image they could get their hands on, set fire to the village, and were on their way back down the mountain, but that doesn't mean they aren't coming back."

For the better part of three days, Sabalah, Marrah, Arash, and the women and babies stayed in the Great Python's chamber. Each evening Adder brought them food, water, and news. Most of the news was good: the villagers had put out the fire before it burned too many houses. The strangers had forced the traders to sail them out of the Bay, and there'd been no sign of them since.

Finally Adder announced it was safe for the mothers and babies to come out of the cave. As Sabalah emerged from the tunnel, the sunlight blinded her. Stumbling down the path, she found an Orefi different from the Orefi she had left only three days ago. Evil had entered the Temple of Batal, and not a rock, stone, stick, or a living being would ever be the same.

11

THE GIFTS OF THE GREAT PYTHON

That evening after they had swept out the broken pottery and scrubbed the floor of the guest house, Sabalah and Arash lit a fire against the spring chill and shared joy as the flames cast shadows on the walls. As Sabalah inhaled the scent of smoke and the warm, musky scent of Arash's flesh, she felt such a combination of grief, fear, mourning, relief, and gratitude that she found herself laughing and crying all at the same time.

As always, the moment came when the river of passion pulled her under, and she saw things no human being could really see. This time it was a pair of yellow eyes that floated in front of her, glowing in the darkness like the eyes of a lion. There was tenderness in those eyes, great tenderness. Afterwards, as she lay curled in the crook of Arash's arms, she could remember nothing except the feeling that she was loved.

Usually after they shared joy, they fell asleep. But tonight they were both restless. Getting up from their bed, Arash went over to the water jar and drank from it. Then he brought it to Sabalah.

"Here," he said, "the night is dry."

Taking the jug from him, she took a long drink of water.

"Awake?" he asked.

"Barely."

"There's something I want to talk to you about. Those Sky-God worshippers could come back at any time."

Sabalah nodded. She'd been thinking the same thing.

"Which means," he continued, "that we need to leave Orefi as soon as we can, because we're not only endangering ourselves, we're endangering everyone here. If we hug the shoreline, it's going to take us months to get to the West Beyond the West. But if we sail straight to Lezentka across open water, it will cut weeks off our journey. Lezentka's a small fishing village that the traders call 'the Gate to the West Beyond the West,' and it's as safe a place as you could wish for. With luck, I think we could make it to Lezentka in about two weeks, including a stop at Gira to re-provision."

"But no one sails across open water. It's too dangerous."

"The pilgrims in the white boat proved it's possible."

"Arash, they had incredibly good luck. It's as if Amonah Herself protected them. They didn't hit big storms even though they started out at the end of the rainy season. They didn't get becalmed and starve to death because they could row when the wind didn't blow. They didn't get lost or end up smashed against rocks."

"We could have good luck too, and even if we didn't, I think it's worth the risk. I've figured out how those Sky-God Worshippers tracked us to Orefi. It's simple: they just asked about us every time the traders put in to shore for provisions. *Have you seen a black-haired, dark-skinned, green-eyed man with a full beard traveling south with a woman whose brown eyes contain flecks of gold?* As time passed, they probably added: *a woman who is with child* to their description of you. We traveled so slowly and came ashore so many times, that we left a wide trail. No one, particularly no one who had spent his life hunting, could miss it, and believe me, the people of the north are the best hunters ever born. They may have left Orefi, but that doesn't mean they've given up. The first time we put in for provisions, we could find them waiting for us."

"Arash, please don't tell me this. I was just beginning to feel safe again."

"Hush, my love." He put his finger over her lips and drew her into his arms. "There's no reason to be afraid. If we sail across open water, we'll lose them forever, and you'll never have to fear them again."

"Do you really believe we'll be safe on the open sea with no land in sight?"

"Yes, that's what I've been trying to tell you. We'll be safe for two reasons. First: we can't get lost because all we have to do is sail straight west. We aren't looking for a shrine we've never visited before. We're simply looking for the western coast of the Blue Sea. Second, once we find it, any trader we meet will be able to give us directions to Lezentka."

"No."

"Please, think it over. I love you and Marrah. I'd never endanger you unnecessarily. The beastmen held me captive for months. I know how they think. They will have sent men to find us who never give up. The Sky-God Worshippers will hunt us to the ends of the earth. Sailing across open water is the safest way to make sure they can't follow us."

He seldom talked about his captivity. It gave his words weight. Sabalah thought of the months of travel that lay ahead of them if they clung to the shoreline. Although they had left Shara in mid-summer, they had barely made it to Orefi before the winter rains began. Did she really want to risk spending the winter in some small fishing village waiting for the storms to stop while the Sky-God Worshippers searched for them? Then she thought about how vast the Sea of Blue Waves was, how great storms often came out of nowhere, how before Marrah was even conceived, she herself had nearly drowned within sight of Shara.

She looked at Marrah who was sleeping peacefully in a basket beside their bed. "No," she repeated. "It's too dangerous. If it takes us another year to get to the West Beyond the West, then we'll travel for another year. We can leave the day after tomorrow if we can get the boat in shape in time, but I'm not risking Marrah's life by sailing out of sight of land. As for the Sky-God Worshippers, we'll just have to travel as fast as we can and pray Batal knew what She was doing when She sent us west."

She went to sleep convinced she'd made the right decision, but the next morning she changed her mind, or rather Adder changed it for her. She had walked over to Adder's house to tell her that they were preparing to leave Orefi and ask the Snakes for help getting their boat in shape.

It was early, and the eastern sky was filled with long pink, finger-like clouds.

She found Adder bent over the cooking fire, kindling the embers back to life with a fan. Rock Snake, who was now living with Adder, was pouring water into a clay bowl of acorn meal. A small pot of honey sat on the table beside the bowl. Some of it had spilled, but the flies hadn't found it yet. Sabalah greeted Adder and Rock Snake in the name of the Goddess, exchanged pleasantries with them about what a beautiful day lay ahead, and then dipped her finger in the spilled honey and sucked on it while she waited for Adder to finish stoking the fire.

From where she was standing, she could see the charred remains of Rock Snake's house. Logs big enough to serve as roof beams were hard to come by, so getting the village back to its original state was going to take time. As she licked the last of the honey off her finger, she wondered if the houses in Orefi would be repaired by this time next year.

At last Adder stood up, wiped the soot off her hands, and suggested Sabalah sit down and have breakfast with them. Sabalah thanked her and declined breakfast on the grounds that she had already eaten. As the acorn mush cooked on the fire, she and Adder sat down on a bench, and Rock Snake came over and sat down beside them.

"You're up early," Rock Snake said, twisting the end of her braid around her finger.

Sabalah nodded.

"Couldn't you sleep?"

"No, I slept well. It's just that last night Arash and I decided we needed to leave Orefi as soon as possible, and I wanted to get an early start. I have some favors to ask."

"Food, water, repairs to your boat?"

"Yes. Is it—"

"Is it possible we can give these things to you?" Adder took Sabalah's hand in hers. "My dear sister, of course it's possible. We'll gladly give all that to you and more. But I can't say I'm happy to hear you're leaving. We've grown very fond of you, and we're afraid of what lies ahead. Those men..." Adder spit on the ground. "Those evil, murderous men are hunting for you and your baby. What if they find you? Who will protect you?"

"No one can protect us, and we're not safe here," Sabalah said.

"No, you're not." Rock Snake took Sabalah's other hand in hers. For a few moments the three women sat silently, holding hands as the wind blew through the open door, bringing with it the sour smell of ashes and smoke-damaged wood. Peering into the shadows, Sabalah saw half a dozen mutilated snake images stacked in a pile against the far wall awaiting ceremonial burial.

"We'd do anything for you," Rock Snake said at last.

"Then help me leave Orefi as fast as possible." Tears welled up in Sabalah's eyes and when she looked over, she saw that Rock Snake and Adder were also crying. The three of them had come to love one another as sisters, and now the time was swiftly approaching when they would have to part. Once she and Arash sailed out of the Bay, Sabalah knew she would never see Adder and Rock Snake again.

Two sisters, not of her blood but of her heart. The pain of their impending separation caught her in the chest and made it hard to breathe. This hurt more than she had thought it would. It was like having to leave Shara all over again.

At last Adder coughed, wiped her eyes on her sleeve, and stood up. "You're right. You have to go. It will tear out a piece of my heart to bid you farewell, but you have no choice." She paused and cleared her throat. "So ... well ... since you must go, I have something for you, some gifts the Great Python commanded me to give you on the day you told us you were leaving Orefi. Wait a moment, and I'll bring the Python's gifts to you."

Walking over to the far side of the room, Adder opened a wooden chest and took out three objects which were, to say the least, a disappointment. For a few moments, Sabalah had entertained the hope that the Python had left her magical charms that would protect her and Marrah as they journeyed west, but she should have known better.

When Adder turned around, she was holding a long, thin stick, a black stone with a hole in it, and a small leather bag. Walking back to Sabalah, she bowed with great formality.

"Beloved Sabalah, Daughter of Lalah, I give you three gifts from the Great Python of Orefi." She handed Sabalah the stick. "Wood from the hair of the Goddess Earth." She handed Sabalah the black stone. "Stone from Her bones, and—" Adder put the leather bag into Sabalah's outstretched hand. "Dust from Her body."

"Dust?" Sabalah said. "You can't mean it?" But Adder did mean it, because when Sabalah opened the leather bag, she found that it was filled with brownish dust that smelled sweetly of lavender and hyacinths.

Biting her lower lip to keep from crying from disappointment, she managed to thank Adder. "I'm honored that the Great Python remembered me," she said, "but what am I supposed to do with a stick, a stone, and a bag of dust?"

"Adder and I have no idea what the dust is for," Rock Snake said. "All we know is that since the Great Python gave it to you, it must have a use, so I wouldn't throw it away."

"As for the stick and the stone," Adder said, "there we can help you." She took the stick from Sabalah and held it parallel to the floor. "This is a weather stick. The tip twists up when the weather is fair and down when a storm is coming. As you can see, although all the bark has been peeled off, it's made of some kind of wood that doesn't grow here. In fact, legend has it that weather sticks don't come from the Motherlands at all. The story goes that long ago some people came out of the Great Western Sea bearing gifts for the Fifth Python. One of their gifts was this stick. The Great Pythons have guarded this weather stick for you for generations. It may look like nothing more than a piece of wood, but it's precious beyond words."

Sabalah took the stick from Adder and ran her fingers down its length. A magic stick that could predict storms. That meant— Before she could complete the thought, Adder spoke again.

"The rock is called a 'loadstone.' If you hang it from something—a rafter, the mast of a boat—the little snake etched on the pointed end will point north."

She indicated a small, wavy line that had been scratched onto one end of the rock. "Loadstones are rare but not nearly as rare as weather sticks. Every once in a while, a pilgrim will bring one to Orefi to offer to the Great Python. We have ... how many, Rock Snake?"

"Five at last count."

"That's right, five." Bending forward, Adder kissed Sabalah on the forehead. "Use these gifts with the blessings of the Great Python, my dear sister. May they guide you to a place where you will find peace and Marrah will be safe."

Three days later, on a fine spring morning when the sky was clear and the wind was fair, Sabalah and Arash bid everyone in Orefi goodbye. As the Snakes danced on the beach singing a song of farewell, they sailed out of the Bay and began to travel west again, not hugging the shoreline but following a course that took them straight down the middle of the narrow gulf that led into the Blue Sea. The loadstone was pointing north. The weather stick, mounted on the mast, said no storms were coming. With luck, they would now move toward the West Beyond the West so swiftly no Sky-God worshippers would be able to follow them.

12

THE VOYAGE TO GIRA

On the second day of their journey, they passed through the narrow end of the gulf and reentered the Blue Sea. At first, Sabalah couldn't believe their luck. Sitting in the stern, she scanned the horizon for dark clouds, but the sky was as transparent as the water. All she saw was a straight wake that stretched out behind them, circling seabirds, pods of dolphins, and schools of fish so thick they looked like submerged islands.

Where had this mild wind come from, this wind that blew them so steadily southwest that it seemed as if Amonah Herself were breathing good luck into their sails? How could the air be so pure, the nights so clear, the weather so fair? How could they be so fortunate?

The tip of the weather stick pointed up as if to confirm that there was nothing to worry about, but how could you put your trust in a stick, even a magic one? She wasn't worried about her own safety or Arash's since he could swim like a seal. She was worried about Marrah who was too tiny to swim if their boat capsized.

She imagined Marrah going under before she could get to her, her small arms outstretched, the terror in her eyes as the water closed over her. Was this the danger the Great Python had warned her to beware of? Was Marrah going to drown even though the midwives had said caul-born babies never could?

She had never been so far from land that she couldn't at least see a strip of brown on the horizon or green branches floating in the water. Here on the open sea, there was no scent of pine trees or earth. Day and night, the wind smelled as if it had been scoured with salt. There was salt on her arms, salt on her clothing, salt in her hair, even the taste of salt in their mouths when she and Arash kissed.

The shore had been a mother who offered her refuge. When she was fishing in the Sweetwater Sea, she had always known that if her boat sank, there was a good chance she could swim back to Shara or at least tread water until someone from the city sailed out to get her. Even during the great storm when she almost drowned, Amonah had saved her by having dolphins bear her back to land.

As long as you could see cliffs, beaches, rocks, an island, a bay to run to if the weather turned foul, you could never get lost. But now, for as far as she could see, there was nothing except water, waves, fish, great flocks of white birds moving north to their summer feeding grounds, and that salted wind that moved incessantly across her body. She had never met anyone except the pilgrims in the white boat who had sailed out of the sight of land; and perhaps, she thought, this was because the legends were true, and almost no one who forsook the shore survived.

Arash tried to reassure her. "Those pilgrims came all the way from the Great Western Sea to Orefi across open water," he said as he sat in the stern combing out his beard with a wooden comb he'd brought from Orefi. "They went back the same way, and I imagine right now they're sleeping safely in their own beds."

"Sleeping safely in their own beds in a land where monsters are taking their children," Sabalah snapped.

When he saw nothing he could say could keep her from worrying about Marrah, he did something so practical and obvious that Sabalah was amazed she hadn't thought of it herself: he turned Marrah's cradleboard into a raft by attaching fish bladders to either end. The most ingenious part of this was that he positioned the bladders so Sabalah could drain the air out of them when she wanted to carry Marrah and blow them back up again when Marrah wasn't strapped to her back.

"You could float all the way to the Stone Gates, little one," he said kissing Marrah on the forehead. Turning to Sabalah he took her in his arms and gave her a kiss of a very different kind.

"Better?" he asked.

She felt his body pressing against her, inhaled the sweet smell of his beard, and for the first time since they left Orefi, she felt desire running through her like a current: hot, strong, and joyful.

"Much better," she said kissing him so passionately that he gasped. "Thank you. I've been so worried about Marrah and now…" She drew him even closer and kissed him again.

"And now," he murmured. If he was going to say something more, he never got around to it, because soon they were kneeling in the bottom of the boat on a pile of blankets and taking off each other's clothes. For a long time they lay together, naked and warm in the spring sunshine, sharing joy in a way they'd never shared it before: very slowly, very tenderly, exciting one another little by little, stopping and starting until they were enveloped in sweet shudders that left both of them breathless.

This time, Sabalah did not feel swept away on a river of passion that took her out of herself. This time she did not see things no human being could see. Instead, she saw Arash looking into her eyes and heard him whispering over and over how much he loved her. This was the old Arash, the tender, playful Arash, the Arash she had lain with for seventy-nine nights in the fields of Shara. This was the man she loved come back to her at last.

"Did you know that babies can swim almost as soon as they're born?" he said as they rose and put their clothes back on. "Babies grow in water inside their mothers, and if you put them back into it when they're Marrah's age, they'll start paddling." He laughed. "Not that I'm suggesting we try it; but there's something about water and babies that go together. I once saw a child born too soon. It had slits on either side of its neck like gills. Sometimes I think we all start out as fish."

"What are you talking about?" she murmured, still distracted by the afterglow of their lovemaking.

"A great mystery," he said.

As he spoke, a flock of shearwaters flew over them, drifting down toward the water and then racing up toward the heavens like a column of black smoke.

"Look!" she cried, and delighted to see how well small things thrived so far from land, she laughed out loud for the first time since they left Orefi.

Perhaps the shearwaters were another sign from Amonah that their journey was blessed, for the wind kept blowing steadily and the weather stayed fair. Little by little, Sabalah stopped worrying and began to enjoy the sensation of skimming across open water. Partly this was because of the beauty of the sea, but it was also because of Arash.

Often when there was nothing on the boat that needed tending to, he took out his *lixah* and sang lullabies to Marrah or some of the songs he had sung to Sabalah when they first met. On one particularly memorable afternoon, they sang the dialogue between two lovers they had sung together last spring at the Festival of the Ewes.

Each day he seemed to grow more loving, more tender. Sabalah sometimes thought that it was as if Arash had fallen in love with her three times: once outside the walls of Shara when he taught her to sing his songs; once on the way to Orefi when he had made love to her so passionately that he had consumed her and swept her away; and once again, here on this boat, his passion turning into a tenderness so sweet that when she lay in his embrace she felt more loved than she had felt since she was a small child cradled in her mother's arms.

Yet sometimes she still had bad dreams. The worst came on the night after Arash made the floating cradle for Marrah. Again she found herself in the Dark Forest running through the darkness. This time there was no path, only branches that lashed her in the face and thorns that tore at her skin. She knew she should stop running and turn around because she was rushing toward something terrible, but she couldn't.

Suddenly she broke out of the forest into a grassy plain that stretched for as far as she could see. The grass was so tall that when the wind tossed it, it looked like the great wave that had capsized her boat on the day Amonah appeared to her and promised her she would bear a child. But in this dream, Amonah was nowhere in sight. Instead, three strange-looking men were running toward her.

They were men like she'd never seen before: tall and pale-skinned with reddish beards, hair white as flax, and eyes as blue as the stones in the necklace her mother had given her on the day she became a woman.

Turn around, Sabalah, Daughter of Lalah! she heard the Great Python's voice cry. *Turn around and run!*

But she couldn't turn. She just stood there, frozen in the grass like a rabbit as the men drew closer and closer and...

She woke abruptly to find herself back in the boat. Arash was on one side of her and Marrah on the other. They were both sound asleep. Directly above the mast, the moon was hanging in the air like a golden kite.

I need to wake up Arash and tell him about my dream, she thought. But when she tried to remember it, she found that it had already gone out of her mind, leaving nothing behind but a vague recollection of tall grass, distance, and danger.

Bad dreams aside, life on the boat was good. Besides the dried fruit, nuts, cheese, hard biscuits, and honey they had brought from Orefi, they had plenty of water and all the fresh fish they could eat. As they moved over that great, trackless blueness, Sabalah felt her mind clearing. In those long, balmy afternoons, with nothing to do except adjust the sails, steer the boat, take care of Marrah, and join Arash in singing the old songs, she found time to look into her own soul where to her surprise, she found a strength she'd never imagined she possessed.

As far as she could tell, that strength had first begun to grow in her in the Python's chamber at the moment she decided to fight to the death to defend Marrah. Before the Sky-God Worshippers had attacked Orefi, she'd been afraid. Now she felt increasingly defiant. *It's Mother strength,* she thought. *Mother fierceness.*

Did all mothers become stronger and braver when the children they loved were threatened? She thought about how mother bears would attack to protect their cubs; how mother lions were more dangerous than anything else in the forest; how even small birds would fly at you and try to peck out your eyes if you disturbed their chicks.

By the time they had been on the open sea for the better part of a week, she had realized two things: First, thanks to her Mother strength, she was no longer afraid of the beastmen or the Sky-God Worshippers who did their bidding. Second, she finally understood the real reason Batal had sent her west to save Marrah.

The attack on Orefi had proved that the Mother People were unprepared for what was coming. In the Motherlands, war only existed as a legend that had no real meaning. There were ancient tales passed down from one generation to another, of battles against ghosts, monsters, and inhuman creatures that attacked by night; but after thousands of years filled with nothing more than local squabbles between villages, almost always resolved peacefully by Councils of Elders, those tales had become as faded and full of holes as a wool cloak left out for the moths. No one took them seriously.

Because they had forgotten what war was and because the Goddess Earth Herself had sent The Divine Sisters to command them to live together in love and harmony, the Mother People had no weapons except the ones they used to hunt with, no walls to keep invaders out of their cities, nothing to stop the beastmen from overrunning them, burning their motherhouses and temples to the ground, and killing every man, woman, and child. The time was swiftly approaching when the people of the Motherlands would need someone to lead them and teach them to fight. They would need a savior, and if Batal's prophecy was true, that savior was going to be Marrah. Sabalah's job was to see that Marrah lived long enough to teach the Mother People how to defend themselves.

It was with all this in mind that she approached Arash one afternoon as he was sitting in the bow dangling his feet in the water. She was glad to find him there, because he had a disconcerting habit of jumping overboard and swimming alongside the boat. Once or twice he had even caught fish with his bare hands, something she'd never seen anyone else do. His swimming abilities were impressive, but it was hard to carry on a conversation with a man who could keep his head under the water longer than seemed normal.

"Arash," she said, sitting down beside him, "do you know how to fight?"

He turned and looked at her with a startled expression. "Why would I want to fight anyone?"

"I don't mean fight someone with your fists. I mean fight with weapons: knives, spears, and the like."

"Do you mean fight with weapons or hunt with them?"

"Fight with them. Do you know how to use weapons to fight?"

"Why do you ask?"

"I'm asking because I need to learn how to use weapons so you and I can defend Marrah if the Sky-God Worshippers attack us again."

There was a long silence. Arash looked down at the water. "No," he said at last. "I don't know how to use weapons. I'm a singer, not a hunter. I can't teach you anything."

He was lying. She could hear it in his voice and in the way he had hesitated before he had answered. He did know how to use weapons, but for some reason he wasn't willing to admit it.

She tried to look into his eyes to see if she could see the lie floating there, but he kept his face turned away from her; and when she touched him lightly on the shoulder, he didn't look up. Instead, he slid into the water and began to swim away from the boat.

He headed straight for the horizon, and for the second time since they left Shara, she thought he meant to leave and never come back. She clenched her fists and gritted her teeth as she watched him swim farther and farther away. *How could he abandon her and Marrah out here in the middle of nowhere! This was an unforgiveable betrayal and...* Before she could complete the thought, he turned and swam back toward her, splashing and laughing and pointing at the horizon. "Look!" he cried.

Sabalah looked in the direction he was pointing, and for the first time since they sailed out of the Gulf of Orefi, she saw land.

There was nothing remarkable about the place where they put ashore for provisions. It was a fishing village much like all the others they had seen on their flight from Shara, except this far south most of the houses were made of stones and mud instead of sticks and mud. Later, Sabalah couldn't recall its name. She only remembered that the meadows that surrounded it were filled with blue borage, pink valerian, and yellow daisies that grew shoulder-high.

The villagers told them they had reached Talpina, the last island of any size before you came to the island of Gira. Encouraged by this news, they set out to sea again as soon as they could fill their water jugs. For three days they followed Talpina's shoreline, moving steadily northwest. The offshore winds were warm, filled with the scent of rosemary, rockroses, and yellow broom. And the sea! Sabalah had never seen such a sea: brilliant turquoise and so clear that it looked more like air than water.

On the morning of the third day, they rounded the tip of the island where a small fleet of fishing boats lay anchored beyond the surf, sailed north hugging the coastline, then turned, put the island behind them, and headed west into the open sea. A little less than two weeks after they sailed out of the Bay of Orefi, they saw the rocky coast of Gira rising out of the sea to greet them.

When she first lay with Arash in the fields outside the walls of Shara, Sabalah had imagined the two of them walking west, following his song map. Instead of walking, they had been forced to sail across open water. Now as their boat approached Gira, she realized they had finally met up with his song.

Standing in the bow with her back to the mast, she began to sing, remembering the sweetness of the words and the sweetness of the nights she had spent in Arash's arms learning them.

When the Queen of the West
calls to her dolphins
the sea trembles,
white foam climbs her thighs.

In the stern, Arash took up the melody, his voice moving in rhythm to the waves.

Gira island of soft nights
Gira island of love
Gira where the maidens dance
Swinging their long black hair

13

SABALAH'S VISION

Rounding the southern tip of Gira, they turned north toward the sacred city of Itesh. As they drew closer, Sabalah felt a growing sense of excitement. In the Motherlands there were three great shrines to the Snake Goddess: Shara, Orefi, and Itesh. Of the three, Itesh was so far west that the Goddess was known there not as Batal, but as Hessa after the little steel-blue grass snake that lived only on the island. Each spring when Hessa shed Her skin, Itesh hosted the greatest religious festival in the Motherlands, and pilgrims came from as far away as the smoking mountain of Omu to wind through the streets in long, serpentine lines, dancing and singing praises to Her.

Unfortunately, they were arriving too late in the year to participate in the Snake Dance, but that night as they entered the Gulf of Hessa and approached Itesh, Sabalah expected to hear the famous drums of Gira pulsing like distant thunder. Instead the city was eerily silent. Its houses were made of rough pieces of granite which glowed softly in the moonlight like a hundred faint stars, but for an instant she saw those houses as something else, something terrible.

Human bones. Piles of human bones.

Her mouth went dry, her heart leaped in her chest, and she felt a terror so great she almost pitched headfirst into the sea. *No! This could not be! Itesh was a city of peace, a city that would endure to the end of time, a city of compassion that had been protected by the Goddess Herself for countless generations.*

She blinked and the piles of bones disappeared. The white stones became houses again. Just houses, some facing the river, some facing the sea. Itesh had not been burned and its inhabitants slaughtered. There were no signs of the beastmen, and yet—

Itesh had no walls, no defenses of any kind. Like Shara and Orefi, it was as open to the sea as a hand extended in friendship. Would the beastmen get this far west? If they did, would Itesh someday be surrounded by high walls? When Marrah grew up, would she have to fight beastmen on this very beach? Would she be forced to defend not only Itesh, but Orefi, Shara, and every other city, village, and temple in the Motherlands? Were those piles of bones a vision of what was to come?

Reaching back, she put the palm of her hand on Marrah's forehead, feeling the warmth of her skin, the softness of her hair. *Little baby,* she thought, *what a great burden you carry.* If only she could spare Marrah the pain of her destiny. For a moment no longer than the blink of an eye, she was tempted to unwrap the Mother Book and see if she could find a prophecy to guide her.

By the time she had managed to put the vision of those bones out of her mind, the wind had dropped off to nearly nothing. They sailed toward Itesh so slowly, they could barely feel the *raspa* moving. The water along the shore must have been too shallow for boats to tie up to docks, because there were no docks. Instead, as they drew closer, they saw that the Girans had set a ragged line of wooden poles in the mud to serve as moorings. The top of each pole was carved with the head of a snake. By the time they got to the first unoccupied pole, Sabalah was ready to get on with the business of securing the boat, but as she prepared to cast a line over the carved top, she was ambushed by such an intense wave of homesickness that she stopped, let the line go slack in her hands, and stood staring at the snake, which seemed to stare back at her accusingly.

"What's wrong?" Arash asked.

"Nothing," she said. "I'm just admiring the river." This was not true, although the Usha River which emptied into the sea just south of the city was certainly worth admiring. In the moonlight it looked like a continuous stream of silver.

The problem was, it also looked like the river that flowed past Shara.

Throwing the loop over the mooring, Sabalah pulled it tight. The wooden snake, worn by water and partially eaten away by salt, had suddenly reminded her of the great painted snake that coiled around the walls of Shara and the beheaded snakes she had seen in Adder's house a few days before they left Orefi. The memory of those snakes had in turn reminded her of her mother and her *aita,* her brothers and sisters, cousins, aunts, uncles, friends, and of Adder and Rock Snake. Were Adder and Rock Snake sitting at their looms worrying about her tonight? Was her mother grieving because her oldest daughter had left Shara without saying goodbye or telling anyone where she was going, taking with her the unborn grandchild she might never see?

She stood for a moment staring at the snake. Its eyes had once been painted bright yellow, but now the paint was so chipped it looked half blind.

When she was a girl, she had longed to travel. She had thought seeing new places would be exciting. That had proved true, but this trip was filled with sorrows that came from more than being pursued by the beastmen and Sky-God worshippers. Again and again, she was being forced to leave the people and places she loved.

Happy people stay home, she thought. *They sleep in their own beds. They don't have to leave their mothers knowing they may never see them again.*

When she was a child, her mother had sung to her in a voice as sweet as birdsong. Her mother's face was kind, her touch gentle. *I will never again be able to bring my problems to her and ask her for advice,* Sabalah thought. *I will never sit across the dinner table from her and listen to her laugh. Marrah will grow up without knowing her grandmother. I will get old in some strange land among strangers, and back in Shara Mother will get old too, and there will always be seas so wide between us that not even love can cross them.* The thought was so painful that tears filled her eyes, but the night was dark and Arash didn't notice.

"We're here," he said cheerfully.

"Yes," she agreed, "we're here." As she checked and tightened the straps on Marrah's cradleboard, she found herself thinking that as much as she loved Marrah and Arash, three people was too small for a family. To be happy, you needed a whole city full of friends and relatives. Itesh, no matter how beautiful it proved to be or how kind its people were, was not Shara and never would be. It was not the way of the Mother People for a woman, a man, and a child to live together in isolation. There was something disturbing about it, something almost sacrilegious.

As they waded ashore, moonlight struck the tops of the waves with lines of pale fire. On the beach, just beyond a row of fishing boats, they were met by two young women who came running toward them laughing.

"Welcome to Itesh!" they cried, stretching out their arms to embrace Sabalah and Arash. "We saw your boat coming in. Everyone else is inside making their evening meals. Sister and brother, are you hungry? Tired? Thirsty? We greet you with love in the name of Hessa and bless the child you bring with you. Tell us what you need, and we'll see that you get it."

"You call me 'brother,' but I'm a stranger," Arash said.

The women laughed and folded him and Sabalah in their arms. "There are no strangers here. We are all children of the Goddess. How could we not love you? How could we not embrace you? We are all of the same blood born from the same great womb."

Those were exactly the words Sabalah needed to hear. The homesickness that lay so heavily in the pit of her stomach began to dissolve. *I think I may like this place after all,* she thought as she embraced first one woman, then the other.

The two were exactly the same height and had the same wildly curly black hair. As Sabalah emerged from their solid, friendly hugs, the moonlight caught them full on, and she saw their faces clearly for the first time. Not only did both have the same hair, they had the same long noses, the same dark eyes, the same heavy brows, the same pointed chins, the same full lips, and the same small, shell-shaped ears. In short, they were twins.

"Are you the famous twin Priestess-Queens of Gira?" she asked, "the ones you Girans call Yashas?"

The twins both laughed at the same instant, their voices so identical that Sabalah couldn't tell where the laugh of one began and the laugh of the other ended.

"No," they said in a chorus, and again they laughed.

"I'm Desta," said the one on the left.

"And I'm Olva," said the one on the right.

"One day," Desta said, "when the Yasha of the East retires, I will become Yasha of the East."

"And when the Yasha of the West retires," Olva said, "I will become Yasha of the West, but that won't happen for years. Both of our Yashas are old but healthy, and Desta and I have a lot more fun not being Yashas."

"Yashas have to sit on the platform during the Snake Dance," Desta explained. "They don't get to dance."

"And they don't get to share joy with strangers," Olva said. "They just sit under the Snake Canopy watching the parade and blessing everyone. During the rest of the year, they preside over the Council of Elders, which isn't easy, because sometimes the Council argues for days about things like whether or not to dig a new well near the old one or put it three hundred paces to the right."

"Boring," said Desta.

"Boring," Olva agreed. Again they laughed in chorus.

"On the other hand," Desta observed, "I'm looking forward to calling up the dolphins when I become a Yasha."

"You're going to get the best of it," Olva agreed. She turned to Sabalah. "When Desta is Yasha of the East, she'll be conducting all the rites connected with birth and life. As Yasha of the West, I'll preside over death and regeneration. Even though I don't get to call up the dolphins, in some ways my training is more interesting than hers. Right now I'm learning how to make potions to soothe grief. Someday when I'm Yasha of the West, I'll be bringing comfort to people."

"Are you learning about the Dark Forest?"

Sabalah immediately regretted the question, but it was too late to take it back. Although she hadn't taken a vow not to talk about the Dark Forest, it seemed likely that she wasn't supposed to mention it to anyone.

She needn't have worried. Both Desta and Olva looked at her blankly. "What's the Dark Forest?" Olva asked.

"Never mind. It's not important." Sabalah flailed around looking for a way to change the subject. "What else does the Yasha of the West do, Olva?"

"Organize the funeral feasts." Olva smiled and her teeth showed white and perfect in the moonlight. "When someone dies, we celebrate their voyage back into the arms of the Dark Mother by eating, singing, dancing, and telling their life story. We all cry for them, of course, but we laugh too. That's Gira in a nutshell: laughter and tears, but laughter most of all. That's the way in all the Motherlands, yes?"

"Yes."

"We've lately come from a funeral feast that lasted for days," Arash said.

"So long?" Desta turned to Olva. "Do we ever have funeral feasts that last that long?"

"Only when a Yasha dies, and that hasn't happened since we were babies." The twins turned back to Sabalah and Arash as if they were both moving on the same pair of legs. "Who died?" they asked in chorus.

"The Great Python of Orefi," Sabalah said.

Desta gasped. "The Great Python is dead? We thought it would live forever."

There was a long silence. Perhaps the twins were so shocked by the news they couldn't speak, or perhaps they were thinking about something else, but it was the kind of silence you didn't interrupt. For a few moments, Arash and Sabalah stood on the beach, rocking from one foot to another as small waves lapped at their feet and the sand shifted under them. Finally Desta spoke. At least Sabalah thought it was Desta. The twins had changed places a few times during the course of the conversation, and she was no longer sure which was which.

"Have you come straight from Orefi?"

"Yes."

"And the Great Python is really dead?"

"Yes."

"You sailed across open water?"

"Yes," Sabalah said, "but how did you know that?"

Olva, or maybe it was Desta, ignored her question. "Did you know that the Great Python was born here in Itesh, and that it had a twin that died at birth?"

Now it was Sabalah and Arash's turn to be surprised. "No, I didn't know that," Arash said. He turned to Sabalah. "Did you?"

"No," Sabalah admitted.

"One twin in the world of the living, one twin in the world of the dead." Sabalah was almost sure that this time it was Olva who spoke. "The Great Python was neither man nor woman; it was the Unifier, the Sacred Bridge between opposites. Tell me, what are your names?"

"I'm Sabalah, Daughter of Lalah."

"I'm Arash, Son of Wanala."

"Sabalah and Arash, did the Great Python give you any gifts before it died?"

"Only a stick, a stone, and a bag of dust." *And the Mother Book,* Sabalah silently added, but she could tell no one about that, not even Arash.

Olva and Desta stopped smiling, and their faces grew serious.

"Did we hear you right? Did you say the Great Python gave you a stick, a stone, and a bag of dust?"

"Yes."

"Wade back out to your boat, get that stick which is fixed to your mast—"

"How did you know it was fixed to our—"

"Unhook that loadstone, Sabalah, Daughter of Lalah. Gather up that bag of dust if you don't have it with you, and wade back here. We'd help you, but the Yashas say you have to bring the gifts of the Great Python to shore in your own hands."

"What? How—"

"Please don't ask questions. Now that we know who you are, we have to take you straight to the Yashas. We can't explain."

"You know who we are?"

"Not exactly," Olva said, "but we know that you've been a long time coming."

14

THE YASHAS OF GIRA

"No, we did not see you coming in a vision or learn about you in a prophecy," the Yasha of the East said, chopping up some onions and throwing them in the stew pot. As the sharp scent of the onions filled the kitchen of the Yasha's motherhouse, Sabalah's eyes began to water and Arash's nose twitched.

Sneezing and crying was not the best way to introduce yourself to one of the twin queens of Gira. Doing her best to fight off the almost irresistible tickling sensation in her own nose, Sabalah tried to distract herself by looking around the room. Except for a few decorative touches, the Yasha of the East's kitchen wasn't that different from Aunt Nasula's. The floor was made of rough cobbles which felt cool under the soles of her sandals. The walls, which had once been white, were smudged with black soot from the cooking fire. Up near the ceiling, a long line of dolphins cavorted in painted waves. In the far corner, she spotted a small altar decorated with fresh flowers. Several ceramic snake tubes protruded from the top of the altar. In front of the tubes, someone had put a dish of milk. No doubt this was the place where the Yasha's house snakes came to be fed.

The presence of snakes in a motherhouse was a good sign since it meant that the place was free of rats, but other than the dolphins and the snake tubes, there were no signs of luxury: only a wooden table capable of seating a dozen or more people; two long wooden benches, both of which looked as if they would rock unsteadily if you sat down on them; twenty or thirty bunches of dried herbs hanging from hooks; half a dozen clay jars filled with water, wheat, and dried fruit; two wheels of cheese; a grinding stone of the roughest kind; a pile of firewood stacked neatly by the clay stove, and the usual assortment of cooking pots, spoons, and knives. As far as Sabalah could see, the Yashas of Itesh did not have special privileges or bigger houses just because they were called "Yashas." Like Aunt Nasula, they worked like ordinary people, and cried like them too when they diced onions.

"As a rule, we don't do prophecy here," the Yasha of the East continued, wiping her nose on the back of her hand. Her hair was gray, her eyebrows bushy, her nose hooked with a little dent in the tip. Several wiry black hairs sprouted out of her chin. Old, respected, powerful, and still chopping onions: that was the way of the Motherlands.

"We leave prophecy to Orefi, Shara, and Kataka. On Gira our specialty is protecting the sacred harmony between the Goddess and her animal children. The city of Itesh rides on the body of Hessa. When Hessa's body moves, all of Itesh moves with Her. The dolphins, who are Her messengers, tell us when She is going to roll over. Hessa moves beneath our city only once or twice every generation, so I doubt you'll get to feel Her sacred power while you're here."

Sabalah was glad to hear that she and Arash weren't likely to encounter an earthquake while they were on the island.

Picking up a bunch of carrots, the Yasha of the East beheaded them with one expert stroke. "Desta and Olva didn't recognize you because your arrival was prophesized. As I believe they've already told you, the Great Python of Orefi was born here in Itesh. Although no one remembers its birth because the event took place so long ago, the Python had a mother and brothers and sisters and aunts and uncles and cousins like everyone else, and two *aitas,* because its first *aita* drowned when the Python was an infant. As far as we know, it didn't leave Gira until it was in its fifteenth year, although again, no one alive is old enough to remember the day the Sacred Snakes came to take it to Orefi.

"In any event, Itesh was the Great Python's birthplace, so it always stayed in touch. A few years ago it sent word that sometime soon a woman would come to us who would need our help. It said we would know her by the girl child she carried on her back and by three gifts it would give her: a loadstone, a bag of dust, and a stick which would be fixed to the mast of her boat. Olva and Desta tell me you sailed into the Bay with the stone, the bag of dust, and just such a stick fixed to your mast. Do you have it with you?"

"Yes, Honored Mother."

The Yasha smiled. "Just call me Njeda. That's the name my *aita* gave me. It means 'Dolphin-born.' Of course at the time, neither my *aita* nor my mother knew I'd grow up to be the Yasha who called the dolphins; but I think they had great hopes for me. Now that stick, please. I'd like to have a good look at it."

Sabalah took the weather stick from Arash and held it out to her. Taking it from her hand, the Yasha of the East ran her finger over the smooth wood. "Such a plain-looking thing, yet so precious, and so powerful that the Great Python itself gave it to you. I can't imagine what you've been doing with it. Is it a sacred stick? Can it part the sea? Charm down birds from the sky? Make an old woman like me young again?"

The Yasha of the East chuckled. Sabalah was liking her more with every moment that passed. She was friendly, warm, welcoming. Whoever had chosen her to be a Yasha had made an excellent decision.

"Not that I'm sure I'd want to be young again unless I could keep the wisdom I've gained over the years." She handed the stick back to Sabalah. "So, seriously, what does this stick do?"

"It predicts the weather. It lets you know when storms are coming."

"Our dolphins do that."

"You can't very well tie a dolphin to the mast of your boat," Arash said.

The Yasha's smile turned into a broad grin. "That's a good point. In any event, you have the stick, and the Great Python told us to do whatever the woman who had the stick asked us to do. So what do you need from us?"

Sabalah was surprised. She and Arash had planned to ask the Yashas of Gira for food, provisions, several nights lodging, and a new sail for their boat, but it had never occurred to either of them that Sabalah might be invited to ask for more. She turned to Arash.

"What else do we need?" she asked. "Can you think of anything?"

"No," he said. "Not really."

Sabalah thought for a moment, ticking off all the possibilities, none of which seemed urgent: Wine? It wouldn't keep. New sandals? Theirs were still in good shape. Salt? They had a whole sea full of salt for the taking. Besides all those things came under the category of provisions, which the Girans would give any travelers who wore pilgrims' necklaces. Why had the Great Python sent such a message to the Yashas? Why had it said they must give her anything she wanted? What could she possibly need that would have been so important that the Great Python itself would had foreseen it? Was it something related to Marrah? Something Marrah needed? But what did a small baby need besides clean diapers, breastmilk, and love?

Safety! she realized. *That's what Marrah needs! She needs to grow up without the fear of being hunted. I need to ask the Yashas to give me something to prevent the beastmen from finding her.* But what could that something be? What would make Marrah safe from pursuit?

Suddenly, she remembered the Python's prophecy: *"A crystal snare. A fish that's not a fish. A baby born on the longest night. Never tell her she was born at Orefi ..."*

That was it! The beastmen had sent the Sky-God Worshippers to Orefi to find a girl child born on the longest night of the year. But what if no such girl child had been born at Orefi? What if Marrah was only one of who-knew-how-many girl babies born somewhere else at some other time?

She took a deep breath. "I need my daughter to be reborn," she said.

The Yasha of the East blinked and did a double-take. "What?"

"I need to find a new birthplace for her."

"I don't understand. Your daughter looks as if she must be at least five months old. Since you came from Orefi, I'm guessing she was born there last winter. Everyone knows the Sacred Snakes of Orefi are the best midwives in the Motherlands."

"I can't tell you when or where she was born."

"Why not?"

"I just can't. All I can say is that, for her safety and mine, I need everyone including her to believe that she was born here in Itesh."

The Yasha of the East put down her knife. "Let me get this straight: you want us to give this baby a second birth, so to speak?"

"Yes," Sabalah said.

"Yes," Arash agreed. "That's exactly what we need."

"Well, as Priestess of the Eastern Temple, I'm the one who would conduct the ceremony, but are you sure about this? My dear daughter, as any woman who has been through childbirth can tell you, one labor for each baby is enough. I've always assumed babies feel the same. Heads squished, little bodies pushed out into the world, exiled from the warmth and love of their mothers' wombs: children are a miracle and the greatest gift of the Goddess, but who given the choice would go through birth a second time?"

"In the name of Hessa, Njeda, give the woman time to explain what she means," the Yasha of the West said, picking the wild onions out of the stew and examining them disapprovingly. He had just entered the kitchen in time to hear the last part of the conversation, and now he stood beside them, feet spread apart, wooden spoon in hand, probing around in the stew pot. With his gray hair, slightly hooked nose, and bushy eyebrows, he looked a great deal like the Yasha of the East, which wasn't surprising since he was her twin. Gira was always governed by twin Yashas. Generally, the Yashas were both identical female twins, but according to Desta, in the past fifty generations at least six pairs of twin brothers and sisters had presided over the Council of Elders.

"Don't take the onions out of the stew, Dviqu," the Yasha of the East pleaded. "Please. If you keep fishing them out, it won't have any flavor."

"They upset my stomach," the Yasha of the West muttered, continuing to pluck the onions out of the stew. "We're old, Njeda."

"Not old enough to give up onions. Stop poking around in the stew. We've got something more important to deal with. Do you understand who this woman who stands in our kitchen is and what she's asking us to do for her?"

The Yasha of the West turned to Sabalah and smiled a wide smile that exposed two missing front teeth. "You must be the woman the Great Python said it was going to send to us, yes?"

"Yes," Sabalah said.

"And if I've heard right, you want that pretty child you're carrying on your back to get herself a new birthplace, correct?"

"Yes."

He turned to his sister. "Well, what are we waiting for, Njeda? The Great Python itself ordered us to give this woman anything she wanted. The moon is full, the Eastern Temple is deserted except for five grass snakes, that rabbit-sized little black-and-white lion you keep as a pet, and the three Sacred Dogs who, as you know, have never much liked the little lion, although I have to admit they will lie down beside the thing. Let's give this pretty little baby a new birthplace right now before the sun comes up. If you can't think of an appropriate ceremony, we'll make it up as we go along, and I'm sure Hessa will understand."

"Is that necessary?" Arash asked. "Couldn't we just agree to tell everyone Marrah was born here on Gira?"

"Arash is right," Sabalah said. "There's no reason for you to go to the trouble of performing a ceremony. I just need you to tell anyone who asks that Gira is Marrah's birthplace."

"That would be a lie." The Yasha of the East frowned. "I wouldn't feel right about lying about something as sacred as a birth."

"Well, I wouldn't mind," the Yasha of the West said. "After all, it's not like it's a lie that's likely to hurt anyone. In fact, if I'm hearing this woman correctly, it's a story that will protect her daughter from some danger she can't talk about. But there's another problem."

He turned to Sabalah. "If we don't give your daughter a real rebirth, then the dolphins won't be able to recognize or protect her if she ever returns to Gira."

"The dolphins?" Sabalah looked from one Yasha to the other. Both were nodding in agreement. "What do dolphins have to do with this?"

"Everything," the Yasha of the East said.

15

MARRAH AND THE DOLPHINS

The Temple of the East was a two-story stone structure decorated with womb signs that included toads, hedgehogs, fish, and large red triangles. That night before the moon set, Marrah was reborn in one of the egg-shaped caves that lay under the Temple.

The ceremony was simple but quite beautiful. The Yashas asked Arash to play his *lixah,* which he did so sweetly that the music nearly brought Sabalah to tears. She could tell he was putting all his love for her and Marrah into his playing, and as she sat on the birthing stool listening to one gentle note follow another, she felt as if he had his arms around both of them. *Nothing will ever hurt you as long as I am with you,* his music promised. *I will protect you and Marrah. I am yours, and you are both mine forever.*

The birthing stool Sabalah sat on was much more elaborate than the simple birthing stool she had sat on to deliver Marrah when she gave birth in Orefi. Decorated with red coils and carved all over with snakes and dolphins, it had a tall back that a woman in labor could lean against when she needed to rest and arms she could grab onto when she needed to push. In the seat there was a large hole representing the sacred passageway through which children came into the world.

The Yasha of the East and the Yasha of the West lay Marrah on a soft white deerskin, took off her clothing, rubbed sacred oil on her forehead, and chanted over her for a long time in a language Sabalah had never heard. To

Sabalah's amazement, Marrah didn't fuss, cry, or try to roll over. She just lay there, grabbing at her toes and smiling up at them as the unfamiliar words moved up and down like music or waves, ebbing and flowing, sometimes as soft as water running over earth, sometimes as loud as surf.

When they finished chanting, the Yashas leaned close to Marrah and whispered more words in her ears, telling her things that only the priestesses of Itesh could tell unborn children. Then they picked Marrah up and handed her back to Sabalah.

"Spread your legs and pass her headfirst through the hole in the birthing stool," the Yasha of the West commanded.

"And yell and moan while you do it," the Yasha of the East added. "No birth is ever completely painless. I've borne twelve children, and although my youngest came the easiest, it still hurt to bring him into the world."

Taking Marrah by the ankles, Sabalah turned her upside down and slowly passed her thorough the hole in the seat of the birthing stool, moaning and yelling as she did so. Marrah did not like this one bit. She squirmed like a fish, her face turned red, and her howls of protest could probably have been heard all the way to Itesh.

Oddly enough, Sabalah couldn't remember what she'd done at the moment of Marrah's real birth, but she did remember the experience had been painful.

"Push!" the Yashas chanted in chorus.

"Push!" Olva and Desta chanted.

"Push!" Arash cried, not to be left out.

Sabalah closed her eyes, gritted her teeth, and pushed. She could feel her womb contract a little, but there was no pain. In fact, the sensation was rather pleasant.

"Quit holding your breath or you're going to faint," the Yasha of the West warned.

Sabalah took a deep breath and tried to bring up memories of Marrah's actual birth. She remembered the smell of the cedar logs burning in the fire pit, the snakes embroidered on the shift the midwives of Orefi had dressed her in, the bitter teas she had drunk. But most of all, she remembered the joy she had felt when she first beheld Marrah and the instant love that had flooded her heart.

"Now!" the Yasha of the East cried.

Opening her eyes, Sabalah found the Yasha of the East on her knees, ready to catch Marrah who was already three-quarters of the way through the hole in the birthing stool. Tightening her grip on Marrah's ankles, she carefully passed her the rest of the way through the hole and into the Yasha's outstretched hands. Again, even though this was only a pretend birth, her heart was flooded with the same great wave of love.

Rising to her feet, the Yasha of the East raised Marrah over her head. By now Marrah was screaming at the top of her lungs, which was just as it should be. A living child always cried as it came into the world.

"Let everyone know that this baby was born tonight in Itesh on the Island of Gira from the womb of Sabalah, Daughter of Lalah!" the Yasha of the East proclaimed.

"Welcome to Itesh, little one!" Desta, Olva, and the Yasha of the West cried. "Blessings, blessings, and more blessings on you, beloved one, dear one, child of our hearts!"

Marrah's face turned bright red, and she gave screech so loud it echoed off the walls. *What are you doing?* that cry said. *Put me down!*

The Yasha of the East smiled, kissed Marrah on the forehead, and placed her back in Sabalah's arms. "You've borne quite a big baby," she said. "We're going to bless her with earth and water now, and I doubt she's going to like that any better than she liked being born. After we're finished, you can nurse her, and with any luck she'll fall asleep."

Kneeling before Marrah, the Yashas rubbed a bit of earth on her forehead and put a drop of saltwater in her mouth to make her part of the earth and the sea. To Sabalah's surprise, Marrah abruptly stopped crying. Maybe she liked the taste of the saltwater. She stared up at the Yashas wide-eyed. *How curious,* she seemed to be thinking. *Who are these big people and why are they talking to me?* Suddenly she made a grab for the Yasha of the West's hair, caught it in her little fist, and pulled.

"Ouch!" the Yasha of the West cried. Reaching up, he gently untangled Marrah's fingers from his hair. Bending over, he gave her a kiss on the forehead. "You're going to be a strong woman," he said, and Marrah smiled as if she agreed with him.

She's going to need to be strong, Sabalah thought. She was again on the verge of worrying about Marrah's future, but before she could put her thoughts in order, a small lion-like animal covered in glossy black fur suddenly jumped up on her lap, put its nose to Marrah's, and began to make a strange humming sound.

"What in the name of the Goddess is that!" she cried. "Is it dangerous?"

"That," the Yasha of the West said, "is Njeda's little pet lion, and it's only dangerous to mice. It eats them just like a snake. Eats the occasional bird too."

Sabalah reached out and stroked the creature's fur which felt incredibly soft. "I've never seen such a thing! It's beautiful. Where did it come from?"

"Who knows." The Yasha of the East shrugged, picked up the animal, and began stroking it. "It just arrived on a *raspa* one day and decided to stay." She scratched the little lion behind the ears, and it began to hum more loudly. Sticking out a small, rough, pink tongue, it licked the Yasha's hand.

Sabalah and Arash both thought the ceremony was over, but it turned out that the most beautiful part of the Giran birth ritual still lay ahead. When Sabalah had nursed Marrah back to sleep, the Yasha of the East led them out of the temple and down to the beach. The seawater was black and smooth as polished obsidian, marked only by the moonlight which left a long, glittering trail. There was no sound of wind or waves; only a deep, holy silence.

Standing on the shore, the Yasha of the East faced the open sea and made high whistling sounds. At first nothing happened. Then slowly the water began to ripple and churn. A silver fin appeared, cutting through the blackness; then another fin and another. Suddenly there were dolphins everywhere, leaping and falling back in a white and black swirl that left Sabalah breathless with wonder.

"Come," the Yasha of the East said. "We must walk into the water and let the dolphins meet you. Once they know you and your baby, they will never desert you. Every mother and child in Gira is protected by the dolphins."

She turned to Arash. “And you too. Don’t hang back. As this baby’s *aita,* you must be introduced to the dolphins. Follow Sabalah into the sea and stand ten or fifteen paces away from her so the dolphins will have room to swim between the two of you.”

With Marrah clasped firmly in her arms, Sabalah waded into the sea followed by Arash and the Yasha of the East. When they were waist-deep, the dolphins began to approach them.

“Can they smell us?” Sabalah asked.

“We think so,” the Yasha of the East said. "We also think they can understand us.” She paused for a moment, then reached out and placed the palms of her hands on Marrah. To Sabalah’s surprise, Marrah didn’t start crying again. Instead, she made cooing noises and stared at the approaching dolphins with wide-eyed fascination.

“Dolphin Children of the Goddess,” the Yasha of the East cried, “I present to you this newborn child, Marrah, Daughter of Sabalah. I present to you her mother Sabalah, Daughter of Lalah, and her *aita,* Arash, Son of Wanala.”

She gave Marrah a nudge. “Walk forward now. You and Arash must stand among the dolphins so they can get to know you.”

Sabalah and Arash took a few steps forward, and as they did so a strange thing happened. The dolphins drew close to Sabalah, gently bumping into her legs and touching her with their long noses in a way that was almost playful; but they fled from Arash as though he were a shark. Their panic was so great and so obvious, that the Yasha called for Arash to come back.

“What’s wrong?” Sabalah asked him. “Why are the dolphins running from you?”

Arash touched the surface of the water with the flat of his hand as if trying to steady himself on it. “I don’t know. If I go back to the beach, do you think you and Marrah will be safe out here?”

“Yes, but I’m sorry.”

“No need to be sorry.” He waded over to her, kissed her on the forehead, and then kissed Marrah on the tip of her nose. “Maybe the dolphins have me confused with something else, a killer whale perhaps.” He smiled wanly. “I’ll have to stop eating so much.”

As Arash made his way toward the beach, Sabalah stood alone, holding Marrah in her arms as one dolphin after another swam up to them showing no sign of fear. Perhaps it was her imagination, but she had the sense they were talking about her in a language she couldn't hear. She wondered if they were related to the dolphins Amonah had conjured up to save her from drowning. It didn't seem likely since Gira was so far from Shara, but as she stared out to sea feeling the gentle touch of their bodies grazing her bare legs, she couldn't stop wondering if Amonah Herself might not come walking toward her over the waves.

The next day, the Yasha of the East summoned Sabalah and Arash to her again. They found her standing on a stretch of deserted beach eating a handful of figs and looking out at the Blue Sea which today was as blue as its name. The sun was high in the sky, and the water was dimpled with small waves that came ashore and retreated leaving behind a net-like foam that glittered in the sunlight.

Not being a woman to waste time, the Yasha immediately got down to business. Finishing off the last fig, she tossed the stem into the sea and looked at Arash. "No one has ever seen the dolphins avoid anyone the way they avoided you when you waded out to meet them last night. They seemed to be terrified. Do you have any explanation for the strange way they acted?"

"No." Arash stared at the sea as if hoping the dolphins might have changed their minds and decided to give him a second chance. "I was disappointed. I wanted them to like me. They were so graceful, and at first they seemed so friendly."

"And you," the Yasha turned to Sabalah, "do you know any reason why the dolphins might have fled from your child's *aita*?"

"No. I was as surprised as Arash was."

"Hmm." The Yasha of the East frowned and looked at Sabalah and Arash for a long time without speaking. Perhaps she was trying to decide if they were telling the truth. If so, she must have come to the conclusion they were, because after a while her face softened and when she next spoke her voice was gentle. "I can only think of two reasons the dolphins fled from Arash: either he eats dolphins—which we all know he doesn't—or the dolphins were confused by his scent. He's the father of Marrah, yes?"

"Yes," Sabalah said.

"That probably explains it. Here on Gira the father of a child is never its *aita*. The *aita* is always the mother's brother or uncle or some other blood relative of the mother. I know that in other parts of the Motherland, fathers become *aitas,* but here they don't. I suspect the dolphins were confused when they discovered your scents didn't match."

The Yasha put her hand on Arash's shoulder. "Don't take it too hard, young man. It's nothing to worry about. I'm sure you'll be an excellent *aita,* and that Sabalah will bless the day she asked you to look after her child."

Three days later, Arash and Sabalah left Itesh, taking its newest citizen with them. From Gira, they planned to travel straight to Lezentka. If the winds were favorable, the weather remained calm, and their luck held, they would step onto dry land again in less than a week.

Not much happened during the crossing except that on the second day out, Sabalah opened the bag of dust that the Great Python had given her and sniffed at it. It still smelled sweetly of lavender and hyacinths, so having nothing better to do, she mixed a small amount with water and dabbed it on the back of her hand. As soon as the mud came in contact with her skin, it turned transparent. Slowly it began to spread until it covered her hand like a glove. When the clear, jelly-like mass began to move up her forearm, she became alarmed and quickly washed it off, but the sweet perfume of its scent lingered for the rest of the afternoon.

"Smell how lovely this is," she said to Arash, holding her hand out to him. "It's like a combination of lavender, hyacinths, and some flower I've never smelled before."

Arash put his nose to her hand and sniffed. "I can't smell anything," he said.

"Nothing?"

"Nothing."

This seemed peculiar, but not very important. Sabalah tucked the bag of dust back in her bundle, and long before they reached Lezentka, she had forgotten that she and Arash could not always smell the same scents.

PART II

THE DARK FOREST

The Goddess Earth will give birth to many kinds of children. Sometimes they will love one another. Sometimes they will conceive children together. Sometimes they will kill each other. The last of the Goddess's children will dig up the bones of their cousins. The diggers will call themselves "Sapiens" and think themselves wise.

—From a page of the Mother Book, which never should have been read

16

WARNING SIGNS

The West Beyond the West

She should have known. That was what tormented Sabalah after it was too late to do anything. All the clues had been there, but she had not seen them.

Except for storms and the attack on Orefi, their journey from Shara had been so free from danger that she had been lulled into believing they were traveling under the special protection of the Goddess. True, they had to wait in Lezentka for nearly a month before they could join a party of traders going west, but that had been only a minor inconvenience. All the way to the painted Caves of Nar, the trails had been wide and well-marked. The land had looked a lot like the land around Shara, and all she had had to worry about was keeping Marrah dry, well-fed, and happy, and finding private places where she and Arash could share joy.

During those weeks, Marrah had changed. Her black hair had grown into a crown of curls, and her sea-blue eyes had darkened to a soft amber. She had begun to put everything she could get her hands on into her mouth, and although she still loved being carried on Sabalah's back, somewhere between the Caves of Nar and Gurasoak, she discovered crawling.

How beautiful those weeks in the south had been, each day filled with sunshine so bright it seemed to lick at the treetops like flame, each night filled with stars and Arash's songs. Every time they made camp, he sang to them in the language of his people. The words of his native tongue were soft and sibilant, full of musical clicks that rose and fell like birdsong.

When they entered the Great Forest beyond Gurasoak, things had become more difficult, but nothing they couldn't manage. They exchanged their sandals for boots and put on leather leggings to keep from being scratched by the underbrush, lit larger fires at night, and kept close track of where they were going since they could rarely see the stars. Long ago, other trading parties had blazed the routes, cutting notches in the trunks of trees to mark the trails. When the traders became confused, Arash always knew the correct fork to take, although how he knew this was something of a mystery.

"I have a good sense of direction," he said. "Trust me."

"You have more than a good sense of direction," the traders told him with frank admiration. "It's like you're smelling the trails and picking the right one."

"Great Goddess, no! I wish I could smell the trails! How handy that would be! No, I lived on the edge of the Great Forest when I was a child. My mother told me never to go in alone. She said the trees ate children." He laughed.

"Mothers often make up stories like that to keep their children safe, but I was having none of it. I was a stubborn boy, born to wander; so one day I went into the forest and promptly got lost. The Forest People found me and kept me with them for nearly a month, teaching me how never to get lost again."

Bending down, he plucked a small, scraggly plant from the side of the trail. "See this? The Forest People call it the *neruhat* which means 'the guide plant.' It only grows where many people or animals have passed. Follow the guide plants, and you can't get lost."

With every day that passed, Arash became kinder and more loving. He was the best of traveling companions: never complaining no matter how long and hard they walked or how little sleep they got. Often he carried Marrah on his back, so Sabalah would be free to gather berries and edible roots. When she returned with a snared rabbit or a basket full of greens, she would find him playing with Marrah or rocking her in his arms and singing to her in his native tongue. Sometimes she found them laughing together as if sharing a private joke only babies and singers could understand.

"While you were out gathering watercress, she tried to pull herself up on my thigh as if she's preparing to walk," Arash would report. Then he would scoop Marrah up in his arms and cover her with kisses.

Although Sabalah never stopped missing her mother and all the friends and relatives she had left behind in Shara, she gradually came to love the Great Forest as much as Arash did. Seemingly endless, it made the forests of the south look stunted. Even at midday in the hottest month of the year, it was cool under the great trees. Taller than any she had ever seen, they seemed more alive than the trees that grew on the shores of the Sweetwater Sea, rising up toward the sky like the pillars of a living temple. Sometimes she wondered if that Dark Forest where souls wandered after death was the twin of this one. Then she would remind herself that the paths she, Arash, and the traders followed led to ordinary places, not different worlds.

Arash taught her the trees of the Dark Forest were called "alders," "hazels," "beeches," 'lindens," and "oaks" in Old Language and *"shruh," "zith," "lash," "niru,"* and *"vuth"* in the language of his people. In Shara the forests were drier and more open, and on moonless nights, the Belt of the Goddess, the Sacred Sisters, and the Path of Spilled Milk shone so brightly you could see the yellow scales on the painted snake that coiled around the city walls. But here the trees grew close together, the air was damp and thick, and the nights so dark, they sometimes made her feel as if she'd gone blind. By day, the light that filtered down through the leaves was as pale as milk. Every once in a while, she caught a glimpse of a few patches of blue sky peeking through the canopy, but these sightings only happened on days when it didn't rain.

Like all dry-land people, Sabalah welcomed rain, as did Arash who took to it like a fish, standing in the open, laughing as his beard was plastered to his face and water dripped off his nose. The traders, who huddled in damp, miserable groups trying to protect their goods from getting wet, didn't share their love of storms; but storms here were such grand and glorious things that Sabalah never ceased to find them exhilarating. First she'd hear the wind rushing through the treetops which swayed back and forth like the masts of boats about to capsize. Then she'd hear tremendous claps of thunder followed by rain drumming against the leaves far overhead. Finally, as lightning flashed all around her, the rain would begin to pour down through the leaves in a deluge that sometimes went on for the rest of the day.

In Shara people believed rain was one of the blessings of the Goddess. If so, this great northern forest must have been particularly blessed since as far as she could tell, more water fell to earth here in a week than fell on Shara in a month.

The last big storm took place shortly before they came to the second great river and parted company with the traders who planned to turn east to trade with the villages upstream. Bidding them farewell, she and Arash journeyed on alone to fulfill Batal's commandment to take Marrah to the most distant part of the West Beyond the West where she would be safe from the beastmen. At first, they continued to follow the trade routes northwest. Then, at Arash's instance, they left the main trail and plunged off into the forest on secondary paths that were so narrow they looked as if they had been made by rabbits.

As they moved deeper into the forest, Arash seemed to grow hesitant, moving more slowly and stopping for long periods of time to stare moodily into the shadows.

"Is there something out there?" she asked him. "Have you seen lion tracks?"

"No," he always said, but he continued to stare.

No had been the answer Sabalah had been hoping to hear. The traders had given them spears when they parted so they could protect themselves from wild beasts, but she had spent her life fishing and collecting wild food, and he had spent his life singing, so neither of them knew how to use spears to defend themselves—unless, of course, Arash had been lying when he told her he didn't know how to fight. By now she was convinced she had been mistaken about that.

"Are we lost?" she asked him after more than two weeks of tramping over nearly-unmarked trails. Have you forgotten how to get to your village?"

"No, I know the way. I just can't do it— "

"Can't do what?"

"I can't ... curse it! This is impossible! I can't!" Ripping off his pack, he heaved it to the ground and strode off into the forest. From the sounds that followed, he must have been beating a tree with a branch because when he returned, his hands were scratched and there were bits of bark in his beard.

"Sabalah, I love you. I love Marrah. I—" Again he stopped speaking, and his face tightened with a misery that made her quickly reach out and take both his hands in hers.

"My dearest Arash, I know how much you love us. Don't worry. You said you knew the way to your village, yes?"

"Yes," he murmured. "It's farther than I remembered, but we're on the right trail. We'll reach the Sea of Gray Waves in a few weeks, then follow the coast north and east to... Aparra." He said the word "Aparra" as if suddenly plucking it out of the air.

"Aparra," she repeated, and was surprised to see tears suddenly stream down his cheeks. So that was what had been bothering him: he had forgotten the name of his own village.

"Yes," he said softly, not bothering to wipe the tears away. "Aparra. Sabalah... " Again he stopped speaking.

"What is it, my love?"

"I wish I could forget the beastmen."

"So do I." Again she thought about how terrible it must have been for him to be their prisoner. Drawing him into her arms, she placed her head against his chest, inhaled the warm, sweet scent of his beard, and felt the beating of his heart.

"Hush." Unstrapping the cradleboard from her back, she hung it on a limb so Marrah, who was sound asleep, faced away from them. Then she drew him down beside her, onto a bed of soft green moss sprinkled with small white flowers. As she ran her hands over his body, feeling the strength of his shoulders, the curve of his hips, the power of his thighs, and the silky softness of his hair, she was overwhelmed by the certainty that everything would work out for the best. She and Arash could never really be lost as long as they were together.

For a long time, she caressed him with her lips and fingertips, not stopping until she felt all the sadness flow out of him. Soon he was grasping her in his arms, moving with her, stroking her hair and her breasts, and murmuring that he loved her, that he would always love her no matter what happened. Love her forever, and protect her.

"Oh sweet man," she murmured. "I don't need protecting." Later those words would come back to haunt her, but at the time they flew out of her mouth and took flight, disappearing into the rustling of the leaves, the scent of his beard, the small circles of sunlight that dappled his body. She felt her spine arch, her lips grow warm, and her own body stiffen against his. Once again, desire rose in a great tide that emptied her mind of everything but the two of them. This time the tide did not sweep her away in its currents. Instead she floated on it, riding it, yet not losing herself in it as wave and wave of joy passed between them.

When at last she lay beside him satisfied, half-asleep, lazily watching the leaves overhead tremble in the afternoon breeze, she realized something had changed: Arash might have forgotten the name of his village, but with every day that passed, he was becoming more and more like he had been before the beastmen took him.

He's healing, she thought. *He's finally coming home.*

She was wrong. He was not healing. Perhaps some part of her suspected this, because the next day, for no particular reason, she found herself staring at the trunk of a massive oak. The oak was so big that if she and Arash had joined hands, they couldn't have encircled it. But it wasn't the size of the oak that had attracted her attention. It was the scratches.

She and Arash had seen similar marks several times in the past few days. They usually appeared at places where the path forked. In fact, they were so often at critical turning points, that if she hadn't known better, she would have thought some kind of beast had been blazing the trail.

Arash explained that the scratches were made by bears who liked to sharpen their claws on the trees, but so far they'd seen no bears nor any traces of them. What they would have done if they had actually met a bear, or worse yet a lion, was a question she did not like to consider.

So no bears, yet the scratches kept appearing. Like all the others, these ran lengthwise down the trunk of the oak, leaving the bark shredded to the quick.

Stepping closer, she spread her right hand, and ran her fingers in the furrows. Five scratches very close together, one of which was off to one side where a thumb would have been on a person. Did bears have thumbs? She was fairly sure they didn't. All the bear tracks she had seen consisted of a tight circle of five oval dots plus claw marks. Still, she wasn't a hunter, and she certainly wasn't an expert when it came to bears. Maybe when bears scratched trees one of their claws drifted to the side.

Turning away from the tree, she began to walk down the trail, hurrying a bit to catch up with Arash. Later she realized that if she had looked at those scratches a little longer, she might have understood everything.

17

ZAKIL

Ever since they stepped onto dry land, Sabalah had slept soundly, and her dreams had been pleasant. Sometimes she found herself walking the streets of Shara, visiting the Temple of Dogs, climbing the cliffs to Batal's temple, or casting her nets into the Sweetwater Sea. On several occasions, she had dreamed she was at Orefi weaving with Adder and Rock Snake or sitting at the table in her mother's kitchen eating dinner with her family. Once she had awakened with the sound of her mother's laughter ringing in her ears. She had been homesick for several days afterwards, but it had been sweet to hear her mother's laugh again even if only in a dream. But just before dawn on the sixteenth day after they parted company with the traders, she woke up screaming. In her nightmare something wild and inhuman had been hovering over her, staring at her with glowing yellow eyes. The beast loved her, but it also intended to kill her.

For a moment she lay there in her sweat-soaked shift with her own screams ringing in her ears. She wanted Arash to hold her until the memory of those horrible yellow eyes faded, but when she called to him, he didn't answer, and when she reached for him, she found he wasn't lying next to her. He must have gotten up to put wood on the fire, but it was odd that he hadn't come back at the sound of her screams. She'd yelled so loud her throat hurt. She felt the spot where he had lain. It was cold, and the deerskins were wet with dew. He must have been gone a long time.

Fighting a growing sense of unease, she turned over to make sure Marrah was still sleeping beside her, only to discover Marrah too was missing. Shallah! Where was she! Throwing off the deerskins, she sat up, looked around, and realized with a mixture of relief and terror that she was still dreaming.

In this new nightmare within a nightmare, she saw Arash standing over her about to plunge a spear into her heart. Arash had Marrah strapped to his back. Marrah looked the same as she did in real life, but Arash looked so different that for a moment she wasn't sure the man who was about to kill her was him. He's taken off all his clothing except his loincloth, she thought. He's shaved off his beard. She shook her head trying to make this false Arash go away, but as Aunt Nasula always said, dreams dreamed you, you didn't dream them.

Frozen in horrified fascination, she watched as all around Arash the pale gray light of early dawn filled the forest. The oak she had been sleeping under looked solid; but Arash's face was emerging from the shadows like the face of a man coming out of deep water, blank at first, then wavering and melting like candle wax. It was a dream face, a face that couldn't possibly be real because Arash's eyes were green, and the eyes of the Arash in this dream were yellow and glowing like the eyes of the beast in her nightmare.

"Go away!" she yelled at the thing that stood over her. But it didn't go away. Slapping her face, she dug her fingernails into the palms of her hands and was surprised to discover that she could feel pain just as she could have if she'd been awake. "Go away! I want to wake up! I want out of this dream now!"

But the dream kept dreaming her, and the Arash, who couldn't possibly really be Arash, kept standing over her looking as solid as the trees. The spear in his hand was quivering; the light was moving across his face. Suddenly his eyes turned from yellow to green, his beard covered his chin again, and his face stopped changing. Sunlight filled the forest, the birds broke into song, and somewhere nearby, a woodpecker began its morning drumming. That was when she realized with growing horror that, impossible as it seemed, this wasn't a dream within a dream after all. She was awake, and the Arash who stood over was real.

For a moment she was so paralyzed with shock she couldn't speak. She stared at him, and he stared back. His lips were trembling, and his left hand, the one that was holding the spear, was shaking. *But he's right-handed,* she thought. As if it mattered which hand he held that spear in. She felt as if someone had let loose a swarm of bees inside her skull. Swallowing hard, she took a deep breath, and tried to gather her wits and understand what was happening.

"Arash?" she said. He was so close now she could smell the scent of the lavender oil they had massaged each other with last night after they shared joy. On his back, Marrah was sleeping quietly in her cradleboard. Anytime now, she would wake up and need to be fed. "Arash," she repeated.

He didn't reply. He just stood there with his spear aimed at her heart. *No,* she thought, *this can't be! He can't want to kill me. There has to be some other explanation.* But she couldn't think of any except that he had gone mad.

Marrah's eyes flicked open, and she gave a small yawn. Putting her thumb in her mouth, she began to suck on it hungrily. Sabalah felt the milk begin to fill her breasts. The *thought my baby is in real danger* hit her like a jar of ice-cold water. Arash had gone mad, and he had Marrah! What was he planning to do with her? Kidnap her? Kill her? She had to get Marrah away from him and run away and hide until he returned to his senses! If only he would speak, explain, do anything but stand there ready to lunge at her at any moment.

Clenching her fists, she swallowed her fear and again tried to think. This time it worked. The buzzing in her head stopped, and an unnatural calmness settled over her. All at once everything seemed to be happening in slow motion. A leaf detached itself from the oak. She watched it fall, taking forever as it rode the morning currents. She had time. There was no rush. She could do this.

Crazy or not, Arash had Marrah. Could she grab the spear out of his hand before he ran it through her? No, not likely. Could she swerve to one side, roll into him, and knock him over? No, he'd be too fast. Marrah would still be on his back, and she'd be on the ground unable to run.

If he had really wanted to kill her, he could have done it while she was asleep. Maybe he didn't know what he was doing. Maybe she could reason with him and convince him to put the spear down. But how did you reason with someone who had lost his mind?

Suddenly she remembered a wild dog that had challenged her one morning outside the walls of Shara, snarling viciously and ready to lunge. She'd spoken to it gently without fear, called it back to itself, and it had stopped barking and let her pass by unharmed. Maybe she could speak to Arash softly and call him back to himself. The most important thing was not to provoke him into killing her, because who knew what he might do to Marrah afterwards. Taking another deep breath, she forced herself to smile at him.

"Arash, what's going on?" she asked in a voice that sounded so bizarrely normal that she could have been asking him what they were planning to eat for breakfast.

He flinched and his eyelids fluttered. Could he be sleepwalking? In a trance? Enchanted? Maybe all she needed to do was wake him.

Suddenly tears began to stream down his cheeks. "I'm supposed to kill you," he murmured, "but ..." His voice broke, and he began to shake. Maybe he was sick. Maybe he was hallucinating. Maybe...

"Why would you want to kill me, Arash?" she asked, keeping her voice low and calm even as another sickening wave of fear crept over her.

Instead of calling him back to himself, the question seemed to make him worse. He lifted his arm as if he were about to throw the spear. "I'm supposed to kill you!" he yelled. "Kill you, do you understand! Kill you!" Marrah began to howl. Resisting an urge to grab her and pull her out of the cradleboard, Sabalah kept smiling at Arash.

"Itik! Rakit iluk! Shakit!" he yelled. He was babbling now. The sounds that were spewing out of his mouth clicked and hissed, at times rising higher than the highest notes she'd ever heard anyone sing. She wanted to clap her hands over her ears, but instead she forced herself to sit there as calmly as possible, all the while thinking: *he's raving, possessed, insane!*

He took a step toward her, then stopped abruptly and stood there trembling like a man being eaten alive by fever. "I can't do it!" he yelled, reverting to Old Language. "I can't hurt you! I'm a failure, a nothing, a clawless traitor!"

"Arash, please, I beg you, calm down."

"The Mordai were right! Humans can't be relied on. Their hearts are too small. They fill up with love too fast. I should have had a Mordai heart like my sisters."

A "Mordai" heart? He had definitely gone mad. Nothing he was saying was making sense. Again she forced herself to smile at him.

"Arash, my love, there's no need to get so upset. You've just had a bad dream. I'm Sabalah, remember? I'm the woman you love. You don't want to kill me. Put down that spear, give me Marrah, come back to bed, and let me hold you."

"Arash?" He said his name with a bitterness that was shocking. Suddenly he turned and heaved the spear toward the opposite side of the clearing. Striking the trunk of a large oak, it stuck there quivering, its point buried up to the shaft. "There is no Arash!"

She stared at him for a moment, once again too stunned to speak. He stared back at her, his eyes glittering with hatred. Hatred for her? For Marrah? For himself? Marrah's howls grew louder.

"You need to lower your voice, Arash. You're scaring Marrah." She looked at the spear, and for an instant she had a sickening image of Marrah impaled on it. "I thought you told me you didn't know how to use weapons," she said softly, fighting the urge to yell at him. *I was right!* she thought. *He said he was a singer, not a hunter. Said he didn't know how to fight. But he did! Where did he learn to throw a spear like that?*

A terrible thought occurred to her: maybe he hadn't gone crazy. Maybe he really had intended to kill her, not on impulse, but coldly and rationally with forethought. How could that be? They'd been best friends, lovers, made a child together. Why would he want to kill her? There was only one reason she could think of, and it was so terrible it made her feel as if all the air had been sucked out of her lungs. "Are you a Sky-God worshipper, Arash? Do you serve the beastmen?"

"No!" He took several steps toward her, seized her by the shoulders, and pulled her to her feet. His grip was firm but surprisingly gentle. The hatred went out of his eyes as quickly as it had come, and again they filled with tears. For a moment he stood there, holding her and letting the tears stream down his cheeks. "I'm not a Sky-God worshipper. I don't serve the beastmen." He spit out the word "beastmen" so bitterly that she had no doubt he was telling the truth.

She wanted to pull away, but instead she continued to speak softly. "Then what's wrong, Arash? What's happened to you?"

"Sabalah, my love, don't ask questions. Just put on your clothes and get out of here before I find the strength to do what the Mordai sent me to do. I won't hurt Marrah. She'll be safe with me."

"Marrah will be safe with you? What are you saying? Are you telling me to leave without Marrah? You know I'd die before I'd abandon her. Please stop talking like this, Arash!"

"I'm not Arash!" Pulling her closer, he gave her a passionate kiss and then held her at arm's length again. "You loved Arash, didn't you? You believed I was him, which means you never really loved me. Why am I jealous? Why does that thought torment me so? You'll probably never see him again. I took his shape and his memories."

"You took his what?"

"I took Arash's shape and his memories."

Was there anything more painful than watching someone you loved go insane? Stay calm, she told herself. *Stand on the outside of his madness. Don't become part of it.*

"Taking someone's memories is impossible, my love. You know it's impossible."

"Impossible? You know nothing, Sabalah! Nothing! Everything you think you know is a lie. I'm not Arash, but I carry him around in my head. Every time I remember something about him, he forgets it. Remember the Python's prophecy? Your Arash is that 'Blind Singer who wanders forever, not knowing who he is.' But I do know who he is, and that's my curse."

She tried to wriggle out of his grip, but he held her fast.

"I remember Arash making love to you in the fields outside Shara as if I myself had made love to you there. I remember the scent of the wild roses, the sheepskins you lay on, the flavor of your kisses, the way you opened yourself to him, the way you adored him. I have his memory of touching your breasts and feeling your nipples growing hard under his fingers, but I wasn't the one touching your breasts all those nights: he was." He pulled her to him and tried to kiss her again.

"Stop!" she cried. "You don't know what you're saying!"

"Listen to me, Sabalah!"

"I am listening! That's not the problem!"

Alarmed by the sound of their raised voices, Marrah's howls grew even louder. Sabalah couldn't bear it. "Give me Marrah, Arash. She's hungry and frightened. I need to nurse her. We can talk about this later."

"Later? You don't understand. There is no later for us, Sabalah. This moment is all we have. All we'll ever have. I'm not Arash, but I've lived inside his head and seen everything he saw. Do you know what it's like for a man to watch another man make love to the woman he loves? Can you understand what it feels like for me to always have Arash's memories of you naked and wanting him? To be haunted by those images and never be able to get rid of them?

"No, I don't imagine you can. Even the Mordai didn't understand that the human part of me would get so tangled up in Arash's memories that I would end up loving you and wanting you as much as he did; how from that moment on, every day I lived, every breath I took would be poisoned with jealousy."

His lips quivered, his voice broke, and he began to sob. "Oh, what's the use? You'll never love me as much as you loved him." Kissing her roughly, he released her and stepped back.

"Get dressed, and leave now. If you still want Arash for a lover, I'll give him to you. That's the only thing I can do to prove how much I love you. I didn't hurt him. All I did was grab him, put my lips to his, and suck out his memories. Arash still eats, he still sleeps, perhaps he even still sings. He's lost in the Sea of Grass somewhere north of Shambah. Maybe you'll be able to track him down. Now go!"

She stared into his eyes trying to find some trace of sanity, but they were as blank as the open sea. Reaching up, she brushed the tears off his cheeks. "Arash, my love," she said gently. "You must calm down. None of the things you've just told me can be possibly be true." Despite the way he was acting, she still felt affection for him. She'd loved him for a long time, and intended to go on loving him once he was himself again. "When the beastmen kidnapped you, they did something terrible to you. I don't know what it was, but you've lost your mind. You can't expect me to leave without Marrah. You can't mean any of this."

"I do mean it, Sabalah. I mean every word."

"Then give me Marrah, dear." Standing on tiptoe, she gave him a kiss on the cheek. "Let me have her, and we'll go away if you insist. But better yet, come sit beside me and we'll pray to the Goddess to restore your sanity."

"Sabalah, I am sane. That's the horror of it." Reaching out, he touched the red crystal in her necklace. "Listen, I stored all Arash's memories in here. I don't need them any longer. If you find him, give him this red crystal and tell him if he swallows it, he'll recall who he is. Now go, I beg you! We're both in terrible danger. If the Mordai find out I let you go, they'll kill me and sacrifice my mother and my sisters to the Ireki."

"Arash, please—"

He shoved her backwards so hard she almost fell. "I'm not Arash, I tell you! My name is 'Zakil.' My mother was a human woman, and my father was of the race who call themselves 'Mordai.' My mother wasn't forced. The Mordai are wonderful lovers, as you know all too well."

Before she could regain her balance, he grabbed her again, pulled her to him, and put his face close to hers. "You lost your mind to pleasure when I touched you, didn't you? Tell me you did. Tell me I was a better lover than Arash. Give me that at least."

"Stop it, Arash! Let go of me!"

"'Zakil.' Say my name. Call me 'Zakil.'"

"No. You have to stop saying such terrible things! You have to remember who you are!" She tried to pull away, but he held her even tighter.

"Sabalah, you're breaking my heart. Can't you love me for who I am? Can't you love me at least a little bit? Have pity on me and tell me you love me at least a little. The only place I've ever felt at home is in your arms."

"Arash ..."

"Every time you say his name, it's like you're jabbing a knife into my heart!"

He was getting worse, not better. Again she tried to pull away, and again he drew her back. Marrah's face had turned bright red. Tears were streaming down her cheeks, and she was screaming at the top of her lungs. *I have to calm him down for Marrah's sake,* Sabalah thought. *Maybe if I can get him talking about something other than his name, he'll stop raving.*

She quit struggling and put her hand on Arash's cheek, which was still wet with tears. "Tell me who the 'Mordai' are, Zakil." She nearly choked on that name, but somehow she managed to continue in the same reasonable tone of voice. "I want to understand. I really do."

Grabbing her hand, he lifted it to his lips and kissed it passionately. "Thank you for that. Thank you, my darling. You ask who the Mordai are? The Mordai are everything I am and everything I'm not. I'm one of them, and at the same time, thanks to my mother, not one of them."

"How can that be?" she whispered, because she couldn't think of anything else to say except to go on repeating that he was crazy. Although she didn't see how her question could have reassured him, it must have, because he grew a little calmer. Dropping her hand, he gave her a weak smile.

"My love, the explanation is simple. Did you think humans were the only children of the Goddess who walked on two legs? The Mordai came here long before humans did. They lived in these lands for countless generations when all the world was still covered with ice. I'm proud of the Mordai part of me. The Mordai are as smart and swift and as beautiful as any beings you'll ever see. They can breathe underwater, and they have webbed hands and a sense of smell so sharp they can scent birds flying overhead at night."

"That's impossible! It's..."

"Please, wait. Hear me out. It wasn't until humans came up from the south and started hunting the Mordai like deer, that they became dangerous. I think the first humans they encountered might have been Sky-God worshippers. Those first humans slaughtered all the Mordai they could find: men, women, and children. The Mordai survivors took the bones of their dead and built a memorial so they would never forget what humans had done to them."

Sabalah stared at him, too horrified to speak. This was worse than she could possibly have imagined. Perhaps he was so far gone in madness that he mistook her silence for encouragement, for he went on with his insane story.

"When the memorial was finished, the Mordai declared themselves the eternal enemies of humans, and then they began hunting them, adding the bones of the humans they killed to the bones of their own dead."

"May the Goddess take this terrible delusion from your mind," Sabalah cried. "Oh, my dear, may She take you in Her arms and give you peace!"

He gave her a look of intense disappointment. "You still think I've gone mad?"

"Yes."

"And you call on the Goddess Earth to save me?"

"Yes."

"Then you still don't understand anything I've been telling you. Don't talk to me about the Goddess, Sabalah. I'm half Mordai, and we Mordai don't worship Her. We worship the Old Ones who live in Lake Calthen, the ones we call the 'Ireki.' Let me make this simple: if the Ireki learn that I've let you live, they'll order the Mordai to track you down and kill you."

"Arash—"

"Zakil!"

She could take no more. This had to stop!

"Zakil, we've talked long enough. Maybe everything you've told me is true. Fine. Let's suppose it is. You say you love me. If you really do, give me Marrah." Reaching over his shoulders, she tried to pull Marrah out of her cradleboard. Marrah reached out for her, but again Arash pushed Sabalah back so hard that she nearly fell over.

"I can't give you Marrah. I never meant to fall in love with you, but I did. The Mordai knew this might happen. They knew my human heart was weak. That's why they're holding my mother and three of my sisters hostage until I return to Lake Calthen with your baby and your tongue."

"My tongue!" He was utterly, violently insane, and he had her terrified daughter strapped to his back. She could not reason with him. She had failed to call him back to himself. She had to get Marrah away from him now!

"I'm supposed to bring them your tongue to prove I've killed you," he said with a matter-of-factness that was more terrifying than his raving. "But don't worry. I have the dried tongue of a deer. I'll take it to the Mordai and tell them it's yours. One dried tongue looks pretty much like another."

Lunging forward, Sabalah threw herself at him and began to pound him with her fists. "Give me Marrah! Give her to me this instant!"

He caught her by the wrists, pushed her back, and held her at arm's length. "No. I'd cut out my own tongue if it would do any good, but I can't give you Marrah. How many times do I have to tell you that if I let you take her with you, the Mordai will hunt you down, kill you, and take her back. The only way you can protect her is to let me take her to them; and the only way you can survive is to get as far from here as you can as fast as you can. Walk back to the trail and follow it north to the Sea of Gray Waves. There is another race of human-like beings who live there who call themselves the 'Watchers.'" They worship the Goddess. They'll take care of you and protect you from the Mordai."

Picking up her leggings and boots he flung them at her. "Put these on, gather up your things, and go to the Land of the Watchers now!"

He gave her no alternative. If you couldn't talk a mad dog out of attacking you, you had to kill it. Bending down, she pretended to pick up her leggings, but when she turned back to face him, she held the spear the traders had given her. She might not be able to throw it accurately, but she could jab it into his neck. The thought of hurting him or perhaps even killing him made her feel ill, but she faced him bravely with her feet apart and looked him straight in the eye.

"Give me Marrah right now, or I'll kill you. Give me my daughter, Arash!"

He took two quick steps toward her, wrested the spear out of her hand, and heaved it into the forest. "You poor, dear, brave, foolish woman. You couldn't kill a rabbit. You still don't believe me, do you? You still think I'm Arash, and I've gone insane? Well then, you give me no choice.

"I didn't steal Arash's body. I simply tricked you into thinking I looked like him. The Mordai part of me can do that, and because I'm also half-human, it was easy. I'm male. I'm about Arash's height. I even have a voice that sounds something like his. But there, the resemblance ends."

Picking up a handful of leaves, he threw them in Sabalah's face. "Look," he commanded. "Look and see!"

The forest around Sabalah suddenly began to whirl. Trees became earth, earth became sky, and Arash became ...

"No!" she screamed. "No! This can't be!"

A tall, handsome man stood in front of her, a man who was human and not human at the same time. He was a little taller than Arash, thinner, lean as a winter wolf, with high cheekbones, a long nose, a slightly pointed chin, and a mane of hair the color of tarnished silver. His skin was golden, burnished with what appeared to be small crystals. On both sides of his neck she saw small slits that looked like wounds, but it was his eyes that set her to screaming again. Arash's eyes were green. Zakil's eyes were yellow, and they glowed like the eyes of the beast in her nightmares.

"This is what the Great Python heard," Zakil said, and opening the slits on either side of his neck, he took a long, hissing breath, exposing a pair of red gills which quivered daintily in the gray light of dawn like the petals of an exotic flower.

18

THE PIECES FALL INTO PLACE

When Sabalah opened her eyes, daylight was streaming through oak leaves. Turning her head, she saw Marrah asleep in her cradleboard. So it had been a dream after all, a horrible dream. For a moment she was filled with relief so intense it brought her to the verge of tears.

A breeze swept through the clearing, and overhead, the oak leaves rustled. Yawning, she turned and saw Arash sitting beside her wringing out a wet cloth which, by the smell of it, had been seeped in the lavender oil they'd brought from Lezentka.

"How do you feel?" he asked.

She peered at his face, trying to bring it into focus, but her vision was blurry, and she had an odd, nauseating sense of disorientation. Everything looked normal except ... She tried to figure out what the exceptions were and came up blank. Maybe she had eaten something spoiled last night. They'd had deer jerky for dinner, but it had been dried and well-salted. The mushrooms, however ...

She coughed and rubbed her eyes, but the blurriness and the unsettled feeling in the pit of her stomach persisted. "I feel terrible." She managed a weak smile. "What happened?"

Arash gave her a worried look. "You fainted."

"Why?"

"I don't know."

"How long have I been unconscious?"

"Most of the morning. I'm not sure you've really been unconscious. I think most of the time you were sleeping."

She shuddered. "I wouldn't call it 'sleeping,' if by 'sleeping' you mean getting rest. I think I may be getting sick. I had the most awful nightmare—the kind I sometimes have when I run a high fever." She groped to recall the details, but they were already fading.

Arash turned around and placed the cool cloth over her eyes. Taking her hand in his, he began to stroke it. She lay back, breathed in the scent of lavender, and relaxed, glad for the comfort of his touch, the coolness of the cloth, and the darkness it brought with it. Her head ached so badly that she was seeing the whirling blue spots that came with pain.

"What did you dream about?"

"It was ridiculous. I dreamed you were—" Suddenly her thumb brushed the space between his thumb and index finger, or rather it brushed the place where the space should have been and found something thin and flexible. Throwing the cloth off her eyes, she sat up so fast she hit her head against the trunk of the tree.

"Who are you!" she yelled. "What are you!"

"Arash."

"Liar! I can tell you aren't him! I can feel the webs between your fingers." Again she squinted, trying to bring his features into focus as they began to melt and flow like wax. Earlier this morning he had frightened her so badly she had fainted, but now in the full light of day her terror was gone, swept away by an upwelling of anger so fierce that she would have gladly run her spear through him if she could have gotten her hands on it again.

"I've got news for you. Your trick doesn't work any longer!" She spit out the words so fiercely he recoiled. "I can see both your faces: Arash's face and your face under his. Your eyes are yellow, not green. Your hair is silver, not black. Your skin looks like you've been rolled in mica. You're a monster, a deceiver, a liar! You aren't fit to say Arash's name, and if you open those slits on the sides of your neck again, I'm going to scream so loud you'll go deaf!"

She leaned forward, thrusting her face into his. "Go ahead. Do your worst. I'm not afraid of you anymore. What were you planning to do? Have another try at killing me when I didn't expect it? Tie me up, take Marrah, and leave me here to starve to death?"

"I didn't have a plan. I could have left while you were unconscious and taken Marrah with me, but if I had, the Mordai would have found you and killed you. I want to protect you. I thought if I could get you calmed down, I might be able to make you understand that you need to leave here as soon as possible."

"Protect me! You call threatening to kidnap Marrah 'protecting me'? Every word you say is a lie!" Jumping to her feet, she grabbed the cradleboard, and strapped Marrah on her back before he could stop her. Picking up the small knife she'd used last night to cut the roots off a bunch of wood sorrel, she faced him with a look on her face that made him step back.

"I'll fight you to the death to protect my daughter. You're not taking her from me. Do you understand? I may be smaller than you are, but I'm quick. I'll slit your throat if you take one step toward us, and if you take this knife away from me, I swear I'll claw out your eyes. What are those horrible red things that make you look as if your throat has been slit?"

"Gills."

"Gills! What are you, a fish?"

"Enough. Stop, I beg you. Please put down that knife. You're upsetting yourself."

"Upsetting myself! I discover that I've been sharing joy with some kind of beast for over a year and you expect me not to be upset! I learn that I've been sleeping next to a thing that wants to kill me and steal my daughter, and you tell me not to be upset! Why isn't Marrah crying? Why is she sleeping through all this? What have you done to her?"

"She's fine."

"What do you mean 'she's fine'? I've been yelling at the top of my lungs, and she goes on sleeping."

"She was hungry and crying. Since you were unconscious and couldn't nurse her, I fed her some acorn mush sweetened with honey."

"What else did you feed my baby! Tell me what else you fed her! If you've hurt her, I'll kill you!"

"There's no need to get so upset. I just gave her a little poppy tea."

"You drugged my baby with poppy tea!"

"I thought it would be better if she slept."

"You're a monster! This is my daughter we're talking about! This is my baby you've drugged!" She gripped the knife so hard the edge of the handle cut into the palm of her hand. If she lunged at him right now, could she kill him before he took the knife away from her? Probably not. The blade was no longer than her little finger. She would have to wait until she could take him from behind.

"What kind of evil creature are you?"

"I'm not evil, Sabalah."

"Don't 'Sabalah' me! Don't you dare say my name! If you're not evil, get out of Arash's body! How dare you strip him of his memories, steal his form, and put on his shape like a festival costume! Show me your real self, Zakil. That's your name, right? As I recall, you said you wanted me to love you for yourself? Well then, show me yourself."

She could see the almost-invisible transparent webs between his fingers more clearly now and small patches of his golden skin burnished with the glittering crystals; but mostly he still looked like Arash, and that made her even more furious. Suddenly she was filled with grief for the real Arash whom she'd loved so much. Arash who had never lied to her. Arash who was good, kind and gentle. In short, Arash who was everything Zakil wasn't.

"Show me your real self. Do it!"

Zakil sighed and put up his hands as if surrendering. "If you insist. I'd hoped I could convince you that what happened between us this morning was a dream, but once a human sees through the veil of illusion, it shreds. I'll never again be able to convince you I'm Arash. You'll always see parts of the real me." He paused and stared at her like a large, miserable, green-eyed dog—or maybe a yellow-eyed dog. The two colors kept alternating in a way that was making her dizzy. Green eyes or yellow: it didn't matter. If he was seeking pity, she wasn't in the mood to give it to him.

"Do it and quit stalling!"

"I don't suppose that there's a chance that after you got used to the way I look, you might—"

"Might what? Love you? Not in this lifetime or my next hundred. I have no idea who you are. I don't even know what you are. Get on with it, Zakil. What else do you have to show me? A tail? A forked tongue? I'm curious. Come on. Throw some leaves in my face. I'm tired of waiting."

"There's no need for me to throw leaves. Most of the enchantment's already come undone. I'm just going to break the rest of the spell you're under and erase the illusion of Arash's body if you're sure that's what you want."

"I've never been more sure of anything in my life."

"Then please try not to scream."

He lifted his arms over his head. For the space of three or four breaths, nothing happened. Then the tips of his fingers seemed to glow. The glow flowed down his arms like honey and everywhere it touched, the veil of illusion dissolved, Arash disappeared, and Zakil took his place. When he had finished, he lowered his arms, and stood there with them at his sides giving her a pleading look that made her feel like slapping him.

She stared at him coldly, searching for some remaining trace of Arash, but Arash was gone. "What are those little shining things on your skin?"

"Scales."

"What are you, half-snake?"

"No, more like part fish."

Suddenly, she remembered the words of the Great Python: *"A crystal snare. A fish that's not a fish."* Why was it never possible to understand a prophecy until it was too late to do you any good! All the pieces were falling into place, all the clues she had dismissed as unimportant. She remembered how Zakil had dived off the side of their boat and swum farther than any human being could swim; how he'd gotten the names of the constellations wrong; how the dolphins of Gira had fled from him; how he'd "forgotten" things Arash would have known.

She remembered how she'd lost her crystal necklace in Ishuna and only found it again after he'd "remembered" how to play the *lixah* she'd gotten for him from the Shrine of the Birds. The next day she'd thought the red crystal had looked paler and then decided it was her imagination. But it really had been paler, because Zakil had sucked the memories of Arash's songs out of it. When the Great Python warned her about the "crystal snare," she'd already been wearing the cursed thing around her neck!

Again she thought of the real Arash whom she'd loved, and how Zakil had robbed him of his memories and left him wandering somewhere in the Sea of Grass where the beastmen could find him, and her anger increased. "Is that all?" she snapped.

"What do you mean 'all?'"

"I mean take off your loincloth. I want to see every part of you. A woman who's been sharing joy with a beast has a right to know how it's made below the waist."

"I'm not a beast. I'm half-human-like and half human. The part of my body below my waist is like any human male's."

"Do you expect me to believe that or anything else you tell me?" She waved the little knife at him. "Take off your loincloth, Zakil, or I'll stab you."

It's a good thing that he didn't smile at that threat, because if he had she might have lost all common sense and tried to kill him on the spot. Instead, he walked over to the other side of the clearing, jerked his spear out of the tree trunk, and came toward her holding it with the point facing downward. For an instant she thought he was going to murder her in cold blood, but instead he turned the spear around and handed it to her.

"Here," he said. "I'm not your enemy. You can kill me any time you want, and I won't fight back."

She stared at him warily. Maybe giving her the spear was another trick to put her off her guard so he could get rid of her and take Marrah. He had his back turned to her. She could throw the spear at him and very likely hit him. But ...

As he began to unwind his loincloth, she watched him, feeling increasingly confused and uncertain. The anger that had blinded her to reason ever since she felt the web between his fingers began to fade a little. Maybe he really did want to protect her and Marrah. It was possible. The forest was huge. She had no idea where they were or how to get back to the main trail. The Mordai, if they really existed, sounded more dangerous than wild beasts. She hefted the spear to shoulder height, then lowered it. *Shallah!* What should she do?

When Zakil turned around, she saw that in this instance at least he hadn't lied. His penis looked ordinary: not big, not small, and at least as far as she could tell, nothing like the penis of anything that swam in the sea, at least not anything she'd ever caught in her nets. It wasn't elongated like the penis of a sea slug, not four handspans long with five heads like the penis of a sea turtle (a possibility that made her wince just thinking about it), not retractable and swiveled like the penis of a dolphin, and not boned like the penis of a walrus or a seal. It didn't even shine like the rest of him. It was just a penis. Which brought up another problem—one she had been trying very hard not to think about ever since she'd found out he wasn't Arash.

"You say your mother was human and your father was a Mordai?"

"Yes."

"And he conceived you with her?"

"Yes."

"Then that means the Mordai can breed with humans the way different kinds of dogs can breed with one another."

"They not only can, they need to." He paused. "Female Mordai, the full-blooded ones, are not ..." Again he paused.

"Are not what?"

"Fertile. At least not often. Human females are fertile all the time. They can have dozens of children if they want to, but Mordai women are only fertile twice a year in early spring and early fall; and their babies frequently don't survive. My father's mother miscarried once and then couldn't conceive again for years. My father was her only child, born when she was almost past the age of bearing children."

Sabalah felt a burst of sympathy for Mordai women. She knew what it was like to long for a child and not be able to conceive. But her sympathy was short-lived, because it made her realize that she was going to have to ask the one question she'd been hoping not to have to ask.

"Is ...?" She couldn't ask him. Not yet. Clapping her lips together, she stopped speaking.

Zakil didn't notice. Bending down, he picked up his loincloth, and put it back on. As he re-tied the knots, she realized that ever since he'd handed her the spear she had begun to see him, not as a beast from a nightmare, but as only a different kind of human being. He moved like a man, talked like a man, had even wept like a man. He was, much as she hated to admit it, attractive. If she hadn't found those webs between his fingers and looked into his glowing yellow eyes, she might have mistaken him for a festival dancer who had dyed his skin with mignonette root and dusted it with mica. On the other hand...

"Zakil, do you have claws?"

He looked at her warily. "What do you mean?"

"I mean that in my nightmare I saw a beast with glowing yellow eyes and claws. For days I've been seeing claw marks on trees. You told me they were the marks of bears, but I don't believe you. So I ask you again: do you have claws?"

"Not exactly."

"What does 'not exactly' mean?"

"It means that I don't have claws, but the full-blooded Mordai do." He spread his hands. "You see my fingernails? They're just ordinary human fingernails. But the Mordai can extend theirs into long, sharp claws; or they can retract them so they look like regular fingernails. This makes them very fearsome in battle."

"Why shouldn't I believe that you have your claws retracted right now?"

"Because I don't. My sisters have claws. Most of the half-human Mordai do, but I don't. When I was a child, everyone used to make fun of me. They called me '*unshuk*.'"

"Which I take it means 'clawless?'"

He nodded.

"The Mordai blazed the trail we're on, didn't they?"

"Yes. They live on the shores of Lake Calthen in a village called 'Hezur Herri.' We're quite close."

"How close?"

"Less than a full day's walk to actually get there, but depending on which way the wind is blowing, the Mordai sentries will be able to smell us long before that. That's why I begged you to leave this morning. If you go on walking with me much longer, it will be too late to save you from them."

"You didn't beg me to leave. You tried to force me to leave without my daughter. You threatened me. You pushed me."

"That was a mistake. I'm sorry."

Sorry? He was apologizing? Her confusion deepened. She lowered the knife, but kept a firm grip on the spear. "Is there anything else I should know about you?"

"Nothing I can think of."

"Oh yes there is. Think harder." She had finally come to it: the question she hadn't wanted to ask.

"I don't know what you mean."

"Let me refresh your memory. You told me Mordai men can conceive with human women. You shared joy with me for months, and still you claim you don't have the slightest idea what I might want to ask you?"

"If you're asking me if you're with child..."

"Of course I'm not asking you that. You and I both know that I just finished my monthly courses. I'm asking you about Marrah. Who's her father, Zakil, you or Arash?"

19

CLAWS

"Arash is Marrah's father."

"Why should I believe you?"

"Because it's true. Three summers ago the Ireki prophesized that a woman with gold in her eyes would conceive a magical child who would be the savior of her people. The prophecy said the woman would live far to the east in a city called Shara. The Mordai immediately sent me to Shara to get you with child. When I finally got there, I wandered the streets for several days disguised as an old man looking into the eyes of every woman I encountered. By the time I looked into your eyes and saw they contained flecks of gold, you were already with child by Arash."

"The Mordai sent you to Shara to get me with child!"

"Yes."

"Are you telling me my baby was supposed to have been born with gills and claws!"

"She probably wouldn't have had claws, but gills, yes."

Shaking with anger, Sabalah hefted the spear to shoulder level again. If he'd made the least sign of resistance, she would have thrown it, but instead he simply stood there looking at her sadly.

"Go ahead. I won't move. That way it will be easier for you to kill me."

She lowered the spear. She couldn't do it. For a few moments she faced him, trying to hate him enough to give it another try, but the only living things she had ever killed were fish and an occasional rabbit. She'd never even slit the throat of a goat meant for her mother's stewpot.

"Go over there, put your clothes back on, and sit down on the bed. I don't want to take the risk of you rushing me and taking away the spear."

"I wouldn't do that."

"I'm not convinced there's anything you wouldn't do. Go now, Zakil."

"Very well." Deliberately turning his back on her, he walked over to the pile of deerskins, pulled on his boots and leggings, put on his tunic, and sat down with his back against the tree, making himself an even easier target.

"Now start explaining and don't lie. I want to know everything: why you were supposed to get me with child, how you knew where to find me, and the exact date you came to Shara. Most of all, I want to know why the Mordai want Marrah so badly that they sent you all the way across the Motherlands to get her."

Zakil shook his head. "That's not a good idea. The truth will just upset you."

"I'll be the judge of that. Start explaining."

He shrugged. "Fine. Remember, I'm just the messenger, so try not to throw that spear at me until you hear me out. I don't know the exact date I got to Shara, but it was less than a week after Arash and you conceived Marrah. I came into your room while you were asleep, saw her already floating in your womb, and knew I'd failed to arrive in time. At that point, she was no more than a glowing pinpoint of blue light, but I had no doubt she was the magical child of the prophecy."

"So then you stole Arash's pack, kidnapped him, took him north to the Sea of Grass, and robbed him of his body and his memories?"

"Yes, but it took weeks. I didn't think there was any rush, so I went slowly so as not to kill him or drive him completely mad."

"Did the beastmen help you?"

"No. I never saw them, or the Tcvali Sky-God Worshippers either for that matter. Everything I told you about the beastmen and the Tcvali came from stories I was told by the Mother People who live along the edges of the Sea of Grass. The Tcvali sounded real enough. The villagers were terrified of them. But I didn't believe the beastmen really existed. I thought the Tcvali had made up tales of men with the bodies of beasts to keep the Mother People from moving north into their lands.

"But when I headed back to Shara to get you, I discovered I was wrong. The beastmen did exist. In fact, there was already a war party of half-human things hiding in the forest outside the city walls waiting to ambush you. Like you, I only got one quick glimpse of them when they passed by us on the trail the night we left Shara, but on two occasions I managed to get close enough to hear them talking to their guides in Old Language. They too spoke about a magical girl child, one who would be the 'savior of her people' and who their shamans predicted would someday destroy them. They knew your name. They even knew Marrah's name. I don't know how they knew all this, but at that point, if I hadn't come along, you would probably have been dead before dawn."

He paused. "Actually, you should thank me for rescuing you. You had a very close call."

"Not a chance, Zakil. Not until rivers flow backwards and trees grow upside down."

"As you wish, but you were lucky it wasn't one of the beastmen who clapped his hand over your mouth that night. The Mordai and the beastmen both want Marrah, but the Mordai don't want her for the same reason the beastmen do. The beastmen want to kill her because their shamans tell them she'll lead her people against them in battle and win. As I said, the Mordai also have a prophecy that predicts she will be the 'savior of her people,' but unlike the beastmen, they don't want to kill her."

"So you aren't planning to take her off somewhere and murder her?"

"No. Please, believe me. I'm doing everything I can to avoid putting her in danger. I love her and want to protect her."

Sabalah felt her spear hand twitch. "Love her, do you? You have a strange way of showing it. Go on. Why don't the Mordai want to kill my baby?"

"She's their only hope. Like I told you, because their women rarely conceive, the Mordai are dying out. They believe that if they can get hold of Marrah and raise her as one of their own, they'll become her 'people,' and she'll become their 'savior' according to the prophecy."

"By doing what?"

"By leading them into battle against human beings and destroying them so they can't keep killing Mordai."

"What!"

"Try to see it from our point of view. The Ireki say that without Marrah, we'll go the way of the great lizards and leather-winged birds. The story of the death of the great lizards and leather-winged birds has been passed down to us from generation to generation. The Ireki say it's the oldest story in the world. They tell it to remind us what will happen to us if we don't succeed in eliminating human beings."

"So it's 'us' and 'our point of view' now, is it? I suppose that's why you can calmly sit there and admit that you Mordai intend to slaughter every human being in the Motherlands, even the ones who've never done you any harm. You really are a beast, Zakil. A talking beast."

"We're not beasts. We just want to survive."

"Be quiet. I've heard enough. I'm going to leave now and take Marrah with me. If you follow us, I'll find some way to kill you just as I'd kill a lion that was stalking me. You and your Mordai relatives have underestimated the love between a human mother and her child." She lifted the spear and took a few steps toward him. "It's the strongest bond in the world. Nothing else can compare with it."

Zakil put the tips of his fingers together in the sign of the Goddess and bowed to her. "In the name of She Who Is Merciful and for your own good and Marrah's, I beg you to listen to what I'm telling you. I'm the only thing that stands between you and the Mordai. Even if you kill me, you'll never get back to the main trail. We entered the Mordai lands several days ago. They know every tree, every bush, every hiding place. They'll hunt you down, kill you, and take her back to Lake Calthen."

"Liar. I think you're bluffing and trying to frighten me just like you did this morning. I bet that lake of yours, if it even exists, is at least a week's walk away. All the scratches on the trees are old. They even have moss growing in them. I think you're the one who's planning to follow me and take Marrah, and I can't risk that."

She drew back her arm and prepared to throw the spear, not for herself but for Marrah. Maybe the Goddess would forgive her for killing Zakil; maybe She wouldn't. But she would rather live for all eternity in the body of a shit-eating fly than risk waking up again to find Marrah strapped to his back.

Yet still she paused.

Throw it! she told herself. *Kill him and get it over with!*

Maybe given enough time she would have killed him, but before she could make herself do it, he slowly rose to his feet.

"Sabalah, my love," he said softly, "put down the spear. We have company."

"Your tricks don't work any longer, Zakil."

"This isn't a trick. Listen and listen carefully. Move slowly, and don't do anything that might be interpreted as threatening. Six Mordai have just come out of the forest, and they're standing directly behind you. One is my half-sister, and one is my cousin. My sister has a freshly killed deer slung over her shoulder. If you take a deep breath, you should be able to smell the blood."

Still convinced that he was trying to trick her into dropping the spear, she took a deep breath and the smell of fresh blood filled her nostrils. For a few moments, she stood there frozen, not knowing what to do.

"The spear," he repeated softly. "Drop it now."

Slowly she lowered the spear and let it fall from her hand. Behind her she heard the sound of voices speaking in strange, sibilant, musical clicks.

"Walk toward me slowly," Zakil whispered, "and try not to show fear. The Mordai can smell fear better than dogs, but we're in luck. The odor of the deer's blood is strong, and when they hunt, they wear mint oil to keep off biting gnats. Come. They don't speak Old Language, so they don't understand what I'm saying to you. If they had wanted to kill you, they would have already done it, but they're confused. They think the child on your back may be the magical child I was sent to bring back to them, but they aren't sure, which means they can't risk throwing their spears at you for fear of hitting her."

Sabalah clenched her fists and began to walk toward him. *I am not afraid,* she told herself. *I am angry. Angry at Zakil. Angry at the Sky-God worshippers. Angry at the beastmen. Angry at the Mordai. Angry at anyone and everyone who threatens Marrah!*

Miraculously it worked. The fear that had been blossoming inside her rolled up until it was no larger than a pebble, and a raw wave of anger took its place, so strong that she might have turned around and attacked the Mordai if she hadn't had Marrah on her back.

When she got within a few paces of Zakil, he reached out, drew her to his side, took her in his arms and embraced her. She stiffened.

"Relax," he whispered. "Try to act as if you find this pleasant. I'm going to tell them you're my mate, but you'll need to look them in the eye. You'll see them as they really are, but they won't know that. They think I'm still tricking you, so you'll need to keep your face as blank as possible and show no fear. If they suspect that I've shown you my real self or don't believe we're lovers, they'll take Marrah and kill both of us—you because you're in the way, and me because I'm a traitor. This is our only chance."

Sabalah turned around and saw the Mordai: three male, three female. They looked almost human, deeply intelligent, recognizable as distant cousins, and yet ... Her mind stuttered and then froze again, not, thank the Goddess, in fear, but in sheer astonishment.

They stood at the edge of the clearing, tall and lean, armed with spears and axes, and naked except for knee-high boots and deerskins which they wore tied around their waists with braided belts. Their yellow eyes glowed like Zakil's, and although they seemed to range in age from fifteen to perhaps as old as thirty, they all had hair the color of tarnished silver. Like Zakil's skin, their skin too glittered with tiny scales, but unlike Zakil's, it was gray and seal-like. Later, she discovered full-blooded Mordai could change their skin color from a grayish-blue to pale gold depending on the circumstances, and that gray was their hunting color.

But it was their hands that set them apart from human beings. All six had long white claws that shone like polished ivory when the sunlight struck them: claws that looked sharp as knives; claws that were fully extended in a way that suggested they were not in a peaceful mood.

Zakil began to speak to them, gesturing at her, himself, and Marrah.

Trying to keep her face blank, Sabalah stared at their claws, thinking how easy it would be for one of them to step forward and rip out her throat, and somewhere inside her chest she felt the first trembling that preceded panic. Again, she tried to summon up anger, but this time she failed. The fear began to rise toward her throat, and she had the sense of falling into a dark hole of terror from which there would be no escape.

Bless them. Love drives out fear.

The words formed in her mind so clearly that she could hardly believe one of the Mordai hadn't spoken. But the voice that uttered them was not Zakil's nor the voice of a stranger. It was the voice of the Great Python. Impossible. But what did it matter.

I am not afraid of you, she thought looking straight at the Mordai. *I bless you. I come in peace. I am not afraid of you. I bless you in the name of She who is the source of all blessings.* Was it working? She had no idea, but as Zakil continued to speak, she went on silently blessing them.

Gradually, her heart slowed, her hands grew warm, and a sense of peace came over her. She felt elated, as if she had drunk a whole pitcher of fermented honey. *I do not have to fear* them, she thought. *Even if they kill me right now, the Great Mother will take my hand and lead me through the Dark Forest to another life.*

Yet beneath those thoughts, she could feel the fear still coiled inside her: fear for herself, fear for Marrah. How long could she keep this up? How long before those fears drove out love instead of the other way around?

The female Mordai with the deer slung over her shoulder—the one Zakil had said was his half-sister—threw the deer carcass to the ground, lifted her head, sniffed the air, and frowned. Then she pointed at Sabalah and said something to Zakil in a harsh tone of voice.

Uttering a two-syllable word that could have only meant *No!* Zakil quickly stepped in front of Sabalah, putting his body between her and the Mordai hunting party. They must have wanted her to come closer so they could smell her and see if she was afraid.

Zakil spoke more animatedly, waving his arms and gesturing at Marrah. Even though she could not understand a word he was saying, Sabalah could tell something had gone wrong. Before, he had been talking in an even tone of voice; now he seemed to be pleading.

Several of the Mordai spoke, apparently asking him questions. Then one of the males said something that sounded like a command.

Again, Zakil said the word that must have meant *No!*

"Unshuk!" the Mordai male yelled. At that the whole group lifted their spears to shoulder height, and Zakil's sister began to speak rapidly in an angry tone of voice.

Suddenly whirling around, Zakil grabbed Marrah out of the cradleboard, pulled out his knife, and held the sharp edge to her throat. Marrah should have been howling her head off by now, but she was so drugged with poppy juice that she lay limply in his arms and only her eyelids fluttered.

"Scream!" Zakil yelled in Old Language. "Scream, but don't try to get Marrah away from me! I'm not going to hurt her, but I have to make them think I'll kill her if they try to rush us. They won't do anything to endanger her. My cousin called me a clawless coward and demanded that I slit your throat and hand over Marrah. When I told him that wasn't going to happen, my sister called me a half-blood traitor. They say they're going to kill you themselves, claw out my eyes, take me back to Lake Calthen, and throw me to the Ireki. I have to buy us time to convince them they're making a big mistake. Scream as if you think this is real!"

One look at that knife at Marrah's throat was all it took. Sabalah screamed at the top of her lungs, but she didn't try to wrest Marrah away from Zakil. He wasn't lying. The Mordai were all yelling now, aiming their spears straight at her but not throwing them. It was clear they intended to kill her, and that the only thing stopping them from doing it immediately was the fear that Zakil would kill Marrah.

"We need to bargain with them," Zakil said. "But we don't have anything but Marrah to bargain with. Sooner or later they'll realize I'm not going to slit her throat. If you're thinking I can plead with my sister to spare me because she's my sister, think again. She's a full-blooded Mordai, and with very few exceptions the Mordai only love one another. The lives of humans, even half-blooded humans, mean no more to them than the lives of rabbits. As far as they're concerned, you're the beasts. They're the real people."

"What are we going to do?"

"I have no idea. Stall as long as we can. Keep yelling at me as if you're trying to make me give you Marrah, but don't make any sudden moves."

Sabalah took a deep breath, threw back her head to yell, and dislodged the empty cradleboard so it swung forward and smacked her on the back of the head. The blow brought everything into focus. It was like waking from a nightmare.

"Zakil!" she yelled. "Keep holding that knife to Marrah's throat! I just realized we have something to bargain with!"

20

Bargaining With Haserre

As soon as the words left her mouth, she realized she was wrong. She and Zakil had nothing to bargain with, because the only thing they could offer the Mordai was something the Mordai could never be allowed to get their hands on.

She remembered the Great Python holding the Mother Book, tapping the image of the snake swallowing its own tail. *Stretch out on the floor face down and embrace the Earth. I'm going to make you take a vow so sacred that if you break it you may die. Repeat after me: I will never tell anyone the Mother Book exists. I will keep its existence a secret, carry it to safety, and defend it with my life.*

The Mordai had dipped their hands into the deer's blood and smeared their faces with it. They were moving toward her slowly now, cunningly trying to cut her off from Zakil since she no longer had Marrah on her back. She had two choices: she could break her vow and perhaps stop them, or she could keep silent and die.

I will die, she thought, *die and keep my vow.* But what would her death accomplish? The Great Python hadn't made her promise to die. It had made her promise to defend the Mother Book with her life. Letting the Mordai kill her wouldn't be a defense. It would be surrender.

Zakil yelled something at the approaching Mordai and moved in front of Sabalah, shielding her body with his. They halted, clearly frustrated.

Stepping forward, his sister smiled, lowered her spear, and began speaking in a softer tone, pleading, wheedling, making her words sound like a caress.

"She's saying that I'm not a traitor, and that she forgives me. She says..."

"That if you give her Marrah, she'll let you live, and you can come home, yes?"

"Yes."

"Do you believe her?"

"I don't know. She's always been treacherous. When I was a child, she killed my dog and ate it."

"Ate it!"

"Out of jealousy, because she thought my father loved me more than he loved her. She felt she should have been the child he loved most. She's the oldest and a full-blooded Mordai. My sisters and I are half-human. She's never forgiven my father for giving her to his human mate to raise after her Mordai mother died, and she's never forgiven me for being born. She's wanted to get rid of me since I was a baby."

Sabalah looked at Zakil's sister, bloody, glittering, swaying back and forth as if she were dancing to the rhythm of her own lies. She looked at the five Mordai hunters who were in motion again, spreading out in a half circle. One had almost reached the point where he could throw his spear at her without hitting Zakil or Marrah.

So it had come to this: she and Zakil were about to die. His sister would take Marrah and raise her as a Mordai. Perhaps if Marrah didn't show signs of being their savior, the Mordai would sacrifice her to the Ireki or drive her out into the forest to starve like an abandoned pet. As for the Mother Book, the best she could hope for was that the Mordai wouldn't bother to take the cradleboard with them, and the Book would rot here undiscovered along with her body and Zakil's.

In that case, Orefi's greatest treasure, the book that the Goddess Herself had dictated to the Third Python, the book in which all things past, present, and future were written, would be lost forever. It would not be there when human beings decided to love the Goddess Earth again and nurse Her back to health.

That was terrible enough, but what if the Mordai took Marrah's cradleboard, opened her pillow, found the Mother Book, and learned how to read it? The Great Python had warned that whoever possessed the Book would possess the greatest power to do good or evil ever placed in human hands. If the Mordai got the Mother Book, those hands wouldn't be human. They would have fingers that ended in claws.

Zakil's sister was still talking, but Sabalah no longer listened to her sibilant clicking. Closing her eyes, she prayed for guidance: *Batal, Amonah, Hessa, Great Mother, help me! Tell me what should I do.* There was no reply. Nothing. Not a word. Not a vision. Nothing.

She was on her own.

"Zakil," she said. "Tell your sister that she's the fool. Tell her that if she kills me, she will kill the Mordai's only hope of surviving as a people. Tell her that if they throw their spears at me, the Mordai will disappear from the face of the Earth like the great lizards and leather-winged birds."

"She'll never believe me."

"Yes she will, because it's true, and I can prove it."

"My love, it's no use. We're going to die here together. We need to protect Marrah. I'm going to pretend to believe my sister's offer. I'm going to walk over to our bed now and put Marrah down on it so she will be safe. The moment I take my knife from her throat and move away from her, my sister will give the command to throw the spears.

"You won't feel any pain. You'll die instantly, my darling, but I won't. They'll only wound me so they can take me back to Hezur Herri alive, blind me, and sacrifice me to the Ireki as a traitor. I love you. I would have given my life to save you and Marrah. I've failed to protect you, and for the rest of the time they let me go on living—which won't be long—I'll feel a grief so blinding that I won't care when they claw out my eyes. What use are eyes when you can no longer see the ones you love? What use are... ?"

"Zakil, shut up!"

Shocked into silence, he closed his mouth and stared at her in disbelief.

"You're being heroic, but we don't need heroism. Keep holding that knife to Marrah's throat and don't move. We aren't going to die either here or anywhere else if I can help it. I'm going to speak to your sister now, and I want you to translate for me. What's her name?"

"Haserre."

"Does she have a living child?"

"No, she's never been able to conceive."

"Good. First tell her the things I told you to say about how she needs to spare my life unless she wants the Mordai to die off like the great lizards and leather-winged birds. Then tell her that I have something to say to her woman-to-woman. Are women powerful among the Mordai?"

Zakil nodded.

"Good. Start talking."

Zakil closed his eyes for a moment as if resigning himself to failure. Then he opened them, turned to his sister, and began speaking. Sabalah could tell from Haserre's reaction that he wasn't convincing her, but she'd expected that.

When Zakil finished, Haserre turned to the others, and they spoke for a while in low voices that sounded like a breeze passing through flutes. As Sabalah stared at them, wondering what they were saying, she had trouble reconciling the beauty of their bodies and their language with their determination to kill her. The only things that made them look like beasts were their claws, their glowing yellow eyes, and the deer blood on their faces that hid the shining of their skin.

Turning back to Zakil, Haserre said something to him in the same soft, wheedling voice she had used before.

Zakil turned to Sabalah. "My sister is now saying that she's sorry for calling me *unshuk*. She says that if keeping you alive can help the Mordai survive, then I'm a hero for not killing you, and that when we get back to Hezur Herri, I'll be honored. She says that she can smell that I love you..."

"Smell it!"

"Yes. She also says that she thinks she can tell by your scent that you love me. She says it must run deep because the smell of your love for me is strong."

"More likely she's smelling my love for Arash."

"Yes, but she doesn't know that. The bad part is that she's said she's willing to accept you as my mate if that's what I want, and to let you come back to Hezur Herri with me to explain how you can save the Mordai."

"Why is that the 'bad part'? It sounds good to me."

"It's bad because my sister has never apologized to me before, and because she still has her claws extended. Don't look at her face. Look at the tips of her fingers. Her claws say she's lying."

Sabalah took a deep breath and silently asked the Great Python for forgiveness. Then she spoke. "Translate for me now, Zakil, and make sure you get every word right. From the way your sister's claws are twitching, it's clear we won't have a second chance to talk our way out of this.

"Say this to her: 'Haserre, I greet you in peace and with blessings. I bring you my daughter who will be the savior of your people, and I bring with her something that will ensure that from this day forth you and all women of the Mordai will bear living children who will grow up healthy and strong.'"

The expression on Haserre's face when she heard this promise was such a mixture of anger, surprise, hope, and pain that Sabalah felt sorry for her even though she knew Haserre was planning to kill her with no more thought than she'd give to killing a rabbit. The longing for a child; the pain of not being able to conceive; the perpetual disappointment and false alarms; the overwhelming grief; the hope that tormented you and refused to fade into resignation: she knew all the sorrows of a woman who could not conceive. How much stronger that grief must be when it came with the fear that, because you and other women who looked like you could not bear children, your people might cease to exist.

Haserre stood for a moment, looking for all the world as if she were going to cry. Then her face hardened, and she began to yell angrily.

"She's cursing you and calling you a liar. She says that it's going to be a real pleasure to kill you, and that she's decided to do it slowly. This isn't working."

"Speak to her softly, Zakil. Tell her that wrapped in the pillow of the cradleboard is a magical book—does she know what a 'book' is?"

"No, and neither do I."

"Then tell her that there's a magical charm hidden in the pillow of the cradleboard that will make the women of the Mordai fertile."

Zakil spoke, and again Haserre responded angrily.

"She says to thank you for telling her about it, and that after she cuts out your heart, she will unwrap the pillow, take out the charm, and carry it back to Hezur Herri. If you have spoken the truth, she says, Mordai women will bear so many children that the Mordai will soon outnumber humans. She says she thanks you for sealing the doom of your people."

"Tell her gently that cutting out my heart would be a bad idea because without me the charm is useless, and Mordai women will go on not being able to conceive. Tell her that I am the answer to her prayers."

"She doesn't pray."

"Then tell her I am the answer to her hopes. Tell her that she has nothing to lose and everything to gain by letting me live. Tell her that I will show her the magical charm which must be handled very carefully to prevent it from being damaged. Tell her that I am the only one who knows how to make it work and that if she takes me back to Hezur Herri, I will prove this; but only if she keeps her promise and spares your life too. If you die, I will tell her nothing no matter how long she tortures me. She must let both of us live, or she will never bear a child."

Zakil's eyes suddenly filled with tears. "You are saving my life even though I deceived you?"

"Don't misunderstand, Zakil. This changes nothing between us. I'll never forgive you for what you did to Arash or for tricking me into sharing joy with you and leading Marrah and me into danger, but you've tried to protect us. When you were forced to choose between being human and being a Mordai, you chose to be human. I honor you for that, and I won't see you killed because of me if I can help it. Now speak to your sister before she gets impatient and skewers me on the point of her spear. And by the way, remind her that if she discovers I'm lying, she can always kill me at her leisure."

Again Zakil spoke. Haserre waited until he was finished and then gestured toward the cradleboard. When she replied both her words and her voice sounded different.

"She says she wants a baby beyond all things. She says if you can make this charm do what you claim it can do, then she is willing to spare your life, but you must show it to her. She doesn't want you trying to escape if there's nothing inside that pillow."

"Do you think she's lying?"

"No, this time I think she means what she's saying. The Mordai have two languages: Rimash, which is the one they use for talking about most things, and *Lu'ka,* the tongue they only use when talking to or about children. My sister spoke about wanting a baby in *Lu'ka.*"

"But still she might be trying to trick us?"

“Yes, but what choice do we have?”

“None I can think of.” Reaching up, Sabalah undid the straps that held the cradleboard and let it slide to the ground, knowing that the moment she bent down to retrieve the pillow, she would make herself vulnerable to the Mordai’s spears. She looked at the tall oaks, the morning sunlight, and three white butterflies that were dancing above a small yellow flower that grew at Zakil’s feet. How beautiful life was. What a precious gift her mother had given her when she brought her into this world.

Turning her back on the Mordai, she knelt and began to unstrap Marrah’s pillow from the cradleboard.

21

THE JOURNEY TO LAKE CALTHEN

As she knelt, she discovered she was still clutching the little knife she had threatened Zakil with. The Mordai either hadn't noticed or hadn't cared. Most likely, they had dismissed it with contempt as too small to do them any harm. Could she prove them wrong, whirl around, throw the knife at Haserre, and cause enough confusion that she and Marrah and Zakil could escape?

No. Even if she did manage to plant the knife in Haserre, the blade was too short to do any real damage, plus there were five other Mordai poised to impale her and Zakil on their spears at the slightest provocation. Flipping the pillow over, she took hold of the case and cut the knot that held the lacings.

A ray of sunlight caught the blade of her knife and the polished obsidian shone for an instant. *Great Python, forgive me. Amonah, Batal, Hessa, forgive me for breaking my vow. I can't let the Mordai take Marrah from me. You can't ask a mother to choose a book over her child. If I die, who will protect her? Who will love her?*

Tugging on the leather laces until they gave, she opened the pillowcase, pulled out the Mother Book, unwrapped it from its waterproof jacket, removed the final layer of doeskin, stood up, and faced the Mordai.

"Nishx ishtel leruahasha ne!" Haserre gestured toward the book with contempt.

"What's she saying now?"

"She's accusing you of trying to pass off an empty box as a magical charm. She wants to know what's inside."

"There isn't anything inside a book except pages."

"Pages? I don't understand."

"The book itself is the 'charm.'"

"She's not going to believe that. You have to show her something."

Sabalah thought for a moment. Haserre's demands were growing more insistent. You didn't have to speak Mordai to know that she was about to decide the whole story of a fertility charm was a lie.

"Tell your sister that this 'box' is full of magical leaves made from the skin of a..." *What could she call vellum that wouldn't make it sound like scraped calfskin?*

"Tell her the magical leaves are made from the skin of ... a Great White Snake that flies through the air like a fish swims through water." *This was idiotic. There was no way Haserre was going to believe this.*

Taking a deep breath, she decided that if she was going to invent a ridiculous myth, she might as well make it as ridiculous as possible. "Tell her that when the Great White Snake flies, birds land on its body, leaving their tracks on its skin like the tracks gulls leave on a beach."

Holding up the Mother Book so it caught the light, she pointed to the front cover. "Tell her this is why the box is stamped with the image of a snake swallowing its own tail."

Zakil looked impressed. "A powerful charm, indeed." Turning, he relayed Sabalah's lie to his sister, who also looked impressed.

"She wants you to show the magical leaves to her."

Opening the book, Sabalah held the spine against her chest and began to turn the pages so the Mordai could see the white velum covered with black writing. Apparently Zakil had believed her story. He'd spent time in Orefi and even spoken to the Great Python. If he didn't recognize the Mother Book for what it really was, there was little chance his sister would. Maybe this was going to work.

As she turned the pages of the Mother Book, a low exclamation of awe rose from the throats of the Mordai and disappeared in a clutter of excited clicks. The hunters shifted from foot to foot like a band of excited children, all except Zakil's sister who stood so still she might have been made of wood.

Gesturing toward the Mother Book, she said something in a tone of voice that sounded almost respectful.

"She wants you to give the charm to her so she can take a closer look at it."

"Tell her 'no.'"

Haserre was obviously not used to being told "no," because again her face hardened and her next words came out as a snarl.

"She says if you don't give the charm to her, she will take it from you by force. Actually she said she would 'rip it out of your puny, clawless hands.'"

"Tell her that I was sealed to this charm by the Great Python of Orefi. Tell her that if anyone besides me touches it, it will lose all its power, and that baby she longs for will never grow in her womb."

Zakil gasped. "Did the Great Python really give this to you?"

"Yes. Will your sister know who the Great Python is?"

"Yes. The Great Python was named in the prophecy of the Ireki as the only being in the world as powerful as they are."

"Good. Then just for good measure tell your sister that anyone who takes this charm from me will be cursed forever by the Great Python's cold curse."

"What's 'the Great Python's cold curse?'"

What have I gotten myself into? Sabalah thought. When she was a child, one of her older cousins had told her that up north in the city of Kataka the priestesses of the Dark Goddess could curse you with a cold fever if you injured the Earth, but that was probably only a rumor brought to Shara by some trader who liked to scare children. Even if a cold curse existed, it had nothing to do with the Great Python.

She fumbled around, searching desperately through all the curses she had ever heard—a half dozen at most, the majority dealing with warts and stomachaches. Finally, she came up with something original. It wasn't brilliant, but at least it fit the occasion.

"The Great Python's cold curse goes like this:
Those who take this charm by force are doomed.
Cold hearth, cold fields, cold heart, cold womb."

Zakil's golden skin turned pale, and his hand trembled.

"Watch what you're doing, Zakil! You almost nicked Marrah's neck! Translate before your sister grabs this book out of my hands and claws it to shreds trying to figure out where the magic in it is hidden. While you're at it, tell her that the Great Python of Orefi greets her through me and blesses her, and that this charm is for all the women of the Mordai, not just for her. We might as well sweeten our threats with a little honey."

Zakil translated. As he spoke, a look of awe came over the faces the Mordai. One by one, they retracted their claws.

Haserre looked disappointed. Clearly, she was an ambitious woman. Perhaps she had thought that if she could take this 'charm' for herself, she could rule the Mordai. It was frightening to think how close she'd come to the truth.

When Zakil finished speaking, there was a long moment of silence. Finally Haserre lowered her spear and gestured to the other Mordai to do the same. Speaking in a quiet voice she pointed at Marrah.

"What does she want now?"

"She says she believes you. She's telling me to take the blade of my knife away from Marrah's throat because since you carry a gift from the Great Python, you and I no longer have anything to fear. She says she is going to let us live and take us back to Hezur Herri."

"How do we know she's not lying?"

"Because she's drawn in her claws."

Sabalah felt such a strong wave of relief that if she hadn't backed up against a tree to shield herself from the Mordai spears, she might have staggered.

Removing the blade of his knife from Marrah's throat, Zakil held her out to Sabalah. "Put her back in her cradleboard. Don't let them get their hands on her, or you may never get her back."

Sabalah crammed the Mother Book back into its original wrappings and stuffed it into the pillowcase. Lacing up the case, she reattached the pillow to Marrah's cradleboard. Then she took Marrah from Zakil, strapped her back in, and covered her with kisses. "Darling," she whispered, "Mama's here. You're safe."

Marrah slept on, limp and breathing softly. For a long time Sabalah had been holding back her fear, but now it all rushed over her at once: Would Haserre keep her promise? Would the Mordai kill her as soon as she turned her back on them? Would Marrah ever wake up?

She began to tremble. *Dear Goddess,* she thought. *The Mordai will smell that I'm afraid of them!* But the Mordai didn't, because Zakil smelled her fear first. Seizing the bottle of lavender oil, he dumped it over her head in a sticky, warm stream.

"I'm going to tell them this is a blessing from the Great Python!" he cried in Old Language. The Mordai must have believed him, because the moment the Mordai words left his mouth, his sister—his fierce, blood-stained, gray-skinned, terrifying sister—smiled.

The trail to Hezur Herri was narrow, twisting, rough, and at times hardly visible, but the Mordai hunters walked along it in long, sure strides as if it were wide and well-traveled as the main trade route between Lezentka and Nar. Haserre led the way, followed by Zakil who appeared to be keeping up a surprisingly friendly conversation with his sister considering that she had recently called him an unclawed traitor and threatened to blind him and sacrifice him to the Ireki. Next came two of the Mordai hunters and then Sabalah with Marrah on her back.

Behind Sabalah, walking so close she could feel his breath on her neck and smell the scent of the mint oil he'd rubbed on his skin, came Zakil's cousin Irgo, a large, silent Mordai with a broken nose and hooded eyes. The remaining two Mordai hunters brought up the end of the procession, walking so silently that if Sabalah had not felt Irgo give her a small shove from time to time to urge her forward, she might have imagined an empty trail stretching out behind her.

As far as she could tell, Irgo wasn't shoving her out of rudeness. On the contrary, he was trying to help her along. The Mordai were stronger than most humans and had longer legs. All of them, including Zakil, walked so swiftly that she often had to run to keep up with them, a task made more difficult by the weight of Marrah, who was finally showing signs of waking up from her poppy juice-induced nap.

After a while Sabalah began to feel like a small child trying to keep pace with grown-ups. Her legs ached, her chest heaved, and her breath burned in her throat. The worst of it was, the Mordai never slowed down. They just went on relentlessly, chatting with one another in their odd, musical language as if they were out for a stroll on the beach.

Could she ask them to walk more slowly? Would they see this as a sign of weakness? She tried to walk even faster and stumbled. Catching her before she could hit the ground, Irgo gave her another friendly push forward.

"Sziz c'ulk," he said. Was he telling her to get a move on? Asking her if she was tired?

"Sziz c'ulk," she repeated, trying to imitate him as closely as possible.

Irgo gave her a startled look. Great Goddess, what had she said? If she survived this forced march intact, she was definitely going to have to learn Mordai.

Finally Marrah made the decision for her. Waking up, she gave a loud wail that said in no uncertain terms: "I'm hungry!"

At the sound of her crying the Mordai came to a stop so quickly that Sabalah ran into the back of the person in front of her—a young woman who had her silver hair braided and coiled like Aunt Nasula's, although Aunt Nasula would never have used a claw to hold the coil in place.

"Uf!" the woman said, turning to Sabalah to glare at her with glowing yellow eyes.

As Sabalah stood there wondering how to apologize, or if indeed she should apologize, Zakil walked back to her.

"The baby needs to be fed," he said.

"Obviously." She instantly regretted snapping at him, but she didn't need to be told Marrah was hungry. What she needed was to sit down before she fell over.

"I can't keep up with them, Zakil. I have to rest."

"Try to keep going a little longer. There's a clearing not far from here. Haserre says when we reach it, you must sit down and nurse the 'magical child.'" He lowered his voice to a whisper. "We have to stop calling her 'Marrah.' We need to give her another name. I just hope it's not too late."

"Why?"

Zakil looked sideways at Irgo who seemed to be paying no attention to them. "Because I am going to help you escape to some place where the Mordai will never find you. If they don't know her real name or yours, it will be harder for them to track you down."

"But you already said her name to your sister a dozen times."

"No, I didn't. I always called her 'the magical child.' Quick: I can only keep this up for so long. What shall we call her?"

"How about ... 'Valina.'" Valina was the name of her cousin who had been serving at the Temple of Dogs on the day the dogs told her she carried Marrah in her womb. It was an auspicious name, pretty, easy to remember.

"Valina she is from now on. And you?"

"I have no idea."

"How about 'Soina?'"

"Where did you come up with that?"

Zakil looked uncomfortable. "It's the name of a little girl Arash loved when he was a child."

She stared at him, amazed. How generous to offer her a name taken from the life of the man she loved. "Soina will do fine," she said quietly. "Thank you."

For a moment they stood there silently staring at each other. Then Marrah gave another howl.

"We have to start walking again."

"They're moving too fast. I don't know if I can make it to the clearing at this rate."

"You have to. Haserre has contempt for humans. She thinks they're weak. So far you've shown her she's wrong. You need to keep showing her that she's underestimated your strength. It's only a little farther to the clearing. Once we get there, you can nurse ... Valina. Valina always goes to sleep afterwards. I'll tell my sister we shouldn't wake her. You can rest as long as you like."

"Is this necessary?"

"You have no idea how necessary. Please. Try. I could carry you both, but that would make you look weak."

"Fine. Lead on."

Returning to the front of the line, Zakil spoke to Haserre who nodded and gestured for the march to continue. Once again the Mordai strode down the trail with Sabalah running as fast as she could to keep up. Fortunately, the clearing proved to be as close as Zakil had promised. Spotting a fallen tree on the far side, she stumbled over to it, removed the cradleboard, and took out Marrah who by now was screaming at the top of her lungs.

"Hush, hush, sweetheart," she murmured, and pulling down the front of her shift, she put Marrah to her nipple. As Marrah sucked hungrily, she sat back and tried to catch her breath. Her feet and legs were burning, and she felt giddy from fatigue and lack of water. Didn't the Mordai ever drink? Maybe they didn't have to. They were part fish after all. Did fish drink? Now there was a puzzle she was not likely to solve in the middle of the Great Forest.

22

HEZUR HERRI

Except for Haserre who occasionally cast a jealous glance in Sabalah's direction, the Mordai seemed uninterested in the sight of their 'magical child' nursing. Presumably Mordai babies nursed the same way human babies did since, as far as Sabalah could tell, the breasts of Mordai women were exactly like human breasts except for a coating of glittering scales. Gathering at the other side of the clearing, the Mordai took out a small board and began to play some kind of game that involved holes and wooden pegs. From the way they acted, they appeared to be gambling, although what they were betting was more than Sabalah was equipped to figure out since the only word of Mordai she recognized so far was *unshuk*.

After a while, Zakil excused himself from the game, came over to her side of the clearing, sat down beside her, and offered her a leather bag filled with water which she emptied in four thirsty gulps.

"I love you," he said as she handed the water bag back to him.

"Don't start in on that again, Zakil."

"I want you to know that no matter what happens, I'll do my best to protect you and Marrah."

"You haven't done a very good job so far."

"You're right, and it's going to get harder. That's why I need to talk to you before we get any closer to Hezur Herri. There are things you need to know."

"Such as?"

"Has it struck you as strange that you're always in the middle of the line when we walk?"

"No, should it?"

"Yes. Haserre should have put you up front where she could keep an eye on you, but instead she has put you between her two fiercest fighters. That's to keep the Mordai sentries from clawing out your throat before anyone can tell them that you've been given permission to enter our lands."

"Did you just say Mordai sentries might claw out my throat?"

"Yes. The Mordai don't allow human beings to enter their lands. Any human who strays past the claw marks that indicate the border is killed instantly. In a little while, probably when we least expect it, Mordai sentries are going to drop down out of the trees onto the trail in front of us. There's a lot of brush, and it's hard to see very far, but they will have been smelling you for a long time. If you were at the front of the line, they might kill you before Haserre could stop them."

"I don't understand. I thought you said your own mother was human. Why wasn't she killed?"

"She is human, but she came to the Mordai lands voluntarily under the protection of my father. Mordai men never force human women to be their mates, but once a woman agrees, she's made to understand that once she enters our lands, she'll never be allowed to leave on pain of death."

Sabalah stared at him in dismay. How would she and Marrah ever get away if the Mordai were willing to kill any human woman who tried to leave their lands? "Hasn't anyone ever escaped?"

"I'm not sure. I once overheard my mother talking to a human woman who had changed her mind. The woman was begging to be allowed to return to her family. My mother told her there were rumors that every once in a while a woman who couldn't conceive was taken back to the Motherlands and set free. My mother said that before the sentries let a human woman go, they always forced her to drink a potion that made her forget all about the Mordai."

"That's awful! Who are you if you can't remember where you've been or what you've done! What kind of potion could do that?"

"I don't know. The ingredients are secret. I think it's made from plants that only grow around Lake Calthen.

Whatever it is, it's powerful. The Mordai know a lot about herbs and potions, and they don't take risks. The point is, they've spent generations hiding from humans. No humans except the mates of Mordai men are ever allowed to see our village or even know about its existence. Which brings us to the next thing you need to know before we get there: You're going to have to pretend to be my mate. We're going to have to live in the same house and lie in the same bed at night. You need to smell of me, and I need to smell of you."

Live in the same house with him? Share a bed with him? Smell of him? Never! The thought of being intimate with this creature that had taken Arash from her made her skin crawl.

"No!" she hissed.

"Wait, please. Hear me out. I won't force you to mate with me. I'll not so much as touch you except to hold you in my arms at night so our smells can mingle. I promise you'll be able to control everything between us except that and the fact that when we're in public, you'll have to pretend to love me."

"I don't love you!" Her anger had faded a little when he had promised to help her and Marrah escape and given them new names, but now it welled up again. "I'll never love you! Get this straight, Zakil: **I do not love you.** Before your sister and her friends showed up, I was seriously considering putting a spear through you, an act which probably would have given me considerable satisfaction."

"Hush. Not so loud. Haserre is looking our way and we can't let her suspect we're fighting. You're supposed to be madly in love with me."

Sabalah opened her mouth to object, but he gestured for her to be silent.

"Please. Not now. If you want to yell at me, wait until we're alone. You've got every right to hate me, but our lives are at stake. We have no choice but to pretend to be mates. Humans aren't allowed to see Mordai in their real form unless they're the mates of Mordai."

"What do you mean 'see Mordai in their real form?' You told me your sister and the others didn't know I could see them as they really are."

"That's what I thought, but I was wrong. My sister isn't stupid. She saw how surprised you were when you first caught sight of her. She didn't smell fear on you, but she saw you look down at her fingers and flinch. From that, she concluded that you could see her claws, which meant that I must have broken the spell you were under by showing myself to you. The penalty for a Mordai showing himself to a human who isn't his mate is death. That was one of the reasons she called me a traitor."

"Zakil—"

"Please. Don't ask questions. We don't have much time before Haserre begins to suspect we aren't just talking about the weather. I need to kiss you."

"No! Absolutely not!"

"Shush, listen. Lower your voice. We need to put on a show of affection right now before Haserre figures out what's going on."

"No," she hissed, "never! You evil, treacherous beast! You're trying to do to me what you did to Arash!"

"I swear by the mother who bore me that I won't take a single memory from you. Just let me kiss you, and then I'll get up and walk to the other side of the clearing."

"Liar! You've kissed me with Arash's lips a thousand times." Again she felt a great wave of grief for Arash wash over her. "You probably sucked out all my memories long ago. Every time we shared joy, you must have taken more of them. You've pillaged my most intimate secrets. I'm surprised I can still remember my own name."

"No, I swear, I didn't. I kissed you, yes, but I didn't take your memories. It isn't done that easily, and it would have harmed you. I left you with all your memories intact, at first because I wanted you healthy and whole when you bore your baby and then..."

He paused. "Oh my love, my dearest love, all I saw when we shared joy was how good you were, how kind, how loving and tender. That's what made me fall in love with you. Kiss me, I beg you. Kiss me now so I can go on protecting you, and I'll never ask again."

Removing Marrah from her breast, Sabalah smoothed down her hair and began to rock her. When Marrah was asleep, she turned to Zakil who was still there waiting for her answer.

"I'd rather put my lips to the mouth of a poison toad than kiss you," she said. "Now go away."

When Marrah woke from her nap, Haserre rose to her feet and signaled for them to start walking again. As before, the Mordai strode down the trail so fast Sabalah had to run to keep up. Fortunately, they didn't go far before two Mordai sentries suddenly dropped out of the trees with their claws extended.

Haserre yelled something, and the sentries immediately came to a dead stop and drew in their claws. Presumably she had just ordered them not to claw out Sabalah's throat—at least Sabalah hoped so.

The sentries approached her and began to sniff at her like dogs. Putting a finger under her chin, the shortest sentry lifted his face to hers and bent toward her lips. Marrah made a soft, cooing sound. Perhaps she was fascinated by the sentry's gills. What a blessing to be so young that you didn't know mortal danger when you saw it.

"Nish c'culnuk sakit!" Zakil yelled, grabbing the sentry by the shoulder and shoving him away from Sabalah.

"Culnuk?" the sentry said.

"Clunuk."

The sentry grinned. *"Clunuk seu sni'lunz xxit, Zaliluh unshuk."* Reaching out, he grabbed a handful of Sabalah's hair.

"Don't scream," Zakil warned, "and don't move."

The sentry ran his fingers through Sabalah's hair, twisted it into a braid, lifted it to his nose, smelled it, and gave her a leering smile that needed no translation.

Smell me all you like, Sabalah thought. *I'm not afraid you, but if you touch Marrah, I'll rip out your gills.* Somewhere, deep inside, she could feel terror, hard, small, and very much alive, but it wasn't rising to the surface. To protect Marrah, she couldn't afford to show fear, so she didn't.

Staring the sentry straight in the eyes, she returned his smile. "So you think I'm attractive?" she said sweetly. "So you think I have pretty hair and that maybe you could persuade me to leave Zakil and be your mate? Well think again. Take me to your bed, and I'll kill you in your sleep. You have to sleep sometime, and there are plenty of rocks around here big enough to smash your skull."

Startled, the sentry dropped her hair and drew back, muttered something to Zakil, and walked back to the head of the line where Haserre and the second sentry were waiting for him.

"Well done," Zakil said. "Heldu says you're no danger to the Mordai, and that as long as Haserre wants to take you to the village, he has no objections. He also says you're pretty for a human woman, but you smell like big trouble and talk like it too, although he admits he couldn't understand anything you were saying. He says that since I'm an ugly, puny, unclawed half-blood, I'm welcome to you."

Sabalah looked at the sentries who stood at the front of the line involved in some kind of extended discussion with Haserre. That had been a close call, much too close.

"Are other Mordai men going to try to kiss me, and if they do, how are we going to stop them from stealing my memories and finding out everything I know including Marrah's and my real names?"

"Stealing human memories isn't easy if you're a full-blooded Mordai. It's easier if you're half human, but even then, only a handful of half-human Mordai can do it without destroying the mind of the human they're entering. I'm by far the most skilled of the lot, which was one of the reasons I was sent to Shara. That's why I took so much time with Arash. I wanted to keep him alive."

"Am I supposed to thank you for that?"

"No." He hesitated.

"Go on. I'm not going to bite you. What else?"

"I told Heldu that you're my mate, and that we have the Right of Each Other's Lips. That means no one is allowed to kiss you but me, but I'm not sure the story that we're lovers will hold up once we get to Hezur Herri. They're going to take us before Tratatu and Ahizpa who will decide whether we live or die. Tratatu will probably believe us because he's my father, and despite the fact that I'm only half-Mordai, he's always liked me better than Haserre. Ahizpa is the one we have to worry about. She's borne six living children, the most in the history of the Mordai."

"I've had a lot of experience talking to wise old women who run things. My Aunt Nasula is the Priestess-Queen of Shara."

"You don't understand. Ahizpa is old, but she isn't wise. She's stupid, capricious, bitter, jealous of youth and beauty, and can be very dangerous, but she's able to make men fertile."

"Did you say that she makes men fertile?"

"Yes. When a Mordai woman doesn't get with child, it's considered the fault of the man."

"Are you telling me I've promised to make all the men of the Mordai fertile?"

"Yes. Can you do it?"

"No, of course not. I've been lying through my teeth to save our lives. I thought you realized that."

Zakil's golden skin went almost white. "No. I thought ..." He looked toward the sentries who still stood at the front of the line talking to Haserre. The one who had tried to kiss Sabalah was flexing his claws like a cat.

"I had no choice."

"But the magic charm the Great Python gave you ..."

"There is no magic charm, at least not one that can help Mordai women bear children. I thought I might be able to find one of the roots or herbs the midwives of Shara use, but I don't know anything about increasing the fertility of men."

"But you showed us the skin of the Great White Snake."

For a moment she was tempted to try to explain what a book was, but that would only lead to questions she couldn't afford to answer. "It's not snakeskin, just calfskin, scraped, bleached, and stretched."

"And the Great Python's cold curse—what about that?"

"Doesn't exist. I made it up."

Zakil, who had faced the Mordai spears without flinching, looked as if he were on the verge of panic. "This is bad. Very bad. My father isn't a stupid man. He speaks Old Language. He's lived among humans and gotten half-blood children on human women. He's going to order you to prove that you can make that charm work. If you can't do what you promised—"

"I have a horrible feeling that you're about to tell me that you'll still love me as they claw out your eyes. If so, please be quiet."

Zakil clamped his mouth shut and stared at her. His fingers were twitching nervously. If he'd had claws, they probably would have been twitching too.

What now? Should she pray to Batal for help? Make a dash for freedom and see if she could outdistance the Mordai who could walk faster than she could run, not to mention claw gouges in oak bark as easily as she could make footprints in sand?

Running was obviously futile and praying to Batal hadn't worked the last time she'd tried it. She had to think, so she thought, and as she did, time seemed to slow down. In a space that seemed to last forever, but which in reality probably only took a few moments, she weighed their options, and to her amazement, found some. The first was time itself. Given enough of it, anything might happen.

"Take a deep breath, Zakil, through your throat or your gills or whatever works best, and calm down. We aren't beaten yet. Mordai women are only able to conceive children in the early spring and early fall, yes? Well, it's late summer right now. That should give us a few weeks, before anyone can tell if my 'charm' works. Actually it should give us more than a few weeks since a woman usually doesn't suspect she's with child until she misses her courses."

"Mordai women know immediately."

"That's not good, but we still have time to escape. I have a plan. To make it work I'm going to have to convince your father and Ahizpa that I possess magical powers."

"Can you?"

"Possibly."

"How?"

"I can't tell you." *Because you aren't ever supposed to know. Because the moment I read so much as a sentence of the Mother Book I will have broken my vow. But what else can I do?*

"But you think you can do it?"

"Yes."

Zakil looked relieved. By rights she should have felt relieved too, but something was still tickling at the back of her mind, something Zakil had said about the Mordai building a monument to their dead.

"Zakil, 'Hezur Herri' is the name of the Mordai village, right? The one on the shores of Lake Calthen that Haserre is taking us to?"

"Yes, that's right."

"What does 'Hezur Herri'—" She stopped, afraid to go on, because suddenly she knew the answer to her unasked question.

"Are you asking me what 'Hezur Herri' means?"

She nodded, suddenly feeling a terror so great she couldn't speak. It was the same terror that had been with her ever since Zakil had showed her his real self, but multiplied a hundred times. Leaping up, it exploded in her like a forest fire. Again she saw the white houses of Gira shining in the moonlight like piles of—

Zakil reached out and put his hand on her arm to steady her. "What's wrong, my love? Why do you smell so frightened? All 'Hezur Herri' means in Mordai is 'The Village of Bones.'"

23

The Village of Bones

In the Motherlands, there were no fortified cities. Long ago The Divine Sisters had commanded the Children of the Goddess to live together in love and harmony, and for the most part, they did. Where fences existed, they were built to keep out deer and prevent goats from eating laundry. Most walls were so low a child could vault over them. Even the walls of Shara would not have kept out a determined rabbit.

But the Mordai did not live under the Peace of the Goddess. According to Zakil, their ancestors had been slaughtered by human beings who did not worship Her. In their bitterness and grief they accused the Goddess of abandoning them. Turning away from Her, they built a wall of brambles around Hezur Herri that was almost as high as the trees that surrounded it. Their wall was like no other wall in the Motherlands: it was a wall made of fear, and when Sabalah first saw it, she had no idea what it was.

Coming to a stop so suddenly Zakil bumped into her, she stood staring in disbelief at the great swath of briars. The leaves stretched toward the sun, shining like small green cups. Hanging from the stems were uncountable numbers of succulent black berries mixed with uncountable numbers of red ones that had not yet ripened. There were so many, she could have picked enough to feed all of Shara within a few paces of where she was standing.

Reaching out, she plucked a handful and put them in her mouth. They were delicious. As their sweetness exploded on her tongue, she reached for more. Marrah was asleep, but when she woke she'd be hungry again. She was still too young to eat the berries whole, but the juice would be a treat for her.

"Come," Zakil urged. "We need to walk on. Move away from the wall before you scratch yourself."

"The wall?"

Zakil pointed at the brambles. "This is the *Marubi.* 'The Wall of Briars' in Old Language. The Marubi surrounds Hezur Herri. In fact the Marubi goes around the entire lake. Now come. Haserre is getting impatient."

Sabalah looked toward the head of the line and saw Haserre glaring at them, her claws twitching in and out. Wiping her berry-stained fingers on her shift, she turned away from the vast tangle of briars, and she and Zakil began to walk again, following the narrow trail that skirted the edge of the wall.

"What purpose does the Marubi serve?"

"It keeps out our enemies."

"Enemies? What enemies? You told me that the Mordai kill any human who strays into their part of the forest."

"But what if we missed one?"

Sabalah felt like telling him no human was likely to get past the Mordai sentries, but she held her tongue. The Mordai were clearly terrified of being attacked. Was it their fear that made them so ruthless?

The Mordai need to put their past behind them, she thought. *The Motherlands are at peace, and they have no reason to be afraid.*

Or did they? Were the Motherlands really at peace if the Sky-God worshipping people like the Tcvali could come down from the north and attack Orefi? Should they build a wall of brambles around Shara? Should there be a wall around every city and village in the Motherlands? Were the Mordai stuck in the past, or were they preparing themselves for what was coming?

She mused on this for a long time as they followed the trail that skirted the edge of the Marubi. Bit by bit, an idea was forming in her mind, but she couldn't quite get hold of it.

At last, they came to a round hole cut in the briars guarded by five Mordai sentries who pulled their claws in as soon as they saw Haserre. The hole was so small and low that anyone entering the Marubi was forced to crawl.

Re-strapping the cradleboard to her chest to protect Marrah from the thorns, Sabalah crawled through a tunnel of brambles and came out to find herself facing another wall made of earth and rocks. This wall was even higher than the Marubi. At its foot was a trench filled with sharp sticks. At the top stood more Mordai sentries armed with spears and axes. There was no hole in this wall, but a narrow path led up its side in a series of steep switchbacks bordered with loose gravel.

Sabalah stared at the wall, trying to understand what the Mordai had been thinking when they built it—a long time ago by the look of it. It was ingenious, fascinating, and horrible. No enemy could make it to the top before the Mordai sentries threw their spears and sent the invaders down to be impaled on the sticks at the bottom.

No beings should have to live behind such a barrier to survive, she thought, and for the first time she was filled with pity for the Mordai. What must it be like to live in fear from the day you were born until the day you died?

Suddenly the idea she had been trying to grasp all day came to her with a clarity so perfect that she wondered why she had not thought of it before. The Mordai fought because they were afraid. They killed because they couldn't trust. They were like cornered animals, beautiful, proud, desperate to survive. If she met their anger with anger, she would provoke their hostility. If she fought them, she would only make them more afraid and more murderous.

Bless them. Love drives out fear.

Again she heard the words of the Great Python, but this time it was her own voice that spoke to her. *Love the Mordai, because love is the way to their hearts.*

By the time she reached the end of the trail, she was out of breath but elated. She knew now what she had to do. She must bring the love of the Goddess back to the Mordai. She must try to give them back the Mother they had lost.

The first thing she saw when she came to the top of the wall were more Mordai sentries; and behind them Hezur Herri, The Village of Bones, the place she had dreaded since that night she and Arash, who had not really been Arash, sailed into the Gulf of Hessa and she saw the houses of Itesh as piles of human bones. Yet now when she looked at the real Village of Bones, her dread was gone, replaced by love, compassion, and pity for these beautiful creatures who were the last of their kind.

Hezur Herri was a small community that huddled at the western end of Lake Calthen like a clutch of birds' eggs. Later she learned there were only about two hundred and fifty full-blooded Mordai left in all the Motherlands. About a hundred and fifty of them lived in Hezur Herri and the rest were scattered along the shores of the Great Western Sea.

The village was laid out in a double row with a wide path down the center that led from the shore of the lake to a large mound of earth of the sort that the Mother People called a "barrow." Barrows were always hollow inside, so this one, given its size, probably served as a temple.

There were one or two small houses, but most of the dwellings were longhouses. The roofs were thatched and covered with bark. The walls were made from saplings that had been woven together with sticks and reeds and chinked with mud. Seen from the top of the wall, the houses of Hezur Herri would have looked like a collection of beautifully woven baskets if it had not been for the bones.

They were everywhere: attached to the roofs, arranged in patterns along the sides of the main path, stacked up in a great mound at the edge of the lake and in another great mound in front of the barrow.

Near the lake, to the left of the mound of bones, was a great circle of still more bones with something big at the center. The thing, whatever it was, looked like an arch, but from here it was hard to tell. To the right of the mound of bones, lying at a considerable distance from everything else, were the ruins of a stone building. Most of it had fallen down, but it looked as if it had originally been built in the shape of a female body: hips, breasts, thighs, and even something that looked as if it might have been an inner womb-shaped room. Had it once been a temple to the Goddess?

Lake Calthen itself was more or less oval in shape, quite large and probably very deep since its waters looked as blue as the waters of the open sea. At present, it was calm, but it was easy to imagine its surface roiled by winter storms, white caps smashing into one another and waves crashing onshore. She was just trying to figure out if the lake froze over in winter when she felt someone give her a small shove. Turning, she found Zakil's cousin Irgo motioning for her to continue down the trail that led to Hezur Herri.

"Sziz c'ulk," he said.

That sounded familiar. Maybe he really had been telling her to move on the first time he'd said those words. Or maybe he was offering to take her for his mate. In any event, repeating the words of a language you didn't speak to an armed man with a broken nose, glowing yellow eyes, and claws—even retracted claws—had begun to seem like a bad idea.

Bless you, she thought. Irgo blinked and looked at her in surprise. Was this a coincidence or had he understood what she was thinking? Maybe her scent had changed. Maybe he was puzzled by her lack of fear.

As she began to make her way cautiously down the trail, which was even steeper than the trail that led up to the top of the wall—Zakil caught up with her. "As soon as we get to the village, they're going to take Marrah away from you," he whispered.

"What!" The serenity she'd been feeling ever since she'd decided to approach the Mordai with love disappeared. "They can't do that! I won't let them take her!"

She felt Marrah stir at the sound of her voice.

"Hush," Zakil cautioned, "not so loud. There are Mordai in Hezur Herri who understand Old Language, so this may be one of our last chances to speak secretly."

"I can't let them have her, Zakil. They'll hurt her."

"No they won't." He put his hand on her arm. "Listen to me. The Mordai never hurt children, never. Children are precious. They get the best of everything: the best food, the best beds, the warmest places by the fire. The Mordai love children. They'll fight to the death before they'll let a child be hurt. That's one of the reasons they hate humans. Long ago, humans killed Mordai children. Each spring the Mordai place flowers on those ancient graves. Marrah will be safe with them, I promise."

"But I won't be with her!"

"You'll only be separated from her for a little while. We'll get her back, and all three of us will escape, but meanwhile you mustn't resist them when they take Marrah from you. Do you understand?"

Sabalah nodded. She had to believe Zakil was telling the truth, or she would not be able to control herself when those beasts touched her baby. *No, not beasts. Children of the Goddess,* she told herself. *Marrah will be safe. The Mordai won't hurt her.*

"You've been brave so far, and you need to go on being brave." Zakil let go of her arm. "You mustn't show fear. You're the one who claims she has a magical charm given to her by the Great Python. You need to make the Mordai afraid of *you.* Do you understand?"

Sabalah took a deep breath. This was so much harder than she had thought it would be. "I understand, Zakil, but I'm not going to make them afraid of me. I'm going to bless them, love them, and lead them back to the Goddess."

"Are you out of your mind? If you try to do that, they'll fall on you the way a hawk falls on a rabbit!"

"The Goddess is with me. I can feel Her arms around me." Brave words, but not strictly true. She could not feel the Goddess's arms around her. In fact at the moment, she would have given anything for the reassuring touch of Arash's hand on her shoulder. But love was the only way. There could be no other.

"Where will they take Marrah when we get to Hezur Herri?" she whispered.

"They'll probably take her to the Children's House."

"There's a house just for children?"

"Yes. It's very comfortable, very safe." Zakil looked shaken. She could see he still wanted to plead with her to make the Mordai fear her, but instead he pressed his lips together and fell silent.

"And where will they take me?"

He didn't reply.

"Where will they take me, Zakil?"

"If they take you into the barrow, that will be a good sign. It will mean they believe your story."

"And if they don't take me into the barrow, where will they take me?"

"Down to that circle of stones beside the lake."

"Will that also be a good sign?

"No."

"Why not?"

"Because it means you'll soon be meeting the Ireki."

"Why is that a bad thing?"

Again Zakil said nothing.

"Why, Zakil? Tell me!"

"Sabalah, my love, you need to understand that you're not on Gira about to meet the Yashas. The Ireki eat humans. In fact, they eat anything that breathes air."

Bless them, she thought. *Bless them*. But this time under the word "*bless*" there was a fear so raw it nearly choked her. Blessing the Mordai was one thing. Blessing monsters who were about to eat you was something else altogether. She wasn't good enough, strong enough, great-souled enough. The Great Python might have been able to do it, but she was only Sabalah, Daughter of Lalah, Mother of Marrah: a simple woman who fished in the Sweetwater Sea so the people of Shara could put food on their tables. Yet, what other way was there?

"You mean the Mordai may decide to sacrifice me to the monsters who live in their lake?" Her voice broke, and she felt tears fill her eyes.

"Hush, my darling. Don't worry. The Ireki aren't going to eat you."

"Why not?"

Zakil took her hand. "Because, my love, I promise I'll kill you before they can get to you."

"No!" she said softly, taking his other hand in hers. "No, Zakil, you must never kill me no matter what happens, not even if you think it will spare me suffering. Life is a precious gift and I want to live to the end of mine no matter what that end may be. If I die, Marrah will never get out of here. Love is my only weapon. It's all I have to offer."

"You can't love the Ireki. They know nothing of love. They were created before love existed. They have no compassion, no sense of the suffering of other beings. They have no souls."

"Everything created by the Goddess has a soul. Trees have souls. Seas have souls. Even rocks have souls." She would have said more, but they had reached the end of the path.

Half a dozen Mordai were waiting for them, all full-blooded, all female. Their bodies glistened with mint-scented oil, their scales shone like stars, their faces were painted with red clay, and they wore crowns made out of what appeared to be human finger bones.

Sabalah took a deep breath of the minty scent, wondering if, besides using it to keep off gnats, they wore it so they'd have some privacy from one another. It must be difficult to live in a village where everyone could smell your emotions. "How do you say 'bless you' in Mordai, Zakil?"

"Sabalah, please—"

"How do you say 'I bless you in the name of the Goddess.'"

"Maite chi Jainkosa izen."

Sabalah walked up the line, passing Haserre who gave her a startled look. Approaching the Mordai women, she smiled.

"Maite chi Jainkosa izen," she said.

"Shuk!" Haserre said. She sounded surprised.

"Shuk," the Mordai women murmured, looking at Sabalah approvingly.

"What did they just say?"

"My sister said you're brave. Actually she called you 'clawed.' The others agreed."

"Now what?"

"Now you need to hold very still and make no sudden moves. You've won their respect. I didn't think it was possible to do it by blessing them, but you have, so don't ruin it by fighting them."

Suddenly the oldest of the Mordai women stepped forward, circled around behind her, and began to unstrap Marrah from the cradleboard. Sabalah's first impulse was to turn and knock her aside, but there were too many Mordai to fight and besides, hadn't she vowed to love them? Love them! Was that possible when they were stealing her baby?

Her stomach heaved and the hairs on the back of her neck stood up. *Help me,* she prayed. *Help me Hessa, Batal, Amonah. Help me love these people.* But she could not love the Mordai women, at least not at the moment, not with her heart beating so fast she felt as if it might explode out of her chest.

All she could do was try to control herself, knowing that if she turned around and attacked the woman who was taking Marrah, the rest of the pack might jump on her and claw out her throat. She couldn't risk it. She had to go on living, because if she didn't, Marrah would be spending the rest of her life in Hezur Herri.

Gritting her teeth, she watched as Marrah was carried over to the waiting group of Mordai, passed from hand to hand, admired, and cooed over. Marrah seemed to be enjoying the attention, smiling and babbling instead of yelling her head off the way Sabalah had expected.

Mordai women, I'm blessing you so you won't smell my fear. Blessing you because I want to love you. But you aren't making it easy. Every instinct of motherhood is telling me to jerk Marrah out of your arms and try to escape. Give me some of that mint oil so I can put it on and keep you from smelling how much it scares me to see you holding my daughter.

Suddenly the women were all speaking at once, pointing first to Marrah and then at her.

"They're asking if you're her mother," Zakil said.

"Tell them 'yes,' and tell them that I love them as I love her."

"You really want me to say that?"

"Yes, quick now, please."

Zakil spoke and the women broke into smiles.

"They say they love Valina too," Zakil translated. "They say to tell you that no matter what happens to you, they'll never harm her."

"You told them her name was Valina?"

"Yes."

"How good is their promise not to hurt her?"

"Good. As I said, the Mordai don't hurt children."

One of the Mordai women put Marrah to her breast and began to nurse her. Marrah sucked greedily. Apparently to Marrah a breast was a breast even if the woman offering it had gills.

"What's going on?" she asked.

"The Mordai women are adopting her, making her a Mordai child. This is the best possible sign. It means she will be safe no matter what happens to us."

"Will their milk poison her?"

"No, I was nursed by my father's niece Neetsik. Neetsik not only nursed me, she nursed one of my sisters."

Before Sabalah could ask more questions, Haserre barked a command. Instantly, the Mordai sentries surrounded her, cutting her off from Marrah and Zakil. She tried to turn and run back to Marrah, but the sentries blocked her path and herded her toward Hezur Herri, poking at her with the blunt ends of their spears.

The main path of the village was lined with Mordai, half-Mordai, and women who looked human. As Sabalah approached, the crowd stood in eerie silence, giving off a scent of mint so strong, it made her eyes sting.

They must be waiting to see if the sentries will turn me toward the barrow or toward the lake, she thought. A kind of dizziness came over her, a sense of walking in a waking dream. This couldn't be happening. Surely—

Before she could complete the thought, one of the sentries poked her in the left side, herding her toward the lake. So they had decided to sacrifice her to the monsters they worshipped. Petrified with fear, she stumbled forward. She was close enough to the arch now to see that it was made from the jawbone of a giant fish whose teeth were as long as her hand. She recognized that jawbone and those teeth. She had pulled those fish out of her nets, flayed them, and tossed them in her mother's stewpots.

The great arch of Hezur Herri was the jawbone of a shark, and not just any shark, but a shark so huge it could have swallowed her whole.

She was so stunned by the size of the thing, that for a moment she forgot everything except that it was impossible for a shark that big to exist. Bless you, she thought, not because she really intended to bless the jawbone of a shark, but because she had been repeating the word so long that it kept going in her mind like a song you couldn't get out of your head.

"Shuk!" the sentry said.

Before she had time to understand what was happening, the sentries had turned her around, and begun to herd her toward the barrow. As she walked up the path, the crowd cheered, children ran up and pulled at her hair, the drummers began to drum, and the Mordai began singing in their high, clicking language. Were they welcoming her? Mocking her? Threatening her?

It didn't matter. Apparently this had been a test to see if she would fall apart and beg for her life. By the grace of the Goddess, she had passed it.

"Maite chi Jainkosa izen!" she cried. "*Maite chi Jainkosa izen,* Mordai people. I come in love. Please don't feed me to the Ireki!"

24

THE PAINTED SHARK

Bless you.

The words throbbed endlessly in Sabalah's head in time to the beating of the drums and the singing of the Mordai who had crowded into the barrow behind her, filling it with the scent of mint and sweat and something musky and dark, which for all she knew was the smell of beasts preparing to attack. She was too stunned by what she was seeing to understand what was going on around her. All she could do was keep repeating bless you to herself to keep from panicking.

There was plenty of reason to panic. She hadn't been driven into the lake to be fed to the Ireki, but she had no idea where Marrah was, and now Zakil was standing in front of a high platform arguing with Ahizpa, the old woman who supposedly had borne more living children than any woman in the history of the Mordai. Since Zakil's father was not up on the platform with her, Ahizpa was probably going to decide if Sabalah and Zakil lived or died, and at the moment their chances of living weren't looking good.

Ahizpa would have been frightening even if she hadn't been yelling at Zakil. She was alarmingly thin with heavily webbed hands, a sharply pointed chin, chipped yellowed claws, and skin so mottled it looked like the hide of a toad. The star-like scales that shone so brightly from all the other Mordai, did not shine on her. Instead her little silver points were veiled with something that might have been dirt. Perhaps this was because she was very old, or perhaps beauty had always escaped her. She might even have been sick, because instead of smelling like mint, she smelled like sour milk.

But it was the predatory look in her eyes that made Sabalah feel as if she were about to be pounced on by an enraged lion. If Ahizpa had had kinder eyes or spoken in a friendly voice, her toad-like skin and strange scent wouldn't have mattered. The Mother People had always valued good nature above physical beauty. But her voice was as harsh as the bleat of a goat, and the glares she was giving Zakil were so threatening they needed no translation.

That would have been cause enough for worry, but the inside of the barrow was so bizarre it made Sabalah feel as if she had stepped into another nightmare. From the top of the wall that surrounded Hezur Herri, it had looked like a pile of hollowed-out earth with a round entrance flanked by large pieces of slate, but the part that could be seen from above ground was merely the roof of a large underground chamber that branched off into many smaller chambers, which in turn led to still more chambers on levels further down.

The walls of the chambers were plastered with white clay like the walls of the temples of Shara, but the Mordai had not decorated them with fruit trees or paintings of young lambs grazing in green meadows. They had decorated them with bones.

The floor under Sabalah's feet was paved with vertebrae that crunched under the soles of her boots when she stepped on them. On either side of her, heaps of skulls climbed the walls in thick columns forming arches. On the ceiling, there were still more skulls laid out in pinwheels that seemed to turn when she stared up at them.

At the entrance to each chamber, skeletons held flaming torches in their fleshless fingers. Were those Mordai fingers? Human fingers? There was no way of telling. As far as she could see, none of the skeletons' hands ended in either claws or fingernails.

Perhaps we're all cousins under the flesh, Sabalah thought. *But what if we're not. What if these are the bones of the humans the Mordai have killed. Dear Goddess, what creatures left these bones behind when they went back to the Mother!*

Suddenly, Ahizpa leaned over the edge of the platform and jabbed her finger at Sabalah. "You there, human!" she said in Old Language. "Come here!"

Startled, Sabalah drew nearer to the platform, doing her best not to notice that every inch was plastered with finger bones, some baby-size. Actually, the baby-sized bones were a good sign. Zakil had said the Mordai never hurt children, so this must be a monument in memory of the Mordai dead, not a monument to some terrible massacre of human beings.

When she reached the base of the platform, she looked up and found Ahizpa staring down at her with open malevolence. The smell of sour milk that wafted off her was so strong it was hard not to gag. Taking a deep breath and straightening her shoulders, Sabalah returned Ahizpa's gaze, doing her best to look friendly.

"Maite chi Jainkosa izen, Ahizpa."

"*Jainkosa!* Who taught you to say the word 'Goddess?'"

"I did," Zakil admitted.

Ahizpa turned toward him so quickly that her long, silver hair flew out behind her like a greasy cape. "You un-clawed idiot! You half-blood fool! You take after your human mother! When Saski came mewling to me with that word, I told her to shut up or I'd have her thrown into the lake." She turned back to Sabalah.

"Why can't I smell your fear?"

Bless you, Sabalah thought.

"Answer me!"

Bless you.

"Is it perhaps because you don't fear me? No, I don't think so. You're doing something. What are you doing?"

Blessing you and doing my best to love you, although I have to say you aren't making it easy.

Ahizpa gave an impatient snort and folded her arms across her chest. "Translate, Zakil. Tell her what I say. Speaking this human language is like dipping your tongue in wormwood."

Zakil gave Sabalah a look of warning that said: Ahizpa will understand everything I say to you. "Soina ..." he began.

Soina? Who was 'Soina?' Ah yes, that was her new name. She'd forgotten all about it.

"Soina, Daughter of..." Zakil paused, "...Daughter of Amonah."

Bad choice! Sabalah hoped Ahizpa had never heard of the Sharan Goddess of the Sea. Apparently she hadn't, because she just kept glaring at the two of them like they were shark bait.

"Soina, Daughter of Amonah, Ahizpa the Fertile Mother of Six, says thus: 'Tratatu, Father of the un-clawed coward Zakil, is not here at the moment. If it were up to me, I would feed you to the Ireki this afternoon, but you are the mother of the magical child of our prophecy, and Haserre says you claim the Great Python of Orefi gave you a charm that can make the men of the Mordai fertile and allow the women of the Mordai to bear many living children.

'Zakil, the un-clawed, half-blood coward, claims you yourself saw the Great Python at Orefi, and that you live under its protection. Personally, I think both of you are lying; but there's no rush. Tratatu has gone hunting. He will return in a few days. Until then, you may sleep in Zakil's bed since he claims he wants you as his mate, ugly human though you are.

'When Tratatu returns, you will return to the place where you now stand and demonstrate that your charm works. If you speak the truth, Tratatu will no doubt argue that we should spare your life. I will argue that you should be sacrificed to the Ireki. There is no room for a priestess of the Goddess in Hezur Herri. I spit on the Goddess who abandoned us and our ancestors in their time of need. I spit on the Great Python. I spit on all humans.'"

Ahizpa suddenly snarled a few words in Mordai.

"Ahizpa insists that I tell you she didn't say 'spit.' She said something far worse."

Sabalah looked up at the angry woman standing above her draped in shabby cobbled-together hides and long strings of bones. "No need to translate, Zakil. I think I know what Ahizpa really said."

And so began Sabalah's life among the Mordai. It was an unsettling combination of the foreign and the familiar, but in many ways, the familiar things were the strangest. When she and Zakil walked out of the barrow, his friends and relatives greeted him the same way her own friends and relatives would have greeted her if she had returned to Shara after a long absence. They laughed, they chattered, they hugged him and patted him, and the children tugged playfully at his clothing.

Three half-human women, whom she later discovered were his sisters, swept him up in their arms and kissed him. An older women who appeared to be entirely human, embraced him so fervently, Sabalah wondered how he could breathe.

"This is my mother," he gasped. "Her name is..."

Zakil's mother had long red hair streaked with gray; dark eyes; skin the color of fall acorns; a round, happy face; a glowing smile. "I'm Saski," she said in Old Language, "Daughter of Bainatu, come long ago from the land of the white cliffs beside the Sea of Gray Waves to dwell among the Mordai with Zakil's father Tratatu. Welcome to Hezur Herri, Soina, Daughter of Amonah. Whom my son Zakil loves, I love."

Releasing Zakil, Saski took Sabalah in her arms and gave her a hug that left her breathless. But that wasn't the end of it. To her astonishment, when Saski let go of her, Haserre stepped forward and hugged her too. Haserre's hug was less enthusiastic than Saski's, and there was resentment and envy in her eyes. Still, it was a hug, and like Zakil's two sisters, Haserre politely kept her claws in.

Somewhat stunned by all this goodwill, Sabalah followed Zakil and his family to the longhouse where they lived only to discover that it too looked familiar. In fact, except for the bones on the roof, it could have been a motherhouse in any of the villages north of the Caves of Nar.

Like the longhouses of the Mother People, one side of the Mordai dwelling was a long corridor that ran the length of the structure. On the other side were half a dozen sleeping compartments and in front of each, a fire pit.

Had the Mordai and the Mother People once lived together in peace? Had they built the same kinds of longhouses when they both worshipped the Goddess Earth? Perhaps, yet there were differences, and as her eyes adjusted to the dim light, Sabalah began to see them.

There were the usual things hanging from the rafters: strips of smoked meat, dried herbs, baskets filled with dried berries which Zakil's mother and sisters had probably harvested from the Marubi. But there were unfamiliar things too: a bundle of bone flutes tied together with a Mordai belt, odd-looking objects made of wood that might be small tables, strings of medicinal plants she had never seen before, and a whole row of small stone jars, which probably contained potions and herbal remedies.

What shocked her most were the weapons. Everywhere she looked there were spears, axes, bows, arrows, knives, clubs tipped with flints so sharp they looked as if they'd cut through your hands if you tried to pick them up. Weapons were propped up against the walls, hanging from the rafters, stacked beside the doors ready at hand. No house of the Mother People would have had so many. Nor would any longhouse of the Mother People have had the image of a shark painted on its walls. The shark was so huge that it did not simply stretch from one end of the house to the other; it ran all the way around from door to door and back again, swimming above anyone who entered like a monstrous hunter. Its eyes were great gobs of yellow, its teeth made of real bones, its mouth a bloody cave of red clay. Even its tail was larger than Zakil.

The moment Sabalah saw the shark and realized it was a representation of the Ireki, she knew neither she nor Marrah would ever be safe in Hezur Herri. The Mordai, who at the moment were being so friendly, could turn on them in an instant, probably would turn on them if she couldn't convince them her "charm" could help their women bear living children.

If I fail, they will feed Zakil and me to those monsters and maybe Marrah too, she thought, and she felt fear rise up in her again, expanding out of control.

Bless you. Bless you. Bless you. This time blessing them didn't work. Her terror kept on increasing until it seemed the shark was circling directly over her, waiting to rip her to pieces. *How much would it hurt? How long would the pain last?*

A few moments more, and Zakil's family would have been able to smell her terror, but then by the grace of the Goddess, something amazing happened.

"Soina?" a voice said.

Tearing her eyes away from the shark, Sabalah looked down and saw Saski standing in front of her holding out Marrah. Marrah healthy and whole! Marrah who smiled when she caught sight of Sabalah, stretched out her small, chubby arms, and burbled with delight! Seizing her, Sabalah pressed her to her breast, hugged her, and covered her with kisses.

"Why have you given her back to me?"

"Nursing children go to their mothers."

Haserre was giving Sabalah a look of such pure jealousy that Sabalah felt pity for her. This pity was soon extinguished when Haserre spit out some words which Zakil reluctantly translated. "Haserre says that it is true that nursing children go to their mothers, unless, of course, their mothers prove to be liars."

"Haserre!" Saski said sharply. Putting her hands on her hips, she began to speak rapidly in Mordai. Sabalah didn't understand a word she was saying, but it was clear she was not happy with Haserre.

"My mother just said, 'That's no way to treat Zakil's mate.' Now I expect Haserre will start yelling at her. After Haserre's mother died, my mother raised Haserre with a love and affection that Haserre never returned. Haserre is proud of being a full-blooded Mordai and has always resented Saski for being human. The two of them have never gotten along."

True to his prediction, Haserre began to yell angrily, pointing at first at Zakil, then at Sabalah. Again Zakil translated, looking more amused than alarmed by Haserre's tirade. "Haserre says: 'His mate, is she? And you believe that? You believe this human came here of her own free will as you did? You believe this priestess of the Goddess came to bear Zakil's children and give her 'magical child' to us?'"

Saski barked out two words which must have meant "be silent," or maybe "I've had enough of your nonsense." Apparently the command of the woman who had raised you had as much force among the Mordai as it did among the Mother People. Haserre immediately stopped talking and gave Saski a strange, elegant bow that involved extending and retracting her claws. Turning abruptly, she stalked out of the longhouse, leaving the leather curtain swinging behind her.

When she was gone, Saski embraced Sabalah again. Then she led her and Zakil to the sleeping compartment that was to be theirs. Three things about it were good: it was relatively large, and the bed, which was made of deer hides stuffed with dry leaves, was soft. Best of all, when Sabalah lay down, the walls that separated it from the main corridor were so high she couldn't see the shark. Yet it offered no privacy. Every word she and Zakil said to one another could be overheard.

For four days, Sabalah lived quietly in Saski's longhouse, scraping hides, thrashing and grinding wild grains, slicing carrots, pounding acorns into flour, taking care of Marrah, and eating with the six families that occupied the other sleeping compartments. The only thing Saski would not let her do was go down to the lake to get water, which was fine as far as Sabalah was concerned since she didn't want to get anywhere near the Ireki.

No one seemed to worry that Sabalah would try to escape, probably because they knew she had nowhere to run to. Even if she got over the wall, she could never get through the Marubi with Marrah on her back, and she would never leave Marrah behind.

At night, Sabalah slept in Zakil's arms, mingling her scent with his. Everything about this was disturbing. He was a stranger. She knew almost nothing about him except the little he'd told her, and yet she had slept next to him for over a year thinking he was Arash. Who was this man? Or more to the point, what was he? When he had looked like Arash, he had felt like Arash; but now his body, like everything else about him, seemed alien and unfamiliar.

She had expected his scales to feel like the scales of a fish, but instead they felt smooth and unusually soft. His silvery hair emitted a strange scent that reminded her of pine needles mixed with cedar bark. When he slept his gills fluttered, and at times his skin grew so cool he seemed to have gone into hibernation like a snake. Then, suddenly, he would grow so warm she had to throw off the deerskin blankets and get up, taking Marrah with her.

As she nursed Marrah back to sleep, she would silently list the things she had learned about him since she entered his mother's house: Zakil was good with his hands. He could sew and carve better than his sisters because he had no claws. He'd made Marrah a small leather dolphin stuffed with goose down, and he had not only made the bone flutes that hung from the rafters of the main room, he could play them. His mother and three of his four sisters adored him, the exception being his half-sister Haserre who sometimes pretended he wasn't there. Arash had preferred his wild greens cooked. Zakil liked to eat them raw.

What did these things tell her about who Zakil really was? Very little. She was still sleeping next to a stranger who for many months had managed to trick her into believing he was someone else.

At least he kept his promise. When she stretched out beside him, he held her tenderly, never forcing his affections on her; and despite the strangeness of it all, as time passed, she began to find his presence comforting.

Sometimes he volunteered information about himself. Since he had lied to her from the moment they left Shara, she was never sure if she could believe what he was saying, but a lot of it seemed to ring true, and knowing anything about him felt better than knowing nothing.

"When I was young," he told her, "the full-blooded Mordai children tormented me until I learned to fight back. They were stronger, but I was more stubborn. I'd grab their legs and hang on. They'd stumble around punching and kicking at me, but they could never shake me off. Finally they gave up and left me alone."

Sometimes he would brag about what a good hunter and excellent tracker he was, about how he never got lost in the forest even on the darkest moonless nights, but like all people who bragged, he went too far.

"Full-blooded Mordai can only deceive humans into thinking they are two things: other humans or water creatures, but I can weave a veil of illusion that can make humans think I'm not there at all."

"Is that how you trapped Arash?" she whispered angrily. "Is that how you captured him and stole his memories?"

"Yes," he admitted.

"This just gets worse and worse." Rolling onto her side, she turned her back to him, drew Marrah close, and stared into the darkness. Although she couldn't see the painted shark, she imagined she could feel it circling around her. "I hate this place."

"I'm sorry."

"I don't care if you're sorry. I don't care anything about you."

"Sabalah, my love, please."

"Be quiet! I've heard enough! I don't need to hear you to brag about how well you can deceive humans!" She stared into the darkness, which seemed to be growing thicker and more menacing by the moment. "Don't call me your 'love' Zakil. My 'love' is Arash. Do you think you can remember that?"

Closing her eyes, she tried to go back to sleep, but sleep was a long time coming. The truth was, despite what she had said, she did care about Zakil. She was terribly lonely and more than a little frightened, and he was the closest thing she had to a friend.

She ran her fingers gently over Marrah, feeling the silken softness of her hair and inhaling the blossom-scented fragrance of her skin. *Nursing children go to their mothers, unless, of course, their mothers prove to be liars,* Haserre had said. And she had lied.

For a long time, she lay awake trying to figure out how to use the Mother Book to convince the Mordai she'd told them the truth, but she couldn't see any way to do this without breaking her vow. Near dawn, she broke down in tears, stuffing the edge of the blanket in her mouth to keep Zakil from hearing. He must have felt her body shaking, because the next thing she knew, he was comforting her.

"Everything will be all right," he whispered, gently stroking her hair.

"That's not true."

"Sabalah, please—"

"I wish you were Arash."

"I wish I were too."

The sadness in his voice made her come a little closer to forgiving him. He had betrayed her terribly, but he did love her in his way, and at least he was a familiar presence here where everything else was so strange and terrifying.

25

Pull and Push

The evening meals had been eaten, the fires banked, and the leather curtains of the longhouses shut and battened down with rocks. In a silence broken only by the sound of humming insects, the crushed bones that paved the main walkway of Hezur Herri shone under a bone-white moon. Beneath the moonlight, Lake Calthen lay like a mirror, so flat and calm that, despite the heat, it appeared to have frozen over.

In that great, shining silence nothing was moving except the sentries who patrolled the top of the wall and three people—two humans and one half-Mordai—who were heading for the ruins of the Goddess Temple. Sabalah was carrying Marrah on her back. She and Zakil were not running or even walking swiftly. There was no reason to hurry because there was nowhere to go except back to the village.

Reaching the shelter of one of the ruined walls, they threw their cloaks down on a patch of small plants that smelled like the mint oil the Mordai spread on their skin. Zakil pulled a small jar of the oil out of his pouch and began to apply it to his face and arms. Although the Mordai used the oil to mask their scents from the animals they hunted and from one another, they mainly employed it to keep off clouds of small biting gnats which were an unpleasant feature of Hezur Herri.

Luckily the mint grew everywhere along the shores of the lake. More luckily, at least from Sabalah's point of view, the gnats were completely indifferent to human beings. They only bit Mordai and half-Mordai like Zakil.

Tonight the moon was so bright she could see the colors of the mint flowers which ranged from reddish purple to lilac. Although there was not enough light for her to make out the leaves, the plants looked familiar. In Shara mint was often grown in the gardens of temples. Perhaps this mint had originally been planted long ago by priestesses of the Goddess before the Mordai turned away from Her to worship the Ireki.

Too worried to pursue this thought any further, she sat down beside Zakil and unstrapped the cradleboard, gently removing Marrah, who was limp with sleep. For a little while, she held Marrah in her arms. Then she put her down on a blanket made of rabbit skins and covered her with a piece of linen. The Mordai worked leather but they didn't weave, spin, or grow flax or hemp. Back in Shara, the cloth that covered Marrah had only been a scarf Sabalah had used to tie back her hair when she went fishing, but here it was something rare and exotic, and Zakil's sisters never tired of admiring it.

For a long time neither she nor Zakil spoke, despite the fact that time was running out, and they had many things they needed to discuss. They looked at the moonlight playing on the stones of the ruined temple walls, at the sweet-smelling mint plants, at anything but one another.

This afternoon, a messenger had arrived to say that Tratatu and his hunting party were on their way back to Hezur Herri and would probably arrive before dawn. As soon as she learned Tratatu was near, Ahizpa had sent word to Saski's longhouse commanding Zakil and Sabalah to come to the barrow tomorrow at noon.

"Ahizpa says that afterwards she invites you to watch a special feeding of the Ireki," the messenger had said grimly in heavily-accented Old Language. "She has a strange sense of humor."

Since then, Zakil's family's attitude had changed. Although to all outward appearances they were as hospitable as ever, Sabalah had caught them looking at her as if they knew something about her that made them profoundly uneasy. That was reasonable. If the Mordai discovered she had lied about the charm—which of course she had—she and Zakil would both be fed to the Ireki. Given that she soon might be the cause of Zakil's death, Sabalah could hardly blame his mother and sisters for wishing they had never laid eyes on her. But their looks said more than that. They were the kind of looks you gave someone when you were keeping a secret from them. What was it? What did Zakil and his mother and sisters know about her that she didn't know? When she asked him, he claimed he had no idea what she was talking about. The problem was, she didn't believe him.

Settling back against the ruined wall of the temple, she took the Mother Book out of the pillowcase and stared at the little snake on the cover. Zakil put out his hand as if to take the Book from her, but she brushed him aside.

"Don't. I can't let you touch it."

"I thought you said it was nothing but pieces of dried calfskin."

"It's much more than that."

"I knew it!" Zakil looked at her triumphantly. "I knew that if the Great Python gave it to you, it must be powerful magic! Show me how it works."

"I can't."

"Why not?"

"Because I don't know. I'm not supposed to try to make it work. I'm just supposed to carry it to a safe place where the beastmen can't get their hands on it. The Great Python made me take a vow never to read it."

"Read it? What does 'read it' mean?"

"This is a book. It talks to me without sound. That's called 'reading.' I know that makes no sense to you, but I'm telling you the truth—far more of the truth that I should tell you, because I need to warn you about something. In a few moments I'm going to break my vow to the Great Python, open this book and read it instead of just opening it and holding it with its back against my chest the way I did when I showed it to Haserre. The instant I read the first word, I may die."

"What!" Zakil started to grab the Book out of her hands and then checked himself. "Don't open that thing," he pleaded. "Don't 'read' it whatever 'read' means. I love you. I want you to stay alive."

"Zakil, dear, I have no choice. I can't wait until tomorrow to read the Mother Book for the first time in front of Ahizpa and your father. I have to know what it says now before I'll know if there's any hope of convincing them that I didn't lie when I promised I could help Mordai women conceive."

She shouldn't have called him "dear," but she was continuing to soften toward him, forgiving him—at least a little—for what he had done to Arash because he was doing so much for her and Marrah. Still, even the fleeting thought of Arash brought pain and longing. *Arash,* she thought, *Arash, if you were only here beside me instead of Zakil. Zakil offers me his love, but I want yours; and if I die when I read the Mother Book I would die with less fear if you were beside me.*

"Sabalah, my beloved, please don't ..."

"Hush, Zakil." She put her fingers over his lips and looked into his glowing yellow eyes, so full of fear for her that he seemed to have no room left to fear for himself. "We have no choice. We can risk my death now or certain death for both of us tomorrow. And besides ... " She paused. "Despite my vow, I don't think I'll die if I read the Mother Book."

"Why not, my love? Why won't you die?"

"Because the Great Python is compassionate. Because I don't think it would kill me for breaking my vow to save the life of my child."

Moving away from Zakil, she closed her eyes and tried to pray, but no prayers came. There was a hollowness in her chest and the weightless rays of moonlight felt heavy on her skin.

The time had come. She could delay no longer. Gritting her teeth and bracing herself for the worst, she opened the Mother Book. To her relief, she didn't die instantly. In fact, nothing happened except that now instead of seeing the cover of the book, she saw a blank page and a nearly-blank page. At the top of the nearly blank-page, a single word was written in Xchimosh:

Pull

Under the word was a red handprint much like the ancient handprints that lined the passageway that led to the Great Python's chamber.

Only one word? She'd been expecting a whole page of prophecies. She'd hoped one might help her convince the Mordai she had magical powers. It wouldn't have needed to be anything special: just some simple prediction or some scrap of knowledge she would have had no other way of knowing. Something like: *Walk around to the other side of the lake and you'll find a bird nest with six speckled eggs in it.* Or better yet: *Ahizpa has a large black mole on her butt shaped like a fish.* But '*Pull?*' Pull what?

She felt almost sick with disappointment. Maybe the Mother Book was protected by a spell that made it impossible for anyone but an initiated Python to read it. Yet if that were the case, why would the Great Python have been so insistent that it not fall into the hands of the beastmen who couldn't read Xchimosh and who probably had never heard of reading for that matter?

"Has it spoken to you?" Zakil asked.

"Yes, I suppose you might say it has."

"What did it say?"

"It said 'pull.'"

"That's all? Just 'pull?'"

"Yes. It's useless. I can't interpret it."

"At least you didn't die instantly."

"No, we'll have to wait until tomorrow for that." She paused. "I suppose I could try reading another page."

"Before you risk that, why don't you try putting your hand in that handprint and pulling? It's about your size. Clawless. Definitely human. Maybe it's sticky."

"Why not? What do we have to lose?" Lifting her left hand, Sabalah let her palm hover over the print, then slapped it down and pulled. She expected it to come right off, but it didn't. Instead, it stuck there as if something were trying to suck it into the book. Frightened, she tried to tug it loose and then...

Darkness, light, darkness. A tunnel, sweeping, circling. Cries of joy, cries of agony, cries of pain. A dark forest, living trees with arms and faces: her grandmother's face, faces of the dead.

Time collapsing around her, something pulling her backwards, taking her to a past so long ago it had no name. She sees Lake Calthen but no sign of Hezur Herri. All the world is frozen solid, ice glittering everywhere brighter than the scales of the Mordai. A great glacier looms on the horizon like a blue mountain, while over the lake, a feathered lizard the size of a lion wings its way through a sky so blue it looks like...

She has no words for such blueness. She watches in awe as the lizard flaps its crimson and purple wings, watches as sunlight ripples down its golden crest. Then...

Snap! As quickly as she had left, she was back in the ruins of the Goddess Temple with Zakil tugging at her wrist.

"Are you dying?" he cried as he pulled her hand off the page. "You're moaning? What happened?"

She stared at him, not able to understand who he was or where she was. Then it all came back to her. Shuddering with cold despite the summer heat, she inspected the palm of her hand, which appeared to be unharmed.

"I went somewhere far away," she whispered. "Somewhere very ancient."

"What are you talking about? You didn't go anywhere. You stayed right here beside me."

"No," she insisted. "I went somewhere long ago, so long ago that I saw the leather-winged birds, only their wings don't look like leather; they're covered with feathers, and they aren't birds, they're lizards."

Grabbing the corner of the page before she lost her courage, she turned it. The next two pages of the Mother Book were the same: one blank, one nearly-blank, only this time the command written in Xchimosh above the red handprint was:

Push

Zakil tried to stop her, but she was too fast for him. Slapping the palm of her right hand onto the handprint, she pushed.

This time there was no whooshing, no forest of living faces, no tunnel. She was simply there—wherever "there" was—standing on a wide path of smooth, gray rock that stretched in either direction as far as she could see, losing itself in two treeless horizons. There were white and yellow lines painted on the path. They ran the full length of it, perfectly straight, perfectly parallel to one another. In the distance, she could see range after range of impossibly tall houses with windows made of a clear substance that shone like ice. Near her, held up by two thick posts made of some kind of strange gray material, she saw a bright green rectangle displaying an arrow and a message written in an unfamiliar script.

EX ...

She was just trying to puzzle out the message when something roared. Looking up, she saw a huge silver bird flying far above her, leaving a trail of white excrement so straight it could have been painted onto the sky with a brush.

Suddenly she heard another noise, louder than the first. Turning, she saw three monsters rolling down the path toward her. They were more brightly colored than rainbows, huge, beautiful, and terrifying. Most of all they were swift, for although they had no legs, they came faster than lions, faster than falling stones, faster than thought itself.

Dashing to the edge of the great stone path, she threw herself into the tall grass. By the grace of the Goddess, the monsters didn't pursue her. Instead as she sat there scratched and shaking with terror, they rolled by as if she didn't exist. Perhaps they had spared her because they weren't hungry, for behind the great, clear, window-like eyes of each monster, she could see people: men, women, and small children. Human beings, all eaten alive.

You should not be here, said a familiar voice.

Looking up, Sabalah saw the Great Python standing over her holding a large staff carved with intertwined snakes.

"I..." Sabalah began.

No excuses! cried the Great Python. *You were warned!* And lifting the staff, it struck her a mighty blow on the head. For a moment she was blinded by pain. Then darkness.

When she opened her eyes, Zakil was holding her in his arms, rocking her and crying.

"Don't ever touch that evil charm again," he said. "Don't ever touch it! I thought you were dead. Oh my love, my darling, I thought I'd lost you."

Disengaging herself from his embrace, she sat up and looked around. It was still night, and she was still in the ruins of the Goddess Temple. Her mouth stung as if it had been filled with nettles, and she had a nasty headache, but otherwise she appeared to be in one piece.

"Where did I go this time?"

"Go? What are you talking about? You didn't go anywhere. You put your hand on that thing and wouldn't let me pull it off. Then you moaned and fell back as if someone had struck you."

"Someone did strike me."

"What! Who hit you? There's no one here but us."

"I..." She started to explain, then stopped. The less Zakil knew about the Mother Book, the better. *You were warned,* the Great Python had said. Warned that she was to tell no one about the Mother Book, warned not to open it, warned not to read it. Warned, not just because the Book contained the greatest secrets ever given to humans by the Goddess, but for her own sake, because the Book was so powerful it could kill the uninitiated.

Fishing it out of the mint plants where it had tumbled when she fainted, she averted her eyes and closed the cover. *I will never open the Mother Book again,* she thought. *Not now, not tomorrow in front of Ahizpa and Tratatu, never, even if it means that the Mordai feed me and Zakil to the Ireki.*

This was an easy vow to make when her head was throbbing and every bone in her body ached; easy when she could still remember the Great Python's staff coming down on her. But when she looked up and saw Marrah sleeping innocently in the moonlight, she realized it was a vow she might not be able to keep.

26

FEEDING THE IREKI

The next morning Sabalah witnessed the *Shruzu*: a Mordai ritual so horrifying that as soon as Tratatu tossed the first carcass into the lake, she knew she would have to open the Mother Book again even if it killed her.

She had already noticed that the Mordai hunted a great deal. They must have been bringing back far more game than they could eat, but in the five days she had been in Hezur Herri, she had been too preoccupied with survival to give this much thought. Like their glittering skin and their gills, constant hunting seemed to be just another difference between Mordai and human beings—interesting but not worth trying to understand if you were planning to escape from their village as soon as you could figure out how to cut your way through the Marubi while carrying a baby on your back.

Thus when Zakil gently shook her awake, she was completely unprepared. Later when she asked him why he hadn't warned her, he said, "Because the Mordai can smell fear, and I knew you'd be afraid."

"Afraid" was an understatement. There were no words in any human language to describe the *Shruzu* except, perhaps, the words the Mother People used for the panic they felt when a volcano opened up and spit liquid fire.

It all began simply enough. After Zakil woke her, she got up, got dressed, changed Marrah's diaper, and took her into the main part of the longhouse where she found Saski and Zakil's sisters cooking acorn mush. All the other families were doing the same thing, making breakfast the way they did on any other day. The only difference was that late last night or perhaps early this morning, someone had climbed up the lodge poles and hung necklaces of bones on the painted shark. Both ends of the longhouse were open and a breeze was blowing, setting the bones clinking together in a way that wasn't altogether unpleasant. Still, bones were bones even if they were the bones of animals, and Sabalah didn't like to look at them, so she concentrated on eating her breakfast, nursing Marrah, and worrying about the fact that she was going to have to appear before Tratatu and Ahizpa at noon to prove she could make Mordai men fertile and Mordai women bear living children.

Usually when breakfast was over, people wandered outside to do chores while she stayed behind and out of sight. But this morning everyone lingered, sitting in groups around the fires, chatting and gambling.

"Why aren't they working?" she asked Zakil.

"Because this is a holiday."

"What kind of holiday?"

He gave her a look which she had come to know meant that he didn't want to say. Finally he coughed nervously and said, "It's always a holiday when the hunters come home with game."

"Does it have a name?"

"*Shruzu*," he said.

"Which means?"

"It just means *Shruzu*. There's no Old Language equivalent." He wasn't telling her the whole truth. She could see it in his eyes.

"How is *Shruzu* celebrated?"

"Wait and see."

She tried asking him more questions, but he just kept repeating "wait and see," so finally she gave up and went back to cracking acorns and keeping Marrah from crawling too close to the fire pit. Marrah was in an exploratory mood this morning, laughing and babbling and grabbing for everything in sight, including a small pot of honey which she tipped onto the floor, making a mess; but as usual no one scolded her. Whatever else you might say about the Mordai, they loved children and always treated them tenderly.

A short time later, she heard the drums start up in a rhythm different from any she'd heard before. As soon as the drumming began, everyone in the longhouse put aside their gaming boards and leapt to their feet. The Mordai's claws twitched and their gills fluttered with excitement. Saski and the other humans and half-humans looked anxious. Zakil looked grim.

Taking Sabalah's hand, he led her outside. A procession was coming down the main path of Hezur Herri from the barrow, getting longer by the moment as more villagers joined it. Leading it was a Mordai male. He had the carcass of a fox slung over his shoulder, and his face was smeared with blood just as Haserre's face had been when Sabalah first saw her.

"Your father?" she asked.

Zakil nodded. "Tratatu," he confirmed.

Tratatu's hair was plastered with red clay, and he wore a net of bones over his body that swung from side to side as he strode toward the lake carrying the fox. The most amazing thing about him was his size. Sabalah had expected Zakil's father to be tall like Zakil, but instead he was unusually short and broad-shouldered with thick, bowed legs.

"Your father is a dwarf?"

"Yes. Dwarfs are sacred. He's the first living dwarf born to a Mordai woman in seven generations. He has powers."

"What kind of powers?"

Zakil smiled nervously. "He's a great lover, a great hunter, and he can hear the Ireki speak."

Sabalah expected Tratatu to stop to talk to Zakil, Saski, and his daughters, but he passed by the longhouse without even glancing in their direction. He was staring straight ahead. His lips were moving but no sound was coming out. This was a state Sabalah recognized.

"Your father's put himself into a trance?"

"Yes, that's how he hears the Ireki. Come now, we need to join the procession."

"What do we do?"

"I sing. You do nothing but walk." Taking her by the shoulders, he looked into her eyes. "Sabalah, my love, listen very closely. We are going to walk to the edge of the lake. Something is going to happen there which may frighten you. No matter what you see, you must not cry out or make any sign that you're afraid. This is more important than ever. If you remain calm, you and I will stand in the barrow in front of my father and Ahizpa when the sun is directly overhead. But if you show fear ..." His voice trailed off.

"What happens if I show fear?"

"If you show fear, there's a good chance neither of us will be standing in the barrow at noon."

"Where will we be standing?"

"I promise you'll be absolutely safe if you don't show fear."

"That's not an answer, Zakil. What's going on here? What am I going to see?"

"Calm down. People are watching."

"They aren't people. They're beasts! They're ..."

Pulling her to him, Zakil shut her mouth with a kiss. At first she fought him, but the kiss was long and sweet and, despite the fact that she wasn't in the mood for it, exciting.

"I hate you," she hissed, but she didn't hate him, not nearly as much as she wanted to. Gradually as his lips kept pressing on hers, she stopped struggling. Finally he let her go.

"I'm sorry about that," he said. "I would never have kissed you against your will, but I figured it would look better than slapping my hand over your mouth. You need to pick up Marrah now and strap her on your back. She'll protect you."

"Marrah will protect *me*?"

Zakil nodded. "Yes, as long as you are carrying her, you won't be..."

"Won't be what?"

"You won't be made a *Shruzu*."

Suddenly she understood. "*Shruzu* means, 'sacrifice' doesn't it? You're saying that as long as Marrah is on my back I won't be sacrificed to the Ireki."

"That's not a question I'm going to answer. Now come along. We need to join the procession before everyone gets to the lakeshore."

"Zakil, tell me right now exactly what's going on!" She pointed at the painted shark that swam around the longhouse walls. "Are we going to be tossed into the lake where that *thing* can feed on us?"

"Not if you can manage to control yourself. Now calm down and see if you can manage to trust me. I know that isn't easy right now, but try."

"Zakil—"

"Please, Sabalah. If you want to live long enough to see Marrah grow up, you need to stop talking and come down to the shore of the lake with me before it's too late." He was deadly serious, and there was a look in his eyes that she had only seen once before on the morning when the Mordai hunting party took them by surprise. Picking up the cradleboard, he helped her strap it to her back, and then placed Marrah snugly in place, her head resting on the pillow that contained the Mother Book. Zakil had recently tied several tiny leather balls stuffed with grass to the rim of the shade, and Marrah batted at them happily, mercifully unaware of what was going on around her.

The *Shruzu* did not take long, but it explained a great deal. As Sabalah had suspected, the Mordai did not hunt simply to feed themselves. They also hunted to feed the Ireki. This feeding took place every time a hunting party returned with game. Often it was a quiet event: just a deer or a few birds thrown into the lake. But when a hunting party returned to Hezur Herri with a great deal of game as Tratatu's had, a *Shruzu* was held.

The *Shruzu* was a religious ritual, so strange and frightening that Sabalah couldn't imagine it being observed anywhere where people worshipped the Goddess. It was not a ritual designed to soothe. It was a ritual designed to terrify.

First everyone in Hezur Herri walked down to the jawbone of the big shark where the hunters threw down their catch in a great, bloody pile. Sabalah had never seen so much game in one place. There were deer, rabbits, birds, squirrels, foxes, weasels, a dead wolf whose paws had been tied together so it could be carried on a pole, a wild boar, and a basket full of tiny bloody things that could have been moles or dormice. It was horrible to see so many of the Goddess's creatures slaughtered.

"Nishak lusxxu zaptana ki!" Tratatu cried.

"What's he saying?" Sabalah whispered.

"He's thanking the Ireki for giving them such a successful hunt. He's saying that he has brought them an offering of the bodies of animals who live on land. The Ireki have told us that all land-living animals are cursed, and that we may kill as many of them as we can find. Only animals who live in water are sacred."

"Humans and Mordai both live on land!"

"Exactly. That's why my father is now saying that if the Ireki want him to give his body to them, he will wade into the lake and let them feed on him. So far, they've never taken him up on the offer, but legend has it they've done so in the past."

"He'd let those things eat him!" Sabalah felt nauseated. Pressing her lips together, she forced herself to look at Tratatu. If anyone needed to understand that the Goddess loved all Her children including him, he did.

Bless you, she thought, but the words stuttered in her mind, and she felt a growing sense of horror combined with terror for Marrah who could never be allowed to grow up among beings who would willingly sacrifice themselves to such monsters.

The drummers were drumming more loudly now, and the Mordai had begun dancing in earnest. This wasn't the dancing of the Festival of the Ewes where people laughed, and swung one another around, and smiled and went off later to share joy. This was the grim dancing of a people who were trying to placate goddesses who were not goddesses at all but huge sharks. As everyone who fished knew, sharks had no compassion. No doubt the Goddess Earth loved them, but sharks loved no one, not even each other. Shark babies ate their brothers and sisters in the womb; mother sharks ate their children; big sharks ate smaller sharks. All sharks wanted to do was eat, and from what Sabalah had seen, they weren't picky.

Suddenly the drumming stopped. Falling on the dead game, the Mordai hunters clawed out the hearts and placed them in another pile. Then, one by one, they threw the bloody hearts into the lake like skipping stones.

At first nothing happened. Then, suddenly, the water began to boil and the hearts were snapped up by giant, dark shapes that slid beneath a film of blood. As the Ireki fed, the Mordai cheered and sang. Rushing forward, they grabbed the carcasses of the animals, dragged them to the edge of the lake, and heaved them into the water.

A thrash of teeth, fins, bloody foam, carnage. Sabalah looked on in horror as the giant sharks ripped the animals' bodies into bloody pieces, biting their own tails and tearing out hunks of each other's flesh in their frenzy. Blood and more blood—a great smear of it filled with unrecognizable bits of beings that had once been birds, deer, wolves.

Pressing her lips together, she willed herself not to vomit. *I'll never be able to eat meat again, she thought.*

For a few moments, the giant sharks fed. Then, as quickly as they had come, they finished their ghastly meal and sank back into the depths of the lake. As the last of the fins disappeared, the Mordai broke into a song that sounded insanely cheerful.

Stunned, Sabalah stared at the singers in disbelief. Only the human women looked upset, particularly Saski. Sabalah wondered how many Shruzus Zakil's mother had witnessed since she came to Hezur Herri. Had she watched human beings and Mordai thrown to the Ireki? If so, did she ever regret leaving her village beside the Sea of Gray Waves where her people worshipped a Goddess of Mercy who never stained the water with blood? *How young were you when you came here, Saski? How soon did you long to go home to your mother's house?*

Zakil put his hand on her shoulder. "You did well," he said. "There aren't many humans who see a *Shruzu* for the first time without trying to bolt and run."

Sabalah nodded. Her mouth was still too dry with fear to speak. Somehow she had managed not to scream or move. She had been terrified, but by a miracle, or perhaps by the grace of the Goddess or the covering stink of the slaughtered deer, none of the Mordai had noticed. At last, she found her voice.

"What are they singing about?" she whispered. "Why do they seem so happy?"

"They're singing an ancient song about how the Ireki saved them from the human beings who attacked Hezur Herri. The song says the Mordai lured the attacking humans into Lake Calthen and—"

"And the Ireki ate them, yes?"

"Yes. On that day, the song says, the Mordai turned away from the Goddess who had abandoned them, tore down Her temple, and began to worship the Ireki."

"The Ireki aren't worthy of worship. They're just gigantic sharks; hungry, stupid sharks who have no mercy, no compassion, no..."

Zakil put one finger over her lips. "Hush, my love. There are people behind you who understand Old Language. When you stand before my father this noon, don't tell him the Ireki aren't worthy of worship, unless you want to come back here."

Sabalah stared at the blood-tinted foam washing up on the beach, and shuddered. Reaching back, she stroked Marrah's hair, trying to draw strength from the fact that Marrah was safe and still completely unaware of what had just happened.

"I never want to come back here," she said. "Never."

27

MINT

Tratatu and Ahizpa stood side-by-side draped from head to foot in bones that clinked every time they moved. Their faces were painted with blood, their hair was matted with red clay, and their claws were out. Sabalah could smell the mint oil wafting off the bodies of the Mordai, the sour-milk scent of Ahizpa, and the dusty, ancient scent of the countless bones that filled the barrow all mixed with the odor of fresh blood.

Before she and Zakil had left for this audience with Tratatu and Ahizpa, Sabalah had been forced to surrender Marrah to Saski who had promised to take care of her until Sabalah returned. Saski's unspoken promise had been that she would also take care of Marrah if Sabalah ended up being sacrificed to the Ireki.

Sabalah clutched the Mother Book to her chest. Behind her she could hear five heavily armed Mordai sentries, including Zakil's broken-nosed cousin Irgo, breathing through their gills. Perhaps the Mother Book would keep the sentries from marching her down to the lake and throwing her in, or perhaps her punishment for opening the Book a second time would be death by shark.

Beside her, close enough to touch, Zakil stood trembling slightly, his fingers twitching as if he were extending and contracting invisible claws. No doubt the scent of fear was streaming off him uncontrollably, filling the nostrils of all the Mordai, including his father. What did Zakil's scent say to them? Did it say "traitor?" Did it say "liar?"

It didn't matter. The Mordai weren't paying attention to Zakil. They were looking at her, caught somewhere between the hope that she possessed a charm that could make their men fertile and their women bear living children, and the hope that she would fail so they could sacrifice her to the Ireki.

Haserre was staring at her with such longing that Sabalah would have pitied her if she'd still been able to feel anything. Ahizpa obviously wanted her dead. As for Tratatu, he seemed to be oddly unconcerned for a man who soon might be compelled to condemn his son to be eaten alive by giant sharks. His glowing golden eyes were half hidden behind his eyelids as if he were sleepy or still in a trance. Sabalah hoped he wasn't talking to the Ireki. She knew what they'd be saying.

"So," Ahizpa said in Old Language, "proceed. Display your powers. Show us how that so-called charm you're holding works." There was such venom in her voice that even some of the full-blooded Mordai flinched.

This was the moment when Sabalah should have panicked, but a strange thing had happened: she had gone completely numb. She could feel nothing now—not fear, not pity, not love, nothing, and she knew why. The instant she had placed Marrah in Saski's arms, she had felt all emotions drain out of her. She was thinking with great clarity now, not that thinking was doing her any good. She might not have been putting out the scent of fear, but she still had no idea what to do next except open the Mother Book and hope for the best.

"Well?" Ahizpa said. "What are you waiting for?"

"I need to chant," Sabalah said, stalling for time.

"Chant then," Tratatu murmured in Old Language. It was startling to hear him speak. His voice was soft, his words blurred as if coming from a great distance. "Chant, use your charm, make us fertile."

Maybe he was on her side. Maybe he wanted her to succeed. That wouldn't be a surprising attitude for a man who had taken a human woman for a mate because the Mordai desperately needed children, even half-blooded ones.

Holding the Mother Book over her head, Sabalah slowly turned in a full circle so everyone in the barrow could see the coiled snake on the front cover. "Oh Goddess of Mercy," she chanted. She was pleased to see Ahizpa flinch at the word *Goddess*. "Oh Sweet Mother of us all, bring the joy of children to the Mordai whom you love as you love all your creation. Let their men be fertile. Let their women bear living babies. Let their numbers grow. Let their longhouses be filled with the laughter of little ones once more."

Realizing that she couldn't keep this up forever, she stopped, although she was strongly tempted to add something like: *Quit worshipping sharks!* For a moment she stood there. Then, praying for a miracle, she opened the Mother Book for the third, and what she hoped would be the last, time. As she did so, something fluttered out and fell to the crushed bones that paved the floor of the barrow. It was nothing much, only a bit of dried mint that must have caught in the Book when she slammed it shut, but as soon as she saw it, she knew the Goddess had answered her prayers.

Last night, it had been too dark to see the leaves of the mint plants that grew around the ruins of the temple. Or rather she had been able to see them indistinctly, but she had not been able to see their exact shape, and taking a closer look had been the last thing on her mind.

Closing the Mother Book, she bent over, and picked up the bit of withered mint. There was utter silence in the barrow. No doubt everyone thought she was bowing to the Goddess and that this was part of the ritual surrounding the "charm."

Tucking the Mother Book under one arm, she examined the plant closely: weak stem; hairy, oval, grayish-green leaves; flowers in whorled clusters. Yes! It was exactly the same mint that grew in the garden of the Temple of Batal in Shara, the one the midwives called *etmak*!

Releasing the bit of withered etmak, she watched it float to the floor. Then she lifted her eyes to the platform where Tratatu and Ahizpa were waiting. Tratatu still appeared to be in a trance, but Ahizpa's claws were twitching impatiently. *I can tell that you'd like to claw out my throat with your own hands,* Sabalah thought triumphantly, *but it's not going to happen.*

"Before I go on," she said, giving Ahizpa a defiant stare, "you must answer some questions."

"I must answer to you!"

"Yes, you must if you wish the charm to work. First, you must tell me if you are bothered by gnats."

"What!"

"Please, answer." For a moment Sabalah thought she was going to refuse. Then Tratatu made a small movement that must have been a command, because, baring her teeth in a nasty grimace, Ahizpa spoke.

"No, the gnats do not bite me."

"Do you have any idea why?"

"Because I smell bad, I suppose."

"Still you are healthy. You have borne many living children, yes?"

Ahizpa drew herself up proudly. "The most children in the history of the Mordai. Six, all healthy, all full-blooded and strong-clawed."

"Do you ever anoint yourself with mint oil?"

"No. Why should I? Since the gnats don't bite me, there's no need."

"You don't hunt? I've heard all Mordai hunters use mint oil to hide their scents."

"No, I've never hunted."

"Why not?"

"Because, you ugly, lying human, I'm lame." Ahizpa spit out the word "lame," as if it were a curse. Actually, Sabalah thought, Ahizpa's lameness had been a great blessing. "Do you have any more questions?"

"Only one." Sabalah turned to Zakil. "You've told me that Mordai women are fertile twice a year: once in early spring and once in early fall. Does some sort of celebration occur when this happens?"

Zakil gave her a startled look. "Yes. There's a great hunt."

"A great hunt during which the Mordai men and women go out together to kill game to offer to the Ireki?"

"Yes."

"And the hunters rub themselves with mint oil to hide their scent?"

"Yes."

"Do the human women who mate with Mordai men ever rub mint oil on themselves?"

"Almost never. There's no need to since they don't hunt and the gnats don't bite them."

Those were the answers she had been hoping to hear! Her emotions came flooding back in a great wave of joy and relief. Again she raised the Mother Book over her head. Again she turned so everyone in the barrow could see it.

"Listen, oh Mordai. Thus speaks the Goddess: *'Blessing on you, my children. I have not abandoned you and I never will. You turned from me to worship the Ireki who are cruel and unworthy of your love, but I am merciful. I understand your pain, and I bring you a message of great joy to comfort you. From this day forth, you must never again use the mint that grows around Hezur Herri. You must not anoint your bodies with mint oil. You must not drink tea made from its leaves. If you do as I command, your men will be fertile again and your women will bear many living children.'"*

Sabalah stopped speaking, and looked up at Tratatu and Ahizpa. The expressions on their faces suggested they had not been impressed. But how could that be? She'd just told them how they could bear living children. Wasn't that what the Mordai longed for?

"Is that all?" Ahizpa snarled.

"All? What more do you want?"

"We didn't expect to hear you babble about mint oil," Tratatu said. "We expected— "

"I've given you a miracle," Sabalah cried, "and you call it 'babble!' That mint that you're so fond of causes women to abort. In Shara pregnant women are even forbidden to walk through gardens that contain it. By slathering yourselves with mint oil, you're killing your children before they're born! It's called *etmak*, and it's deadly poison!"

"It's true that a few people have died from eating no more mint oil than you can hold in the cup of your hand, but we don't eat it, we use it to keep off gnats. We aren't fools. We know the power of herbs and potions."

"You don't understand. You don't have to eat it to be poisoned. The oil passes through your skin!"

"Ridiculous!" Ahizpa snapped. "It may pass through your weak, ugly, human skin but nothing passes through ours. You appear to have forgotten we Mordai have scales, beautiful silver scales instead of that mush that holds you together."

She turned to Tratatu. "I've been gathering herbs and making potions longer than she's been alive, and I've never heard of such a thing. She's lying. That box she's holding either doesn't contain a charm or, if it does, she doesn't know how to make it work." She jabbed her finger at the sentries. "Take it from her!"

Before Sabalah could react, a sentry stepped forward and snatched the Mother Book out of her hands.

"No!" she cried. She made a grab for the book. The sentry shoved her in the chest so hard she nearly lost her balance. "No!"

"You see!" Ahizpa said triumphantly. "This lying human said that if we touched her so-called charm, something terrible would happen. But look! Nothing has happened, nothing at all! She isn't under the protection of the Great Python. There's no Great White Snake that flies through the air. There's no Cold Curse. There's only a puny, clawless human woman standing before us next to her puny, traitorous, clawless, half-human mate, and they both stink of fear."

"Tratatu," Sabalah cried. "Don't listen to her, I beg you! She's wrong. I've told you the truth. The mint oil—"

Tratatu opened his eyes. They were wild, deep, gold, and glowing, and there was no mercy in them. "The Ireki are telling me they're hungry," he said. "They're saying it's time they were fed."

28

The Second Judgment

"Forgive me," Zakil pleaded. He stretched out his arms, and Sabalah impulsively moved into them. She wanted to forgive him and go back to the Mother free from anger, but part of her couldn't. Zakil was the reason she had lost Arash; the reason she had had to give Marrah to Saski; the reason why she was about to die a death so terrible she couldn't think about it without experiencing a cold, creeping horror that made her feel as if she were about to faint. Still, his embrace was a comfort. It would be good not to die alone. Or would it? Could she bear to listen to his screams as the Ireki tore them both limb from limb?

Maybe we should kill each other now, she thought. But life was precious, suicide was forbidden by the Goddess, and besides, the Mordai had thought of this possibility as they had thought of everything else. She stared over Zakil's shoulder at the interior of the nearly-bare sleeping compartment where they had been confined to await the moment when Ahizpa and Tratatu would lead them to the lake to be sacrificed. There was nothing they could use to do harm to themselves—not a knife, not an axe—only her pack, a bowl of berries, a jug of water, a small wooden stool, and the deerskin blankets that covered their bed.

When she'd first arrived in Hezur Herri, Zakil had promised to kill her before the Ireki could eat her. She'd proudly rejected his offer, telling him that she wanted to live to the end, no matter what that end might be. Now...

The bitter taste of fear crawled up from her stomach into her throat until she felt as if she might choke on it. *Think, think, think,* she told herself. She had to find some way out of this if not for her own sake, then for Marrah's. She couldn't die and leave Marrah to grow up among the Mordai. Who would raise her? Haserre would be bad enough, but what if they gave her to Ahizpa? Who would sing her lullabies in Sharan and tell her about her grandmother, and aunts and uncles? Who would kiss her before she fell asleep and keep her safe from the beastmen?

Disentangling herself from Zakil's embrace, she sat back on her heels, took a deep breath, and prayed: *Dear Goddess, give me a clear mind. Help me figure out what to do.*

Perhaps the Goddess answered her prayer, because she suddenly felt less afraid. Pressing her hands together to keep them from trembling, she coughed and licked her lips which had gone dry.

"Zakil, what are the Mordai going to do to us?"

"Sacrifice us to the Ireki, my love."

"No, I mean exactly **what** are they going to do? What happens when humans, or in your case half-humans, are sacrificed? Will they claw out our hearts?"

"No, this isn't a *Shruzu*."

"Will they throw us into the water alive?"

"It's best you don't know."

"No, it's best that I do know. Tell me."

Zakil opened his mouth, but before he could speak the leather curtain that shut off their sleeping compartment from the rest of Saski's longhouse was thrown aside, and Tratatu entered. He had been terrifying enough when he stood on the platform beside Ahizpa with his face smeared with blood. Now his claws were dyed yellow, his hair was stiffened with ashes, and his entire body was painted with small sharks that swam from his ankles to the band of shark teeth he wore around his neck. At the sight of those sharks, Sabalah felt her stomach heave and the bitter taste of fear again crawled up into her mouth.

"Father!" Zakil cried.

Tratatu nodded to Zakil but did not answer. Turning to Sabalah he addressed her in Old Language. "Your name?"

Sabalah hesitated for a moment, then remembered. "Soina," she said.

"Daughter of Amonah? Do I have that right?"

"Yes."

"Interesting that you should be the daughter of a Sharan sea goddess. What's your real name, and who's your real mother?"

"Since you're going to feed me to sharks, I see no reason to answer that."

"Heh," Tratatu grunted, and to her surprise he sat down on the bed beside her. "I thought that would be your answer. Listen to me, whoever you are, I think you've been condemned unjustly."

"What!"

"Be silent. I can only afford to stay here a few moments, and we have a lot to discuss. Did Zakil tell you that in my youth I almost got myself sacrificed to the Ireki? No? Well, I did. I was young, rebellious, and eager to see the world, so I went into the lands of the humans and spent how long?"

"Two years?" Zakil said in a choked whisper.

"No, three. I spent three years wandering through the Motherlands disguised as a human and when I got back, Ahizpa's mother accused me of betraying the Mordai. I only escaped because I'd brought home a human woman to mate with. As you might have guessed, her name was Saski, and when she entered Hezur Herri, she was already carrying Zakil in her womb. The Mordai don't kill fertile males. We're too rare.

"During my years in the Motherlands, I had an easy time of it since the Mother People believe dwarfs are under the special protection the Goddess. At one of the first longhouses I visited, they gave me a pilgrim necklace made of shells like the one you're wearing. I was fed and coddled and entertained. In winter I slept by their fires and grew fat. In summer, I walked farther east than any Mordai except Zakil here. Among the places I visited was Kataka, the city where they teach the secrets of the Dark Goddess. Perhaps you've heard of it?"

Sabalah nodded. A faint hope was beginning to blossom in her, but she pushed it aside. She had to keep thinking clearly. Tratatu seemed friendly, but if he had intended to spare their lives, he wouldn't have come to them with sharks painted on his body. What was this about? Why was he telling her all this? What did he want?

Pulling out a small pouch, Tratatu took out a strip of dried meat and began to chew on it. As he ate, he stared at her through lidded eyes. "So?" he said at last.

"So what?"

"So, do you still claim to be under the protection of the Great Python?"

"Yes."

"The Great Python's not doing much for you, is it? Here you are, about to be thrown into the lake, and the Great Python hasn't lifted a hand to protect you, nor has your supposed mother, the Goddess Amonah. Tell me, are you expecting Amonah to walk across the water and save you from the Ireki?"

"Perhaps," Sabalah said defiantly. "It's happened before."

"Oh it has, has it? Well I wouldn't count on it happening again. You're not the first Goddess-worshipper to be sacrificed to the Ireki. You may have noticed that Ahizpa hates humans. Every time our sentries catch one trying to sneak into Mordai lands, it's into the lake. Humans killed her father."

"Who was trying to kill them," Zakil said.

"Be silent!" Tratatu ordered. "This is no time to rehash ancient feuds." He turned back to Sabalah. "So, I ask you again: do you claim to be under the protection of the Great Python?"

"Yes. You can ask me as many times as you want, and my answer will always be the same."

"Good."

"Good?"

"Good, because I believe you. You see, when I was in Kataka I was shown a thing called a 'book.' I'm very possibly the only Mordai who has ever seen one. Or perhaps I should say that until you arrived, I was the only Mordai who had seen one, because now everyone in Hezur Herri has seen a book. Unfortunately for you, they didn't know what it was, but on closer inspection I did. I take it that this is a book of prophecy, yes?"

Sabalah pressed her lips together and didn't answer. She had no intention of telling him anything about the Mother Book, not even that it was a book.

"You're stubborn," Tratatu said. "I find that admirable. No doubt the Great Python made you promise not to let anyone know what you carried with you when you came to the West Beyond the West. But let's assume I'm right. If your so-called charm really is a book, then I want to know what's in it, and since I can't read Xchimosh..."

Sabalah flinched involuntarily at the word.

"Ah! I'm right! It is a book and it is written in Xchimosh! This must mean it's a book of prophecy which you can read." He leaned so close she could see a small crack in his front teeth. "I want you alive, do you understand? I don't want you to be sacrificed, but I have no power to stop it. I can't overrule Ahizpa. You're going to be fed to the Ireki and so," he jerked his thumb at Zakil, "is my son. I can't save him either."

"Then why did you come here? Did you come to torment us? To gloat?"

"No, I came to tell you that if you survive the swim, I won't let them throw you back."

"Survive the swim? What does that mean?"

Tratatu looked at Zakil. "You didn't tell her?"

"No," Zakil said, "I thought it better not to."

"Well tell her," Tratatu said, rising to his feet. He turned back to Sabalah. "There's not a chance in a hundred you'll survive, but you claim to be under the protection of the Great Python, so perhaps a miracle will take place. If you make it back to shore, I have the power of the Second Judgment, and I'll exercise it."

Before she had time to reply, the leather curtain was swinging and Tratatu was gone.

After his father left, it took Zakil a long time to speak. "They're going to take us out into the middle of the lake and dump us in," he said at last. "The Ireki prefer their food alive. They enjoy seeing their prey thrash around in terror as it tries to escape. Fear is their salt. They savor it."

"Dear Goddess," she whispered.

"Once we hit the water, we can try to swim to the beach. If we make it and are able to run to the arch, it's supposed to be a sign the Ireki have spared us."

"How many people have made it to the arch?"

"None. No one, human or Mordai, can outswim the Ireki. Most are torn apart immediately. Some have swum quite a distance before the Ireki have eaten them. One or two have bled to death on the beach." He paused. "I don't want to describe that to you. Let's just say that parts of them were... missing."

Sabalah felt as if she were going to throw up. Gritting her teeth, she told him to go on.

"Under ordinary circumstances, even if we got to the beach in one piece, we'd never make it to the arch, because we'd have to run through a line of sentries who'd beat us senseless. When we regained consciousness, they'd throw us back into the lake where the Ireki would finish off what was left of us."

He smiled grimly. "The good news is that my father has promised that if we get to the beach, he'll exercise the Second Judgment. I think that means he'll order the sentries to let us run to the arch without being beaten."

"You **think** that's what he means? You don't know for certain?"

"No, but it doesn't really matter. We'll never make it to the beach."

"Why not? Why should we give up hope?"

"Because the only way to keep the Ireki from eating us is to walk to shore on the bottom of the lake instead of swimming. Walking on the bottom confuses them. But you can't walk because you can't breathe underwater. I can, but I'd never leave you behind."

"Zakil, if there's any chance you can survive, you should..."

"No. I love you. I'll die with you."

"Zakil ..." But she could see that there was no use trying to explain to him that love was supposed to be about life, not death.

For a while, they sat in silence. Finally, Sabalah got to her feet and began to pace around the sleeping compartment looking for anything that might help them escape. If she could find a sharp stone, she might be able to cut a hole in the wall, not that that would help. The longhouse was guarded by Mordai sentries. The best she could hope for if she and Zakil crawled through a hole in the wall was death at the end of a spear, and she'd decided not to die.

Stooping down, she picked up her pack, went back to the bed, sat down beside Zakil, dumped out the contents, and examined them. The sentry had taken her knife before he led her out of the barrow. All that was left was extra clothing, a few strips of dried meat, a doll she had made for Marrah out of twigs and acorns, the weather stick, the loadstone, the pouch of dust the Great Python had given her, three or four packages of herbs, and the fringed skirt, earrings, and blue stone necklace she'd brought with her from Shara.

Pushing everything aside except the pouch of dust, she picked it up, opened it, and inhaled the scent of lavender and hyacinths. This dust had been the third and final gift of the Great Python. Adder had warned her not to throw it away because it must have a use, but except for mixing it with water and perfuming her arm with it, she had never been able to figure out how to use it. She had a vague memory of the dust-and-water mixture doing something strange when she smeared it on her skin, but she couldn't remember exactly what that something had been. The only thing she recalled was that it had a stronger odor when it got wet, and that even so, Zakil had not been able to smell it.

Coating your body with something the Mordai couldn't smell might have come in handy if their sentries had been trying to track her down by following her scent, but since they'd already caught her, she couldn't see how it mattered if they could smell her or not.

She closed the pouch and put it aside. Perhaps the Great Python had believed she would need the dust when she reached the Sea of Gray Waves, a prospect that was seeming less likely with every moment that passed.

As she turned to look at the rest of the things she had dumped onto the bed, she heard drumming. The rhythm was strange, violent, terrifying. *You will die!* the Mordai drums seemed to be saying. *You will be eaten alive! There is no escape from the Ireki!*

Dizzy and trembling with panic, she clutched at the blankets, trying to anchor herself to the bed as the entire room spun around her. Could a person die of fear? *I cannot faint. I must keep thinking. Dear Goddess, show me some way out of this!*

"They're coming for us." Zakil's voice trembled.

Taking a deep breath, Sabalah put herself in the hands of the Goddess. Either she would die or she would not die, according to Her will. What was death after all but a return to the Mother? The pain of being eaten alive would be terrible but mercifully brief. After that, there would be sleep and then a new life in a new form. Perhaps she would come back to this earth as a songbird or a flower. Perhaps she would return to Shara in the body of a newborn child.

Mastering her panic, she took Zakil in her arms and held him. "Zakil, would it help if I told you that I care about you?"

"Yes," he murmured.

"I won't lie to you, not when we're both facing death. I don't love you, but I do care about you. I care about you a lot, and I don't want you to die." It cost her nothing to say those words. She *had* come to care about him—not in the way he cared about her, but as a fellow being who was suffering with her and going to die with her. Compassion had always been the greatest gift of the Goddess. No matter what happened next, it was the one thing neither the Mordai nor the Ireki could take from her.

Zakil grew calmer. As he relaxed in her arms, her mind again began to race. *Think, think, think. A bowl of berries, a jug of water, a skirt, a necklace, a pair of earrings, a loadstone, some extra clothing, a weather stick, a doll, a packet of herbs, a few strips of meat, a pile of blankets, a pouch of dust.*

The drums grew louder. She could hear the procession approaching: the chanting and singing of the Mordai, the cries of the children, the barking of the dogs.

There was only one thing on that list she didn't know how to use. Letting go of Zakil, she picked up the pouch, opened it, and plunged her fingers into the dust. It was soft, fragrant, as finely powdered as pollen. Could it be pollen? Was she supposed to mix it with water and drink it? She probed deeper and felt something hard. Pulling it out, she brushed off the dust and examined it.

"What is it?" Zakil asked.

"A piece of bone. It looks as if someone carved it into a shape, but I can't tell what it's supposed to represent because it's broken."

"Perhaps there's another piece in the pouch."

Plunging her fingers back into the dust, Sabalah felt around again. She was about to give up and dump the dust on the bed, when she encountered another small, hard object. Blowing off the dust, she held it up to the light.

"Here's the missing piece," she said.

"Put the two of them together and see if they match."

Picking up the two fragments of bone, Sabalah placed them side by side in the palm of her hand and pushed them together. They fit, and when she saw the shape they formed, it was all she could do to keep from screaming with joy. Leaping to her feet she grabbed the bowl of berries, dumped them on the floor, and emptied the pouch of dust into the empty bowl.

"Bless the Great Python!" she whispered. "Quick, Zakil! Bring me the water jug! I think we have a chance!"

29

SACRIFICED

Blinding sunlight, heat, not a breath of wind. Lake Calthen was smooth as a mirror of polished silver. As Sabalah and Zakil walked down the main path of Hezur Herri toward the water surrounded by armed Mordai sentries, the air seemed heavy with menace, and the hope Sabalah had felt only moments ago grew thin.

She looked over at Zakil who was trembling so hard he could barely walk. His body, like hers, was coated with a clear, jelly-like substance that smelled like lavender and hyacinths, and something else she had not smelled the first time she'd mixed the dust with water. On that occasion, the two of them had been sailing toward Lezentka blown west by a warm breeze, and the mixture of dust and water had smelled sweet to her. Zakil hadn't been able to smell it at all. Now beneath that same sweet scent, the mixture gave off the odor of something dark, rotting, and fish-like. It wasn't the salty smell of freshly-caught fish, but the stink of decayed ones barely concealed by the scent of the flowers. It was, she thought, the smell of death.

This wasn't going to work. She had been insane to think it might. She and Zakil had made a terrible mistake: they had turned themselves into shark bait. Fortunately, he still couldn't smell the nauseating odor that was wafting off of them and neither could their Mordai guards, but she could. She was leading Zakil to a horrible death. This was her punishment for opening the Mother Book.

She gagged, fighting to keep down the bile that was rising in her throat. Did anyone else in this crowd feel sick at the thought of the two of them being torn to pieces? If so, they were doing a good job of hiding it. If you hadn't known this was a sacrifice, say if you'd been looking at this procession from the top of the wall or even from the ruins of the Goddess Temple, you might have thought a festival was going on. The humans and half-humans of Hezur Herri were throwing flower petals at them as the full-blooded Mordai danced and chanted, their scales glittering, their red gills opening and closing like the wings of butterflies.

How strange and beautiful the Mordai were, even Ahizpa who was decked out in a cape of bones decorated with red feathers that fluttered as she moved. *Red flower petals, white flower petals; white bones, red feathers. Red flapping tongues. The bloody white teeth of sharks ...*

Again she felt as if she might vomit. *Stop it!* she commanded herself. Stop it! As the petals fell on her in a steady rain, she tried to think of Shara; of the great painted snake that wound around its walls; of her mother Lalah who'd cried that day they'd brought her out of the water half-drowned and who must have been crying ever since over her lost daughter; of Aunt Nasula who had told her anything was possible as long as she was still young; of her *aita,* Uncle Bindar, who had wiped her forehead with lavender water and called her his "dear child"; of Arash—dear Arash—whom she'd loved for seventy-nine nights and whose memories she wore around her neck.

But when she thought of Marrah crawling toward her, happy and smiling, her grief and fear and nausea became so great that she stumbled and would have fallen if Zakil hadn't caught her arm. She searched the crowd desperately, hoping for one last glimpse of Marrah's face, but all she saw were the faces of strangers.

"Be brave," Zakil urged in a voice that had no courage in it.

Be brave? What choice did she have? If she fell or refused to go on, the Mordai would simply pick her up, toss her into a boat, take her out into the middle of the lake, and throw her to the Ireki. If you were walking to your death, you might as well do it with your chin held high, hide your fear, and pray for a miracle even if you knew you weren't going to get one.

She tried to put the thought of Marrah out of her mind, but she couldn't. At least Marrah was too young to understand what was happening. If the Mordai were merciful, they would never tell her how her mother had died.

In front of them, the crowd of dancers and drummers parted, and she saw they had finally reached the edge of the lake. She had expected that she and Zakil would be forced into a dugout with a mast and a leather sail or a round shava made out of pieces of cowhide stretched on a wicker frame, but the Mordai boat that was going to take them to their deaths was a sturdy raft made of oak.

She knew at once why they were being taken out on the lake in a raft, why the Mordai never fished, and why there were no other boats pulled up on the beach. The raft was big and strong because the Ireki were bigger and stronger. Their massive jaws could chew a piece out of any ordinary boat and sink it. The Mordai sentries who took sacrifices out to the Ireki had no intention of sacrificing themselves.

Later she had trouble remembering exactly how she and Zakil got onto the raft or how they got to the middle of the lake. Did they wade through the ankle-deep water of their own free will or were they forced at spear point? Was the trip to the center long or short? The terror of those moments was completely erased by the greater terrors that came after it. She could only recall calm blue water and the bones of Hezur Herri shining in the distance with deadly whiteness. And the arch, of course. The arch was the stuff of nightmares.

At last the raft stopped. For a moment there was nothing but sunshine and the soft slap of waves beneath the floorboards. For a moment, she was able to convince herself that the Mordai had changed their minds. And then ...

"Isur tak!" one of the sentries yelled, and all at once she was in his arms. Before she had time to struggle, he threw her into a deerskin that was being held taut by two of his companions. Then she was in the air again, flying above the sentries like a bird as they tossed her up and down. Each time she rose screaming, she could see Zakil also being tossed.

"Sa, ifun, chit!" A great cry rose from the sentries as she was flung higher than she could have believed possible if she had had enough wits left to believe anything. Then came the

flight over the lake in a great arc, her arms flailing, her legs kicking as though she were trying to swim in air, her hands opening and closing, trying to grab onto emptiness, followed by the shock of hitting the water and a descent into darkness.

She came up choking and gasping to find Zakil beside her.

"Swim!" he yelled. Turning toward Hezur Herri, they began to swim frantically away from the raft. For a moment or two, it looked as if the Ireki might not appear. Then the first great fin came rushing toward them, cutting through the surface of the lake like the blade of an axe.

Suddenly the head of an enormous shark rose out of the water. Its teeth were longer than a man's hands, its jaws so wide Sabalah could have stood in them with her arms outstretched and not touched the sides. But it was the size of its body that caused her to stop swimming and freeze in terror.

She had seen dozens of sharks, but they had all lived in saltwater, not in lakes, and even the biggest ones were no longer than a *raspa.* This shark, if it really was a shark, had a black back rippled with white, smooth as wet stone. It was huge, impossibly huge, bigger than a longhouse, bigger than a temple. It didn't belong to any world she knew. It was a monster left over from the time of the great lizards, something that had lived and grown under the surface of Lake Calthen for thousands of generations.

The Old Ones, Zakil had told her. *We worship the Old Ones.*

"Down!" he yelled, jerking her under as the giant shark headed straight toward them. He held her there as the white belly of the creature passed over them close enough to touch. The tip of one of its pectoral fins parted her hair. Then she was out of air, fighting against Zakil's grip, struggling back up toward the surface as more of the creatures surrounded them and began to circle.

She saw three gaping mouths huge as gates, three white tongues long as beds, teeth like temple stones, and behind them three red caverns. In less than an instant she and Zakil would be gone, torn apart, eaten.

Only...

Only, it didn't happen because, instead of attacking them, the sharks stopped.

"Swim!" Zakil yelled.

This time, she needed no urging. Turning away from the Ireki, she began to swim toward Hezur Herri as fast as she could. The sharks didn't go away, but they didn't attack either. They just followed at a distance and kept circling.

Sabalah and Zakil swam on. As they drew nearer to shore, Hezur Herri appeared to grow larger. Now Sabalah could see the slates in front of the barrow, now the ruined Mother Temple, now the faces of the people on the beach. The Mordai weren't drumming or chanting. They were standing in absolute silence watching Zakil and Sabalah's progress in disbelief.

The great sharks moved closer, then suddenly pulled back.

"Eat them!" a shrill voice cried in Old Language. Sabalah looked toward shore and saw that Ahizpa had run down to the edge of the lake. Apparently she was trying to get into the water because Tratatu had come up behind her and was holding her back. "Eat them, Old Ones!" she screamed. "Eat them!"

As if obeying her command, one of the great sharks came straight at Sabalah with its mouth wide open. For a second she saw the sunlight glint off its white teeth. Then its jaws clamped down, not on her body but on her hair.

She felt a strong jerk that almost snapped her neck. All at once, most of her hair was in the shark's mouth, and it was swimming away with it. *A shark ate my hair! No one will ever believe ...*

No one would ever believe anything about her if she didn't start swimming again. She and Zakil had almost reached the beach. A dozen strokes. A dozen more. Coughing, sputtering, inhaling water, she swam desperately toward Hezur Herri.

Putting down her legs, she felt her feet touch the muddy bottom of the lake. She took a step, staggered, fell back, swam a few more strokes, and then found her balance and ran through the shallows onto the beach. When she looked over her shoulder, Zakil was running out of the water behind her, and the Ireki had disappeared.

Giving a great whoop of joy, Saski ran forward and threw her arms around Zakil. "My son!" she cried. "You were spared!"

"Throw them back!" Ahizpa yelled. Running up to Sabalah, she grabbed her by the shoulders and tried to force her back into the lake. As the tips of Ahizpa's claws dug into her shoulders, Sabalah lowered her head and butted her in the chest. Ahizpa fell with a clank of bones, and then got up, furious but unhurt.

Before she could grab Sabalah a second time, Tratatu pushed Ahizpa aside, and signaled to the Mordai sentries to put down their spears. "I exercise my right of Second Judgment!" he commanded. "Don't beat them. Let them walk to the arch unharmed."

That was all Sabalah and Zakil needed to hear. Gripping one another's hands, they staggered up the beach to the arch and fell in a heap under it.

Kneeling beside them, Saski offered them a skin of fermented honey. "Drink deep," she said. "The Ireki have spared you. This has never happened before."

She turned to Sabalah. "You told us the truth when you claimed you were under the protection of the Great Python. There's no other explanation for this miracle." She looked over her shoulder warily, and then, to Sabalah's astonishment, she quickly put the tips of her fingers together in the sign of the Goddess. "Bless you for extending the Great Python's protection to my son. Soina, Daughter of Amonah, I owe you a great debt that I will repay sooner than you can imagine."

Before Sabalah could ask her what she meant, Tratatu came over to them. Offering Sabalah his hand, he pulled her to her feet and turned her to face the crowd.

"My people!" he cried. "Behold the human woman the Ireki have blessed: Soina, Daughter of Amonah, mother of Valina our miracle child; Soina a priestess of the Goddess who has chosen to serve the Ireki instead; Soina, who will live with us forever here in Hezur Herri and guide us through her prophecies!"

"What!" Sabalah cried.

Turning her around roughly to face him, Tratatu pulled her down to his level as if to bless her with a kiss. "Be quiet," he warned. "Don't be a fool. There are still many who would like to see you and Zakil thrown back into the lake. I don't know how you kept the Ireki from eating you, but I doubt it will work a second time."

"It was a miracle," Zakil said. Sabalah was impressed with how well Zakil lied, but then he knew what she had momentarily forgotten: neither he nor Tratatu nor any of the Mordai could smell the stuff they had smeared themselves with before they were led out to be sacrificed. She had not been sure when she found the little broken image of a shark in the dust the Great Python had given her that the dust was a shark repellent, but she had hoped it was, and her hope had been realized.

Lifting the palm of her hand to her nose, she inhaled the fishy scent which she was now sure was the odor of dead shark. In Shara, those who fished sometimes towed dead sharks behind their boats to keep live ones from eating their catch. She'd done it herself once or twice.

The Great Python must have known the Mordai were going to sacrifice her and Zakil to sharks. Had that prophecy been written in the Mother Book? If so, it was possible that the Book really did contain all things, past, present, and future. No wonder the Great Python had said whoever possessed it possessed the greatest power to do good or evil ever placed in human hands.

She looked at Tratatu who was busy arguing with Zakil in Mordai. He had just announced that she was staying in Hezur Herri forever, but she would prove him wrong. She should have died out there in the lake. She hadn't, which meant she was alive for only one reason: the Great Python had wanted her to live so she could escape from Hezur Herri, taking Marrah and the Mother Book with her.

"Carry it to the West Beyond the West," the Great Python had commanded on the day it gave her the Mother Book. *"Carry it until you find a people who will know how to keep it from falling into the wrong hands. I can't tell you anything about these people, but you will recognize them when you meet them. They are not like us,* ***really*** *not like us. For all I know, they may not even be human. The Mother Book says they have three eyes: one blue, one brown, one dug out of the ground."*

One blue eye, one brown, one dug out of the ground: at least when she met them, they shouldn't be hard to recognize.

The Great Python might have wanted her to live so she could flee from Hezur Herri, but in the days that followed her escape from the Ireki, Sabalah was hard pressed to figure out how to get over the wall and through the Marubi without leaving both Marrah and the Mother Book behind. Tratatu kept the Book in his house. Every day he brought it to the barrow and ordered her to appear before him and Ahizpa and read a prophecy from it. Every day she refused, which meant she was forbidden to see Marrah or hear a word about her. Zakil always walked to the barrow with her to give her courage, but although everyone else in Hezur Herri was allowed to enter, he had to wait outside.

"Think of your daughter as dead," Ahizpa told Sabalah on the third day.

"Where is she?" Sabalah demanded. "What have you done with her?"

"We've given her to Haserre," Tratatu said. "Read us a prophecy and maybe we'll let you see her. Read us a page, and perhaps we'll let you nurse her."

"Read us nothing, and you will die of old age before you look on her face again." Ahizpa leaned forward a little and the smell of sour milk streamed off of her. "Or perhaps you won't die of old age. Perhaps you and your clawless traitor lover will just die."

"You don't frighten me," Sabalah said, but that was a lie. Ahizpa did frighten her. She frightened her terribly.

On the fourth day, her longing to see Marrah grew so great that she gave in. Opening the Book, she held it upside down and pretended to read. *"Birds heavier than stone will cross the Great Western Sea. Songs will be sung by invisible singers. There will be mushrooms brighter than the sun."* These were the prophecies the Great Python had told her on the day it gave her the Mother Book. Surely there could be no harm in repeating the Python's words to Ahizpa and Tratatu.

Closing the Book, she looked at them defiantly. She had not read a word. She had not broken her vow again. "Now let me see my daughter."

That afternoon Haserre had brought Marrah to her and watched her enviously as Sabalah nursed and petted her and cooed over her.

"Did you miss me, darling? Did you miss, Mama?" Marrah stretched out her hands and laughed a laugh of joy that almost broke Sabalah's heart.

"Your time's up," Haserre said, pulling Marrah out of Sabalah's arms and kissing her. Marrah, who loved everyone, threw her arms around Haserre's neck and nestled into her breast.

Oh my darling, Sabalah thought, *if they take you from me, will you forget me? Dear Goddess, what should I do? Guide me! Help me!* But no one guided her and no one helped her, and if the Goddess was listening, She didn't speak.

But others in Hezur Herri did speak. They were brave and compassionate, and they risked their lives to talk to one another. Neither Sabalah nor Zakil knew they existed, but each time Sabalah was summoned to the barrow, they stood in the crowd growing more and more frightened for this young priestess from the Motherlands who was being bullied and threatened by Ahizpa and Tratatu.

30

Song Sung by Invisible Singers

There were thirteen of them: eight human women, three Mordai women, and two Mordai men; and they all kept a secret so dangerous that if anyone in Hezur Herri had discovered why they were meeting in the ruins of the ancient Goddess Temple, they all would have been sacrificed to the Ireki. Their secret was an old one, perhaps as old as the earth itself: they worshipped the Goddess.

The eight human women had been raised in the Motherlands, and had not changed their religion when their Mordai lovers brought them to Hezur Herri, although they had pretended to. The five Mordai came from families that had never stopped worshipping Her. Although they had all found one another over the years, they had never before met in a single group for fear of being discovered. But this afternoon one of the Mordai men had overhead something that made it imperative for them to act as a group and act quickly. He was Zakil's cousin Irgo, the sentry with the broken nose who had tried to help Sabalah keep up when Haserre marched her to Lake Calthen. No one except the twelve people standing around him knew Irgo spoke Old Language fluently; and no one but they understood how much he hated the Ireki who had once devoured a human woman he had secretly loved.

Tonight just after dusk, Irgo had visited every longhouse where the Goddess-worshippers lived. Sitting down in front of their fires he had chatted with them as he might have done on any other evening, but in the middle of each conversation he uttered the following phrase:

"I saw an owl yesterday night."

Trying to keep their faces impassive, each of the twelve had replied: "Are you sure?"

"Yes," Irgo had said. "I'm sure. It was a white owl."

"It's rare for them to come so far south and very early for them to have turned white," each of the twelve had replied. "What time of night did you see it?"

"After the moon set." Then, abruptly changing the subject, Irgo began to discuss an upcoming hunt. He had uttered the prearranged signal that indicated an emergency, not just any emergency, but one so dire that everyone in Hezur Herri who worshipped the Goddess needed to come to Her ruined temple as soon as the moon set.

The signal was clever and not likely to be noticed by those who worshipped the Ireki.

Owls were sacred to the Goddess in the West Beyond the West where Mother People all along the shores of the Sea of Gray Waves raised tall stones to Her, but they were also common.

Thus alerted, the Goddess-worshippers of Hezur Herri had secretly made their way to the ruins of the temple. Now all thirteen of them stood in a circle holding hands.

One of the human women in the circle was Zakil's mother Saski. Neither Zakil nor his half-Mordai sisters suspected that Saski was keeping such a dangerous secret from them. If Saski had ever confessed to Tratatu how much she longed to return to her own people and the little Goddess temple that sat in the center of her village, Tratatu would have either killed her on the spot or fed her to the Ireki.

Once, only once, had Saski made a mistake that could have cost her her life. This had happened when Zakil had emerged unharmed from the lake and, overcome with relief and gratitude, she had put the tips of her fingers together in the sign of the Goddess when she thanked Sabalah for saving him. Fortunately for her, no one but Sabalah had noticed, but Saski still shuddered when she thought what would have happened if Tratatu had been looking their way.

There was need for haste tonight. The longer the thirteen of them stayed together, the more likely they would be discovered. Yet, before Irgo told them why he'd summoned them, they had something to do, something that would remind them why they were willing to put their lives in mortal danger.

Whenever they met out of the hearing of the rest of the villagers, the secret Goddess-worshippers of Hezur Herri recited the Six Commandments of The Divine Sisters. Now, as they stood in a circle in the darkness clutching one another's hands, they began to whisper:

Live together in love and harmony.
Cherish children.
Honor women.
Respect old people.
Remember that the earth and everything on it is
part of the living body of your Divine Mother.
Enjoy yourselves, for your joy is pleasing to Her.

To these commandments which were as old as the Mother People, perhaps as old as the first people to stand on the Earth and love Her, the secret Goddess-worshippers had added three more commandments that had come from the years they had spent living among the Mordai:

Do not kill beings who speak and walk upright.
Do not sacrifice living things that walk, crawl, swim, or fly.
Love and forgive everyone no matter what they look like or what they have done.

Of these new commandments, the third was perhaps the most crucial. Lack of forgiveness and love, the Goddess-worshippers agreed, was what had made the Mordai turn away from the Goddess and spurn Her blessings.

When their whispers had died back into silence, Irgo spoke. "Dear ones, I've called you together tonight because we must help Soina and Valina escape as soon as possible.

I've learned that tomorrow Tratatu and Ahizpa are going to call Soina to the barrow again, and Tratatu is going to demand the same thing from her he's been demanding since the Ireki spared her and Zakil: that she reveal the powers of the charm she brought to Hezur Herri, the one she says was given to her by the Great Python of Orefi.

"If Soina refuses, Tratatu and Ahizpa have decided to give her one more chance, perhaps more than one; but if she remains stubborn for another week, they will take Valina from her permanently. Then they will lame Soina so she can never leave Hezur Herri. The laming will happen very quickly, without warning. Two sentries will be ordered to hold Soina while Ahizpa cuts her hamstrings. If after that, she still refuses..."

Low moans of horror and disbelief rose from the Goddess-worshippers. Some looked out at the lake where deep beneath the surface, the Ireki slept with open eyes.

"Tell us what to do," Saski said, and Irgo told them.

The next day, Tratatu and Ahizpa called Sabalah to the barrow and demanded another prophecy. Again Sabalah refused until Haserre appeared, cuddling Marrah in her arms.

"Do you want to hold your child?" Haserre's voice seemed softer and the envious glint was gone from her eyes. Later, Sabalah remembered these changes in Haserre, but at the time, the only thing she cared about was Marrah.

At the sight of her mother, Marrah stretched out her arms and began to cry piteously. Sabalah felt her sore breasts filling with milk. *My darling,* she thought. *My dear one. My baby.*

Her resolve crumbled. Opening the Mother Book, she read the first few lines that came to hand: *"In the West, a people will call the Blue Sea 'Our Sea.' In the South, the dead will be preserved beneath pyramids of stone. In the East, a flash of white light will fill the sky, and a great city will instantly become ash..."*

"Nonsense!" Ahizpa cried. "Absolutely useless nonsense! You aren't reading prophecies. You're making them up!" She turned to Haserre. "Take the child away."

When Haserre had left the barrow with Marrah, Ahizpa turned to Tratatu. "Well," she said, "what did I tell you?"

"You were right." Tratatu glared at Sabalah. "You understand that you *will* read us this entire book, yes? You understand that you cannot escape, that you will live out the rest of your life here? We are in no hurry. In time, we will break you, bend you to our will, and force you to read this book to us. We may even force you to teach us Xchimosh so we can read it ourselves."

Sabalah did not reply, but Tratatu saw the rebellion in her face.

"You still hope to escape?"

Again she said nothing.

"We must extinguish that hope." He paused. "If you cooperate we will let you sleep next to Zakil. If you don't, we will separate you from him, take your daughter away from you permanently, and do something to you so terrible that you'll spend the rest of your life regretting your stubbornness. I'm not going to tell you what your punishment will be. I prefer to leave it to your imagination.

"Still, I am merciful. I will give you one more chance. Think about what I've said. Do you want to read the prophecies in this book to us of your own free will, or do you want to be forced to? Tomorrow we will call you back, and you can give us your answer."

Stepping down from the platform, he took the Mother Book from her, and opened it. "Read this line," he said, shoving the book in front of her. "Read it right now, and spare yourself a lot of trouble and pain."

Sabalah looked him straight in the eye. "I don't have to read it," she said. "I know what it says: *Hear all people: Tratatu of the Mordai will die on the shortest day of this year.*"

That was a lie, but what did it matter? She had lied and they hadn't believed her. She had broken her vow and read them real prophecies, and they still hadn't believed her. So why not tell Tratatu the date of his death? Maybe tomorrow she'd make up a death date for Ahizpa. What did she have to lose? They were going to take Marrah from her no matter what she did.

Grabbing the book from her, Tratatu slammed it shut. "Foolish, stupid woman!" he said. "The Ireki have already told me how I will die. I will live to be very old, and then... " He paused. "Then I will have the honor of being eaten."

In the back of the chamber near the door, Irgo stood in the crowd listening to Tratatu's threats and Soina's defiance. Here was a true priestess of the Goddess. Would he die to protect her? Yes. Long before she left the barrow, he was already outside walking toward Saski's longhouse.

As they made their way back to his mother's house, Zakil gripped Sabalah's hand firmly, although inside he was shaking with terror. She should not have told Tratatu the date of his death, but she was stubborn—the most stubborn female he had ever encountered. He couldn't help admiring her for standing up to Tratatu and Ahizpa, yet at the same time, he wished she would give in.

"Sabalah," he said.

Before he could go on, she interrupted him. "Don't ask me to break my vow, Zakil, because I already have."

"What!"

"I read them real prophecies, and they thought I was lying. In a way, this makes things easier. Since they don't believe me, I might as well refuse to read them another word." She laughed grimly. "You might say Ahizpa and Tratatu are helping me keep my vow to the Great Python."

Sabalah's revelation that she had actually been reading from the Book was so upsetting that Zakil could think of nothing to say except to tell her again that he loved her.

"Thank you," she said. "That helps." But she did not reply that she loved him, and it was clear that, although he kept hoping, she never would.

When they got to the longhouse, they were surprised to see Saski standing outside. Usually this time of day, she was off working in the gardens, but today she greeted them as if they had just returned from a long trip.

"Zakil, my darling!" she cried, and throwing her arms around her son, she put her lips to his ear. "I'm going to take Soina off to weed the carrots. I want you to wait a while and then follow us carrying my digging stick so it will look as if I've forgotten it, and you're bringing it to me."

"What are you saying, mother?"

"Don't ask questions. Just do it." Stepping back, Saski kissed Zakil on both cheeks and then turned and embraced Sabalah. "I worship the Goddess," she whispered. "No one must know this. You need to come to the gardens with me, so we can speak without being overheard."

Sabalah was not as surprised by this revelation as she might have been if she had not seen Saski place her fingertips together in the sign of the Goddess on the day she and Zakil came out of Lake Calthen in one piece. Still it was shocking to be told outright. She had lived among the Mordai long enough to know what they did to traitors.

Kissing Sabalah on the forehead, Saski embraced her again. "I'm going to help you escape," she whispered. "Do you understand? Don't speak. Just nod."

Sabalah nodded. Then, looking around to make sure no one was watching, she quickly put the tips of her fingers together.

The carrot patch was as far away from the immediate vicinity of Hezur Herri as you could get without climbing the wall. Located near a small stand of willows, it was usually deserted since once carrots got going, they needed very little tending. Not long after Saski and Sabalah arrived, Zakil appeared carrying Saski's digging stick.

"What's all this about?" he asked.

Pulling a carrot out of the ground, Saski brushed off the earth and threw it into her basket. "Tomorrow Soina is going to give Tratatu and Ahizpa a prophecy they'll be able to confirm."

"I'm going to tell them where to find three gold rings that have been lost for over twenty years," Sabalah said as she tugged at a weed. "One will be found here in the carrot patch, one in the ruins of the Goddess temple, and one ..." She paused and looked over at Saski. "Where did you say the third ring will be found, Saski?"

"On the finger of one of the skeletons in the barrow."

"No," Zakil said, "that's much too obvious. Someone would have seen it long ago. How about burying the third ring near the refuse piles?"

Saski looked pleased. "That's an excellent idea, my son. You're quick-witted." Bending down she pulled up several more carrots. "I'm going to miss you."

Zakil could not see his mother's face, but Sabalah could. There were tears in Saski's eyes.

"Miss me?" Zakil said.

"Explain Irgo's plan to him," Saski said, and Sabalah explained.

31

THE MARUBI

Zakil's mother stood in the middle of the room turning in slow circles. Where was the Book? It wasn't on Tratatu's table where Saski had seen it the last three times she'd come to spend the night with him. It wasn't hidden under the acorns in the big basket by the door. He hadn't stuffed it into the thatch or piled his clothing on top of it. She'd even looked under his pillow, carefully rolling him onto his side while praying that he wouldn't wake up.

Luckily Tratatu hadn't awakened, probably because he'd been drugged. She hadn't given him the half-empty cup of fermented honey that sat on the floor beside his bed, but it contained poppy juice: she'd stake her life on it.

In fact, Saski thought, *I am staking my life on it. If Tratatu wakes, he'll catch me going through his things. He'll demand to know why. What could I possibly tell him that wouldn't get me fed to the Ireki? I can't say: 'Tratatu, my dear mate, I came here intending to drug you with poppy juice so I could steal the Mother Book and take it to Soina, but unfortunately someone else got here before me.'*

Who had given Tratatu that cup of fermented honey? Had it been Ahizpa? Had Ahizpa taken the Mother Book?

Saski paced from one side of the room to the other trying to think of another place to look. She couldn't afford to give in to panic. She had to think. How could Irgo's plan have gone so wrong? It had seemed simple enough: This afternoon Soina had gone to the barrow and pretended to read the prophecy of the three golden rings, demanding that if it proved true, Ahizpa and Tratatu would allow Valina to spend the night with her. Sure enough, the rings had been found right where the secret Goddess worshippers of Hezur Herri had buried them. Now Soina, Valina, and Zakil were waiting at the Marubi, and she was going to have to come to them empty-handed.

Walking over to Tratatu, Saski stared down at him. His eyes were closed, and he was snoring softly, his gills fluttering. Ever since she was a young woman, he had been her mate. In many ways she loved him, but for most of her life, he had been her keeper as well as her lover. Years ago, they had stood together outside the Marubi, and he had warned her that once she entered Hezur Herri, she would never be allowed to leave.

She had been young, inexperienced, passionately in love with this strange creature who seemed more magical and exciting than any of the men in her village. Giving him a long, loving kiss, she had laughed and told him that staying with him forever was what she wanted most in the world. Then she had fallen to her knees and crawled through the opening in the Marubi, climbed up one side of the great earthen wall and down the other, entered Hezur Herri of her own free will, and never left.

What had she been thinking that afternoon? How could she have abandoned her mother and her *aita* and all her relatives to go off with a stranger? Why had she decided to live the rest of her life with people who had turned away from the Goddess to worship the Ireki? She would give anything to go back to her village and gaze on her mother's face one more time, but that was impossible. Tratatu was the greatest hunter in Hezur Herri. If somehow she managed to escape, he would track her down and either kill her on the spot or take her back to the lake and throw her to the Ireki. Even though he loved her and she had given him three children, that wouldn't stop a man who had sentenced his own son to death.

Since she couldn't set herself free, she'd hoped to help Soina and Valina escape. Now that plan was in tatters. Soina had vowed she would not leave Hezur Herri without the Mother Book, and it wasn't here.

"What have you done with it?" she asked Tratatu who was so heavily drugged his eyelids didn't so much as flicker at the sound of her voice. There was nowhere else to look. The Book must have been stolen by someone, and Saski decided it was time to leave before that someone came back and found her.

Outside, it was drizzling steadily, wetting the roof bones of Hezur Herri, and turning the main path into a creek. Pulling her cloak tightly around her, Saski sloshed through the puddles and followed the earthen wall until she was out of sight of the lights of the village. A little farther on, she came to the foot of a trail that led to the top of the wall. The trail was hidden by brush. Narrow and given to surprising turns, it snaked back and forth as if it had been designed to force anyone who attempted to follow it to plunge over the edge and roll back into Hezur Herri.

It was so dark she couldn't see her feet, so she had to move slowly. Usually the top of the trail would have been guarded by a sentry who would have turned her back at spear point and reported her attempt to escape to Tratatu. But tonight, the sentry on duty was Irgo.

When Saski got to the top, Irgo was nowhere in sight. He must already be with the others as they had planned. Making her way down the steep, equally treacherous path on the far side of the wall, she climbed into the trench and waded through waist-deep water, threading her way through a forest of sharpened sticks. The water was cold, so by the time she climbed out on the other side, she was shivering, not to mention coated with mud from head to foot. But mud and cold were the least of her worries.

The Marubi rose up in front of her smelling of rotten berries and mold. Like a fool, she reached out to it and pricked her finger on a thorn. Putting her wounded fingertip in her mouth, she sucked on it and kept on trudging through the mud.

At last, far from the official entrance, she came upon the secret Goddess-worshippers chopping at a dark tangle of briars. When she appeared, they didn't say a word. They just kept chopping. There was a courage in their silence that Saski admired. They had taken a vow not to endanger Soina and Valina by making any sound they could avoid. Chopping a hole through the Marubi, they had all agreed, was going to make noise. There was no use adding to it by idle conversation.

Behind choppers, Soina and Zakil stood quietly waiting for the hole to be big enough to crawl though. Tonight Soina had Valina strapped to her chest instead of to her back. Valina was sleeping soundly thanks to a small sip of poppy juice that Soina had reluctantly agreed to give her to keep her from crying and betraying them to the sentries. Poppy juice was the only part of their plan that seemed to be working tonight.

Soina and Zakil had spread mud on their faces so the sentries would have more trouble spotting them. They were both dressed in leather to keep from being torn to shreds. Irgo was standing next to Zakil. Saski wondered if he'd been able to distract the other sentries. Were they drunk on the blackberry wine he'd brought them, or were they up on top of the wall making their usual rounds? In either case, there wasn't a moment to be lost.

Approaching Soina, she pointed at the hole. "Crawl in now," she whispered. "Go at once, and may the Goddess go with you." She reached out to embrace Soina, but Soina stepped back.

"Where's the Mother Book?"

"Tratatu didn't have it. I looked everywhere."

"What do you mean Tratatu didn't have it? He took it away from me today like he always does. I saw him carry it into his house. Where else could it be?"

"I don't know, but it wasn't there. I think someone stole it. You'll have to leave without it."

"No! I can't! We need to go back and find it!"

"That's impossible. Do you want to be lamed, lose your daughter, and get everyone who's helped you thrown to the Ireki? Go now before it's too late."

"No! I promised the Great Python I'd carry the Mother Book to safety. If you can't find it, I will. I'm going back. Maybe Ahizpa took it. I'll sneak into her sleeping compartment and—"

"Are you out of your mind! Ahizpa's six full-blooded children and their mates live in her longhouse with their children and their children's children. Her five dogs are almost as vicious as the Ireki. Ahizpa lets them out at night. Not so much as a mouse has ever gotten past those dogs in one piece."

"Please," Zakil pleaded, "we can't stand here talking. My mother's right. We have to leave now. Irgo says that in a few moments the sentries are going to get to this part of the wall. They'll look down and see us."

"You can do what you want, Zakil, but I'm going back to Hezur Herri to get the Mother Book."

Before Soina could move, Irgo stepped forward and put the point of his spear against her throat only a handspan above Valina's head. "Take a step toward the wall and I'll shove this through your neck before Zakil or anyone else can stop me," he said in Old Language. "I'll claim I caught you trying to escape. I'll claim we all caught you. Then I'll hand Valina over to Tratatu and Ahizpa and feed your dead body to the Ireki."

"Get that spear away from my daughter!"

"Lower your voice, Soina, or you're going to get us all killed."

"Irgo!" Saski whispered. "What are you doing?"

"I'm sending Soina and Valina where they need to go: away." With his free hand, he gestured toward the hole in the Marubi. "Zakil, get in there. You've agreed to lead Soina and Valina to safety."

"No!" Zakil hissed. "I'm not going anywhere as long as you have your spear pointed at Soina's neck."

"For the love of the Goddess," Saski pleaded, "listen to Irgo, my son. Go and take Soina and Valina with you."

"Kill Soina, Irgo, and you'll have to kill me too."

"That's just what I'm planning to do to you, cousin, if you don't get into the Marubi right now," Irgo said coldly. "First I'll kill her, then I'll kill you. Then I'll take Valina back to Hezur Herri. This would be a waste of both your lives, not to mention the worst possible fate for Valina, don't you agree?"

"Saski told me you worshipped the Goddess," Soina snarled. "She told me you spoke Old Language because it's the common language of the Mother People. I thought you'd become one of us. Where's your compassion? Where's your love? Where's your reverence for living things? The Mother People don't kill each other."

"I look forward to spending long winter nights quietly discussing this problem with Saski, but right now ..." Irgo turned and poked at Zakil with the tip of his spear. "Go, Zakil, before my patience runs out, and I remember how much of a full-blooded Mordai I really am."

"If I go, you won't hurt Soina and Valina?"

"Not if you go now."

Without another word, Zakil walked over to the Marubi, fell to his knees and crawled into the tunnel of brambles.

"You next," Irgo to Soina.

"I don't believe you'll really kill me."

"Just try me." Lifting the spear, he put its razor sharp edge against her chin and cut.

Soina gasped. The cut was tiny but painful. Before she could recover her wits, Irgo pushed her toward the Marubi. "Go!" he commanded.

What choice did she have? Checking to make sure Marrah was tightly strapped to her chest, Sabalah lowered herself to her hands and knees and crawled into the jagged hole in the Marubi, leaving Hezur Herri, the Mordai, and her false name behind her. As the brambles closed around her, the last of the starlight faded, leaving behind near total blackness. Up ahead, she could hear Zakil scuttling through the tunnel. She was shaking with anger—anger at Irgo, anger at Saski, anger at Zakil, anger at every Mordai and every human and half-human who lived in Hezur Herri. But mostly, she was angry at herself. Leaving the Mother Book behind was the worst thing she had ever done, worse even than breaking her vow not to read it.

I've failed, she thought. *Failed so badly, I deserve to be cursed forever. The Great Python gave me the most important task ever entrusted to a human being, and I've proved unworthy. I've let the Mordai take the Mother Book from me!*

For a moment she considered crawling back and confronting Irgo, but the tunnel was too narrow to turn around in, and when she looked over her shoulder, she saw that the Goddess-worshippers had already blocked the hole with brambles.

What if she went back anyway? What if she clawed her way through the brambles, fought Irgo, eluded the sentries, reached Hezur Herri, and entered Ahizpa's longhouse without alerting the dogs? Perhaps the Mother Book wouldn't be there. Perhaps she would lose Marrah trying to find it: Marrah, who still had to be saved from the beastmen. Marrah, who was the only thing in her life she'd ever done right.

Dear Goddess, she prayed, *forgive me,* but again there was no reply, only mud, fear, and the pain of the cut on her chin and the blackberry thorns scratching her face and tearing at the exposed flesh of her hands.

For what seemed like forever she crawled through the darkness doing her best to protect Marrah from the brambles. Finally, up ahead, she saw a faint circle of starlight. She'd paid a terrible price, but she'd made it. Marrah was safe, and Zakil was waiting to guide them to safety. She could see the toes of his boots.

"Zakil?" she whispered, pushing herself out of the Marubi. But it wasn't Zakil waiting for her. It was Haserre.

Reaching down, Haserre grabbed her hands and jerked her the rest of the way out of the tunnel. Behind Haserre, Sabalah saw Zakil standing next to four heavily armed Mordai women who were holding torches. *He had betrayed her!* Before she had time to feel the full horror of his betrayal, the Mordai women threw down their weapons and dropped to their knees.

Sticking the ends of their torches in the mud, they put their fingertips together in the sign of the Goddess.

32

The Circle

Zakil ran to Sabalah and threw his arms around her. "Is Marrah alright?" Sabalah drew back the leather hood that had protected Marrah from the thorns of the Marubi and saw that she was still sleeping.

"Marrah's fine," she stammered.

She stared at the kneeling women, the flickering torches, the weapons they had thrown aside. Haserre was kneeling in front of her with her head bowed; Haserre, who had hated her, mistrusted her, wanted to kill her from the moment they first met. Was this a trick? Why hadn't Haserre already run her through with a spear or clawed out her throat?

Will she kill me? Will she take Marrah from me? The questions sprang to her lips, but she was so torn between fear, hope, and shock, she couldn't speak.

Bowing until her forehead touched the mud, Haserre spoke in Mordai, clicking and hissing softly in a tone of voice Sabalah had never heard her use before. *"Sush ruanzi Jainkosa kala nalasha Lu'ka nomin't aala."*

Zakil let go of Sabalah and stared at his sister in amazement.

"What's she saying, Zakil?"

"She's saying you're the true messenger of the Goddess. She's saying 'thank you.'"

"Thank you for what?"

"Thank you for giving her a child."

Suddenly all the Mordai women were laughing, smiling, and crying tears of joy. *"Nalasha Lu'ka nomin't aala. Nalasha Jainkosa,"* they murmured.

"They say fifteen Mordai women took your advice and stopped using the mint oil. Eight came into their time of fertility early. Haserre and these four are now with child. They are thanking you for giving them children. They want you to know that, thanks to you, they've turned away from the Ireki and now worship to Goddess who made them fertile. They're begging you to bless them in Her name."

Stunned, Sabalah stared at these Mordai women who after so many generations of separation had rejoined the Mother People. She thought of the years she had spent wanting a child and the happiness she had felt when the sacred dogs had placed their muzzles on her belly. There was no joy like knowing there was a baby in your womb. Nothing compared to it.

Putting the tips of her fingers together, she said the only words of Mordai she knew: "*Maite chi Jainkosa izen:* I bless you in the name of the Goddess."

Suddenly the Mordai women were on their feet, hugging her, kissing her, clasping her to them, cooing at Marrah and admiring her. Reaching out, Haserre stroked Sabalah's hair, so dark, so different from her own. "Soina *Andragai,*" she said, kissing Sabalah on both cheeks. *"Ima."*

"Haserre's just called you her sister, and not just any sister but a full-blooded Mordai sister. She also called you her mother."

"Her mother!"

"Haserre's real mother died giving birth to her. I think she's adopting you."

Bless you, Haserre, Sabalah thought. Bless you. The Blessing of the Goddess had worked after all. It had seemed so weak when she first met the Mordai, yet it had driven out hatred. Love really was more powerful than spears or claws.

"How do you say 'daughter' in Mordai, Zakil?"

"Try *'alaba.'*"

"Alaba," Sabalah said and was rewarded with a smile so bright and hopeful that for a moment Haserre's face seemed to shine in the darkness. Putting her hands on either side of Sabalah's face, she spoke for a long time in Mordai. Finally, she kissed Sabalah on the forehead, stepped back, and gestured for the other women to pick up their torches.

"Haserre says she and her companions are going to help you and Marrah escape from the lands of the Mordai. She says if you try to go on alone, Tratatu will track you down, take you back to Hezur Herri, and sacrifice you to the Ireki; but they can cover your scent with theirs and take you on paths no one else knows, ancient paths sacred to women. Will you go with them?"

"What about you?"

"I'm to stay behind. Haserre says that she knows now that I am not a clawless coward but a brave brother who must return to Hezur Herri and pretend to be angry with you. Haserre is going to lead you to a human village that lies near the Sea of Gray Waves. My job will be to steer Tratatu and his hunters in the opposite direction."

Taking Sabalah in his arms, he hugged her close and kissed her. "I'll miss you, my love," he whispered. "I'll miss you terribly."

"I'll miss you too, Zakil." To her surprise, Sabalah felt tears streaming down her cheeks.

"Riku lat xuna, Ima Andragai," Haserre said. She was holding a small clay bottle marked with a design that looked as if it might represent the brambles of the Marubi. *"Shna lertantho sethha lat."*

"What's she saying, Zakil?"

Zakil frowned and did not answer.

Haserre held the bottle out to Sabalah and spoke again. She seemed to be pleading for Sabalah to do something.

"What does she want?"

"She wants you to promise that after she has taken you to safety, you'll drink what's in that bottle. She says she will lead you out of the lands of the Mordai and deliver you to your own kind whether or not you make this promise, but she begs you on the lives of her unborn children and all Mordai children to come, to drink that potion when the time is right."

"What is it?"

"She says it's *lertantho,* the Elixir of Forgetting."

"Is that the potion you told me about? The one you said the sentries force infertile women to drink before they allow them to leave the lands of the Mordai?"

"Yes, but Haserre promises no one will force you to drink it. She says you don't need to be afraid. It's a very weak mixture that will only make you forget the last few weeks, which means you won't forget the vision Batal gave you of the beastmen, or Arash, or the vows you made to the Great Python, or any part of your journey from Shara except the part where you and I parted from the traders and set off together for Hezur Herri."

"How do I know she's telling the truth? How do I know that if I drink what's in that bottle, I'll be able to remember my own name? You stole Arash's memories. Why shouldn't she try to steal mine?"

"Because without your memories, you'd be no use to the Mordai. You wouldn't be able to read the Mother Book. You wouldn't even know what it was. If I didn't think my sister was telling the truth, I'd be knocking that bottle out of her hand instead of pleading with you to do as she asks."

His voice broke, and for a moment he stood there trying to get himself under control. "As soon as you swallow the first drops, you'll forget I ever existed. You won't remember how much I love you, how I held you in my arms and mingled my scent with yours to keep you safe, how I said I would rather die than abandon you and Marrah. You won't remember that I turned traitor to my own people and showed you my true form. Zakil, the half-human Mordai with gills and golden eyes who loved you more than his own life, will no longer exist even in your dreams. The only good I can see in this is that by forgetting me, you will also forget I deceived you, and thus you may finally be able to forgive me."

Sabalah looked from Zakil to Haserre and back again. "As far as I can see, there's nothing in this for me but the danger of losing my entire past and forgetting who I am. Why should I take the risk?"

"Because you're generous and compassionate and would not want to destroy an entire people by accident. The Mordai who live in Hezur Herri are among the last of their kind. The only way they've survived for so long is by staying hidden. No humans, no matter how good-willed, can be allowed to know where they live or even that they exist. The Mother People are peaceful, but imagine what might happen if the beastmen learned of our existence and sent the Tcvali to slaughter us."

"Shimza riku lat xuna lertantho Valina, Ima Andragai," Haserre said, falling to her knees, bowing her head, and

holding the bottle up to Sabalah. *"Riku lat xuna lertantho, Ima Andragai."*

"Again my sister is asking if you will promise to drink the *lertantho*—not now, but once you have taken Marrah to safety."

"How do I know she's telling the truth? How can I be absolutely sure that this potion will not destroy all my memories and leave my mind as blank as the mind of a newborn child?"

"It's simple. You must trust us."

Trust them? Trust the Mordai? There was no way Sabalah could decide except to look into her own heart, and when she did, she was surprised to find that she did trust them after all. And yet...

Reaching out, she took the bottle from Haserre and helped her to her feet. "Zakil, tell your sister that I accept the potion, and that once I have made sure Marrah is safe, I'll consider drinking it. That's all I can promise."

Zakil spoke for a long time to Haserre in Mordai. When he was done, Haserre leaned forward and kissed Sabalah on both cheeks. *"Eskertu,"* she murmured.

"My sister believes that once you have thought it over, you will do the right thing. She says 'thank you.'"

Zakil put his lips close to Sabalah's ear. "In the years to come, you will not remember me, but perhaps someday we'll meet again, and I'll be able to persuade you to love me for who I really am. Perhaps we will meet on Gira."

He began to sing to her in a soft, sweet voice that sent chills down her spine:

Gira island of soft nights
Gira island of love
Gira where the maidens dance
Swinging their long black hair

"Perhaps," Sabalah said, but she didn't think it likely. She would take Marrah to safety, love her, care for her, and protect her from the beastmen until she was old enough to protect herself. Then she would journey to the Sea of Grass and search for Arash. No matter how many years had passed, she would find him and bring him home to the village where his mother's bones lay. It was Arash she loved, Arash who had first sung to her of Gira and the lands that lay beyond

Shara. She could feel the red crystal that contained his memories lying warm against her flesh. She would not risk forgetting him even to save the Mordai.

"If you do not choose to drink the *lertantho,* will you ever be able to forgive me for deceiving you?" Zakil whispered.

"You're already forgiven," she told him, and stepping back, she put the tips of her fingers together and blessed him in the name of the Goddess who had compassion for all living beings, even those who made mistakes.

Just before dawn when the sky above the tall trees had taken on the color of the pearls the divers of Shara brought up from the bottom of the Sweetwater Sea, Haserre called a halt. By that time they were already far from Hezur Herri. The ground was marshy and the air smelled of salt and the sea.

Putting down her pack, Haserre opened it and drew out a small package. For a moment she stood there holding it in her hands as she spoke in Mordai. Sabalah did not understand what she was saying, and since Zakil was no longer with them, no one could translate for her.

She only recognized three words: *Tratatu, Ima,* and *Andragai;* but when Haserre handed her the package and gestured for her to unwrap it, she knew as clearly as if she spoke Mordai what Haserre had said: "Here, sister, is the Mother Book which I took from Tratatu."

Giving a cry of joy, Sabalah hugged the Mother Book to her chest. On the cover, the little snake turned forever in its eternal circle from death to life, from life to death, and back again.

33

THE VISITOR

The strange woman standing beside Marrah's bed had golden eyes and golden skin burnished with shining crystals. In her arms she held a golden-eyed, golden-skinned baby. Two golden-eyed, golden-skinned children stood beside her.

"I've come to thank your mother for my children," the woman said in Old Language. She spoke slowly as if searching for unfamiliar words. There was music in her voice, a sibilant sweetness like the click of water flowing over small pebbles. "Where is she?"

"Mother's gone to Hoza to watch the raising of the Goddess Stones."

"When will she return?"

"I don't know."

"Has Sabalah ever told you about me?"

"No."

"Then she must have done it."

"Done what?"

"Never mind. Just tell her Haserre came to thank her."

"I will."

But Marrah never did tell her mother about the strange woman, because when she woke the next morning she realized she had been dreaming. No real women had golden skin. No children shone like silver in the moonlight.

No babies had tiny claws.

AUTHOR'S NOTES

Freshwater sharks are currently found in Nicaragua, Asia, and Australia.

Megalodon sharks, which lived 2.6 million years ago, were 45 feet to 59 feet long, weighed 50 tons, and had teeth seven inches long.

The Mordai: Although the Mordai are fictional, I have chosen to imagine that they and other human-like creatures survived in small numbers in the forests of Europe well into the era when Sabalah makes her journey to the West Beyond the West. Paleoanthropologists have found a number of ancient species which they agree were human-like. The best known are the Neanderthals (Homo neanderthalensis), which appear to have interbred with humans as may have the lesser known Denisovans (Denisova hominins). Other human-like ancient beings include Homo floresiensis, Homo erectus, Homo habilis and Homo naledi. We don't know by what names these cousins of ours called themselves or if any more remain to be discovered, but as I began to write about them in The Village of Bones, I came to wonder if perhaps small bands of human-like survivors were the original inspiration for the stories of fairies, gnomes, elves, and other magical creatures which appear so often in European folk tales.

The Mother Book and the *Sibylline Books*: My description of the Mother Book was inspired by the legend of the Sibylline Books. According to Dionysius of Halicarnassus, the Cumaean Sibyl offered to sell nine books of prophecies to Tarquinius, the last king of Rome. When Tarquinius refused to pay the high price she demanded, the Sibyl destroyed six of the books. Fearing he might lose them all, Tarquinius bought the last three, which were consulted by the Romans at moments of crisis for the next thousand years.

Weather Sticks: Weather sticks are not fictional. They were used by some groups of Native Americans to predict changes in the weather and the arrival of storms and can still be purchased today. Made of a thin rod of birch or balsam fir and mounted outside, a weather stick will twist up when the weather is good and down when it is changing for the worse.

Curses: *Rak* and *Shallah* are Sharan curse words that have no English equivalents.

Resources:
The Earthsong Series is set in a fictional world based firmly in real-world archaeology and paleoanthropology as described in *The Language of the Goddess* and *The Culture of the Goddess* by Marija Gimbutas, Professor of European Archaeology and Indo-European Studies at UCLA. To learn more about the goddess-worshipping cultures of Neolithic Europe visit http://marymackey.com/the-civilization-of-the-goddess.

To learn more about Mary Mackey and the Earthsong Series, find her on Facebook or visit MaryMackey.com

ACKNOWLEDGMENTS

I owe a special debt of gratitude to novelists Pamela Berkman and Dorothy Hearst who read every version of this novel in manuscript. Their suggestions and criticisms were invaluable. I am also deeply indebted to the late Maria Gimbutas, Professor of European Archaeology and Indo-European Studies at UCLA, whose research on the Goddess-worshipping cultures of Old Europe has never ceased to inspire me. Finally, I want to thank my agent Barbara Lowenstein who first suggested I write a prequel to *The Year the Horses Came* and Angus Wright, my husband and companion of thirty years, who has never ceased to encourage me, and who bore with good humor and patience the long hours I spent shut away in my study working on *The Village of Bones*.

Photo Credit: Angus Wright.

MARY MACKEY is the author of fourteen novels including *The Village of Bones: Sabalah's Tale, The Year the Horses Came, The Horses at the Gate,* and *The Fires of Spring,* all of which tell the story of Sabalah and Marrah's struggle to save the Goddess-worshipping cultures of Neolithic Europe from nomad invaders. Her novels have appeared on the *New York Times* and *San Francisco Chronicle* bestseller lists, been translated into twelve languages, and longlisted for the James Tiptree, Jr Literary Award. She has also written seven volumes of poetry including *Sugar Zone*, winner of the 2012 PEN Oakland Josephine Miles Award for Literary Excellence. A screenwriter as well as a novelist and poet, Mary has sold feature-length scripts to Warner Brothers as well as to independent film companies. She sometimes writes comedy under her pen name Kate Clemens. At present, she lives in northern California with her husband Angus Wright. You can learn more about her, read her blog interview series *People Who Make Books Happen*, and sample her work at www.marymackey.com. Her literary papers are archived in the Sophia Smith Special Collections Library, Smith College, Northampton, MA.

IF YOU LIKED *THE VILLAGE OF BONES,*
YOU MAY ALSO ENJOY…

The Year the Horses Came
Earthsong Series Volume One

Now grown to womanhood, Sabalah's daughter Marrah sets out with her nomad lover Stavan to fulfill the Snake Goddess's prophesy that she will "be the savior of her people," only to be captured by the Beastmen who want her dead.

The Horses at the Gate
Earthsong Series Volume Two

Initiated into the mysteries of the Dark Goddess, Marrah, now Priestess-Queen of Shara, uses magic and cunning to defend the city from an attack by the Beastmen.

The Fires of Spring
Earthsong Series Volume Three

A generation after the invasion of the Beastmen, Marrah's daughter Luma and Luma's friend Keshna come of age as female warriors. Luma's twin brother Keru has been captured by the Beastmen who have taken possession of his spirit, turning him against his own people. Learning that he is still alive, Luma and Keshna set off on a perilous journey across a land of warring tribes to rescue Keru from the clutches of the Beastmen's evil shaman Changar.

The Last Warrior Queen

The year is 3643 B.C.E. The great matriarchal cities which have dominated the earth are about to disappear as hordes of nomads overrun the fertile valleys of Mesopotamia. Born into one of these tribes is Inanna, a woman who speaks the language of plants and whose touch can heal. Led by her powers to the City of the Dove, where love is sacred and sex is an act of worship, Inanna fulfills her destiny by becoming a great warrior queen.

KEEP READING

To enjoy an excerpt from Mary Mackey's novel

The Year the Horses Came

Marrah's Story

The Year the Horses Came

MARRAH AND THE BEASTMAN

The coast of Brittany: 4372 B.C.E.

Marrah walked toward the sea holding her child necklace in her hands. Behind her came the drummers and flute players, the dancers and singers, the young men and women bearing baskets of white flowers, the crowds of friends and relations, and the children, tumbling over each other for a better view. There was nothing organized about this walk to the sea, nothing solemn, although the day when she became a woman was the most important day of a girl's life. Like almost all religious events in Xori, this one was noisy and chaotic, a ragged procession of barking dogs, mothers with babies on their hips, old men dancing the dances of their youth, and young people laughing and talking.

As Marrah's bare feet touched the stones of the beach, the noise stopped and a sudden hush descended, for this was the moment when she was passing from the Bird Goddess's keeping into that of the Sea Goddess. The silence was so deep she could hear the sound of the waves striking the far side of the small rocky island that lay some distance offshore. It was not a loud sound, more like someone breathing and exhaling softly, but when she heard it she felt as if the Goddess Amonah Herself were calling to her. The island was only a large boulder of ragged white granite, but everyone in the village regarded it as an especially lucky place. Gray seals sometimes came to sun themselves on its rocks, the best fish were caught in its waters, and precious bits of flint were often found washed up on its beaches. For these reasons, and perhaps for others, the island was especially sacred to the Sea Goddess, and every girl who came of age went out to it alone to toss her child necklace back into the water and then sit awhile praying and meditating. *But first,* Marrah thought, *the birds must come and give me leave, for the birds are signs of the Goddess Xori's grace, and without them no one can prosper.*

The silence lasted for a long time as everyone stood quietly, waiting for a sign. At last it came: the gruff *kow-kow-kow* of a seagull, Marrah's namesake, the best possible omen. Then like an added benediction, a cormorant flew by. At the sight of its long bill and brown wings, a murmur of satisfaction rose from the crowd. Cormorants could use their wings underwater; what better sign could there be of harmony between Xori and Amonah?

The music and noise took up where they had left off. As the drummers called to each other and slapped out new rhythms, Great Grandmother Ama's three youngest grandchildren came forward: Hatz, a round, comfortable-looking man in his early twenties who was one of the best cooks in the village; and the twins, Belaun and Hanka, who fished with Uncle Seme. The three of them carried Hanka and Belaun's boat, a sturdy dugout with an image of Amonah carved on the bow. The Goddess had the body of a fish and the face of a woman, and no sailor would have thought of setting out to sea without Her.

"Climb in," Hanka said as she handed Marrah one of the wooden paddles. "I think you know how to steer one of these things by now." At that everyone laughed for when Marrah was only a child of five, she had climbed into this very boat, paddled away from shore, and nearly drifted out of sight before Sabalah had spotted her and raised the alarm.

Marrah got into the dugout and made herself comfortable. As Hanka and Belaun pushed her into the water, the crowd pelted her with white flowers until she was floating on a sea of blossoms.

"Come back as quick as you can," the children called after her.

"Why? Will you miss me?"

The children laughed and threw more flowers. "Hurry," they insisted.

"It's the food," Hanka said. "They can't touch it until you get back."

"That's right," Marrah's brother Arang yelled, "it's the pudding and the honey cakes. Can't you smell them, sister?"

Marrah could smell them; in fact the scent of the honey cakes was making her stomach rumble, but her newfound dignity required that she paddle slowly toward the island as if feasting were the last thing on her mind.

It was a short trip, but an exciting one. Almost all the excitement was in Marrah's mind. The sea was unusually calm, the sky clear, the water as blue as a necklace of callais, but with every stroke of her paddle, she felt as if she was becoming more of a woman. Never again would her mother or Uncle Seme stand on shore and call her back. This was her sea, her boat, her sky, and she could go wherever she wished, even paddle over the rim of the horizon to the very edge of the world if she felt like it.

When she reached the island, she tied the dugout to a rock with a piece of woven cord, knotted her child necklace into the corner of her skirt so her hands would be free, and waded ashore. She looked around, hoping to see some seals, but there were none in sight. Feeling mildly disappointed, she began to climb cautiously up the slippery rocks. On the seaward side there was a level area—not a beach, really, for sand had no chance of staying on the island during the winter storms—but more of a ledge that projected into the water. There, alone and facing the sea, she would say a prayer and throw her childhood necklace to Amonah.

The climb was steep, and the narrow linen skirt was no help. Soon she stopped and tucked the hem into her belt. She was so preoccupied with placing her feet securely on the wet stones that she didn't bother to look at the view, which she had seen many times. After she had passed the roughest part of the seaward slope, she turned and saw something that brought her to a stop again. She shaded her eyes with her hand, looked down at the beach, and gave a low whistle of alarm. There seemed to be something—no, *someone*—lying on the rocks: a dead someone by the look of it, face down and surely drowned.

What kind of disaster was this? Breaking into a run, she stumbled the rest of the way down the slope. When she reached the body, she stood over it, gasping for breath. The dead man—for the body was too large to be that of a woman—lay sprawled and limp among bits of seaweed and wreckage washed up by last night's storm. He was tall, perhaps the tallest man she had ever seen, and he was dressed in a hooded, cape-like garment made of a strange material that looked like matted brown fur. The cape covered his entire body except for his hands, which were pale and waterlogged.

She stared at his hands in horrified fascination. On every finger he was wearing a ring of some sort, most carved from bone, but two of copper. Copper was the yellow color of bones and death, sacred to the Bird Goddess in her most terrible form. In the land of the Shore People, it was only worn for religious ceremonies. She shuddered. A dead man in copper rings lying on her beach! No girl's coming-of-age had ever had a worse omen than this. It was as if the Goddess Xori were cursing her, as if She were saying, "Throw Amonah your childhood, Marrah, and I'll throw a dead man back at you."

She knelt down, mustered all her courage, grabbed the dead man's shoulder, and heaved him over on his back. As he turned, his hood fell back, exposing his face. With relief, she saw he was no one she knew, but how strange he looked! He was old, so old that his hair and beard had turned a strange yellow-white, and yet there wasn't a line on his face. It was a thin face, lean and strong-jawed, with skin so pale she could see the veins in his eyelids. In his ears he wore more copper rings: five or six at least, plus two small gold ones. Around his throat hung a necklace of fierce-looking teeth from some animal she didn't recognize, a copper pendant shaped like the sun, and another shaped something like a deer, only more stocky, with thick legs and hair on its head instead of horns. There was even copper in the hilt of his knife, and what a knife! So long you'd have trouble using it for anything practical and tucked away at his side in a scabbard as if he never went anywhere without it. There was no one in her village who could make a knife like that, and who would go hunting in copper necklaces that would rattle together and scare off the game? It was all very confusing.

She was about to rise to her feet when she saw a movement so quick and faint she would have missed it if she hadn't been staring directly at his face. His left eyelid had fluttered, and even as she watched, it fluttered again! He was alive! ...

www.ingramcontent.com/pod-product-compliance
Lightning Source LLC
LaVergne TN
LVHW010000300125
802532LV00005B/175

9781530804573